RED DEATH

JEFF ALTABEF

FIRST EDITION SOFTCOVER
ISBN: 1622533208
ISBN-13: 978-1-62253-320-6

Editor: Lane Diamond

Printed in the U.S.A.

www.EvolvedPub.com
Evolved Publishing LLC
Cartersville, Georgia

Printed in Book Antiqua font.

Other Books by Jeff Altabef

What Others Are Saying about Jeff Altabef's Books:

WIND CATCHER:

"This is an enjoyable read for all ages that goes by as fast as the authors can unspool it."

– Kirkus Reviews

"*Wind Catcher* stands out from the crowd. It's... a powerful young adult adventure steeped in Native American legend and tradition."

– Midwest Book Review

"A page turning thrill a minute, Wind Catcher kept me guessing until its final pages. Age appropriate YA literature at its best. Don't miss it!"

– Judy Murphy, Masters School Librarian

BRINK OF DAWN:

"Wow! Simply, wow! How's that for a review? Any reader, young adult or not, who enjoys fantasy, thrillers, adventure, stories with a strong female protagonist, or simply a great work of fiction will love *Brink of Dawn!*"

– Readers' Favorite Book Reviews

"This book is enthralling and leaves you begging for more!"

– 5 Girls Book Reviews

SHATTER POINT:

"The book combines my favorite aspects of my favorite authors into one: James Patterson—the master of the psycho killer who kidnaps girls; Patricia Cornwell—scientific thriller; and Dean Koontz—really spooky plots."

– No Holding Back

"There are twists and turns galore in this book and once you think you have it all figured out, another curve ball is thrown at you. If you love a good mystery suspense, this is the book for you."

– Bookie Monster

"From genetic manipulation and twists of fate to cold-blooded murder, scenarios change with a snap but succeed in bringing readers along for what evolves into a wild ride of not just murder and mayhem but social inspection."

– Midwest Book Review

Introduction

In a sweeping adventure like this one, set in a faraway time, you will find many new characters and places to love. To aid you in keeping track of them all, author Jeff Altabef has created a handy "Cast of Characters," which we've included immediately following the last chapter.

We've added links to the "Cast of Characters" at the end of each chapter, to make it easier for you to reference if necessary.

If you prefer to review it before starting the story, as we know many of you will, please just click the link below.

Cast of Characters

We really love this dystopian adventure, loaded with memorable characters that are sure to stay with you long after you've finished reading the story. The characters really are the heart and soul of this story. Yet the author also raises some interesting questions about the nature and fate of humanity, which make the story all the more compelling.

We think you're going to enjoy it as much as we did.

Dave Lane
Managing Publisher/Editor

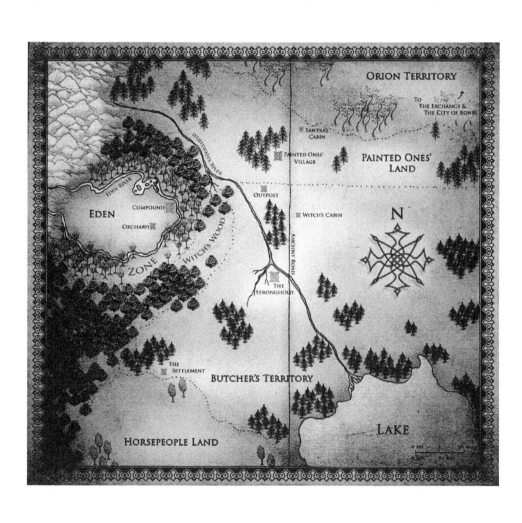

CHAPTER 1
AALISS

A aliss nearly growled, her mood foul. Weary from a long day, she wanted nothing more than to crawl into bed, stuff her head under a pillow, and fall blissfully asleep. Instead, she found a note perched on top of her bed like a bad omen. She sighed and carefully unfolded the paper and read her young brother's precise handwriting.

He wanted her to come to his lab, and although he phrased it like a request, he was really summoning her.

For a long moment she stared at her bed, tempted to slip under the sheets, but she really had no choice. Wilky would wait for her all night and the next day until she came for him, and she didn't want him sleeping at the lab again.

She trekked across the Compound to his lab and stood before him.

Wilky crossed his arms against his thin chest. He was a good-looking boy with bright blue eyes, the family's jet-black hair, strong features, and a thin muscular frame. "We're starving them."

Aaliss glanced behind her brother and into the holding pen. Three Guests her age, two girls and one boy, sat slumped with their backs against the wall.

They do look gaunt.

Somehow the unwanted thought bullied its way into her mind before she could prevent it. Wilky had a way of doing that—making her see the world differently, the way *he* saw it—and now, when she looked at the captives, she saw only skin and bones and desperation.

She waved at the Guests in what she hoped would be a dismissive gesture, but she failed miserably and felt a little foolish. "They're Soulless, Wilky. The devil has claimed them. We're not supposed to worry about the Soulless."

Her words sounded hollow even to her, and a chill swept down her spine. She had begun to doubt Eden's most fundamental teachings, which scared her. Once doubt crept in, where would it lead?

Wilky stayed silent and intensified his glare until his eyes carved straight through her chest and into her soul. He might be thirteen, but he had the eyes of someone much older and wiser, someone who knew truths he should never have known.

Time ticked on, the two locked in a silent tug of war Aaliss knew she would never win. Born stubborn, Wilky would stay, arms crossed and eyes glaring, for as long as it took for her to cave in.

A fire three years ago had claimed their parents, and she had been responsible for him ever since. Sometimes she wanted to strangle him, but he was her brother, and she loved him, and the two had forged a team of sorts. Piers, their oldest brother, completed the group, but he was... well, he was Piers, and that made him more of an honorary member of the team than a full-fledged participant.

They do look hungry.

She sighed. "Okay, I'll find Piers and see if he can rustle up some food. But you know I'll get into real trouble if a Priest catches me sneaking into the Parsonage."

Wilky shot her a sideways glance and a small smirk.

They both knew she was too highly trained, too skilled to get caught.

"This can't wait until tomorrow?" she asked.

He shook his head.

She groaned as she left the lab, retraced her steps through the Labyrinth, slipped her way to the stone circular staircase that led to the Parsonage, and cringed when she saw a full moon through a narrow window. She didn't believe in superstitions as much as other people she knew, but a full moon portrayed an ominous sign. She didn't scare easily, but the devil used the moon to create mischief, and a full moon meant danger.

No one else traveled the staircase at this time of night, so she crept up the steps unseen until she reached the top landing and a locked door. Unlike the other doors into the tower, which were made of wood, a heavy steel door protected the Parsonage where the Priests lived. A red light glowed by the handle, with a keypad to its side.

She approached warily and peered through a small window. The full moon reflected back at her as if spying on her, waiting for her to be discovered. She had no excuse to visit the Parsonage this late, and if the High Priest caught her, she would get in trouble. If he suspected dark motives, her punishment would be severe. Still, she had come this far and could not disappoint Wilky. She said she'd go, and she kept her promises.

She pressed six on the keypad three times, and held her breath as the light turned from red to green. The combination for the lock changed daily, but a glitch in the system allowed three sixes to work every time.

Wilky had told her the secret.

She had no idea how he had discovered it. She assumed he must have overheard someone talking about it, but when she asked him, he would not say.

"I must be crazy," she muttered to herself, and exhaled as she edged the door open just far enough to peek down the hallway.

Flickering candlelight danced through the corridor, casting shadows that looked like living creatures, as misshapen and dangerous as those that lived in the Zone—the heavily wooded buffer area between Eden and the Soulless.

Aaliss patrolled in the Zone. As a Guardian, part of her job was to make sure the Soulless never learned of Eden's existence. In that darkness, she was one of the dangers for the unwary. Not so here in the Parsonage. Priests ruled in Eden.

She focused on her destination and ignored the shadow creatures, willing them away. *You are not real.* With no one in sight, she slipped into the hallway and glided toward the fourth door on the left.

A tall, thin Priest knelt at a small wooden altar in the small chamber. Two years older than Aaliss, the handsome nineteen-year-old wore the robe of the newly initiated Priests. He had many of the same features as Wilky—chiseled chin, short straight black hair, and bright blue eyes—but that revealed only part of her brother's story.

The fire that took their parents had severely damaged the other half of Piers's face, the side not visible from the doorway. Half his body had been badly burned, leaving him disfigured and suffering with weakness and pain in his left leg and arm.

Relieved to find him alone, she entered the small prayer room and silently closed the door behind her. As the smallest and plainest chamber in the Parsonage, it had just enough space for the small altar, a chair, and perhaps four people standing close together. Although simple and small, it was Piers's favorite place to pray. She'd known she would find him here, as he always prayed before he went to sleep.

He knelt on alternating black and white marble tiles. All the floors in the Parsonage were made from the same tiles—white for truth and purity, and black for lies and evil. Just like the Priests' robes—the initiates wore black with white sashes, and the fully-ordained Priests wore white robes with black sashes. Only black and white existed in Eden—gray and the doubts that accompanied it had no place here.

She crept toward him, shadow-quiet, a sly smile creasing her lips. She could move like a ghost when necessary.

His lips moved as he concentrated intently on his prayers. He knelt at the altar, his back rod straight with his head bowed piously.

When she had snuck close to him, she poked him on the shoulder.

He leaped forward with a start and let loose a soft shriek.

She forgot about the moon and the shadow creatures, and laughed freely while he scowled at her. It felt good to laugh; she so rarely laughed anymore.

"Are y-you crazy?" he stammered as he straightened his black robe. "You almost sent me to the next world!"

"You're always so easy to startle." Her smile faded as she studied her brother's face and lifted her hand to touch him. "You have a bruise on your cheek."

He looked away before she reached him. "What are you doing here? You could get into real trouble."

She balled her hands into tight fists. "Did *he* do that to you?"

"I spilled the Sacred Drink yesterday. I was careless. My leg gave out, so I had to be taught a lesson. The Book of Jacob tells us it is a sin to waste food."

"But it was an *accident*. He has no right to hurt you. Doesn't the Book also tell us to be kind to our fellow Edenites, always, especially those who are hurt? 'Care for your brothers and sisters, always, for in this world you are each others' keepers against the Soulless ones.'" She narrowed her eyes. "I'd like to teach him a lesson about following the ways of the Book."

Piers turned and gently wrapped his arms around her shoulders. "It's okay, Ally. It doesn't hurt, and I spilled the Sacred Drink. Besides, he *is* the High Priest. The Creator speaks through him. Sometimes he must be severe to teach the proper lessons. There's a plan, and the Creator has given us the High Priest to explain it to the rest of us. These mysteries are hard to understand, but we must accept them."

She softened in his grip and spoke false words. "You know what's best." She still wanted to teach the High Priest a lesson, maybe punch him in that round face and feel her knuckles crush his flat nose, but she told her brother what he wanted to hear. Life was hard enough for Piers without adding to his burdens.

He smiled with the only side of his face that could, but it made her feel better.

When he released her, he stepped backward and frowned. "Your hair looks long."

Guilt ripped through her. As a daughter of Eden, she knew the consequences of bending the rules—shame and humiliation if caught by a Priest.

She smoothed her black hair. "Hair grows. I've been gone for two weeks!"

"Your hair is almost touching your shoulders. You know the Word. Vanity is a sin. You should cut it before anyone notices."

"Yes, *Father,* if you say so." She bowed her head.

He failed to take the bait and renew one of their old arguments. Instead, he asked, "So, why did you risk coming here? I planned to see you and Wilkiford tomorrow."

She frowned. "It's our Guests in Wilky's lab. He's upset. He says we're starving them, and I think he's right. They're thin, Piers, and they have a wild look in their eyes. It's not right to treat them that way."

He raked his hand through his hair and started pacing, limping slightly, his left boot swooshing quietly against the marble floor. "Do you care about how the rancher treats the cattle or the farmer the chickens?"

"Don't sermonize to me, brother!" Heat flushed her face. "These people are human beings. I've spent time with them. I've gathered some of them. They have no souls, but they're not livestock."

He stopped pacing and let his arms drop to his side. "Yes, but the Creator has stripped away their souls. They're not like you or me. They are the *Soulless.* He's punished them for their wickedness! We risk His wrath if we have anything to do with them. It's all written in the Book of Jacob. 'Though the Creator has saved but a few of us for His greater glory and the promise of a new beginning, ever be on your guard.'"

No one quoted the Book like Piers. His piety had become almost all-consuming since the fire, and Aaliss hated it. Before the fire he was fun, daring, even rebellious. Now he'd wrapped himself up so tightly in the Book that none of the old Piers had room to breathe.

"I know all about the Book, brother. I listen to the Reflections every night when I'm not on patrol. It's easier to believe the Soulless are damned here in the Parsonage. You don't spend time with them, or gather them from the Zone for our experiments." Tears rushed unbidden to her eyes. "You know how Wilky gets. When he grabs onto something he won't let go."

"I understand. Our Wilky is a special boy." He sighed. "What do you want from me?"

"All I need is a loaf of bread. Everyone knows food is plentiful in the Parsonage. The rest of us aren't so lucky."

"It's important that we Priests have enough energy to care for Eden's spiritual soul. I don't...." He paused when he saw the tears in her eyes. "I suppose it's natural for Wilky, of all people, to become attached to the Soulless. Stay here. Let me see if I can find something in the Pantry."

He limped from the room, careful to close the door quietly behind him.

Left alone, Aaliss studied the two portraits that hung on the wall behind the altar. One depicted Jacob, the original *Guardian of Eden*, and the other, the High Priest. Both wore identical robes and expressions. She wondered how long it had taken the High Priest to copy the prophet's confident yet solemn face.

The weasel would have wanted it just right.

Both sets of eyes seemed to stare at her, boring into her, questioning her. Unnerved, she slipped to the window. The view from the Parsonage stretched to Eden River and the Zone beyond. The moonlight sparkled off the river, but the Zone crept beyond it like a long black shadow. Her heart raced as her keen eyes searched for the evil the full moon would surely bring.

She wondered about the world outside of the Zone. *The Zone is wild, but what lies beyond it?*

The Priests told stories of the Soulless, describing them as wicked, uncivilized, cannibals even. But how could they know? None of the Soulless she had gathered or killed seemed much different from the Edenites. And no one ventured beyond the Zone. The land of the Soulless was forbidden, a place shrouded in mystery.

Piers returned carrying a round loaf of bread in a fine but plain linen cloth. "The moon has no power over us. We are Believers. Purity, Faith, and Strength."

He understood her better than anyone else, and sometimes she thought he could read her mind. "I know, brother. Purity, Faith, and Strength."

Would his opinion change after a night in the Zone under a moonlit sky?

He triumphantly handed her the bread as if it were a trophy. "This was all I could find."

"Thanks. I knew you would help."

He held onto the bread for a few seconds before releasing it to her. "I'm going to speak to Wilky tomorrow. This cannot continue. He has to understand the difference between Edenites and the Soulless. It is not good for him to get so...." He seemed to search for the proper word. "...Confused."

CHAPTER 2
AALISS

Aaliss watched as Piers shuffled down the hallway and into the flickering candlelight. She'd be happy to leave the Parsonage. She never felt comfortable here. She always got the odd sensation that the Parsonage was more dangerous than the Zone—a silly notion, but it rippled through her now.

Piers stopped a few paces from the door and gave her the "all clear" signal.

For a moment the firelight lit his scarred face and the shadows played their games, creating a version of Piers Aaliss didn't recognize— morphing him into something wicked.

That's not my brother. It's simply the shadows and the full moon up to their tricks.

She shook her head to clear it, eased her way into the hallway, and headed in the opposite direction from her brother, back toward the circular staircase. She moved swiftly until she noticed light seeping from the cracks in the doorway that led to the corner room, the one closest to the staircase. Someone had left the door open by the slightest amount.

Her heart hammered against her chest as hushed voices escaped from the other side of the door.

She glanced back at her brother, who waved her on toward the staircase, yet the door with the light and the voices pulled her. The staircase led back to Wilky and her bed and rest. She wanted to go that way, yet her eyes focused on the sliver of light inviting her to the other door.

She couldn't just turn away from the voices, so she crept toward them and quieted her breath to sharpen her hearing. The words became clearer as she drew closer, and she glimpsed into the light.

The High Priest stood with his back to her, but she'd recognize him anywhere. As a large man, his ample flesh waggled when he spoke, and he still wore the purple robes from preaching the Reflections only a few hours earlier. If that wasn't enough to identify him, she saw the thin braid that fell halfway down his back like a serpent. As a direct descendant of Jacob, he never cut his hair. Everyone else in Eden had short hair. Only the male Blood Relatives were allowed to wear their hair long, and tradition decreed that they must always wear it in a braid.

When she was a child, she dreamed of yanking that braid. Now she wouldn't mind doing far worse to the High Priest as payback for all the vicious things he had done to Piers.

The High Priest spoke in a hushed baritone voice. "The Creator works in mysterious ways. He has fulfilled the prophesy through the strange boy. We have what we need."

The large bulk of the High Priest blocked the second speaker from view and muffled his words. She inched the door open to better hear the conversation and perhaps see the identity of the second speaker, but the High Priest stood in the way like a boulder.

"Malachi, are you sure we have the formula?" asked the mysterious voice.

"Yes, I'm certain. It was right there in front of us for hundreds of years, though it took that strange boy to find it. A simple mushroom and a flower, and the cure works instantly. The Red Death will have no power over us. Our blood will remain pure. We have been delivered."

She inched the door open, desperate to see the face of the other speaker. She wanted to know who this 'strange boy' was that he kept mentioning.

"This changes everything. How quickly can we make the cure?" The second voice became clearer and sounded familiar, but she still couldn't identify it.

The High Priest shifted his weight as if he stood on uncertain ground, and lowered his voice. "Making the cure will not be a problem, but we must be careful. The cure presents us with a unique opportunity. Eden Day is less than three months away. Everyone partakes of the Sacred Drink at the high festival. We could slip the cure into the drink and inoculate the entire community without them knowing."

She pushed the door open another inch to hear the reply, her heart dancing in her chest. If the High Priest turned, he would spot her, and she would spend a long time underground in the jails. It was possible he'd never release her.

"The Creator speaks through you," the mystery man said. "If we secretly slip them the cure, then we can claim responsibility for this miracle. Our power would be absolute."

The High Priest chuckled. "Exactly. We could march two or three Soulless among the people without fear. The prophesy will be fulfilled, and no one will dare question us. Ever."

She gripped the bread hard, breaking the crust as sweat soaked her back. She glanced at her brother, who still lurked in the hallway as a lookout. Unaware why she had stopped, he waved for her to continue to the staircase, but she could not move. She needed to hear more.

The High Priest turned, and for a heartbeat it seemed as if he would walk out the door and straight into her. Luckily, he stopped halfway and grabbed a cup from a table.

"What about the boy and his family?" asked the stranger. "They will know the truth. They create too large a loose end."

The world stopped spinning.

The boy and his family? Her mind spun. *Are they talking about Wilky and my family?*

The High Priest answered, "Do not concern yourself with them.

Jacob has shown me the answer in a vision. Now I understand why He told me to assign the boy as a researcher at such a young age. Tonight will be their last. The scarred one is still useful. His devotion is strong, and I can bend him. Also, it would look too suspicious if the entire family vanished. Some remember the unusual circumstances behind the fire and the popularity of their parents."

The High Priest moved to the side, sliding just enough to reveal the face of the second speaker.

Aaliss's stomach soared and she tasted bile.

"Agreed." Her uncle, President Aibel, smiled with a slight lift of his chin, as he raised a pewter cup of the Sacred Drink to toast the High Priest.

A jolt ripped through her, and her knees buckled. The High Priest and her uncle meant to murder them tonight. Rage burned inside her.

Do I have time to save Wilky?

She glanced at the door to the staircase, not sure if she should run or confront them. If she entered the room and shut the door, she could hurt them both badly, and then kill them. They deserved a painful death, and it wouldn't take long. Yet Wilky's safety had to come first. The High Priest's men could already be on their way to the lab, and Wilky would stand no chance against them without her.

Piers's voice wafted down the hallway. "Father Isaac, what are you doing up at this time?" He shifted his body between Aaliss and the Priest to shield her from view.

Jacob's Braid!

She cursed the full moon. She had no time to spare for the High Priest and her uncle — she'd have to come back for them.

With her head spinning and chest heaving, she dashed toward the staircase and plunged back into the darkness. No lock barred entry from this side of the door. After all, no one worried about the Priests leaving the comforts of the Parsonage.

The High Priest heard voices in the hallway. He wobbled to the door and looked for the source, but found the corridor empty. Doubting his own ears, he turned back to the President, who poured another cup of the Sacred Drink.

Crumbs on the otherwise spotless floor crunched under his sandal—a few bits of bread on a white tile.

"Curious," he muttered to himself.

Aaliss raced forward taking the stone steps two at a time. She automatically switched into her Zone state, senses on high alert, and stopped only when she reached the ground floor and listened for the sounds of pursuit. No shouts, footsteps, or doors slammed—no sign that anyone had noticed her.

With any luck, the High Priest expected them to be sleeping in their residence. That should buy them some time, maybe enough to escape.

She pulled open the door to the Compound and plunged forward into the building's sprawling ground floor. She sprinted forward until she reached the shiny steel door that led to the Labyrinth, and unlocked the door with a key from a chain around her neck.

As she reached for the doorknob, a deep voice grumbled from behind her, "Hey, you, what're you doing out so late?"

She had been reckless in her haste and silently chastised herself. Caught, she turned and smiled, her boots squeaking against the tiled floor as she came face to face with two Monks.

Monks patrolled the hallways late at night, looking for unholy behavior. Most people feared them. Their authority stemmed from the High Priest, which made them virtually all-powerful.

She faced two Monks who could not look more opposite from each other.

One cast a big shadow, literally. Big and burly, he towered over her, a red cloak straining tightly around his broad shoulders. He held a whistle in his hand, but upon seeing Aaliss, he pocketed it in the folds of his cloak, and an unfriendly sneer twisted his ugly face.

The second one was short and thin with a long face and scary-looking hollow eyes.

"I'm just headed to the Labyrinth." Aaliss tried to appear annoyed, rolling her eyes and tapping her foot. "I've got work that can't wait. They treat us like slaves."

The big Monk stepped toward her. He smelled of that night's dinner, which, in truth, hadn't smelled good when it had been served. "What's that you're carrying?"

Jacob's braid!

She'd forgotten the bread. "It's just something for... for my brother. He missed dinner tonight because he's working late." She tried to keep her tone light, as if being caught with food was not a major infraction of the rules, but it was.

The Monk's beefy fingers flipped open the linen wrapping. "Priest's bread." He smiled at his partner. "Thievery is a major sin, Abner. What should we do with her?"

Abner smirked, his long face turning cruel as he looked Aaliss up and down with nasty, appraising eyes. "She's cute. I'm sure we can think of some way for her to do her penitence."

Aaliss acted on instinct and tossed the bread at the big Monk's face. When he lifted his paws to catch it, she kicked his left knee hard. The blow buckled the brute, dropping him to his knees, and she swung her right elbow into his temple. The Monk groaned and wobbled, and she immediately chopped the edge of her hand against the base of his neck, which sent him to the floor unconscious.

Abner tried to grab her, but she caught his wrist and brought his arm down hard against her knee, dislocating his elbow with a sick popping sound. He groaned, and she grabbed him by the shoulders and rammed his head into the steel door. The Monk staggered back a step, his nose bloody, and she knocked him unconscious with a roundhouse kick to the head. Just to make sure he was out cold, she booted him hard in the ribs, and and grinned slightly at the sound of bone breaking.

You deserved that and worse, you pig!

The Monks would never have approached her if they knew she was a Guardian, but she was young, in plain dress, and didn't have any weapons, so they had been none the wiser.

She dragged them one at a time to the other side of the steel door, and remembered to grab the bread right before it closed. She bound their hands with the rope they used to cinch their cloaks, and tied their feet with their bootlaces. They'd be unconscious for a while, but eventually they'd wake and bring others.

Time was short, but she'd known that already.

Three stories below ground level, the Labyrinth consisted of a honeycomb of tunnels and labs where a dozen different research teams worked. Wilky was the youngest researcher in Eden's history and, accordingly, assigned the smallest, least convenient space—farthest from the entrance door and closest to the Zone.

She flew down the concrete steps, praying he would be safe. No one else was working in the Labyrinth at this time of night, so she expertly wove her way past dark labs and through empty hallways. She held her breath when she reached his workspace, used her key, and shoved open the heavy metal door.

He calmly sat on a stool waiting for her, safe.

She exhaled. "I've brought food, Wilky, but we've got to go." She pushed the bread toward him, her hands shaking. "Something terrible has happened."

He casually slid from the stool and took the bread.

"You don't understand. They're coming for us. We've got to run!"

Wilky strolled past a desk littered with a dozen test tubes, two microscopes, and one computer, and stopped at the holding area. Two-inch thick glass walls separated three holding pens. One contained the three starving Soulless, one held a single girl about the same age as Aaliss, and the third was empty.

Aaliss glowered at him as he opened the food delivery chute and dropped the loaf into the pen that housed the three Guests. It landed softly, and the largest of the three, a boy a few years older than Aaliss, snatched the bread and broke it into pieces to share with the other two.

She started to urge Wilky on, but then noticed some provisions by the door that opened to the tunnel, which led to the Zone—four woolen cloaks, four leather satchels, her small crossbow, a two-foot curved short sword, and her full-body black ostrich-skin jumpsuit. The ostrich skin was extraordinarily soft and warm, and well broken in. It was her most precious possession—her Guardian uniform.

"How did you know we needed to leave?" She placed her hands at her hips. "Did you overhear something and not tell me?"

He ignored her question and asked one of his own. "Piers?"

She shook her head. "I couldn't get him, but he'll be fine. They won't harm him. I heard the High Priest and our uncle talking. They need him for *appearances*. You and I, on the other hand, they'd rather not have around."

His eyes became suddenly wet, and tears trickled down his cheeks.

She hadn't seen him cry since the fire, and her heart twisted. "He'll be okay, Wilky. Don't worry about Piers. Our brother knows how to take care of himself."

He nodded, but she thought he didn't really believe her, so she added, "We don't have much time. I'll come back for him later. We'll figure something out."

He pointed at the girl who sat alone in one of the holding pens. "Need," was all he said.

She sighed and shook her head. "We can't bring her. We have to move quickly, and she'll just get in our way. All we need is each other."

He stood firm by the door to the holding pen, and said, "*Need!*"— with more conviction this time.

She knew that *look* on his face; no one could argue with him when he got that look. One time he went four days without washing because he didn't like the texture of his soap, of all things. She had to whittle off an inch and practically sand it to make it smooth enough for him.

She could drag him along by the ear, but they would get caught that way. He needed to move and move quickly, which would only happen on his terms.

"You know the alarm will ring when I open the door to the tunnel. All the Monks will know something is wrong!"

He folded his arms against his chest.

She sighed. "Do we need the other three or just this one?"

He shook his head. "Only the girl."

"Okay, we'll take her, but we have to go now!" She stomped her foot in frustration, retrieved two gas masks from the table, and checked to make sure they had a full two-week charge. That's the maximum amount of time they would have together, as they could not risk being in contact with the Soulless girl unprotected.

The Red Death was easily transmitted through air, so just being near a Soulless would cause infection. Those contaminated died young, never lasting beyond the early twenties. If an older person encountered the disease, death came almost instantly. No known symptoms foretold the disease except what showed in the eyes. The children all knew the rhyme: *...eyes turn red, you'll soon be dead.*

Aaliss watched Wilky as she changed into her jumpsuit.

He held two beakers in his left hand and a dropper in his right. He squeezed fluid from each beaker into the steel door's lock. Smoke spiraled upward and an acidic odor filled the room, as the metal fused together and melted the lock.

"Nice work, Wilky." Fully dressed, she approached the holding pen with her key in hand, and looked back at her brother. "Are you sure we have to take her? This is crazy. She's going to slow us down."

"*Need!*" He grabbed his cloak and glared at her.

She regarded the girl again, whom she'd gathered two days earlier. The girl had been odd and constantly talked to herself in a language Aaliss did not understand, but she'd taken direction and seemed harmless.

Aaliss donned a gas mask and made sure Wilky had his on securely, and then she opened the glass door and waved for the girl to follow her.

The girl tentatively stepped forward.

Wilky gave the girl a cloak and a satchel, and motioned for her to follow him.

Aaliss unlocked the door to the tunnel into the Zone. Dread filled her as she peered back at the lab.

A large framed picture of Jacob hung by the door. Underneath the photograph was the Guardians' sacred motto: *The Soulless are Not Human. To Kill in Jacob's Name is Just.*

Red lights flashed.

An alarm blared.

She grabbed her supplies and turned to push them forward, but Wilky and the girl had already started to run—straight toward the Zone and the full moon.

CHAPTER 3
PIERS

*P*iers smiled as bright sunlight kissed his face. The pain in his arm and the weakness in his leg had vanished, and he stood tall and straight, strong and whole. He rubbed both sides of his face and felt nothing but smooth skin — the scars had disappeared. His toes brushed lightly against the soft grass in the courtyard on a perfect spring day.

Rebecca stood beside him — lovely Rebecca, his Rebecca. Red highlights sparkled in her short wavy brown hair, and her wide chocolate eyes shined lovingly. They both wore plain ceremonial wedding robes the color of freshly fallen snow. A yellow rosebud hung from Rebecca's neck, fastened by two strings of white twine twisted together. The flower symbolized their love, and the twine the life they would lead together.

Piers's parents hovered next to him, with Aaliss and Wilky at their side. They all looked happy, dressed for a great celebration and feast.

Admiring Edenites gathered for the festivity and crowded the rest of the open space. The scene felt familiar to Piers, having dreamed of this moment with Rebecca many times before....

Before the fire?

A harp played soft music in the background, signaling the beginning of the ceremony.

Piers turned to face the High Priest, who plastered a wide grin on his doughy face. He was clad in his rich purple ceremonial robe, the one reserved for significant festivals such as this.

The High Priest nodded to the harpist so he could begin the service, but the music didn't stop. The harp grew louder, its notes turning from light and whimsical to harsh and discordant, as if a child were scraping his hands across the strings.

Piers winced, and a scowl darkened Rebecca's beautiful face. The noise grew louder still, splitting his ears.

The High Priest grabbed him by the shoulders and spun him around. His eyes blazed crimson as he slapped Piers hard across the face.

Piers tasted blood and woke with a start to find two Monks inches from his face.

One had a nasty welt on his neck, and the other shook him. "Wake up, scar face!"

The large Monk with the bruised neck grabbed him by his sleeping shirt and yanked him to his feet. "Time to get up, *Father*. The High Priest would like a word with you."

Piers barely had time to grab his simple black robe from the bedpost and slip it over his head, before a harsh shove sent him skittering into the bed of the novice who slept next to him. Six other novices shared the sleeping chamber. Though they all appeared to be asleep, he knew they were faking. No one could have slept through that commotion.

The two Monks took turns pushing him into the hallway and toward the High Priest's office.

He had difficulty keeping up with them as he dragged his bad leg, scraping it against the floor. By the time he reached the office, sweat drenched his sleeping shirt and anxiety rippled through him. He had never heard of a Priest being treated with such disrespect. What could he have done to deserve such shabby treatment?

The big Monks rapped on the door three times.

Piers cringed at the loud noise. He tried to calm his thumping heart with a few deep breaths, but with little success — it felt as if it would explode in his chest.

There must be some mistake.

The High Priest bid them to enter.

The smaller Monk opened the door while the large one tossed Piers forward with a heave.

Piers stumbled into the office, fell to his knees, and braced himself with both hands against the floor.

The High Priest sat on his tall throne chair behind a massive oak desk. The chair had armrests shaped like lions' heads, and velvet cushions the dark red of dried blood. The desk looked sturdy and simple with straight, clean lines that glistened with the sheen of hundreds of years of careful polishing. Two white candles flickered on both sides of the desk.

In contrast to the simple desk, the rest of the office was ornate: elaborate wall sconces provided soft yellowish light, carved cherry paneling stretched halfway up the walls, and paintings of dozens of past High Priests hung above the wood paneling. All the men were memorialized in the same pose, and with the same solemn expression on their faces.

"That's not necessary, Josh." The High Priest sounded friendly, but his eyes burned hot. "Help our friend up and bring him over here."

Josh, the big Monk, yanked Piers to his feet, dragged him to a chair opposite the desk, and shoved him onto it.

"You can leave us now." The High Priest dismissed the Monks with a wave of his hand and a phony smile. When the door shut, he turned his attention to Piers. "Is this the first time we've had an official meeting in my office?"

Piers wiped sweat from his forehead with the sleeve of his robe. He wanted to vomit, but he choked down the acid that rose in his throat. "No, your Grace, I was here three years ago, after the fire."

"Ah yes, how could I have forgotten?" The High Priest folded his hands contentedly on the desk. "That was a bittersweet day — the bitter news about your parents, offset by your sweet decision to join the priesthood. I trust you haven't regretted your choice?"

"No, I have not." The question alarmed Piers.

"That's so good to hear, my son. I knew we could count on you."

We?

A shadow glided from the corner of the room, and Piers's heart skipped two beats.

The shadow morphed into a man. Gray hair speckled his neat black goatee, slate gray eyes glimmered in the candlelight, and a thin braid shifted on his shoulders. He moved silently and confidently in his black ostrich-skin suit, which showed the well-sculpted lines of his arms and torso. Two curved short swords hung from both of his hips.

Piers knew him instantly, although he had never met him.

They called him the Viper — the Priest in charge of the Guardians, the High Priest's nephew, and a Blood Relative. Stories swirled about him — horrible, violent stories.

Piers dismissed them as exaggerations, or myths even, but watching him now, he believed every one of them, and a frost spread throughout his body.

"We can count on you, can't we?" The High Priest ignored the Viper, who remained ominously silent.

Piers nodded. "Yes, of course. I'll do... anything you ask."

"Do you know the story behind this desk?" The High Priest leaned forward. "It's very special. It's the Desk of Jacob, the very same desk where he penned the Book of Jacob. The Creator spoke to him while he sat behind this desk. No one can lie in its presence." The High Priest lovingly rubbed the desk's smooth surface with his pudgy hands. "Do you believe that, Piers?"

Piers tried to focus on the High Priest, but it was impossible with the Viper skulking toward him, so he ended up dancing his eyes between both men, never settling on one for long. "If you tell me it is true, I will believe it with all my-my soul." His voice cracked as fear threatened to consume him.

"Where are your siblings?"

The Viper glided even closer, his arms within reach.

"I don't... know. They should... be sleeping."

"They should be sleeping, yet they are not. When was the last time you saw your sister?"

They must have caught Aaliss with the bread.

Piers regained a measure of control and sat straighter. Only his desire to protect his sister could overcome his fear. "Aaliss visited me tonight. She was worried about the state of the Guests in my brother's lab. She thought they were starving. I gave her a loaf of bread for them. It was my idea and my fault. I accept full responsibility." He lowered his head in submission. He could have refused her, should have refused her. Now he just hoped he could take all the punishment for the rule breaking.

The Viper moved closer still.

Piers smelled apples and imagined the man's breath against his neck. He tried not to tremble, but his hands shook like leaves in the wind.

"You gave a loaf of my bread to the Soulless?"

"Yes, your Grace. I beg for your forgiveness." He kept his gaze downcast.

"What else did you do with your sister? Did you conspire with her to betray us?"

He lifted his eyes. The High Priest's face had turned purple, and Piers's stomach lurched.

What else has she done?

He spoke quickly in one burst. "No, your Grace, I just gave her the bread. She would never betray Eden."

The High Priest shared a glance with the Viper and the purple drained from his face. "Oh, but they have, Piers. Your sister and brother have betrayed us. They made a deal with the Soulless. They freed a Soulless girl and fled to the Zone." The High Priest rubbed his hand through his hair. "They went arm-in-arm and face-to-face with a Soulless girl. They took no gasmasks. I can only imagine how the Dark One tempted them, but now they are traitors and contaminated, their souls forfeit."

Only a slight tremor in the High Priest's left eye betrayed his dishonesty, but the news had shocked Piers so much, he couldn't be sure whether he'd imagined it.

His body felt as if it had turned to liquid. If he had not been sitting, he would have ended up on the floor in a puddle. "There must be some mistake, your Grace." He leaned heavily against the desk, an apple-sized lump having formed in his throat. "Aaliss and Wilky would never betray us. It makes no sense. Why would they submit to the Red Death? Their souls will have been taken."

"The Dark One works in mysterious ways." The High Priest nodded to the Viper, who grabbed Piers's arm.

He struggled, but the Viper held him firmly and jerked his scarred arm hard toward the desk.

"Now, tell me everything," said the High Priest. "Where are your sister and brother, and what are their plans?"

He stammered, "Th-there must be-be a mis-mis-mistake. I know nothing." Blood pounded inside his head and drowned out any thoughts.

The Viper slid the nearest candle toward his arm.

Piers struggled more fiercely, but he couldn't free himself from the Viper's iron grip. "N-n-not the fire."

Images of the fire three years ago flooded his mind's eye. He remembered carrying Wilky through the smoke and then racing back for Aaliss, who was trapped in her room by a burning beam. He had kicked it aside, pulled her out, and pushed her toward the front door and safety. Then when he had turned to his parents' room, he heard screams and tried to reach them, but the flames had grown too large and wild. They jumped everywhere, burning higher and hotter, blocking his path. They leaped at him, eagerly licking his body, consuming him. He remembered strong arms carrying him away as his parents screamed, and then darkness had overtaken him.

The Viper pulled Piers's arm over the flame.

As he cried out, the smell of charred skin replaced the scent of apples.

The High Priest smiled beatifically, drumming his fingers on the Desk of Jacob as if listening to a concerto only he could hear.

CHAPTER 4
AALISS

Aaliss slammed the tunnel door shut.

Thud!

And with that ominous sound the unthinkable had become real. Her Guardian code would never open the door again, and without the tunnel, they were stranded in the Zone with the Soulless and the full moon. She could take care of herself, but Wilky would be practically defenseless in the wild.

Being responsible for him had become second nature to her, but she could manage him in Eden, a safe place filled with quiet rooms where distractions wouldn't overwhelm him. The Zone was different. Dangers filled the Zone, seeping into the very trees and grasses, and the Red Death made even the air lethal.

How am I going to keep him safe here?

Wilky and the Soulless girl bent at the waist, gasping for breath from the sprint through the tunnel.

He looked fragile, and she worried that the rough world outside of Eden would swallow him whole.

She cursed her uncle under her breath. That snake had betrayed them. She had never trusted the High Priest, his low character as obvious to her as a foul stench, but she had hoped for more from her uncle. Admittedly, they were never close, but to betray his own kin? A special place in hell waited for him, and she wanted to be the person who sent him there. She'd die happy, if only she could strangle the life out of him first.

You'll get yours, Uncle, even if I have to die to do it.

Revenge would have to wait, however. She groaned and pounded the door a half dozen times. It felt good to hit something, even if it *was* just a steel door.

The door blended seamlessly with the surrounding forest, as if it belonged to a thicket of shrubs and small trees. A computer projected the camouflage onto the steel. It changed with the time of day and the seasons, thus always ensuring an almost perfect match to the surroundings. Only those trained to find the slight tells could actually see them—tiny imperfections that differentiated the digital image from the natural forest that surrounded it. Everything about Eden involved trickery and deceit, even the way in.

She frowned and turned to face Wilky and the Soulless girl. Speaking more to herself than her brother, she said, "Okay, which way shall we go from here?"

The Zone consisted mostly of dense forest. Mature oaks, maples, and evergreens competed for space with giant gray ghost trees. Ferns, mosses, and thick grasses covered the forest floor.

"We could travel along the main way." She pointed to a path straight in front of them. "Or we could venture out to the north." Barely visible, the thin northern trail wasn't wide enough even for Wilky's slim frame. "We need to put as much distance between them and us as possible. They probably have four teams of Guardians in the Zone. The Monks should have radioed them by now, so they'll likely converge on us by way of the main path. But if we go north, the going will be slow and noisy, and you don't have the proper training to navigate that narrow trail. Any fresh team they send after us will easily track and overtake us."

Wilky frowned, but she had always told him the truth, no matter how difficult, and she refused to change now. Lies were for other people, scum like the High Priest and her miserable worm of an uncle.

No lies in my family, not between my brothers and me.

Wilky spun in a slow circle, and trembled. This was his first time in the Zone.

Fear is a good thing. There's much to fear here.

She spotted two Eyes perched in a nearby oak. One pointed at the tunnel door, and the other away from it. Battery-operated Eyes peppered the Zone, transmitting images to the Compound. She unsheathed her blade, climbed up the tree, hacked at the cameras to knock them from their perch, and watched as they tumbled to the ground, useless.

She jumped from the tree and stomped on them with a satisfied grin on her face.

The Eyes were only one of the obstacles they would have to overcome. The Edenites had added all sorts of traps to the buffer area. Aaliss knew what to look for—strategically placed mines, spring traps, and poisonous gas canisters, all designed to prevent the Soulless from wandering too close to Eden—but Wilky had no idea what was dangerous, and he might trigger one without realizing it. She'd have to keep him close.

He tugged at her arm. "Water."

She sheathed her blade. "We don't have time for a drink now, Wilky. I've got to decide what to do, and we need to move fast."

He crossed his arms over his chest and shot Aaliss that familiar stubborn look again.

"You've got to be careful in the Zone. Dangerous creatures roam out here. You have to do what I say and follow close behind me and try not to make much noise." Aaliss turned to the Soulless girl.

The girl stood mesmerized by the closed tunnel door, as if she couldn't quite understand what had happened to the tunnel.

Aaliss grabbed her shoulders and spun her around. "Listen, you, I don't care if you follow us or not, but if you come with us, you do as I tell you and you keep quiet. I'll leave you behind at the first hint of a problem. I'm not going to risk our lives for a Soulless girl."

The girl stayed mute with a glazed look in her eyes.

Wilky tugged on Aaliss's arm. "Eden River!"

She shook her head. "We can't go back to Eden, Wilky. The river is mined, and even if we made it back they would find us. Who knows what story they've spun? They'll brand us as traitors and execute us. Our necks will be on the headman's block in no time. We need a plan first, and maybe some help."

A howl tore through the night from the forest just in front of them, and a chill crept into her blood.

It's a firefox!

Their distinctive cry sounded longer and higher-pitched than regular foxes. Extremely dangerous, they usually traveled in packs. The size of wolves, they had strong jaws with two rows of razor-sharp teeth, and amber eyes that glowed in the dark. Their fur started deep red at the base, lightened to orange, and then blazed bright yellow at the tips. When the sun hit the fur just right, the animal appeared as if were on fire. Beautiful, if only they gave you time to appreciate it before they went for your throat.

Aaliss glared at the full moon and stepped closer to Wilky. He'd be defenseless against one of the predators. "It's getting late, and the moon's lost most of its power by now. We should be all right."

She scanned the forest in search of the firefox. She didn't see any signs of the animal, and turned to....

Wilky and the Soulless girl raced toward the river, crashing through brush and stomping long grass.

"This is crazy," she muttered as she ran after them. "The river is a dead end!"

Within a few minutes, Wilky skidded to a stop where the forest ended and the river began.

Eden was only a half-mile across the water, yet it felt a lot farther away. As a peninsula, Eden connected to the mainland by a narrow strip of land littered with landmines called the Bridge. Only a fool would try to cross the Bridge without the map pinpointing the landmines, and they didn't have it. Eden River protected Eden's other three sides, its water fast and wide, and also treacherous with numerous mines. The fishermen could navigate those explosives, the information passed down from generation to generation, but they never shared that knowledge with outsiders.

From here she could see the massive wall that circled the city, the tops of the four towers that stretched above the wall, and the pitched roof of the cathedral that stood in the center. A few lights twinkled from the Parsonage, and her ire rose.

"I bet the High Priest is making plans to capture us." She turned toward Wilky. "Now what? I told you we can't go back to Eden!"

"We take Eden River that way." He pointed downriver.

She grinned, surprised at her brother's quick thinking. "Good idea! The current will carry us a few miles downriver. As long as we stay along the bank, the mines should be no problem, and they won't know where to look for us. We'll need some dead wood to make a raft."

She had always thought of the river as Eden's protector. Its fast currents and mines kept unwanted visitors from the community, shielding the Edenites from the Soulless and the Red Death. Now the river had become their ally, the only chance for two Edenite runaways and a Soulless girl. Perhaps the moon still had some power left, turning things upside down.

Another firefox answered the first's howl. The shriek came from their left, hungry and close.

Aaliss rested her hand on the hilt of her sword. "Sounds like a hunting call. Let's move fast."

They had no problem finding dead wood along the riverbank. Using rope from their satchels, they bound four long, wide branches together.

Aaliss pointed at a rocky portion of the riverbank that jutted into the water. "Let's launch the raft from there."

She studied the river with trepidation and tried to see how deep the water flowed, but no luck. She couldn't swim, and the current moved swiftly. She watched as white water splashed up and over nearby rocks, and a tree branch raced downstream. She followed the branch's path until it crashed into a rock and split in half.

The river flowed south. She had never gone south before, having been warned away from that part of the Zone. Even though she'd finished first in her class, she had only been a full Guardian for less than a year, so her superiors prohibited her from patrolling the most dangerous parts of the Zone, and everyone considered the southern sectors the most dangerous.

Another firefox howled to their right, and the hair on her neck stood on end. This one sounded even closer than the last, and she felt the trap tightening around them—at least three beasts hunted them.

Bending low, she tapped the water with her hand, testing it.

Will it save us or drown us?

"The water's cold, Wilky, but not too cold. I'll stand in the river and hold the raft steady. You and the Soulless girl jump on. Be careful to stay on top. We'll take it downriver for as long as we can last and avoid those rocks."

Another howl. Tall grasses by a nearby tree swayed, and a flash of red mingled with the green in the moonlight.

Wilky edged away from the forest. Even he realized the firefoxes were close now.

They snarled and she smelled their wild fur. Better to risk death in Eden River than face a hungry pack of firefoxes.

Aaliss huffed, pushed aside her fear of drowning, plunged into the water, and battled to keep her footing on the slippery riverbed. The water reached her waist and the cold knocked the breath out of her.

"Come on, Wilky, I've got it steady." She clenched her teeth.

He clumsily jumped on top of the raft while the Soulless girl nimbly swung her body next to his.

Once both of her passengers were safely on their stomachs, Aailiss kicked off the riverbed and deftly pulled herself up to join them. She thanked Jacob that the wood stayed afloat as the strong current raced them downriver.

She chanced a look over her shoulder and found four disappointed firefoxes sulking along the bank. Their amber eyes sparkled in the moonlight as they howled their displeasure at a meal missed.

She exhaled, wrapped her left arm around her brother to help him cling to the raft, and watched Eden with a heavy heart as they floated downriver.

When the towers and the Compound disappeared, she muttered under her breath. "They'll pay for this."

Aaliss lost all feeling in her right hand and both feet, which dragged in the river. Her teeth chattered incessantly, and her left arm and shoulder had cramped under the strain of holding her brother tight to keep him safe.

"We have to g-get off the water. It's t-too cold." She kicked with her feet, pushed hard with her right hand, and guided the raft to the bank, where she beached it onto rocky sand.

They had lasted half an hour on the river, having traveled six miles or so.

Good enough.

She shoved the raft back into the water, hoping to throw off anyone who would pursue them.

The full moon still cast enough light to guide them. "Let's follow this path." She pointed to an active deer trail. "We need to put distance between us and the river. Try to be quiet."

This part of the Zone felt different from the areas she usually patrolled. Although it had the same trees and vegetation, more giant ghost trees dotted the landscape. The trees' massive size and broad branches created wide swaths of clear space on the ground.

An eerie silence settled into these woods as the three of them traveled quietly for a long time, until Wilky began to stumble from fatigue.

She stopped in a grove of four vast ghost trees. She liked to camp among the giant trees. The higher branches were usually safe from predators and an easy place to hide.

"Okay," she said. "We've traveled far enough. Let's make camp here. We'll climb up and sleep in our hammocks. It'll be light soon, so let's get a few hours of rest. We'll start out again at daylight."

She helped her two charges up the largest of the four trees. They climbed thirty feet and settled on an intersection of three wide branches. She removed hammocks from their satchels, firmly secured them to the tree, and placed hers close to Wilky's.

She whispered to him, "Okay, everything is quiet, and we're safe for now."

He had difficulty communicating, but if he grew familiar with his surroundings, and she removed much of the outside stimulus, the words would come.

"We don't need to rush, but there are things I need to know."

He nodded.

"I overheard the High Priest and our uncle talking. They said you've discovered a cure to the Red Death. Is that true? Have you figured it out?"

He smiled slyly.

Edenites had been searching for a cure from the beginning, more than eight hundred years. The idea that her sweet, slightly odd brother could have solved the mystery sent a jolt through her. It was both miraculous and shocking at the same time.

"How did you do it?"

"I saw it." He spoke slowly, each word strained. "It came like a dream. I saw the virus in the microscope, and then I saw the cure. I can't explain it any better." He shook his head, obviously frustrated.

She could see that he wanted to say more, to explain it to her in a way she could understand, but he simply couldn't—not now, in the middle of the strange forest and the giant trees. Maybe he'd be able to later, when things became more settled.

If things ever become more settled.

"What's the cure? They said something about a mushroom and a flower. Is that all it takes?"

"Everyone can be cured."

Aaliss paused to consider his words, not sure she understood their meaning. "Everyone can be cured?" she repeated. "Does that mean that the Soulless can live free of the disease? And we don't have to worry about catching it?"

The moonlight twinkled in his eyes. *"Everyone."*

"That's incredible!"

The Priests had always discussed a cure for the Red Death in terms of an inoculation, a drug that would shield Edenites from the curse. They'd never mentioned the possibility of curing the Soulless, and the fat pig of a High Priest certainly said nothing about that.

"The High Priest and our uncle plan to cure the Edenites on Eden Day," she said. "They want to add your cure to the Sacred Drink and make it seem like a miracle, but that wouldn't work with you hanging around. You could tell someone that you developed the cure, and then their miracle would become yours, not theirs. They assumed I would know what had happened and would protect you."

She sighed as the truth of their circumstances fully dawned on her. It was even worse than she suspected. "We're too dangerous, too much of a threat to their grand plan to keep alive. They'll do anything they can to find us and kill us."

Wilky shrugged, and the Soulless girl turned her head toward them.

"What's her name? I can't continue calling her the *Soulless girl*. She must have a name."

Guardians never asked the Soulless they captured their names. Names were dangerous—Edenites had names. Better to refer to them simply as "Soulless."

"Gemma."

"Can she speak our language?"

The girl stared blankly into space, and Aaliss wondered if she knew what was happening.

"Yes," Wilky said. "She uses our words, only she mixes up the sounds a little. If I listen closely, I can understand her."

"So she understands what we say?"

"Yes."

"And we still need her?"

Wilky didn't say anything, but she knew his answer by the stern expression on his face.

Glancing at Gemma, she spoke loud enough for the girl to hear.

"She can come with us, but I'm not responsible for her. If she gets in the way or causes trouble, I'm cutting her loose."

She lowered her voice and whispered to her brother, "Try to get some sleep. It will be light soon. I'll wake you in a few hours."

"Can't sleep."

Her heart ached. He sounded so small and young and scared.

"Sing to me," he said.

"We should be quiet now. Just close your eyes."

"Can't sleep. Sing to me."

New places and things frightened Wilky. He had a hard time managing them.

She could only imagine what effect their predicament and the Zone had on him. She hated to sing, but if singing would make him feel a little better, she could not refuse him. "Okay, just for a moment."

He closed his eyes and she sang him a song, a lullaby their mother sang to them when they were young.

> Sleep and let God attend thee,
> He's sent Guardians to protect thee,
> Soft the darkness comes a creeping,
> The Red Death comes a sneaking,
> You will be safe while you are sleeping.
>
> ~~~
>
> Angels watch over thee,
> Jacob keeps the Dark One away from thee,
> Soft the darkness comes a creeping,
> The Red Death comes a sneaking,
> You will be safe while you are sleeping.

The gasmask distorted her notes, but the song worked. By the time she finished, both Wilky and Gemma had fallen asleep.

The night sky started to lighten and turn gray. She didn't expect to fall asleep, but exhaustion overtook her. Right before she drifted off, a troubling thought tried to break through her fatigue.

The forest is too quiet, even for this hour.

She was too tired to understand what it meant.

CHAPTER 5
EAMON

Eamon studied the faces around the campfire, worry etched on his own as he wondered whether this would be the last time they would all gather together. He sat between his two older brothers, King Dermot and Prince Fintan. Dermot had lived six winters more than Eamon had, and Fintan one, yet *he* was the planner and worrier. Often he wished he could be more like them, but he never stopped fretting about tomorrow, the next season, the next winter.

All the council members, twelve in total, joined them this night, forming a loose circle around a campfire that had started to lose its intensity. They met in the Courtyard, in the middle of the Stronghold, a small city protected by a sturdy stone wall. The Stronghold stood in the center of Dermot's kingdom between the Outpost to the north and the Settlement to the south.

When Eamon realized everyone had stopped talking and were looking at him, he remembered what they had been discussing. "We'll have to slaughter more cattle this year. The tribe's grown since last winter." The answer was obvious to him.

"The herd's also added numbers this year, my Lord," added Keenan, the Cattle Master. Built broad and strong like a steer, he had been Cattle Master for three years, and Dermot trusted him. "I reckon we could cull the herd by another twenty over last year and still maintain the size."

All eyes turned toward Dermot. His reign had already lasted six years, almost an eternity. The Sword of Power lay across his lap, a long sword so heavy that it required two hands to wield it in battle. Its blade gleamed in the firelight, and the many rubies in the gold and silver hilt sparkled brilliantly. An inscription, written in a language no one understood, ran down both sides of the blade and glimmered in the firelight. The smithies could no longer make a weapon like the Sword of Power. That knowledge had been lost. They made other swords, fine ones, victorious ones, but none so grand. Only the King could wield the Sword of Power, the tribe's finest.

"Twenty more will do." Dermot sounded tired, his energy waning with the dying fire.

"The butchers will need help," Eamon added, always worried about the repercussions from their decisions no one else seemed to consider. "We lost four to the Red Death this year, including the prior Master."

Everyone spit when he mentioned the Red Death, to ward off evil spirits.

Clay the Cleaver, the new Butcher Master, nodded his head gravely. He had lived only seventeen winters, but Dermot had judged him most capable. He was Keenan's younger brother, although the relationship was impossible to tell by looking at them. Clay resembled a cleaver, wiry of build, face thin and angular, with small black eyes sharp and dangerous.

The tribe's main industry involved livestock, so the number of their cattle and the quality of their butchering made a big difference in their fortunes. Prices at The Exchange where they bartered with other tribes varied. Known for offering the best meat, the Butcher Tribe fetched the highest prices, earning them more silver for the supplies they needed, such as steel for their smiths and wine for their feasts.

Dermot turned toward Fintan. "How many new swords have you added to your ranks this year, brother?"

"Thirty, but our northern neighbors grow increasingly bold by the day. We can not be left unprepared if they develop the nerve to attack us." Emerald flecks in Fintan's dark brown eyes flashed angrily in the firelight.

Eamon knew Fintan wanted to say more, but that he felt uncomfortable discussing it at an open council meeting. Eamon could see it in his brother's eyes, the clenched jaw, and the tense muscles in his shoulders—he had plans, ambitions. Eamon could guess what his brother wanted, but would surely find out later.

"With thirty new swords, you can temporarily spare ten." Dermot glared at Fintan, which silenced his protest before he voiced it. "Your new soldiers can practice their steel work on the cows, and then you can have them back."

The full moon shone down on them. The council met on the evening of each full moon, and this meeting had been longer than any Eamon remembered. He glanced at Dermot, looking for signs of the Red Death even though he knew he was being foolish. Only red eyes warned of the disease, and his brother's eyes had thankfully remained his natural brown. Still, his imagination played evil games on him.

Have the edges of his eyes turned red? If I stare closely enough, will I see crimson?

He shook his head to clear away such nonsense.

"That's the final item for us tonight." Dermot lifted his face and gazed at the stars. "May the herd forever be strong and the heavens guide us in all matters!"

The council repeated the short prayer and the meeting ended. The members dispersed, except for Eamon and his two brothers, who remained by the fire.

Fintan and Dermot were shorter and wider than Eamon. Both had long brown hair pulled back in a thick ponytail, unlike Eamon whose hair fell to the top of his shoulders in a curly mop. Eamon shared the same oval face and angular features with his brothers, but the lines of his face had a certain softness that his two brothers lacked, which had earned him the nickname *Eamon the Handsome* among the Stronghold's women. His eyes also burned a deep blue, while both Fintan and Dermot had their mother's chestnut-colored orbs. Eamon could at least remember that his father's eyes had been blue. He couldn't recall much about his mother, just a warm feeling, really, but Dermot had told him of her brown eyes, and that was good enough for him.

When the three were alone, Fintan pleaded his case, as Eamon knew he would. "We should attack the Painted Ones now, Derry. Let's teach them a lesson and take the fields to our north!" Fintan swung his head back and forth from one brother to the other, looking for support and finding none. Undaunted, he pressed on. "They have good fields, fertile land. We could grow corn and wheat for our herds. We'd become more prosperous and our power would grow!"

Eamon knew what Fintan desired — power for the tribe and glory for himself. Not necessarily in that order.

Some things never change, eh, Brother?

Dermot listened quietly to his brother's fervent plea, and when Fintan finished, Dermot glanced to the heavens. After a long moment, he turned back to Fintan, his expression hard as steel.

The older brother Eamon loved had vanished, replaced by the king of the Butcher Tribe, and as such, he ruled with certainty. "I will not be the one to break the peace, Fin. We have enough lands, and our time in this world is short enough as it is."

Fintan turned away from his brothers.

Dermot continued in a conciliatory tone. "Still, I will not ignore threats to our security. Send two more guard units to patrol the northern boundaries. To *patrol*, Fin. We will not break the peace. Understood?"

"Yes, my king." Fintan's voice simmered. "If you would excuse me, I grow weary from this long night of council."

Dermot nodded, and Fintan stalked off.

Eamon watched him leave. When they were children, Dermot urged his brothers to balance their studies between warcraft and learning, but they separated at an early age. Fintan excelled at swordplay and at other weapons, while Eamon read the more advanced books and did the more difficult calculations with the same natural ease Fintan showed with a sword or a bow. Eventually, they stopped competing against each other and focused on what each did best. Still, some wounds never truly healed, and both brothers held their grudges.

"You know Fin will start a war. It's just a matter of time." Eamon frowned at Dermot. "It's all he thinks about."

"Maybe, but the weight of this sword is heavy. He will not defy me." Dermot tilted the sword's blade upward and smiled wryly. "Was I any different when I was his age?"

"How can you say such a thing? You've led us in peace for four years now!"

Dermot placed a hand on his shoulder. "You were young when I first started ruling, and don't remember those early days well. We fought wars for the first two years of my reign, with the Horsepeople to the south and the Painted Ones to the north, before I finally made the peace."

"But those wars were necessary!"

"Were they? I thought so at the time, but as I think about them now, they could have been avoided. War can be intoxicating, the high indescribable, but it doesn't take long before you realize the cost—the lives ruined. Not just the deaths, but also the injuries—those who lose an arm or a leg, or maybe the death of a brother, a father, a friend. That can hurt as much as any wound."

Dermot shook his head and lifted his hand from Eamon's shoulder. "Some images haunt my dreams, but you can't go back, only forward and learn from your mistakes. There's nothing I can do about them now. I'm old, Eamon. I've already lived twenty-three winters—more than most."

Eamon spit repeatedly. "We don't say the number out loud! You know it only invites the Red Death." After another dose of spitting because he had mentioned the curse, his mouth had gone dry.

"Numbers cannot hurt me, brother. What lives inside me and grows by the day is the problem." Dermot prodded the fire with the blade from his great sword. Sparks flew in the air and the flames recovered some of their lost vigor. "I need you to promise me something."

Eamon sensed a trap—all this talk of death and age, and now a promise—so he spoke carefully. "What would you have me do, my Brother?"

Dermot bore his eyes into him, carving past skin, bone and blood, and into his soul.

Eamon had seen him use his gaze as a weapon many times, but never aimed at him. He had to admit, it was effective. He felt some of his resolve wither.

"When I pass, I don't want you to challenge Fintan in the Circle of Destiny. He will be our next king."

Eamon's face turned as hot as the embers of the fire. "I've been training! I'm getting much better! I might best him." He had spent much time practicing of late. His arms had grown stronger, and his skills had greatly improved, not that Dermot had noticed.

Dermot nodded. "Your sword is quick, and of your courage there can be no doubt, but Fintan's sword is faster and his shield stronger. He's been preparing for this moment his entire life. You have spent much of your time in studies. You are not to oppose him in the Circle of Destiny."

Has he no faith in me?

Eamon felt the sting of Dermot's words. "If not me, there's no one else. The cousins are still too young. He will be king and lead us into war."

"Your life is too important to be wasted. Your work with the Books of Wisdom is essential to the tribe's future. We must collect our knowledge to guide future generations, or they'll be destined only to repeat what we have done, and never advance. No one but you can finish them. Promise me, Eamon."

Eamon looked away and tears welled up in his eyes, not because of the promise his brother sought, but because of the truth of his words. The Red Death would take him soon, as it did everyone but the witches. Dermot had always been there for Eamon. He could not imagine a world without Dermot.

There must be some way to break the cycle. If anyone deserves to cheat the Red Death, it's Dermot. Surely the heavens will recognize this.

"Promise me," Dermot persisted.

How can I refuse him when his end is so near?

Eamon managed to put a stoic expression on his face as he tossed a rock on the fire. "If it's your wish, then I so promise."

"Good. Now, tell me how the books are coming. Do we have enough paper?"

Eamon stared at the campfire. "They're all underway. We're mostly finished with the book on livestock. That was my first priority, but all the others have been started. If we're careful, we should have enough paper. Jillian's letters are small but legible." He shrugged. "Of course, it depends on Renny the Round. You know how much our Master Builder likes to talk. His words are more numerous than the stones he uses for the walls."

Dermot laughed at the small joke, and Eamon joined him, the tension broken between them.

"Shall we go inside?" asked Eamon. "The hour is late."

"No, I'd like to watch the sun come up." Dermot sounded distant.

"Shall I call for Bree or Shannon to keep you company? I can't keep up with you. I don't know which one you favor."

"No, they sleep peacefully in their beds. I don't want to disturb them. You stay with me. We can watch the sunrise like we did when you were small. Besides, they don't call *me* Eamon the Handsome."

Eamon glared at his brother, sending invisible barbs at him that, if real, would have skewered him. "I can't help what they say. I'm a warrior, just like you and Fintan."

Dermot chuckled, his face soft and warm. "I know you are. I only tease you. You are as ugly a brute as we are."

"I'm happy we settled that." Eamon leaned back on his elbows and stared up at the starry sky. The full moon seemed to smile down on them, and lifted his spirits. "Derry, do you really think the gods watch us from the heavens?"

"Haven't we decided this already?"

Eamon laughed. They had repeated this conversation so many times it felt as comfortable as his favorite shirt. He hoped this would not be the last time.

Dermot flexed his right hand with a pained expression on his face.

Eamon knew the Red Death had no symptoms beyond the red eyes, yet he wondered if his brother could feel it burning in his blood.

CHAPTER 6
FINTAN

Fintan trudged to his sleeping quarters, kicking stones as he went. The sweet smell of burning firewood followed him like a long shadow. He had wanted to ask Dermot one last time to attack the Painted Ones, but he knew his stubborn brother would rule against him.

Soon I'll get my chance, Brother — even if I have to wrestle that sword away from you.

The Stronghold's three large stone residence halls loomed only a short walk from the campfire. The largest housed the female members of the tribe and the Nursery where all the children younger than ten slept. The second largest hall contained the remaining males, and the smallest but most elaborate was reserved for the royal family, council members, and other significant leaders. Wisps of smoke spiraled from the main chimney of each.

A crow's call sounded from behind the Women's Hall.

Fintan grimaced and wearily headed in that direction, feeling heavier and more tired than he had only moments earlier. As he neared the edge of the stone building, a strongly built man stepped from the shadows and hurled a dagger at him. The moonlight reflected off its spinning steel blade, and he snatched the knife inches from his chest by clasping both palms against cold steel.

He tossed the dagger back to his friend. "If you kill me, Eamon will rule next. You'll be turned into a scribe and be forced to battle ink bottles all day." He chuckled. "I remember when they tried to teach you to read and write. You were lost like a sheep that had wandered away from the flock."

Cormac grinned. "I practically tossed the dagger underhand." Fintan's best friend since childhood, he had a wide stonemason's chest, a long pointy nose, an unkempt black beard, and small onyx eyes that glittered in the moonlight. A copper pin in the shape of a sword affixed to his leather cloak identified him as the Captain of the King's Guard.

At least Dermot let me name my own Captain.

At the time, Fintan thought Dermot would listen to his plans to attack the Painted Barbarians. He thought his brother would let him prove himself before he died, and even fight beside him on the same battlefield. Foolish ideas. His brother would never change and allow Fintan to seek the glory he deserved. Dermot wanted to keep all the glory for himself.

Cormac said, "So what of our plans? Did you discuss them with your brother after the council meeting?"

"The King would rather not attack our friends to the north. How ironic that the *Blade of the Butcher Tribe* refuses to break the peace." Fintan leaned against the wall, its rough edges pressing against his back. "I managed to convince him our northern neighbors are a threat to our security, so he's willing to send additional patrols to protect us, but he does not want the patrols to break the peace. That would make him very angry." He pursed his lips into an exaggerated frown.

"Patrols are not enough! The Painted Ones are weak. We should take those fields with our steel." Cormac pounded the wall. "Dermot is old and scared. This is our time! We should take what we desire. When was the last time he led us in battle?"

"Four long years have passed since he led us against the northern barbarians. Four years since he made the peace he now holds so dear. It appears he's more interested in his *Books of Wisdom* than the good of the tribe."

"What good are those stupid books on animals and plants? Your brother favors scribes and weaklings. How much silver have we wasted on paper and ink? Why? We should burn those books and write a new one full of our conquests!" Cormac's voice grew louder. "A book written in the blood of our enemies!"

Fintan grinned as he imagined the cover. "We'll call it *The Book of Conquests*, with our names scrawled across the cover in blood. I like it. That will be the first thing we'll do when I become king. In the meantime, while my brother lives...." He paused, stared meaningfully at Cormac, and shrugged. "We are subject to his pronouncements and sworn to follow his commands. Still, the border territory is dangerous. Cattle could be stolen. A patrol might be attacked. These things have been known to happen."

Cormac flipped his dagger in the air, caught the blade with the tip of his finger, and spun it back in the air again. "But what if they don't attack us?" A sharp gust of wind brought an icy chill into the air, and Cormac pulled his leather cloak tightly around him. "Time grows short. Winter approaches. We can't attack once the first snow falls."

Fintan shrugged. "Dermot's old. If he doesn't want to protect the tribe, then it's our responsibility to take his place. You remember the lessons we learned together as children? The tribe must come first. We must always protect the herd so it remains forever strong."

"Yes, but *everyone* loves Dermot—*Dermot the Kind, Dermot the Just, Dermot the Blade of the Butchers.* Few would stand with us against him."

Fintan narrowed his eyes. He didn't need to be reminded about Dermot's popularity among the people. It wasn't easy being the younger brother of a hero. Four years ago he had wanted to fight against the Painted Ones, but Dermot had refused him, saying he was too young, and kept all the glory for himself. Fintan could only prove himself with a new war, but Dermot kept the peace, so the tribe would have only one *Blade* and one hero, and no chance for him to best his older brother.

He hitched up an eyebrow. "What if our beloved King died suddenly? Such a thing would be very tragic."

Cormac's grin threatened to take over his whole face as he flipped the dagger back into the air. "Yes, with Dermot gone, only Eamon could oppose you."

Fintan looped his arm over Cormac's shoulder. "I have no worries about *Eamon the Pretty Boy*. He spends all his time with the scribes and weaklings. He's nothing, but Derry is another story. We'll need to be clever. I understand the poisonous red berries grow this time of year in the Witch's Woods to the North. We can trust Scotty the Snake. Tell him to retrieve some for us. Have no fear, my friend. One way or another, we'll be heroes."

"I want to be called *Cormac the Conqueror* in our book."

"That doesn't seem very likely. They usually remember just the kings."

"They sing songs of *Poland the Punisher*."

Fintan chuckled and playfully shoved his friend toward home. "True, but there's only one *Poland the Punisher*. Maybe you can have a small mention. Nothing too...."

Cattie hid among the shadows and held her breath. The straps of the leather satchel cut into her hands, but she dared not move or drop her load of firewood. From the safety of her hiding spot, she watched Fintan and Cormac stalk off into the distance, and a small smile spread wickedly across her face.

CHAPTER 7
P'MINA

P'mina wiggled against her sister's iron grip. She'd rather scale the steep cliff north of the village, to reach the teal- and gold-colored flowers that only grew in the mouth of those caves, than be stuck with her sister this night. And that was usually her least favorite thing to do; she only climbed that cliff when someone had a fever high enough that it might kill them, and only after she had tried all the other plants she knew that reduced fevers.

"Why can't you ever sit still?" Kalhona asked. "You're going to make me mess up."

P'mina knew there was little chance her sister would slip up as she expertly worked the needles and dyes. As the best Artist in the Painted Ones Tribe, even people from other tribes recognized her talent.

Kalhona plunged a needle a little deeper than necessary.

"Ouch!" P'mina glared at her sister with the angriest look she could muster.

"That wouldn't have happened if you'd sit still. It's been a long night. Don't make it any longer." A crooked smile creased Kalhona's face.

P'mina helped her sister work through the long line of customers this night, which had stretched on longer than any other she could remember. She had hoped that Kalhona would be too tired to work on her, but she wasn't that lucky, and it would not have mattered. Whether she got the tattoo or not, she was still doomed.

On every full moon, tradition required the female members of the Painted Ones Tribe to receive a new tattoo memorializing the tribe's history. Together these markings created a mosaic depicting tribal history going back hundreds of harvests. They reserved only their right arms for personal, not tribal, stories, and tonight her sister painted P'mina's right arm.

Usually she looked forward to getting a new tattoo, but not this one.

On a girl's tenth birthday, she received a tattoo of a ghost tree on her right arm. Small differences in the tree, such as color, branches, size, and placement of leaves, indicated a particular family, and flowers represented children. Only members of the tribe could accurately read the details. Kalhona once tried to explain all the subtle variances to her, but P'mina could never keep track of them all. In truth, only the Artists understood them with certainty, and even they disagreed from time to time.

The Artists decorated each woman, moon-by-moon and harvest-by-harvest, with details telling the story of her life—her loves, losses, victories, and defeats. The more colorful her arms, and indeed, her entire body, the happier her life was thought to be.

P'imina didn't feel quite so happy as tears pooled in her eyes. She didn't want to cry, but the night had been long, and the weight on her heart heavy. "I don't want to leave."

"You must go." Kalhona lifted the needles. "It's a huge honor. We're having a special feast and everything. You have no choice."

"If it's such a big honor, then you go!"

"Why are you always so difficult?" Kalhona resumed her work, but softened her voice when tears started rolling down P'mina's face. "I'm sorry, sister. I didn't mean to yell, but you know this *is* a big honor. We only swap girls with them once every ten harvests, and only if you're thirteen. I'm too old. You and the other girls will represent our tribe and help the Orion folk understand our ways."

"They're monsters! They treat their women like slaves. They think women can't do anything but cook, clean, take care of young ones, and be wives!"

"Since when have you followed the rules?" Kalhona smirked. "You've learned all there is to know about plants—which ones are edible and which are good for medicine. That's very important." She touched the tattoo she had added to P'mina's tree after the last harvest—a vine with a variety of colorful flowers, which depicted her knowledge of all things floral—and chuckled. "I'm sure you'll be running things over there before long."

Why is this so hard for her to understand?

"Shyla says they punish their women if they don't behave. She says the Orions are mean and horrible. I don't want to go!" She wrenched her right arm from Kalhona and wrapped it around her chest stubbornly.

"You can't believe everything old Shyla says." He sister lowered her voice and leaned close. "She's had the red eyes for three days now. She won't live long enough for the feast."

"Shyla wouldn't lie to me!" P'mina shook her head defiantly. Shyla wasn't her friend, but she had an honest face.

"Maybe not, but what about Talia? She has a big family, and at last harvest's Awakening Feast she couldn't have been happier." Talia had been swapped ten harvests earlier and was the sole survivor who hadn't succumbed to the Red Death. Yet.

P'mina's face flushed with heat. Talia lauded her six children over everyone in the tribe as proof of her happiness, which was more than annoying. Besides, she was sure it was really an act. "Talia's a nit and has always been one. I won't get to see you or anyone else. Aren't you going to miss me?"

"That's not true! I'll see you each spring at the Awakening Feast, and maybe at The Exchange also. You'll tell me everything that's happened, and I'll tell you all about us. I'll spend all day adding to your tattoos and...." Kalhona paused and looked around, as if making sure no one could hear, and whispered, "You'll be redeeming the family. From now on, everyone will talk about us with pride instead of those whispers and looks we still get sometimes because of Mom."

Finally, she speaks true.

"They will never forget about our mother. We will always be *witchborn* to them. They can pound dirt!"

Kalhona shot her a sharp look, so P'mina lowered her voice. "It wasn't Mother's fault that the Dark One made her a witch. She left right away, and no one's heard from her since. There have been no curses or dark magic or anything. They can all pound dirt!" Talk of her mother pulled strong emotions from her. Her face now burned with a mixture of anger, shame, and sadness, but mostly longing for the mother she missed. "She didn't even have time to say goodbye."

"You don't remember how it was, little sister. One day she woke and her hair had turned red. The Dark One claimed her in our hut while we were sleeping! She left right away because it was the safest thing for her to do. You were in the nursery, and she couldn't just walk in and say goodbye. Think of the other children. Many days of whispers and looks and rumors followed." Kalhona gently reclaimed P'mina's arm and resumed work on her tattoo. "Some wanted to banish *us*, too."

"Do you ever think about her? Do you think maybe she's still... alive?" P'mina's voice cracked, but a trace of hope gleamed in her mind. Her mother could be anywhere, and P'mina would do anything to see her again.

Kalhona sighed. "I try not to think of her—I don't want to tempt the Dark One—but I did hear a rumor once." She wiped the excess dye and blood from P'mina's arm and leaned in close to her sister's ear.

P'mina took a shaky breath and tried to calm her racing heart. Kalhona never spoke about their mother, and now she might know where to find her. Just the possibility of seeing her again sent P'mina's head spinning.

"I met a trader at The Exchange from the Butcher Tribe. He told me about a witch who lives off the Ancient Road north of their lands. I don't know if I believe him, and even if he told me the truth, I doubt she's our mother." Kalhona shrugged. "There are other witches, but she's the only one I've ever heard of close by."

Kalhona released her arm, and P'mina examined the new tattoo—two interlocking, identical round faces shined down on her ghost tree like two moons, one white, the other caramel. The white one frowned with a blue teardrop falling from the left eye, while the caramel one smiled. The Painted Tribe was famous for their blond hair, fair skin, and blue eyes. P'mina and Kalhona shared all three of these traits, though their hair differed. P'mina's fell long and straight, whereas Kalhona kept her hair short with waves. The Orions generally had darker skin and black curly hair.

"Do you like it? You have the only one with a blue tear." Kalhona had tattooed the other twenty-one girls who would be swapped with a similar image, but P'mina's big sister had kept this special detail for her alone.

"It's beautiful. I'll always think of you when I see it."

Kalhona grabbed her hand. "Listen, just behave for the next couple of weeks before the feast. Think of it as a new adventure. You love adventures."

P'mina hopped from the stool and beamed a cheesy grin. "Of course. I'll be the perfect angel."

"Promise me you won't do something stupid to embarrass me."

"Yes, Kally, I promise." She kissed her sister on the cheek. "Do you need help cleaning up?"

"No, you can go. You always put things away in the wrong places. It'll be faster if I clean up on my own."

P'mina stepped into the crisp fall night, and the cold air refreshed her. She lifted her gaze to the star-filled sky, and a light cloud passed before the moon, making it seem as if it had long straight hair. Or at least that's what she imagined.

She smiled. For the first time in months, she realized what she would do. The certainty felt good, as if she had discovered a secret trove of plants she needed for her medicines.

She looked to the woods that formed the border with the Butchers and spoke softly to the night and the moon. "Sorry, sister, some promises are not meant to be kept."

CHAPTER 8
VIPER

The first orange rays of sunlight peeked through the treetops as the Viper emerged from the tunnel. A light breeze swayed the branches of the nearby trees as if the forest were welcoming him, so he smiled in return. It felt good to be back here, where he felt at home—where no rules, no social constraints, and no laws held him back. He enjoyed the freedom to be his true self in the Zone, which brought him closer to his forefather, Jacob. If he had his way, he'd never go back to Eden. One day soon, with the cure and Jacob's help, he'd live out his wish. First, he had to make sure the girl and boy didn't disrupt his plans.

Plainly put, he had to kill them.

The door swung shut behind him as Jonas, his old instructor, lumbered to join him.

The Viper regarded him carefully in the morning light. Jonas's short, mostly white hair barely covered his head, gray stubble dotted his face, and he limped slightly on stiff legs. A few inches taller than the Viper, Jonas's black ostrich suit stretched tightly against thick arms, a barrel chest, and a bulging stomach. In his day, he had been deadly with the battleax slung on his back, but his best days were behind him. Still, Jonas retained certain enthusiasms that would come in handy.

The Viper squatted and scanned the immediate area, his keen senses surveying the grass for clues. He understood these forests well and knew instinctively what was natural and what looked out of place.

Jonas pointed to the cameras on the floor, his voice raw. "No one has seen them in the Zone besides these Eyes?"

"No one." The Viper remained still, and swept his gaze across the scene as he stroked his goatee.

Jonas stomped toward the north. "There's no way the three of them used this trail. It would look like a cattle stampede if they had. They must have gone toward the main path."

The Viper stayed where he crouched. *Has Jonas always been so clueless, or have his skills slipped so much in the past few years?* "Look at this grass. It's trampled down, but there are no marks leading to the main path." He pointed in the opposite direction. "It looks as if they went toward Eden River."

Jonas trudged toward the river. "You're right, Gabriel. They definitely went this way, and it looks as if they moved in a hurry."

"I'm not surprised." He pulled a few blades of grass from the ground and sniffed. "There's a partial track from a firefox. From the size and smell of it, I'd say he's a full grown male."

Jonas shook his large mug. "How do you do that? It's almost like you're part hound. I sure hope the firefox hasn't done our job for us. I'd hate to have gotten up so early and have nothing to kill."

"I knew I brought you for a reason."

"Two reasons, actually." Jonas ticked them off with thick fingers. "One, I like killing as much as you do, *Priest*. And two, you know I can keep a secret. Those kids were wearing gasmasks in the video feed. We could just bring them in, but you want them dead. Why?"

"There's a third reason I brought you, old man." The Viper stalked past Jonas and bumped into him with his shoulder as he went. "As long as you get your drink, you don't ask a lot of questions. Don't make me regret my decision."

Jonas kept his mouth shut, rubbed his bloodshot eyes, and shadowed the Viper.

The Viper followed the messy trail to the river's edge, where it took him only a second to spot drag marks that led to the water. "Very clever, little rabbit. They made a raft from loose driftwood and used Eden River to escape the firefoxes and go south. They launched it from there." He pointed at a partial boot print in the dirt.

Jonas stood with the toes of his boots hanging over the riverbank. "I hate the south! Good chance something else will get them before the day's done."

"You shouldn't underestimate our little rabbit. She graduated at the top of her Guardian class."

Jonas shrugged. "I've seen the reports and heard the stories. Her scores rivaled your own, but she's young and inexperienced. She's never even stepped into the southern part of the Zone before, and she's burdened by her weird brother and a Soulless. They'll offer no help and will only slow her down. She'll need luck to survive."

The Viper dragged his hand in the river, let the frigid water lap over his fingers, and smiled as it bit against his warm skin. "Maybe, but for now we go after them. The water's frosty. They couldn't have lasted long on a raft in the middle of the night. We'll follow the bank south and find where they beached it."

"Who's leading the team in the southern part of the Zone? We should radio them to close the circle, just in case the kids survived the night." Jonas pulled a radio from his pocket.

"Samuel."

Jonas frowned and rubbed the stubble on his head. "I don't like him. He's not like us. I don't trust him to keep his mouth shut."

"If he becomes a liability, we'll get rid of him and his team and blame it on the girl. But first we have another more pressing problem." The Viper pointed to a large thorny bush a few feet away. "There's a firefox sleeping under that bush."

Jonas squinted, and after a long moment, the corners of his lips turned upward. "It's damn hard to spot, but I see it now. We could quietly go down the bank here, and it won't bother us. They usually sleep during the day."

"Yes, but with it so close to the tunnel door, it could cause a problem for my Guardians." The Viper felt a jolt of adrenaline and grinned; a firefox was a worthy adversary. "What type of Priest would I be if I left a full-grown firefox where it could harm members of my flock?"

He heaved a heavy stone into the bush.

Almost instantaneously, the firefox appeared, snarling and angry, amber eyes blazing even in the daylight.

The Viper unsheathed both his short swords and kicked another rock at the beast.

The animal bolted forward before the stone landed. It leaped at him, jaw open, both rows of teeth razor sharp.

The Viper moved fast, sidestepping the charge and slicing both of his short swords into the animal's side.

The animal landed hard on a pile of rocks and yelped. Its front right paw broke from the fall and blood gushed from the gashes in its side. It couldn't stand, but it still lunged toward him—jaw working feverishly, snarling, wanting to bite, to taste, to kill.

Jonas chopped his long battleax down and cut the predator in two.

Blood splattered onto the Viper's ostrich suit, and he smiled. The morning was off to a good start, and he had more important quarry to hunt.

CHAPTER 9
EAMON

Eamon usually enjoyed breakfast in the Feasting Hall. Having slept outside last night, worrying about the Red Death and Dermot for endless hours, he now felt a bit worn down and not quite his usual self. At least the energy in the large chamber lifted his mood. A fire roared in the fireplace on the far end of the room, and six long wooden tables stood equally spaced throughout the hall. Fresh straw littered the floor, and a stack of oak logs rested neatly next to the fire.

Everyone ate in the Feasting Hall. Broad-backed smithies sat next to chicken farmers who bumped against scribes and tanners. Before Dermot had started his reign, royals and a privileged few took their meals in a separate dining room in the Royal Hall, but early in his rule Dermot banned that practice in favor of the camaraderie of shared meals among all members of the tribe. Even some of the prominent families now ate beside the lesser ones.

Eamon liked the change, but not everyone agreed. He wondered how long it would take Fintan to reverse the decree.

Eamon spotted a dozen Little Ones serving in the hall, all in their plain gray tunics, and more worked the kitchen. Children who lived ten to thirteen winters spent most of their time in school, but they also helped with different chores, the most common of which involved the Feasting Hall. When younger, he'd worked in the kitchen and the Feasting Hall.

The Master Cook jokingly called them his *Army of Little Ones*, treating them much like soldiers, teaching harsh rules about discipline when needed, a cane never far from his hand. The previous Master Cook treated them the same way and so did the one before him. No one knows what happened before that.

Eamon sat alongside Dermot on one end of the hall, farthest from the fireplace, scrambled eggs and roast pork piled high on wooden plates in front of them. Newly baked loaves of bread and jugs of fresh milk and sweet spring water completed the meal. The time was late for breakfast, so most people had already left the hall to begin their day.

Dermot seemed content to stay planted. He teased Kelly, his seven-year-old cousin, threatening a royal decree to outlaw pigtails, her favorite hairstyle. Kelly's face tinted pink as she struggled for the right words to protest while Dermot laughed and playfully tugged her hair.

The door opened, and Fintan sauntered inside with his shoulders swinging confidently. His full-length cowhide cloak drifted in his wake as his longsword swayed at his hip.

Cormac, as usual, walked a step behind.

Eamon thought it odd that Dermot had allowed Fintan to name Cormac as the Captain of the Guard. Older, more experienced soldiers had proven their courage with Dermot years earlier, but Dermot let Fintan choose his friend.

It hadn't made sense... until last night. As a young king, Fintan would need someone he trusted as his Captain.

Dermot must have known Fintan would succeed him last spring when he let him choose Cormac.

Anger flushed his face. *When did he decide Fintan would be the next ruler? Has it always been obvious to him that I'm unworthy to be the next king?*

As the duo strolled across the room, Eamon scanned the Feasting Hall, glancing at the faces out of habit. They told him the mood of the people—who seemed content, and who held grievances. People usually guarded their emotions around him, but their masks vanished when they thought no one was looking at them.

A pair of brown eyes caught his attention. They belonged to a young woman, who kept her gaze fixed on Fintan as he approached the table.

"May we join you, my king?" Fintan asked Dermot with his usual cocky grin and a small nod of his head. Courtesy required him to ask the King's permission before sitting at his table, although in this case it was a mere formality.

"By all means, Brother." Dermot waved at the bench opposite him and Eamon.

A Little One brought two large plates, carefully placing them in front of Fintan and Cormac. The youngster stumbled as he turned to leave.

Fintan chastised him. "Careful, boy, or you're headed to the stables. We can't have you spilling all the food."

The Stable Master sat nearby and bellowed, "We can always use a new Little One. He'll have to hand in that fancy tunic, though. It'll get stained when he shovels the dung."

Everyone seated at the table laughed heartily at the boy's embarrassment. His face flushed scarlet as he bowed his head and muttered "sorry" while quickly backing away. In his haste, he almost smacked into another Little One, but a young woman noticed the imminent collision and guided the flustered boy safely to the side.

Eamon saw the self-satisfied grin planted on Fintan's face, and his stomach soured. "Perhaps he stumbled on your boot?" He knew full well the answer to the question, and what type of king his brother would become.

Fintan's grin grew even wider and stretched almost from one ear to the next. "It's not my place to clear a path for him. He has to learn these things on his own."

Cormac chuckled.

Eamon shook his head and noticed the brown-eyed girl still looking at Fintan. "It appears you have a new admirer, Brother. At the next table, the girl with the brown eyes can't seem to take them off you. I think she works in the Nursery." He nodded in the girl's direction.

A bit of ash smudged her forehead. Straw-colored hair framed her oval face, a few strands of which brushed in front of intelligent eyes and bumped against a longish nose.

Fintan and Cormac turned to stare at her.

She confidently returned their attention, surprising Eamon with her boldness.

Fintan turned back around. "I don't recognize her. She's not my type." Sticky bits of yellow toppled from his full mouth as he forked more eggs.

"You never know, Brother. Believe me, sometimes during a feast, strange things happen." Dermot chuckled. "Girls who start off as not your type end up irresistible by night's end. If I didn't know better, I'd swear some of them make deals with witches."

"It would take more than a deal with a witch for me to be interested in that girl." Fintan slashed into a large chunk of roasted pork with a knife, and speared it with his fork, ending the conversation.

A young woman burst into the Hall, and the commotion made Eamon look up. Her long raven hair drifted behind her pretty round face as she rushed toward them. A young girl, just barely of age, followed closely behind.

Eamon nudged Dermot in the ribs. "Jillian looks troubled."

She stopped before their table and spoke so rapidly her words ran together. "My Lords, there's a problem. I can't find Gemma."

Dermot lifted both his hands with palms faced outward. "This isn't the first time our sister has wandered off. She's always turned up before. When was the last time you saw her?"

"Five days ago. She usually turns up in the south with the sheep when we can't find her. Something about the animals soothes her. I assumed she went south again and would return in a week or so, but this time is different. This morning Noreen told me she saw Gemma enter the Witch's Woods. Why would she go that way if she wanted to go to the Settlement? It's in the opposite direction from the road to the south."

Jillian grabbed the young girl and thrust her forward. "It's okay. Tell them everything. They won't be angry with you."

Noreen swayed nervously and kept her eyes fixed downward as she spoke, her voice squeaky. "Four days ago, I saw Princess Gemma crossing the creek and heading for the Witch's Woods. She was skipping and singing. I figured she would just go by the edge and come back. I didn't know she was missing until I spoke to Jillian this morning. I swear that was the last time I saw her." She reluctantly lifted her eyes. "Gemma, I mean, my lords."

Kelly pulled on Dermot's cloak, her face splotchy, tears brimming her eyes. "You have to get Gemma back. The Witch's Woods are scary."

The Nursery Master often told children horror stories about the Witch's Woods to discourage them from venturing into the dangerous forest.

Dermot spoke in a reassuring voice. "Don't worry, Kelly. Gemma's just gone missing for a little bit. We will find her. Everything's going to be all right."

Tears spilled down Kelly's puffy cheeks, but she managed a small brave smile.

"Any idea why she'd head to the Witch's Woods, Eamon?" asked Dermot.

All eyes turned toward Eamon. Gemma was his twin, a rare thing among the Butchers, but beyond that, Gemma was unique among her people. She spoke in her own language, which only Eamon and Jillian fully understood, and more than that, she saw the world differently from everyone else. Details had a way of overwhelming her. She'd spend an entire day distracted by the color of a common daisy, forgetting to eat or do any of her chores. Often Jillian found her in a field or by the Naming Tree or Whitewater River or any one of a dozen places lost in thoughts that seemed to be far away. She was irresponsible that way, but little children loved her. They loved her *funny* language and the wide smile she always wore to greet them.

"I don't have any idea why she'd go into the woods." Eamon wished he understood her better. He had tried his entire life, but she remained a mystery.

"We'll search for her." Dermot stood. "Fintan, grab your twelve best Horsemen. We'll meet at the edge of the Witch's Woods by the stone bridge. May the heavens guide us. The Witch's Woods is no place for Gemma."

The Witch's Woods is no place for any of us. Eamon shivered with a slight chill.

Those who went in often never returned.

Five days might as well be an eternity.

CHAPTER 10
AALISS

*A*aliss spun in a slow circle and found herself in an unfamiliar place. Hulking buildings, hollowed out and ruined like vast metallic skeletons, stretched toward the sky all around her. The air smelled sour, as if rotten food had been left outside. Debris, glass, and an odd white powder littered the ground.

She bent low and rubbed the powder between her fingers. It felt like sand, but it looked whiter and finer than any sand she'd ever seen. She looked up at Wilky, who stood next to her, his face tense.

"What is this, Wilky? Where are we?"

His voice trembled. "Bo-bones. The City of... Bones."

Aaliss let the powder drop from her hand and jumped upright. "Is this place real or imaginary?"

"Real."

A cackle came from a dark alley sandwiched between two ruined buildings.

The noise scared her, but curiosity nudged aside the fear. "You stay here. I want to see who made that sound."

Wilky shook his head. "D-Don't."

Aaliss unsheathed her short sword. "Don't worry. I just need to see."

She stalked toward the alley and heard another cackle, followed by female voices that chanted something she could not understand, which only piqued her interest more.

When she reached the opening between the ruined structures, she saw a small fire. She inched forward, careful to keep to the side.

Three shapes stood near the outskirts of the flames, but from this distance the silky blackness made them appear like shadows.

She should leave. Nothing good was happening here, yet she felt pulled, as if someone tugged her forward. Her heart started to thud against her chest and her breathing turned shallow. She crept forward, stepping lightly on the white powder, straining to see clearly.

Wilky grabbed her hand and pulled her to a stop.

She frowned at him and whispered, "I told you to stay back."

"Must go."

She glanced at her frightened brother and then back toward the fire. "Just a little farther."

Wilky tugged on her hand, but she ignored him and moved closer still.

Suddenly the chanting stopped. The flames blazed higher and lit the scene. Three witches with blood-red hair and crimson cloaks stood behind the fire. One held a banner of a red raven, and another lifted a crying baby in the air.

The child's wailing pierced through the distance and knifed its way through Aaliss's skull. She cringed as the sound caused her pain, and stood frozen. She didn't want to look, yet she could not turn her eyes away.

One witch lifted a knife and the baby stopped crying. The white powder at their feet turned red, and the three women stared down the alley right at her.

The one who held the baby cackled. "Our master has led him to us. The boy is here. We need the boy."

The other two witches started chanting, "Give us the boy!"

Wilky pulled Aaliss's hand with all his strength.

The boy? They want Wilky! What have I done?

A pack of firefoxes appeared behind the witches and bolted forward, as if the crones had given them a silent order to kill them.

"Run!" Aaliss turned and pushed Wilky forward. They raced from the alley, leaped over a pile of rocks, and skidded down a main street.

The pack was gaining on them, howling with excitement at such easy prey.

She shouted for Wilky to run ahead, and turned to buy him some time. Half a dozen firefoxes closed in on her — fifty feet then twenty. In a heartbeat they would be at her throat.

She readied herself for their leap, hoping to take down a couple.

Wilky stepped between her and the pack.

"What are you doing?"

The animals stopped short. They snarled and nipped at the air, but fear shone in their eyes.

She didn't understand it, but they were afraid of Wilky.

The three witches moved behind the firefoxes, a look of triumph on their faces. "We have the boy."

Aaliss braced herself. "No!"

Wilky turned and wrapped his arms around her waist.

Heat flooded her body, and....

She bolted awake, heart racing, gasping for air. The vivid dream had seemed so real, but she awoke in the hammock and found nothing unusual except an odd stain on her suit. Something warm, wet, and foul had splattered against her stomach.

Grimacing, she blinked her eyes against the morning glare. It was later than she had planned on waking, and she silently cursed herself for being so careless. She needed to be more disciplined, especially with Wilky's life at risk, but that wasn't what bothered her most. She glanced at her stomach and confirmed her fears — the odd stain was really a bird dropping. She had done far worse than waste sunlight.

She felt as if an ice cold snake slithered up her spine. She looked upward and found a mature terrawk sleeping forty feet above her, as still as a statue.

"Great," she muttered, surveying the four-tree grove, careful to stay quiet.

They had camped amidst a terrawk nesting ground. Almost a dozen of the large birds rested among the higher branches of the ghost trees, and more were likely hidden among the leaves. Now she understood the silence from the night before. The creatures in the forest knew to keep clear of the nesting grounds. She had violated one of the most elementary of the Guardians' rules: always thoroughly scout your campsite.

Among the deadliest creatures in the Zone, terrawks were extraordinary killers. Once, Aaliss had watched four birds take down a full-grown buck in a few frenetic moments. The deer never had a chance. It swung its antlers at them, but they converged in an organized attack, one pecking at the eyes, the largest ripping at the throat, while the other two tore at the rest of the beleaguered animal. Within minutes the birds had stripped the deer to nothing but bone, a few shreds of muscle and sinew, and antlers.

Mature terrawks stretched three feet long, had a six-foot wingspan, pointed red beaks, and razor-sharp talons. Their gray feathers provided perfect camouflage, blending into the ghost tree's bark. They tucked their beaks and talons away as they slept, rendering them almost undetectable.

Aaliss should have known they nested here, and now her mistake could cost them dearly.

Terrawks hunted at night, usually sleeping during the day, but noise would wake them. And they would not wake happy, especially if they thought something threatened their nest.

She glanced at Wilky and Gemma. Thankfully, they were awake, wide-eyed and ashen. They knew danger hovered above them even though she was sure Wilky had never seen a terrawk before.

She placed her finger to her lips.

He nodded.

She reached for her crossbow, careful not to swing the hammock. The small weapon stretched only the length of her forearm. Its wooden housing contained ten bolts with fast-acting poison tips. One bolt could paralyze a full-grown man, and slow down anything bigger. Once fired, a spring automatically loaded the next bolt into the crossbow, but firing at the terrawks was a bad idea—a *terrible* idea, really. Each bolt would take down one bird, but too many of the predators nested among these trees for the three of them to escape. Still, the weight of the crossbow in her hand made her feel better, less helpless.

The branches below them were wide and strong. If they moved shadow-quiet, they might climb down without the birds noticing them. She could do it, but.... She glanced at Wilky and her heart twisted. She might get down unheard, but Wilky and Gemma would need a lot of luck.

Still, she could think of no better alternative.

She whispered to Wilky, "Our only chance is to get down quietly and back out of the grove."

He shook his head and turned toward Gemma. He nodded to her, and they both covered their eyes with their hands.

Blood raced through Aaliss's head and the noise sounded like a waterfall. "We can't stay here," she whispered angrily.

Wilky kept his hands over his eyes.

She tried to calm herself and steadied her breathing. Sometimes he got this way, and it took patience to get him to come around.

The wind blew and the hammocks swayed. Wilky's squeaked—the metal clamp must have been rusted.

A terrawk to her left stirred, turning its beak toward them, interested in the source of the noise. The wind gusted again and the squeak sounded like a high-pitched wail.

Her heart galloped in her chest. She clutched the crossbow as a second bird swung its beak in their direction.

One more gust and we'll never leave the hammocks alive.

Time slowed. She aimed the crossbow at the nearest bird, which perched no more than forty feet away, and used her training to ward off a rising wall of panic. Panic would kill her—would kill them all.

She heard her instructor's voice in her head: "*Stay calm. There's always a way out. You just have to think of it.*"

The hair on her neck started to prickle as an early warning that the wind would soon gust. Another squeak from Wilky's hammock, and they were goners. But before the wind blew, she heard a different sound—faint but real.

Someone slashed a blade to clear underbrush, hacking at the dense foliage.

The terrawks started to stir. The one directly above her snapped its head toward the oncoming clatter. Four terrawks in the tree to her right shifted in their branches. A sharp squawk sounded high above them as an immense gray bird in the top most branches shifted. Aaliss had never seen a terrawk this huge before, its beak almost completely blood-red.

The noise grew louder and became more human sounding: boots trampling plants, a blade slicing hedges, legs brushing against branches.

The huge terrawk launched itself with two mighty beats of its wings and circled high above the nest.

Frozen, Aaliss wanted to warn the newcomers, but she couldn't risk putting Wilky in danger. A cold sweat beaded across her forehead as two more birds joined the first and began circling.

Voices drifted to her from just outside the clearing. "Are you sure our orders are to kill her on sight? I can't believe she'd betray Eden."

Aaliss listened closely to hear their conversation.

"Our orders come directly from the Viper. He's already in the Zone with Jonas. He was clear. They're to be treated as dangerous. Aaliss in particular is lethal. He said we're not to hesitate to kill them, but if she surrenders, I can't see why we would need to kill her."

She felt as if she'd been punched in the gut. Samuel, one of her friends, clamored toward them with orders to kill her. They had patrolled together many times, and she liked his quirky sense of humor. Now he hunted her, and even worse, the Viper searched for them.

Three Guardians stumbled into the grove. Samuel led the way, hacking a path with his short sword, followed by a woman holding a crossbow.

Aaliss recognized her as Estienne, another friend, but she didn't know the third Edenite.

Young, he lingered behind the other two, holding his sword at his side and taking short, tentative steps.

The four circling terrawks screeched and dove at the unsuspecting

Guardians like arrows. Other birds launched themselves from the ghost trees.

Two simultaneously struck Samuel, who cried out.

Estienne launched a bolt from her crossbow but it missed wide, and other terrawks ripped at her flesh.

The youngster turned and ran.

Samuel and Estienne followed him—a jumble of blood, torn flesh, feathers, wings, beaks, and claws, mixed with screams of pain, panic, and terror.

The cries receded from the grove as the three Guardians fled.

Aaliss turned to give Wilky the all-clear signal, but Wilky and Gemma had already started to climb down.

She quickly joined them as more screams rose from the forest. She moved toward them to help, but Wilky tugged on her arm. He was right; she couldn't help them now. She had to protect Wilky, and it was too late anyway.

She sighed, turned, and ran out of the grove with Wilky and Gemma at her heels. She concentrated on her footing over the uneven ground, using her sword to cut a path wide enough for the three of them. She veered far from the ghost trees and stayed under the more protective cover of the oaks and maples. Angry branches snapped back at her as she ran, favoring speed over stealth.

When air started to come in gasps, she stopped and turned, and her world ceased spinning. "Wilky, what have you done?"

Wilky and Gemma were panting from their strenuous flight, but that wasn't what had panicked her.

Wilky had discarded his gasmask, and now stood unprotected only a few inches from Gemma—only a few inches from certain death, from being infected with the Red Death and having his soul stripped from him.

She dropped to her knees, tears welling up in her eyes. "Wilky, why?"

The dam broke and her tears fell.

CHAPTER 11
WILKY

Wilky stared at his sister, his feet stuck to the ground as if sunk into a mudhole. Details began to intrude in his mind and crowd out Aaliss's face—a paw print on his left that led to a snapped branch. The snapped branch led to other snapped branches, then to other paw prints. Slightly to the right of one paw print, a green worm with yellow spots ate a leaf from an oak tree. Eight brown circles dotted the leaf in a rough circular pattern that wasn't quite symmetrical; the dots made a perfect diamond pattern.

Gemma smelled acidic. She smelled like worry.

A light white cloud floated overhead in the shape of a large horse. He liked black horses best, but he had never seen a completely black one. Always some white or gray or brown mingled with the black; even if no one else noticed it, he always did.

Gemma was breathing so loudly.

The greens and browns and yellows closed in on him in a kaleidoscope of colors.

He closed his eyes and bit his lip, fighting hard for control. He wished he were back in his lab or his small dwelling among the familiar, safe, and quiet, where all these colors and smells would not haunt him. He concentrated on his breathing, counting his inhales and exhales, all the while trying to ignore the different fragrances in the air.

When he opened his eyes, he focused solely on his sister.

Tears streamed down her cheeks and fell on both sides of her gas mask as she yanked at her short black hair. The ostrich suit had a white-greenish stain on the stomach, but he refused to take in the details.

Still, he felt his mind wander and couldn't stop some of the minutiae from leaking in. The stain had more white than green, and the dropping looked as if it had fallen from a distance and thus splattered across the suit. He could calculate how far in his head if he tried.

He bit the inside of his cheek hard until he tasted blood, regained control, and heard his sister's pleas.

She cried "Why?" over and over again, her voice hoarse between sobs.

He stamped his foot in frustration. Images flooded through his mind, but he couldn't find the words to match them. He saw Eden and knew they could not return. Not now. Maybe someday, but now darkness and shadows covered Eden. The light that had always shone around it had vanished as if sucked from the world. Even Piers was cast in darkness.

Their futures lay out here with the Soulless. He saw bits and pieces of it—just flashes of scenes that stuck in his mind, scenes he memorized down to the smallest details.

He had known the terrawks would attack. He saw the attack in a vision just before he woke. He had warned Gemma and closed his eyes to it, but it didn't matter. He had already witnessed the carnage, already seen the blood and the feathers and heard the screams. The image had now become part of him, stuck in his mind like a pebble in a shoe he could never remove. He had also been with his sister in the City of Bones and saw the witches. He knew they meant trouble, but how he and they fit together remained a mystery.

He summoned his strength and stepped close to his sister, his boots crunching on fallen leaves and twigs.

The wind gusted and rustled her hair, and she wiped her cheeks with her hands. Dirt had smudged her palms, bits of brown and green clinging to them. Her crossbow lay on the ground with a bolt in position.

A bright red cardinal called from a nearby tree, and a fat gray squirrel bounded from one tree to the next, chattering his displeasure with the world. He clung on to a branch and then scurried away, followed by another squirrel, this one black. The black squirrel's tail was bushier than the gray one, but shorter.

No!

He refocused on Aaliss. "Don't need the mask anymore," was all he could say, and he struggled with those simple words. He couldn't explain the certainty he felt or how he knew the mask offered no protection.

His sister stopped crying and laughed. "You've taken the cure! The Red Death has no power over you! I should have known."

He knew she wanted him to say yes, maybe even *needed* him to say yes on some level, but she had to know the truth. Just like she always told him the truth, he would be honest with her. Their future lay here with the Soulless, away from Eden. The gas masks couldn't help them anymore. They would have to find a different way. This was the only way to make her believe.

"No." He shook his head. "No cure yet. We can't go back." He spoke gravely and shook his head. "Can't go back."

He stroked his sister's hair. The textile sensations flooded through his fingers, but he maintained control and focused all his attention on her, willing her to believe him.

"We can never go back?" She looked weak and small at that moment, not the way she normally appeared, but the way she sometimes seemed when she thought no one else was looking.

"No. It's all right." Wilky thought it would be all right, eventually, in ways he had seen but could not understand. He had no way to communicate this to his sister except for the simple statement. He smiled crookedly at her, doing his best to reassure her without words.

Aaliss stared at him for a long moment, and then she took off her mask and let it tumble to the ground.

He knew she would.

CHAPTER 12
CATTIE

Cattie stood in her usual spot as far away from the Master's prying eyes as she could, her mind lost in thought, her body tired from working late the previous night. She was supposed to be watching a dozen two-year-olds, but the children might as well have been on a different planet. She had more important matters to contemplate.

Just when she thought her day could not get worse, her younger sister, Maeve, ambled over to her side. "What are you planning?"

Cattie frowned at the sight of her. Even now, after working the morning shift, she looked striking. A pink string drew her blonde hair off her face in a low ponytail, and her wide eyes contained five different shades of blue. Cattie had counted them when they were children, becoming increasingly jealous with each shade. Her own brown eyes were the singular color of mud.

Maeve slowly rocked an infant in her arms. Fussing only a moment ago, the baby now cooed quietly.

"Why would you ask me that, Mae?" Cattie added a chill to her voice.

"I know that look. You're planning something. Whenever you get that look, you dream up a new plan to escape the Nursery and move up." Maeve rolled her beautiful eyes.

"I have no idea what you're talking about."

Two of Cattie's toddlers wrestled over a toy wooden soldier. The bigger one yanked it away from the smaller one and started beating him on the arm with it.

Cattie growled in their direction but didn't budge to intercede, and the children paid her no mind.

Let the little brats settle the matter on their own.

Maeve chuckled. "There have been too many schemes to count. Although my favorite is when you tried to persuade the King's cousin, Brion, that you were a good witch and should be re-assigned as his personal tutor so you could teach him magic."

Cattie felt heat flush her cheeks. "Okay, so I've had some bad luck. I can't help it if I have ambition to do something better with my time than tend to these monsters."

The larger toddler stopped beating his friend with the toy soldier, smiled mischievously, and bounced it off the smaller one's head. The small boy let loose a loud wail.

Forced to act before others stepped in, Cattie scolded the small crying child. "That's what happens when you lose. He's bigger and stronger than you." She handed the wooden toy to the larger toddler, who grinned. "You're a good boy. You took it fair and square."

Maeve wrinkled her nose. "Do you think that's the best way to handle the situation? Teach them they can get whatever they want if they beat each other up for it?"

"Yes, dear sister, I absolutely do think that's right. They should learn the truth about how things work. It's no use teaching them how things *ought* to work."

The Master rang the bell for a shift change. At twenty years old, he kept the Stronghold's youngest children safe — over a hundred charges — the future of the Butcher Tribe.

"Thank goodness," muttered Cattie as she strolled outside.

Maeve must have returned the newborn to his crib because she rushed after her sister and touched her arm when Cattie had reached the Courtyard. "It's beautiful out. I love the fall weather. The leaves have just started to turn colors and the light is just right. It's so clear and the air is so crisp." She spun around in a circle, and the bottom of her blue dress ballooned outward.

Annoyed at her sister's good mood, Cattie blurted out, "Prince Fintan has eyes for me." She spoke before thinking and immediately regretted it. She hadn't meant to tell her, but sometimes Maeve just being Maeve goaded her.

She's always so darned happy!

Maeve grabbed her arm. "Prince Fintan, the King's brother? I didn't know you were friends. When did this happen?"

Cattie stared hard at her sister and whispered even though no one stood near them. "You have to promise me you won't tell anyone what I'm going to tell you. Swear on mother's blood."

Maeve shifted on her feet and clutched her hips. "I swear. Now tell me everything! I knew you were up to something."

"Not here."

She led Maeve away from the Feasting Hall and toward the deserted space under the Naming Tree, an ancient ghost tree that towered above the buildings in the Stronghold. Carved into its bark were the names of every member of the tribe. The practice stretched back to the beginning of time, and thousands of names reached high into the tree. When they stepped under it, Cattie scanned the higher branches, not sure where her name appeared, but sure it would be remembered long after she joined the tribal leaders in the stars. She just needed a little bit of good luck for once.

When she stopped, she stared up at her sister, who had crossed her arms against her chest. "I overheard a conversation last night that changes everything. Prince Fintan spoke to Cormac, the Captain of the King's Guard, in whispered tones. They thought no one could hear them."

When she paused, Maeve pressed her. "And what were they saying?" She tapped her foot anxiously. "It can't be that you just saw them talking. I know you. You were spying on them and overheard something you shouldn't have heard."

Cattie smiled, a hint of mischief playing with the corners of her mouth. "You don't need to know the details. Let's just say I overheard something important they wouldn't want our king to discover."

"And you plan on blackmailing Prince Fintan?" Maeve's tone conveyed her displeasure, as did her face, which changed color from peaches and cream to a splotchy scarlet.

"Blackmail is such a strong word, sister. Once Fintan knows I share his secret with him, I'm sure he'll fall madly in love with me. He'll see that he can trust me, and that I'll be the best choice for him as his princess. A coupling ceremony is sure to be in our future." Cattie chuckled at the thought and spun in a circle with her arms stretched wide. "I'll never have to work in the Nursery again. I think you should wear your yellow dress, the one with the flowers."

Maeve's normally sweet voice turned toxic. "I don't like this plan one bit. I don't trust those two."

"You don't have to like it, sister. Just keep your mouth shut." Cattie pinched her sister's arm, just so Meave knew that she was serious.

"Oww!"

"Remember, you swore on our mother's blood, and that's the strongest oath you can make. Everything will work out so long as you don't ruin it."

She'd get her happy ending. She just needed a good plan.

CHAPTER 13
P'MINA

P'mina trudged toward the nursery past clay huts with their brightly-colored fabric roofs. Each family had their own color, every shade of the rainbow except red, which was bad luck. The huts reminded her of a field of wildflowers, each one distinctive and beautiful.

The Orions had no colors. They used the same straw-colored dried thatch on all their roofs.

P'mina kicked the ground. *They lack creativity and imagination. How can I be myself among them?*

The tribe bustled with energy as they prepared for the Renewal Feast—Spinners spun thread into brightly covered decorations; others cleared the round ceremonial space in the center of the village; the great stack of fire wood needed for the giant bonfire grew steadily by the wheelbarrow.

The Artists performed the most important task, adding to the Mother's Banner that would wrap around the festive space. It told the story of the Painted Ones with exploding colors and images of wars, treaties, harvests, and families. The history was so exacting that each female member of the tribe had her name added to the banner when she received her first tattoo, so she would forever be remembered as part of the tribe. Her name would stay on the Banner, but after the Renewal Feast, she'd be an Orion, never to be thought of as a Painted One again.

Her sister Kalhona worked on the grandest image on the banner—the Tree of Life—the most beautiful painting P'mina had ever seen. Her earliest memory revolved around it: her mom had held her at an Awaking Feast while she stared at it with her mouth agape, then she whispered that P'mina's name would one day show up on that tree in a place of importance, because she was *special*.

A fond memory ruined. Soon her name *would* be added to that tree as one of the girls who was swapped with the Orions.

I'm special because they're giving me away.

She clenched her hands into fists, turned her back on the Banner and her sister, groaned, and marched to the nursery.

Most toddlers were playing outside in the short grass enjoying the sunny day. P'mina spotted Tania almost immediately. Her curly blonde hair fell down to her shoulders in an unorganized mop around a round, happy face, clear hazel eyes, and small button nose. As usual, she smiled with real joy in her eyes.

P'mina stooped low and called out her name.

Tania twisted, grinned and raced forward, unsteady on her feet, giggling as she wobbled. She opened her arms as she got close and shouted, "Peema," which was as close as she could come to properly pronouncing P'mina's name. She jumped into her aunt's outstretched arms and laughed with delight as P'mina spun her in circles.

P'mina breathed her in, and she smelled like happiness. P'mina gently placed her on the ground and watched as she spun unsteadily for a moment and then plopped down on her ample backside.

Smiling and laughing, she shouted, "Peema!"—her favorite thing to say, though in truth she was so young she could say little else.

"Your Aunt P'mina loves you very much."

Tania giggled and opened her arms for another hug. "Love Peema," she said and fell into another tight embrace.

"And I love you, Tania. Very, very much." P'mina fought hard to keep the tears from her voice.

Last night Kalhona had been wrong when she said P'mina could not recall what had happened when their mother had turned into a witch. P'mina did remember some things: the nasty looks, her aunt's anxiety, and the hollow feeling in her stomach that never quite left. Now she worried about Tania and what she would have to face after P'mina left the tribe.

Knowing others were watching them, she bent low and whispered. "People might say bad things about me, but you tell them to pound dirt. You had nothing to do with it."

Tania replied happily, "Pounds dirts!"

"Your momma loves you. I know she's not as nice as I am, but she loves you very much."

Tania looked quizzically at P'mina, her eyebrows raised and her cheeks pinched together. "Peema loves me."

"Yes, I do, and so does your mother." She felt tears start to moisten her eyes. "I'll find a way to look after you, but it'll be our secret."

Tania grabbed P'mina's nose. She loved to grab noses, ears, hair — really whatever she could reach.

P'mina grabbed the girl's hand and playfully munched on Tania's chubby fingers. "Now don't forget. Always eat the blue berries and never the green berries."

Tania scowled. "Green berries bad!" She stuck out her tongue to prove it.

"I must go, sweetie. Don't forget that I love you." She turned to leave, but Tania grabbed onto her leg and refused to release her. P'mina had to pry her fingers off her leg.

Tears welled up in Tania's eyes. She was such a happy child that the tears surprised P'mina.

"Don't cry, sweetie," P'mina whispered, her own voice husky.

Tania banged her hands on her legs and her face turned red. "Peema!"

One of the caregivers walked over and said, "Is everything okay?"

"Everything's fine." P'mina did her best to regain her composure. "I just wanted to see Tania before I hunt for the red berries they need for the dyes. It'll take all day, so I won't see her later."

Tania started to cry in a hurricane of tears, and waved her arms as if she knew the truth was very different.

The worker lifted the girl and stroked her back. "Don't worry, Tania. P'mina will see you tomorrow. Isn't that right, P'mina?"

Fearful she would start to cry, P'mina had already turned and hurried away. She retrieved a satchel of supplies and her spear from her hut. Her spear functioned as part walking stick, part weapon, and part tool for harvesting plants in the forest. She swept her eyes across the small living space for the last time. She didn't want to leave, but she'd rather find her mother than be forced to live with the Orions.

She sighed heavily and then she marched toward the woods, hoping to slip away unseen, but her luck did not hold.

A voice called after her, "P'mina, where are you going?"

She froze.

Merina, an annoyingly clingy girl her age had called after her.

P'mina spun and plastered an artificial smile on her face.

Merina jogged toward her. "What're you doing?" she asked, out of breath.

"Oh, I'm just gathering some red berries for Kalhona. She needs them for the Mother's Banner."

Merina grinned and skipped around her, her bright yellow dress swinging out from her knees. "This is our month before the feast. We can do anything we want! Let her get her own berries, and come with me. I'm going to ride one of the horses." She clasped her blue-stained fingers in front of her. She worked with the dyes, which always left a trace on her hands.

"I'm the only one who knows where to find the berries she likes." Anger laced P'mina's words.

Why are Merina and the other girls so content with the swap? How can they be happy to leave?

"How long is it going to take? Maybe I'll come with you."

Although Merina was the closest thing to a friend P'mina had in the tribe, she would never confide in her. "It might take all day. You'll be much happier with the horses. Enjoy your riding." She turned to leave, but Merina caught her by the arm.

"How come you aren't as happy as everyone else? The tribe is treating us special, like heroes. I even got sweet iced milk yesterday at dinner. Of all of us, P'mina, I would think that you'd be happiest."

P'mina spit out the words fast, hot, and angry. "And why would I be the happiest?"

Merina smiled, oblivious to the anger tinting P'mina's words. "After what happened with your mother, this is your chance to do something good for the tribe. Everyone will remember you instead of your mom. Her sin will be completely forgotten."

"My mother did nothing wrong!" P'mina stomped her foot. "Besides, Kalhona and I have done plenty good for this tribe."

Finally understanding the raw anger in her friend's voice, Merina stepped backward. "Sure you have. You both have. Just some of the older girls talk, but with the swap, no one will mention it again. You'll be special just like the other twenty-one of us."

"I have to go. Enjoy the horses." P'mina started to leave, but Merina stopped her again by grabbing her arm.

"That's a heavy bag you're carrying." An odd twinkle lightened her eyes. "How long are you going to be away?"

P'mina's heart sank. If Merina figured out her plans, all would be lost, so she said the first plausible explanation that entered her mind. "Sometimes I need tools to cut away plants to get to the red berries." She added hastily, "I'll be back by nightfall, and tomorrow I'll go riding with you."

Merina stared at the bag for a long moment.

P'mina's hands turned clammy. She was sure Merina would ask to see the tools, but to her relief, Merina's smile returned.

She released P'mina's arm. "See you tomorrow, then."

Relieved, P'mina hustled away before Merina could ask any more questions. Once she reached the forest's edge, she turned and saw

Merina still standing where they had been talking, looking at her, her lips turned down in a frown.

P'mina gave her a half-hearted wave, spun on her heels, and hiked through the familiar woods. She had spent much time in these woods, harvesting plants of value, for food or medicine or as dyes for the fabrics. She stopped at times, looking at her favorite gathering spots, thinking back to her time spent with Loiana.

Loiana had known the most about plants in the tribe. She spent years teaching the other girls her secrets, but P'mina was always her favorite student. That was until the Red Death took her at the beginning of summer. P'mina missed her terribly. Loiana never called her *witchborn* or treated her poorly because of her mom. She would have understood why P'mina needed to run.

The sun dipped lower in the sky as P'mina reached the Ancient Road. Narrow and made from crushed rocks fused over time, it was no wider than two people could walk side by side. The forest encroached on the sides, but she could still see far in both directions.

"Which way shall I go? Mom could live either way." She stood squarely on the path and turned in both directions. Finally, she placed her hands on her hips. "I'm going to need some help, Mom!"

Then she remembered spinning with Tania. Inspired, she dropped her spear and her satchel, closed her eyes, and spun in quick tight circles until she felt dizzy. When she opened her eyes, she staggered around like Tania had, and sat on the road, facing north.

Once her head cleared, she smiled. "Thanks, Mom! I'll see you soon!"

She walked north, confident she would soon be reunited with her mother, confident all would be right with the world, confident she had made the right decision.

CHAPTER 14
VIPER

The Viper twirled a small paring knife in his fingers, expertly carved a strip of meat from the freshly killed rabbit's haunches, and flipped it to Jonas, who gladly caught it in his callused hand. The meat tasted good and fresh, the blood warm and thick.

Jonas tossed the strip high in the air and let if fall into his open mouth, a splash of crimson splattering his chin. "I love fresh meat, especially when it's still warm." He wiped the blood with his sleeve.

"I remember the first time you took me on patrol. We ate that deer within minutes of taking her down." The Viper grinned. "You had a mouthful of blood before I even knew what had happened. You looked like a boy with a blueberry pie."

"Yes, that's when I knew you were made of the right stuff." Jonas reached his hand out for another slice of rabbit, but the Viper ignored him and studied the forest instead.

"The trail continues east." He pointed to a snapped branch up ahead. "They must have traveled along the deer trail while it was still dark, but we're gaining on them." He tossed the remaining rabbit carcass into the woods and followed the trail, while Jonas lumbered behind him.

They moved quickly, the trail easy to follow—broken branches, turned dirt, even a footprint or two marked the way.

They might as well have cut their path with a sword.

The Viper felt oddly disappointed the hunt wasn't more challenging—although young, Aaliss had generated a reputation. She was considered a prodigy, and he expected more. The numerous ghost trees with their wide umbrella of branches even made for easy traveling.

The Viper hesitated, squatted, and poked at what caught his curiosity with the end of a stick. "See this terrawk dropping?" He pointed to a white-greenish blob in front of them. "It looks recent, and there's another one over there, and another just beyond it."

"That's a lot of activity." Jonas surveyed the branches of the nearby trees and whispered, "It's sure gotten quiet in this part of the woods."

The Viper pointed to the grove of ghost trees up ahead and crept forward as silent as a shadow, practically drifting over the ground. Jonas followed carefully behind, but he made too much noise for the Viper, so he scowled at the big man. "You stay here. Try to be quiet."

Jonas crossed his arms and muttered, "It looks like a nest to me. Terrawks love the higher branches of the ghost trees, but if you want me to stay behind, then I'm staying right here."

The Viper scolded him with a glare and stalked forward. When he reached the edge of the grove he paused. This was the largest terrawk nesting ground he had ever seen. Over a dozen birds slept in the branches. He quickly scanned the grounds and easily spotted the trail Aaliss and company had created when they fled. A small bit of woolen cloak snagged on a nearby rose bush might as well have been a sign.

How did you escape these birds, little rabbit?

The Viper widened his gaze and found a second disturbed area on the far side of the grove, this one violent. Fresh blood littered the ground, but no bodies.

He returned to Jonas, who looked uneasy, his eyes constantly darting toward the grove and the sky. "It's a nest, all right. There must be more than a dozen of the big birds. It seems as if our rabbit left the grove unharmed."

Jonas shook his head. "How could that be? Three kids and a dozen terrawks? That doesn't sound right. Those birds should have ripped them to pieces."

"A diversion entered the nest from the other side of the grove. I spotted blood, which would explain why Samuel hasn't answered the radio."

Jonas shuddered and glanced upward toward the trees. "That's a bad way to die."

"Come on."

The Viper led Jonas in a wide arc around the nesting grounds, easily finding the new trail Aaliss had made in her hasty retreat from the grove, and within minutes they heard someone crying.

The Viper unsheathed both his swords and whispered, "I'll go around and cut them off. You come straight at them. Give me five minutes, and we'll have them surrounded."

Jonas nodded as he pulled his long axe from his back, twisted his hands on the ash handle, and peered down the trail eagerly.

The Viper's blood raced as he sprinted ahead to trap Aaliss. He moved with the forest, always traveling on the balls of his feet, careful to blend with the sounds around him. Branches bent quietly in one direction but snapped in the other. He smiled as he completed the half circle. His senses sharpened as adrenaline flooded his blood, and anticipation burned through him.

She was upwind; he smelled fear, and the scent thrilled him. Those he hunted should be afraid, and the rabbit had to be killed. He had no choice. Jacob had a glorious plan for Eden, and she would only screw it up. He simply acted as Jacob's instrument, and as such he was righteous, all-powerful. He knew this rush came directly from Jacob himself—it was divine; it was right; it was his purpose.

He pulled back one last branch and cleared the brush.

Jonas had already marched onto the scene with his heavy battleax clutched in his right hand, looking eager to draw blood.

The Viper held his swords ready to strike in an instant. He expected to find the rabbit and two defenseless kids, but instead he stared down at a young man slumped against the trunk of a ghost tree, weeping uncontrollably.

In shock, his eyes looked glassy and unfocused. When he lifted them to the Viper, a bit of recognition took away the dull edge, and he staggered to his feet, his black ostrich suit torn along one leg and one arm.

Disappointment stretched across Jonas's body tighter than his suit. "Who in Jacob's name are you? Where's the girl?"

The young man swung his head between both men, but he fixed his gaze on the Viper. "I'm John, one of the novices."

The Viper sheathed one of his swords and stepped forward, still holding the other. "I remember you. You're Ike's boy, right?"

"Yes sir." John tried to stand, but the effort seemed too much for him because he only made it halfway up before he collapsed against the tree and slid to the ground. His right arm had been badly hurt, his suit smeared with blood, his gasmask fixed crookedly on his face.

"You're with Samuel's team, right?" asked Jonas.

John nodded.

"Well, where's Samuel?" Jonas slipped his axe back into its strap on his back. "What in Jacob's name happened to your team?"

John turned toward the Viper, who had glided toward him. "We came upon a nest of terrawks, sir. They were everywhere. One moment we were hacking through the forest, and the next all I could see were beaks and talons and feathers. And blood... so much blood." He hung his head and wept.

The Viper prodded him to continue. "And...."

"So we ran. I was in the lead and got away, but Samuel and Estienne didn't make it. When I realized they weren't behind me, I turned back, but it was too late. I wanted to help them—I really did—but they were already dead. The birds covered them. They were eating them!" John retched onto the ground by the tree.

"What about Aaliss and the others?" the Viper asked. "Have you seen them?"

"No. I've been here since the attack. I don't know how long it's been." He cast his eyes down. "I should have helped them, but all I could think to do was run."

"Can you stand?" the Viper asked.

John struggled unsteadily to his feet.

"Can you lift your right arm?"

John tried to raise his arm, but it shook with effort. He couldn't lift it above his waist, and a new batch of tears flowed down his cheeks.

"Grab your sword with your left one then." The Viper felt the rush building in his blood. He knew it would soon boil unless he satisfied it.

John moved woodenly, in too much shock to question the Priest of the Guardians.

The Viper struck, quick and hard. His sword sliced into John's neck, and blood spurted in a wide arc as the young man fell to his knees. The Viper grabbed him by the shoulders and stared intently into his eyes as the light left them.

Jonas chuckled. "What about the safety of your flock and all that nonsense you told me this morning?"

"I am a Blood Relation. Jacob's blood flows through me. I do His bidding."

"Why make him hold the sword?"

He frowned. "He was one of ours. He deserved to die with a weapon in his hand."

"And now we can blame all these deaths on Aaliss."

"If that's His will, then so be it. It's not my place to question Him."

CHAPTER 15
WILKY

Wilky watched as Aaliss inhaled and filled her lungs with unfiltered air from the Zone for the first time. "The air smells different from back home. It's fresher and cleaner."

Wilky noticed it too. So many different fragrances filled the forest—the trees, the mosses, the animals. They could overwhelm him and carry him away if he let them, but he refused to let that happen. They were still in danger, and he had to help. He had to focus on Aaliss, nothing but his sister—the black back of her Guardian suit, her perfect posture, the way the sun hit her hair....

She interrupted his thoughts and sounded troubled. "Wilky, will we lose our souls now that the Red Death has us? I don't feel any different. I'm still the same person I was yesterday, right? What happens after we take the cure? Will our souls return?"

She glanced at him for answers, but he offered none. She had to wrestle with these questions on her own. With time she'd figure it out, and that was the best way.

"If we keep our souls, then what makes us different from the Soulless?" Aaliss kept walking and muttered the Guardian's sacred motto. *"The Soulless are Not Human. To Kill in Jacob's Name is Just."* She stopped short, and he almost walked into her. "Are all the lessons wrong?"

He thought about her question. Not all the lessons were wrong. When he looked at the core teachings he saw light. It was the rottenness around the edges that perverted everything, making it hard to find the light in the center.

Aaliss shook her head as if she was banishing unwanted thoughts, which Wilky knew was exactly what she was trying to do. He knew she'd fail miserably, because once she locked onto a problem, she never gave up until she solved it. She might push it away from her mind temporarily, but she'd come back to it and decide the truth on her own.

He heard a branch snap and looked up to see a yellow finch alight from its perch. Three beats of its wings and it started to rise. Another bird, this one dark and larger....

Aaliss thought about the Priest of the Guardians and clutched her short sword a little tighter. "The Viper's our main problem." She knew he hunted them, and she quickened her pace. "Samuel said he's in the Zone and after us. There's something scary about him. Every new Guardian has to patrol with him at least once before they let you become a full-fledged Guardian. Nothing special happened when we went out together, but he seemed to look through me as if I wasn't there. He holds the records for all the tests new Guardians have to go through, and you hear stories about him all the time: how he loves to hunt, how superhumanly fast he is, what an amazing tracker he is. They say he's never lost his prey, but that can't be true. If we're going to survive we'd better avoid him. But I have this sick feeling that he's close."

A handful of ravens suddenly took flight not far behind them. She grabbed her crossbow, and the hair on the back of her neck stood on end.

"Viper is bad," Wilky agreed.

"Have you ever met him?" She doubted he had, but maybe Wilky had seen him at the entrance to the tunnel.

A shiver shook Wilky's body. "Never, except in dreams." His face drained of color, and for a minute, a haunted look crossed her brother's eyes.

"That's right, Wilky. He goes into the Zone by himself. Some of the older Guardians say he was born in the Zone, and that he's more Zone than Edenite."

Aaliss's heart skipped a beat as two chipmunks raced across their path.

I need to settle down.

She continued her one-way conversation. "The way I figure it, we need to make that cure. That way the Red Death will have no power over us, and we could eventually go back home." She glanced at her brother for confirmation. He was looking into the forest, but she thought he was still paying attention, so she continued. "If we find the flower and the mushroom we can make the cure, right?"

"Yes."

"Good. Now we just need to find the ingredients. When we make camp, you'll have to describe them to me so we can both decide where to look. I'm not sure what we're going to do with Gemma, but we'll figure that out as we go."

The plants near them shook and a maple tree swayed. A sixteen-point buck bolted in front of them, running full out. The massive animal crashed through the forest in a frantic desire to escape something, but what?

She stopped. "That's odd."

She scanned the forest around her, listening intently, holding her breath. Then she heard it—faint but real—and the air flew from her lungs. She spun and looked at Wilky and Gemma.

Exhaustion played in their features—their shoulders sagged to the ground, their eyes downcast. Dusk had just fallen, and it had been a long day.

Until that moment, she had hoped to make camp soon.

"What's wrong?" Wilky said.

I can run for it. If I start now, I'd get out of the path in time, but Wilky and Gemma could never do it. Even if they were fresh they might not be fast enough.

"Wilky, we've got a big problem. A Devil's Storm is coming right at us. Those nasty Flesh Eaters are riled up, and we can't get around them. Usually I'd find some water to cross or a ghost tree to climb. They'll strip any other type of tree, but they won't touch a ghost tree. But the last one is too far back, and I don't see any other ones. Jacob's braid!" She swore as she twisted in place and hoped for divine inspiration.

The Flesh Eaters were three-inch long, red beetles, with angry, hungry mouths and sharp stingers in their tails. They didn't have eyes, and navigated by smell with long antennae that swooped out in front of their heads. Usually calm and ordinary, they ate vegetation and other bugs, but during a Storm they raced for miles at a feverish pace, eating only flesh. No one knew why they stormed, but when they did, they swarmed over every living animal in their path, taking it down to the bone in seconds.

And now the three of them were right in the path of a Storm. Her knees buckled, and her mind went blank.

"Fire," Wilky suggested, as the clattering from the Storm grew louder. It sounded like a million tiny drummers beating against bone drums.

"Fire would work. The Flesh Eaters won't go into the flames.... Yes, if we use it as a shield they'll go around us, but how are we going to make a fire big enough to hide all three of us in time?"

Wilky fumbled in his leather satchel and retrieved a clear glass bottle.

Life flooded back into her body. "You have a bottle of Liquid Fire?"

Liquid Fire was extremely volatile. One spark and it burned intensely for a short time with searing hot, blue flames.

"You're amazing!" She grabbed the bottle and kissed him on top of his head. "Stand by the oak, and I'll spread the liquid fire in a wide arc around us. We can't make a circle because we'll need a way out after the

Devil's Storm is gone. The blue flames will burn hot, but the forest is wet. With some luck the entire woods won't go up, and we'll escape out of the opening after the Storm has passed."

She poured the liquid fire carefully, making sure not to spill any on her suit. Uncertain how wide to stretch the arc, she settled on fifteen feet.

She joined Wilky and Gemma by the tree as the red swarm appeared in the distance.

Gemma clutched her hands to her ears.

Millions of angry Flesh Eaters raced toward them, the clatter of their hard shells and the snapping of hungry mouths louder than a hard rainfall. It was an evil sound punctuated by desperate cries of animals fleeing from the Storm's path, and from those that failed to escape.

Aaliss held a match at the ready and waited for just the right moment. If the flames burned out before the Flesh Eaters passed, they would still be doomed. She could only guess how long the blue flames would shield them. She stared hard into the distance until the red wave closed in on them. It didn't look like millions of individual beetles, but rather a single monster—a red tide that rolled fast, the Flesh Eaters running over each other's backs to surge forward, their hard shells colliding against each other, their greedy mouths searching for meat.

She imagined what it would feel like for the bugs to swarm over her, eating her flesh to the bone, and her hand started to tremble. She could wait no longer, so she lit the match and tossed it into the Liquid Fire.

The flame exploded to life, a wall of blue leaping before them, protecting them from the angry red monster.

The bugs reached the flames and parted as if an unseen general had given a silent command.

She turned and watched the Flesh Eaters reconnect behind them. For a moment she worried they might double back, and held her breath, but they continued their march northward.

She grimaced at the smoke, unsheathed her short sword, and grabbed her crossbow. They had lost any chance they might have had of escaping the Viper. The blue flames and the smoke would act like a beacon—he was hunting them, and soon he would find them.

She had to be prepared. No one was superhuman, not even the Priest of the Guardians. Her instructors had often compared her to the Viper, as his scores were just a hair better than hers. In the end, he was only human, and a bolt would take him down just like it would anyone else.

They trained me to kill. I just need a steady hand and a clean shot.

The Viper scrambled up the branches of a ghost tree. Jonas followed, swinging his battleax into the bark, using the weapon to hoist his bulk onto the lower branches.

"I hate Flesh Eaters," Jonas said. "I saw them take down a deer a few years back. They had it to the bone within a minute—a quick death but not a good one. It was hard to look at."

The Viper paid him no mind. The High Priest insisted that he not go alone on this sortie, and now he had started to regret his decision to bring Jonas. Maybe he should have brought one of the other Blood Relations in the Guardians—Mathew was younger and quieter than Jonas and could keep a secret.

He climbed higher, wedging his boots into knots into the tree, and searched the forest looking for signs of Aaliss. "They aren't that far ahead of us. They should be right in the path of the Storm. I don't see any other ghost trees or rivers they could use to shield themselves."

Jonas sat on a branch with his back against the tree trunk. "It would be a pity if we came all the way out here and found nothing but bones." He rummaged inside his satchel. "By Jacob, where's my bottle? Did you take it?"

The Viper scowled at him. "When we return to Eden you can drink as much Sacred Drink as you want. Until then you stay sober."

Jonas grumbled. "You are a hard man, Gabriel. We had better make quick work of these kids."

The Viper pointed toward the east. "For Eden's sake, that rabbit is clever. Look over there, only a half-mile in the distance. Blue flames! Only Liquid Fire makes flames like those. Those flames should protect them against the Flesh Eaters, but it won't protect them from us."

The army of Flesh Eaters raced around the trunk of the ghost tree. For some reason no one understood, the tree's bark repelled them.

A squirrel sat on a nearby branch, staring down at the bugs, safe from the carnage. The Viper swiped at it with the flat side of his short sword, knocking it from its perch. It twisted as it fell, and the Flesh Eaters took the squirrel to the bone almost before the animal touched the ground.

We're close. The rabbit will soon be mine.

CHAPTER 16
VIPER

The thrill of the hunt pulsed through the Viper's veins. The end was so close. He could breathe it in the air.

The rabbit is getting sloppy. She must be weary.

While she surely tired, he only grew more powerful, energized by the euphoric feeling that always seared through him right before a kill. And now he felt the heat more than ever before. He was practically on fire.

Jacob wanted him to kill—no, he *demanded* it.

"Hurry up, old man, we're almost on them."

The Viper flew ahead, the acidic stench of Liquid Fire burning his nostrils as he raced over smoldering ash. The trail blazed in front of him.

He dashed around a red maple and jumped over a dead branch, and slowed to a crawl, letting Jonas, who was huffing loudly, catch up. He pulled back a branch from a sapling and peered into a clearing.

Just ahead, a boy and girl sat on a large rock outcropping eating purple fall berries, looking like a king and queen on a rocky throne. They appeared spent, their heads drooping as they leaned back on the rocks.

Purple smears stained the girl's cheeks and a vacant look dulled her eyes.

The boy concentrated hard on the handful of berries between them, staring at them, mesmerized, as if they were divulging secrets only he could see.

It was odd that the boy had discarded his gasmask. Still, it mattered not. He'd kill the boy and his sister either way.

He studied the rest of the clearing for signs of Aaliss. The sun hung low in the sky, casting dark shadows, shadows she could use to hide. "Where are you, rabbit?"

Jonas moved close behind him. He smelled of sweat and grease and something else—not fear, but desperation—and the scent gave the Viper pause.

"They're sitting ducks." Jonas leaned close to him. "It couldn't be easier."

"Yes, but where's the rabbit? She wouldn't leave her brother unprotected. She must be nearby."

"She probably doesn't even know we're following them. No doubt she went off to piss in the woods or hunt for game." Jonas nodded toward the boy and girl. "All we have to do is grab the brother, put the steel edge of my axe to his throat, and she'll come running. We'll promise to bring them back to Eden safely, and when she disarms, we finish them all. We'll be back in Eden tomorrow by midday."

A voice in the Viper's head warned him to be careful—he'd always recognized it as the voice of Jacob—so he didn't budge. Instead, he stared into the dense forest that ringed the rock outcropping—so many places for a rabbit to hide in those thick shadows.

"Come on, Gabriel. I'm not afraid of a girl in these woods. I'll be on her brother in a few seconds. I'd rather take him while there's light. Let's go!"

"If you want to snatch the boy, I won't stop you. I'd rather wait until nightfall. I want to see the rabbit before I move."

Jonas snorted as he stumbled into the clearing, grinning while he held his great axe in front of him.

The boy and girl glanced at Jonas, but neither one yelled or ran. *Something's wrong. They should be shaking. Why aren't they afraid?*

Still, he felt confident the rabbit would soon be his. If she lay in wait, she would show herself before Jonas reached her brother, which would provide him all the advantage he needed. Once he took her down, the boy and Soulless girl would be no challenge. Soon, she'd be his.

If Jonas had to pay a price for his eagerness, then so be it. Jacob held his fate in his hands.

A soft breeze blew against his face, and it felt as if Jacob had kissed him.

Aaliss realized her mistake and cursed.

She'd hoped the Viper would come forth, but he stayed hidden. Instead, Jonas alone rumbled his way into the opening. She couldn't let him reach her brother, but when she let a bolt fly, the Viper would see the trap and know her location. He would gain the advantage, and he already had too many advantages to start with.

She squinted her eyes, furious with herself.

Jonas looked like an angry bear in his black ostrich suit. His gait unsteady as he lurched forward stiffly. The muscles on his right hand twisted the handle of his weapon, and he looked anxious for blood.

Aaliss realized how brave Wilky had been during the entire ordeal. Jonas must be a terrifying sight for him—more than twice as wide as Wilky himself and carrying a razor-sharp axe—yet he stayed seated, trusting his sister completely, having confidence she would protect him. *He has misplaced his trust.*

She could deal with Jonas, but the Viper would be so much harder. A lump formed in her throat as she steadied the crossbow.

She scanned the clearing desperate for signs of the Viper. If he just showed himself, she could fire at him first.

Jonas had reached the base of the rock formation, and she could wait no longer. She let loose a bolt and sank it into Jonas's left thigh.

He stared down at it, grimaced, and then looked at her.

At first, she doubted whether the poison had worked. Maybe he was too big.

Then the big man wobbled. He raised his axe to fling it at her, but his strength left him and it clanged uselessly against the rock. He followed a second later with a loud thud.

She spotted movement on the far side of the clearing out of the corner of her eye. A branch snapped, or maybe she had imagined it, or maybe the wind had gusted. It mattered not; either way, they had to run.

She leapt from her hiding spot.

Gemma bolted in the direction where Aaliss had seen movement.

A shadow obscured Wilky's face as he swung his gaze between Aaliss and Gemma.

"No, Wilky. Don't chase her. She's going the wrong way! Let her go! Come with me!"

He stood frozen for a heartbeat, and then raced after Gemma.

Aaliss groaned and ran after them, fully expecting to be taken down by the Viper at any moment. She twisted around an oak, and jumped over a bush when she heard horses approaching. "Wilky! No!"

Horses meant Soulless, and Soulless were almost as dangerous as the Viper.

She almost grabbed him before they broke free of the forest, but he had a step on her as they cleared the tree line and emerged onto a grass field.

Six horsemen approached with leather cloaks and longswords hung from their hips.

Wilky stopped.

Gemma ran to them and shouted, "Fintan!"

Aaliss's mind swirled as she assessed the situation in a heartbeat. She *saw* how the battle would play out before it began. Her brain just worked that way, and it was her best advantage. She didn't have to *think* about what to do; her mind kept her one step ahead of everyone else. People were predictable, and all she needed was the smallest clues to know what they would do.

The lead horsemen rode aggressively with a hint of a smile on his lips. He thirsted for power, was overconfident, and would blunder ahead at a full gallop.

The rider behind him grinned foolishly and leaned back in his saddle. Arrogant and pampered, he had no desire to be first.

The last horsemen struggled to keep control of his animal. Weak, he would bolt at the first sign of trouble.

Aaliss mapped out her plan. She'd shoot the lead horsemen in the throat. The second rider would slow and give her time to reload, so she could take him in the chest with another bolt. She wouldn't have time to get off a third shot before the next horsemen closed in on her, so she'd have to duck low as he swung his sword at her head, slice her blade into his leg, and pull him from the saddle. If she moved fast enough, she'd be able to mount the horse, urge it forward, catch the fourth rider by surprise, and kill him with a thrust into his chest. The last two would turn and race away. The entire fight would take no more than two minutes.

She pulled back the crossbow's elastic cord and a bolt slotted in place. Before she shot, however, came the one wildcard she could never account for.

Wilky jumped in front of her and cried, "Stop!" He waved his hands in her face to prevent her from letting the bolt go, and within seconds it was too late.

The horsemen surrounded them, and her chances of killing them plummetted.

CHAPTER 17
FINTAN

Fintan and the horses started the day fresh and full of energy, but that was hours ago. After a long day in the field, the horses trudged along like they were pulling plows, as tired of the fruitless search as Fintan and the other riders.

Fintan gnawed on a piece of dried beef.

Cormac's gray colt tried to turn around when Cormac loosened his reins to complain to Fintan, "I'm starving. What are you eating? Give me some!"

Fintan grabbed another strip of meat from his bag. "You should have brought your own food." He shot Cormac a smug smile and popped the strip of beef into his mouth.

Cormac's eyes rested on Fintan's saddlebag, and he spoke with a sinister grumble. "What else do you have in there?"

Fintan smiled mischievously. "My saddlebag has my stuff. You have your own bag."

"I didn't know we'd be out all day looking for Gemma." Cormac lowered his voice. "Crazy girl, Gemma."

"That's my sister you're talking about."

The search party traveled in a loose formation heading north, with

Fintan and Cormac in the center. So far they had found nothing, having stayed on the edge of the Witches' Wood without venturing too deeply into the forest.

Eamon's group had gone south, and Dermot led the party that searched deepest into the woods, which was fine with Fintan because the Witches' Woods scared him.

When they started the search he proclaimed that they should look along the outskirts since Gemma wouldn't travel in too far. Everyone knew the real reason he didn't want to tread too deeply, and no one objected.

"I've heard you call her worse," Cormac retorted, looking miserable. "Do you have any more food?"

"You'll never find out." Fintan laughed. "Get any closer, and we'll duel to the death." Fintan playfully half-pulled his sword from its sheath.

He wouldn't fully unsheathe it. Among the Butchers, once someone unsheathed a sword in anger, it must taste blood to be re-sheathed, lest one risk the displeasure of the heavens. Hasty warriors had been known to cut themselves to keep the heavens satisfied. Better to lose a little blood than suffer the consequences of vengeful gods.

Cormac snorted. "We should be heading back soon, anyway. The light is fading, and we've found no trace of Gemma. Maybe Dermot or Eamon have already rescued her, and we're just out here riding for pleasure."

Fintan re-sheathed his sword. "That would be my luck. Waste an entire day and one of my brothers gets to play the hero." He lifted his gaze toward the darkening sky and found something curious. "Look at that fire."

Cormac reined up close to him. "Blue flames? I've never seen a fire with such bright blue flames."

"Those blue flames are a sign from the heavens!" Fintan shouted for the benefit of the entire search party. "We must investigate!" He spurred his horse forward.

"And then we get some food," muttered Cormac, and his horse snorted its agreement a second later.

Fintan raced toward the blue streaks. He doubted they had anything to do with the heavens, but he needed a story to tell in the Feasting Hall and this might be a good one. Or at least it would be a good place to start a story. He could make it more interesting if he had to.

The flames disappeared, but still he raced in their direction.

"The flames are gone, Fin!" Cormac shouted over the sounds of the galloping horses. "Let's go back to the Stronghold."

"Not until we see the blue ashes." Fintan urged his horse onward. The forest peeled away, replaced by a meadow. He spurred his horse faster, and then he saw Gemma run into the clearing.

"Look!" He pointed to his sister. "The heavens have truly given us a sign!"

His spirits soared as the search party cheered. Visions of his welcome back at the Stronghold as a hero danced through his imagination. Finally, he had bested Dermot, and he felt as if he were flying.

As they raced forward, two strangers garbed in unusual clothes ran into the clearing after Gemma.

"Surround them!" ordered Cormac.

The deafening sound of the horses' hooves filled the air until they surrounded Gemma and the two strangers.

Gemma sprinted excitedly to Fintan's horse, shouting at him, waving her hands, a wide smile on her face.

Fintan had no idea what she was saying. He never bothered to try and understand her, finding her language tedious.

Shoving her behind his horse, he studied the two odd-looking newcomers. "What do you plan on doing with that toy?" He pointed to the small crossbow aimed at his chest.

The boy pushed the girl's hand down, and the weapon pointed safely to the ground.

The girl spoke for both for them. "My name is Aaliss and this is my brother, Wilky. We are peaceful travelers."

The horses anxiously danced in place around them, snorting heavily from the hard gallop and the tension in the air.

"You've captured my sister and now you say you come in peace?"

Aaliss hesitated as she skittered her gaze across the horses, and finally said, "We found Gemma and brought her here to safety. We did no harm to her."

Cormac laughed. "She lies! It's clearly written on her face!" Cormac might not be book smart, or really smart in general, but he had a talent for reading people.

Fintan had no doubt he was right about the girl, and neither did the rest of the horsemen. A general murmur of agreement echoed from the others.

"What are we to make of these two—a skinny boy and a girl with a man's haircut? Perhaps we should run them through and leave them for the wolves?" Fintan's horse danced and seemed to whicker at the suggestion, while the other horses tightened the circle around the siblings, making escape an impossibility.

Fintan basked in the glory of the moment. No one could deny this accomplishment, and he had many witnesses.

"Why don't you come down off that horse, so we can settle the matter between us?" Aaliss slung the crossbow over her shoulder and unsheathed her short sword.

He roared with laughter. "Look, she threatens me with her toy sword. She might be crazier than my sister."

She waved the blade at him and encouraged him to dismount. "We'll see how crazy I am."

Gemma tried to jump between them, but Fintan shoved her back and toppled her to the ground. She uttered her gibberish, but he didn't pay any attention to her.

Cormac seized Wilky with a rough hand and brought his longsword to his neck. "Drop your toys, and I won't hurt him."

A drop of blood trickled down Wilky's neck and onto his steel.

The strange girl narrowed her eyes. She looked as if she wanted to lunge at Cormac, but the blade he pressed against her brother's neck held her still. Steel kissed skin, and a slow red trickle meandered onto the boy's shirt.

She dropped her sword and her crossbow, holding her palms out to show them she had no more weapons. "Harm him and I'll kill you."

Fintan wasn't sure why, but a cold shiver knifed through his body.

The Viper watched from the shadows, quietly cursing under his breath. The rabbit ran right into the arms of the Butcher Tribe. He was so close to finishing her, just a heartbeat away before they burst into the clearing.

He breathed deeply and looked toward the heavens. Jacob wanted him to continue; he felt it in his blood. The hunt had become more difficult, but Jacob would find a way to help him. Jacob's way wasn't always easy, but it was always right.

Yes, he would have to spend time amongst the Soulless.

Still, my sword will taste the rabbit's blood. It will just take more time, and be even sweeter because of it.

CHAPTER 18
EAMON

E amon had spent the entire day certain that Gemma had fallen victim to some horrible end. As the hours wore on, his imagination turned ever darker, until he pictured a pair of demons feasting on her body. Upon entering the Stronghold, he had heard the good news and raced to Gemma's room, where he flung open the solid oak door to find Gemma and Jillian sitting on the edge of the bed in the small room. He inhaled for what seemed like the first time all day and brushed shaggy brown hair from his eyes.

"Are you okay?" The simple question left much unsaid, but his tone filled in the rest. He scrutinized his sister, looking for signs of harm or injury, and found none.

Gemma jumped from the bed, darted forward, and flew into Eamon's arms for a tight embrace. "All is well."

Still pink and wet from a recent bath, she wore her favorite green dress, the one with dozens of different flowers sewn on it that looked as if a rainbow had been mixed in a pot and poured over the fabric. Gemma embroidered flowers on all her clothes, her stitches impeccable and the colors always bright.

Eamon glanced at Jillian, who shook her head, and he got the distinct impression that all was *not* well. He trusted Jillian way more than Gemma.

He gently pushed his sister away from him. "What happened to you? Where have you been?"

She spun in a tight circle—the small room had little space for spinning. Just enough existed for the bed, a night side table, a small dresser, and dozens of dried flowers she hung on every inch of the walls and from the ceiling. Gemma's room was unique, just like her.

Once she finished the circle and faced Eamon again, she spoke in her special language. "I've seen so many different things. Beautiful things! Scary, dark ones too."

"Start at the beginning, Gemma." Jillian sounded tight. "Tell Eamon where you went."

"Oh, it was wonderful. I traveled the entire Witch's Woods. There's a wide river at the end. The water gushes, making white crests, and the roar is so loud it's hard to hear your own thoughts. And there's an underground tube to a far away land."

"What underground tube?"

"It's a bit smelly, but it goes on forever. No colors, just a big circle in the ground that's lit by strange white light. No flames or candles, just light. The tunnel travels under the water and connects to the land beyond."

"A circle in the ground? Could you take me to find it?"

She shook her head. "No. There's this door that vanishes into the forest. I stared at it for a long time, but I'd never find it again, unless the Eyes were still there, but I don't see how I could find the Eyes even if they were still there."

"There were eyes by the door?"

"Oh yes, big unblinking ones. The tube connected to these rooms. The walls were smooth and filled with more weird light and metal boxes with words and numbers that glowed." She frowned. "Other people were there also. I don't know what tribe they came from, but they were sad and hungry until Wilky gave them the round bread."

Eamon glanced at Jillian, who tried unsuccessfully to hide her grin behind her hand. Realizing the tale would only become more bizarre, he settled on the bed next to her. "This is some story."

"Oh, it only gets stranger," quipped Jillian. "Tell Eamon about the message."

"That's the best part. Wilky gave me this message especially for you. He said that it's not too late. He's discovered a cure to the Red Death. You just have to help them find the ingredients." Gemma spun in another circle, laughing. "It's really good news."

"He knew my name."

"Yes, he did. Isn't that weird? He's really nice but a bit peculiar."

"*He's* the peculiar one?" Eamon chuckled. "Did he happen to mention what he needed to make this *cure*?"

"Not to me. I saw him talking to his sister, but I couldn't hear what they said." Gemma shot her brother a sly smile. "I don't like her as much as Wilky, but I bet you will. I was too worried about the nasty birds with the big red beaks to concentrate on what they were saying anyway. Aaliss didn't see the birds at first, but once it was light, you couldn't miss them. Still the birds were not nearly as scary as the red field of crawling things. That was terrible."

Eamon shook his head, raised his eyebrows, and glanced at Jillian. It was a look they sometimes shared when they talked with Gemma.

Jillian shrugged in response and ran her hands through her hair.

Gemma continued chatting for a long stretch, during which she relayed a very disjointed account of her travels. When she tired, she lay down on the bed, pulled a quilt decorated with scores of flowers to her chin, and fell asleep.

Once Eamon and Jillian entered the hallway, he said, "She has a great imagination. I wonder if we'll ever know what happened to her."

"The strange thing is that she believes everything she told us. I can tell when she's having fun with us, and this time she believes every word." Jillian's eyes twinkled. "What if she's telling the truth?"

Eamon grinned. "That there's an underground tube with strange white light and metal boxes with glowing words at the end of the Witch's Woods?"

Jillian grabbed his arm, stopped him short, and stared deep into his eyes. She moved in close, and he felt her breath against his lips. "Not that — the *cure*."

Eamon shrugged. His mind had been stuck on the same thing — a cure could save Dermot. Just the thought of it made his heart race. "I don't know. Her story is so unreliable. How can we trust any part of it?"

"Yes, but what if...?"

She went back to check on Gemma, and he continued down the hallway to find Dermot.

What if this Wilky knows a cure for the Red Death? Is there time to find the ingredients before Dermot succumbs to the disease?

His mind whirled so quickly, by the time he reached Dermot's door, his head started aching and he felt dizzy. He knocked heavily.

"Come in, Eamon."

Dermot's room was substantially larger than Gemma's, his being the grandest in the Stronghold. It contained a four-poster bed, a giant chest of draws, two large windows that overlooked the Courtyard, and a fireplace. Dermot sat in one of two high-backed wooden chairs, gazing through the windows. The curtains were dark and heavy, but Gemma had managed to stitch her flowers on their border — her way of showing her love for Dermot when he became king.

"How'd you know it was me?" said Eamon.

"No one else knocks like you." Dermot kept his eyes focused on the window and looked drawn and uneasy. "Sit with me before we go to the Feasting Hall."

"Did you see Gemma?" Eamon wondered if their sister's condition weighed heavily on him. "She has some interesting stories to tell."

"I did. I was relieved to find her unharmed." He grinned at Eamon. "Fintan's tale is quite riveting. It seems to get more heroic with every telling. Soon he will have scaled a mountain, raced through magical blue flames, and fought a rogue band of tribeless men, instead of simply stumbling upon our sister and collecting a boy and girl."

Eamon smirked. "Who knew our brother was such a talented

storyteller? Soon we'll have songs written about his great victory.... *But what of Gemma's stories?* What do you make of *them?*"

Dermot sighed and returned his gaze to the window. "I love her dearly, but I can't understand her. Not like you can. I catch a few words, but the rest sounds like nonsense to me. Jillian translated a bit, but it's hard to figure out what's real and what's fantasy—a tube in the ground and a moving red field? I'm just happy she's safe."

"What about... the message for me?"

"What message?" Dermot arched his eyebrows.

"Gemma says this Wilky left me a message by name, that he's discovered the cure to the Red Death. I haven't spoken to him, but...." Eamon looked down. He didn't want Dermot to see the desperation in his eyes. He so wanted the story to be true, needed it to be true before Dermot's time had run its course. He knew he sounded foolish even repeating it, but still.... "She said we just need to find the ingredients to this cure and—"

"That's something! There's no cure for the Red Death. It's what happens when you get old. It's what has always happened. Listen, Eamon, I have to tell you something."

He didn't like the sound of his brother's voice, and suspected bad news.

"This morning my eyes flickered red, just for a moment. They returned to brown, but they *flickered*. It won't be long until I wake with the Red Eyes. Maybe, tomorrow...." Dermot shrugged—no sadness darkened his face, only acceptance.

Eamon wanted to question him. Surely he had seen wrong, but to what end? If not tomorrow, then his eyes would turn the day after or the week after that. The gods would not spare Dermot. They were cruel and spared no one.

"Then I must speak with this Wilky right away," he said. "Maybe Gemma tells the truth! Perhaps he has found a cure."

Dermot grabbed his arm and held it tight. "I don't fear the Red Death, Brother. When I pass I'll join Father and Mother in the heavens, where I'll keep an eye on you and Fin and Gemma. I'll send messages.

Just make sure you're listening." He released Eamon's arm. "Besides, Fintan claims the boy and girl threatened him. It's a high crime to threaten a royal. They'll be in the Basement for a long time before he lets them out. They're his prisoners until he decides their fate."

"But they didn't even know he was a prince. Surely we can make some allowances for their actions."

"It makes no difference. Their fate is his to decide." Dermot glanced back out the window. "I *will* miss this place."

"Derry, this can't be the end."

"All stories end, Eamon, and there are worse fates than death. Come, Brother, let's get something to eat." Dermot slapped him on the back and strode to the door. "I'm starving, and I can't wait to hear the *new* details Fintan's *remembered* about his heroic adventure."

Eamon trudged after his brother, but Jillian's voice resurfaced in his head.

What if Gemma's story is true?

He had to know, and he had no time to waste.

CHAPTER 19
P'MINA

P'mina had started to regret her decision to run away as the almost full moon floated high in the night sky. Normally it would have lit the forest, but clouds drifted in front of it, dimming its brightness so only a fraction of its light reached the forest floor. Having never stayed in the woods overnight, she longed for the warmth and safety of her hut as her fraught nerves amplified the forest sounds around her. She became convinced that a pack of wolves was close, until a squirrel ran out from under some fallen leaves, and an owl's screech made her jump like a small child frightened by a ghost story.

The Ancient Road stretched far into the distance. Built in the time before tribes, no one knew who originally constructed it or where it ended. Still, she clung to a shred of confidence that she had chosen the right way. Her mother had given her the direction, after all, so she must lie just ahead.

She clutched her spear until her hand hurt as fatigue and doubt clouded her mind. The cold had also started to bite through her rough-spun woolen cloak, which only made matters worse.

The Ancient Road narrowed ahead of her, as tree branches reached onto the path like dark skeletal arms that wanted nothing more than to grab unsuspecting travelers. The song of a nearby warbler startled her, but when the bird's song died away, something else replaced it, something bad—a snarling, snapping sound. She spun.

Two amber eyes shimmered in the darkness, illuminating the vague outline of a firefox.

The last remaining bits of courage drained from her body as she stared at the wild, angry-looking creature. She stepped back, holding the steel point of the spear between herself and the animal.

Unimpressed, the firefox grew bolder and trotted toward her.

She did the only thing that came to mind—she screamed and ran. Stumbling forward in the dark, she churned her legs, and felt as if she were running through a bog. As she raced forward she spotted another set of amber eyes in front of her in the distance.

Much to her dismay, they noticed her and started toward her, too.

Without any other choice, she surged forward, but every step brought her closer to the firefox in front of her. Then she saw a path off to her left and, racing even faster, leaped onto the path. Branches and hedges brushed against her on all sides, scratching her face and arms, and she stumbled over uneven ground.

Both firefoxes ran behind her now, and she envisioned their snarling snouts, long rolling tongues, and rows of razor-sharp teeth. Her lungs burned as she pumped her knees so high they almost reached her chest.

She smelled the creatures' sour breath, her heart threatening to explode, but then she glimpsed orange firelight in the distance. The light became her beacon.

She followed a bend in the path, and abruptly stopped.

A red witch stood in front of a small campfire, holding a torch and a spear much like her own.

Tears sprang to P'mina's eyes. "Mother!" She ran and jumped into the open arms that welcomed her.

Strong arms wrapped around her as she buried her head into the witch's chest. "I knew I would find you," she sputtered.

The witch whistled, and the firefoxes stopped snarling and snapping their jaws.

P'mina separated from the witch.

Affectionate brown eyes specked with red peeked through a hood from a scarlet robe. "Come on, sweetie, let's get you inside."

P'mina noticed the old, partially ruined, stone and wood cabin behind the witch. It had a sturdy door, but the mostly grass thatch roof did not quite cover the entire building.

"I can't believe you found me." Honey and warmth dripped from the witch's voice. The firefoxes stayed outside as the woman closed the door behind them. A small fire blazed in the fireplace and a kettle hung from a black metal bar. "You must be starving. I've made some stew."

The smell of meat and vegetables caused P'mina's stomach to flip happily. She hadn't eaten anything but a small snack of nuts and berries at midday. A wide smile spread across her face. She had found her mother. The world was right and true and good.

Her mother pointed to a simple wooden table with two benches. "Please, darling, take a seat while your mother gets you a bowl."

P'mina happily sat on the bench as her mother left to tend to the kettle. Stress, worry, and years of anguish all melted off her at once, and she immediately decided she liked the small room. The fireplace looked wide and inviting, and the straw spread across the floor added warmth and a sense of hominess to the place. She couldn't spot any decorations, but she noticed, with some satisfaction, a number of dried plants in different wooden bins at the far side of the room.

"I know all about plants, just like you," she said.

Her mother returned with two full wooden bowls, one in each hand, and carefully placed the bowls on the table, one in front of P'mina. She spoke in a high-pitched, sweet tone. "Eat. It will make you feel better. Then we can talk all about plants and whatnot."

P'mina obediently picked up the wooden spoon and dove into the stew. It tasted even better than it smelled.

Her mother smiled and pulled back her hood.

P'mina involuntarily sucked in her breath at the sight of the lush, blood-red hair that cascaded around her face. She had never seen anyone with red hair before.

"I said for you to eat your stew, sweetie." Her mother's voice had turned noticeably cooler.

P'mina scooped another spoonful of stew into her mouth, not wanting to anger her newfound mother. She was indeed beautiful, more beautiful than P'mina had imagined, with a fair complexion, oval face, and bright red lips.

"Have you lived here the entire time since you left the tribe?"

Her mother smiled. "Not the entire time, but mostly."

When P'mina ate another spoonful of stew, her mother's smile deepened.

P'mina pointed to a banner above the fireplace. "That's a pretty red bird, Mother."

"That's my banner, the Red Raven." Her mother unclasped her robe and let it fall away from her shoulders and onto the back of the bench.

Something struck P'mina as odd, but it took her a moment to realize what seemed amiss. "Where's your tree and all your art?"

No tattoos graced her mother's neck and arms.

"They vanished when the red eyes and hair came."

A lifetime of achievements had been wiped away in one night. P'mina frowned. It didn't seem fair. "No one told me about that, but I guess we can get Kalhona to give you new ones. She's the best Artist in the tribe." A warm, sleepy feeling started to settle into her body.

"Sure, we can get Kapohona to do it, if you like."

P'mina's heart jumped and her eyes widened as the firelight danced wickedly in her moth— No, in the *red witch's* face. The room suddenly turned hot and filled with sharp shadows and malice. She fought hard to keep awake. "Who are you? You're not my mother."

The witch pulled the bowl of stew away from P'mina. "No, sweet child, I'm not your mother. My name is Santra, and I know someone who will pay plenty for a pretty little Painted One."

P'mina eyed her spear, which she'd left near the door, next to the witch's spear.

She realized now that the two spears were not alike at all. The witch's spear was longer, made of dark wood, and a spike protruded from it a third of the way up. It looked well used — stained brown and red, like a mix of old and new blood.

She struggled to keep her eyes open, but blackness circled in on her....

CHAPTER 20
PIERS

Piers walked stiffly down the long hallway toward his siblings' dwelling, a grimace fixed on his face. He searched for room 833 in the almost pitch black hallway and held his arm still as he went. When his robe rubbed against the new burn, he saw stars. The medical Priest had put a numbing salve on it, which had helped for a short time, but the effects had mostly worn off now. A part of him welcomed the pain, knowing Aaliss and Wilky must be facing far worse than a burned arm. He should be with them, protecting them, but instead he was stuck in the comforts of the Compound with a burned arm and a shattered heart.

Only trace amounts of moonlight filtered through the windows on the ends of the long corridor. Although he could barely see in the darkness, he kept his flashlight switched off. He had no need for it during this part of his nocturnal sortie. He knew the way by heart and had no trouble navigating the long dark hallway.

He'd snuck out of the Parsonage after all the other novices had fallen asleep—well, all but one. He thought Zeke might have seen him leave, but he was a solid enough guy, almost a friend, so Piers thought he would keep his mouth shut. Still, it didn't matter.

What choice do I have?

He recalled the events of the prior day as he hobbled down the hallway.

At sunrise, two Monks retrieved him before the other novices woke.

Piers feared another encounter with the Viper, but instead, he faced the High Priest sitting alone behind the Desk of Jacob.

A pleasant smile played on the obese Priest's face, and he greeted Piers as if they hadn't been together under such different circumstances only a few hours earlier.

The High Priest's eyes beamed warmly, but his voice sounded cold. "Last night was necessary, Piers. I know you might not understand that now, but in time you will. Jacob wanted me to test you, so I could be certain as to your loyalty." He leaned forward. "I had no choice but to follow His wishes. I suspect Jacob has big plans for you. I have big plans, too, but first we must get through today. You will sit beside me for this morning's prayers while I explain your siblings' treachery. It is important that the Community understands the treason stopped with your brother and sister. I know you are innocent of any dark deeds. Now the Community will also know you are pious when I place my hand on your shoulder. It is the best way for me to communicate my faith in you to them. Do you understand?"

"You want me to stay silent as you condemn my brother and sister as traitors."

The High Priest clasped his hands in front of him. "That's exactly what I want, and exactly what you shall do. I knew there would be no problem. After all, the evidence is unquestionable, and I know you had nothing to do with their crimes, *right*?"

The last few words hung in the air like an invisible dagger, which the High Priest could sink into Piers's neck at any moment.

He nodded his head numbly, unable to speak.

"Good, Piers. Good. I know you are loyal. See yourself out. I need to pray before the morning sermon and hear what Jacob wishes of me."

Just like that, the meeting ended.

Later that morning, prayers started off routinely, but the High Priest cut them short. When he reached the conclusion, he forced a grave tone into his voice as he informed the Community about Aaliss and Wilky and their traitorous ways.

He rambled on for half an hour and hit all the important points: the Dark One convinced them to join the Soulless for personal vice; the Red Death had contaminated them; they had become enemies of everything good and holy; anyone caught helping them would be treated as harshly as the traitors themselves; the evidence against them was undeniable.

He broadcasted the sermon to every breakfast hall; nowhere within Eden would be safe for them now.

Piers sat next to the High Priest, silently enduring the man's hand on his right shoulder as his fingers dug into his flesh. It took all his willpower not to vomit.

His uncle, the President, sat on the other side of the High Priest and nodded as the High Priest condemned his niece and nephew.

The High Priest said they would be captured if possible, but he had authorized lethal force to subdue them, if necessary. With the Dark One involved, he could take no chances. Jacob would decide their fate. It was in His hands now.

Piers's stomach twisted into knots. With each hateful word, the knots tightened. He knew the charges against his siblings were false. They had to be false. They would never make a deal with the Dark One. They had to be innocent. Yet he still couldn't fathom how the High Priest could have made this mistake.

The High Priest was supposed to be infallible. It was the Edenites' most sacred rule — *the High Priest speaks with Jacob's voice in all matters.* Jacob spoke directly to the High Priest, guided him in all things, and the High Priest in return ruled over the Community. His word was beyond reproach, but how could that be true when he proclaimed Aaliss and Wilky traitors?

Piers wanted to stand and shout his defiance, proclaim their innocence to the entire Community, call out that the High Priest was somehow mistaken, that it was all a grave misunderstanding. But he had no proof. Without proof he feared he would sound crazy or, worse yet, under the influence of the Dark One. No, he had to find a better way. First, he had to discover what really happened and find proof of their innocence. He was the oldest. This responsibility fell on him.

He would not fail.

He felt tired, as if all the light from his soul had been sucked away, and what had been bright and true and good had become gray and dark and foul.

When he reached apartment 833, he removed a key from his pocket and checked both sides of the hallway to make sure no one lurked in the shadows. The Monks had taped a big red capital letter *J* to the door, indicating that a crime had been committed and no one could enter.

He ignored the tape, unlocked the door, scooted inside, and closed it behind him.

Safely inside, he steadied his nerves, switched on the flashlight, and swung it in a wide looping arc.

The chaos and mess startled him. The Book of Jacob made it clear that dirtiness and clutter were grievous sins to be punished severely. Monks sometimes investigated different apartments on suspicion of untidiness.

Rumors swirled that they had other motives for the searches, dark motives, but Piers had always dismissed the rumors. The High Priest's actions were supposed to be pure and above suspicion, and therefore, the Monks who reported to him could be nothing less.

Now, as he surveryed the room, he suspected otherwise.

The Monks had upended furniture and books and smashed picture frames on the floor. The place looked as if a twister had ripped through it, everything tossed about except the dual portraits of Jacob and the

High Priest. Every dwelling had both pictures, and now they looked oddly out of place, perfectly straight and centered on the living room wall—serene in the midst of chaos.

The simple dwelling consisted of a living room, two bedrooms, and one bathroom. Before Piers moved to the Parsonage he had shared one of the bedrooms with Wilky. Everything in their room had to be maintained in a certain order. If he switched one book with another or replaced one crookedly, his brother would melt down until Piers restored it. Some nights it took hours to determine what was wrong.

Now, he'd do anything to get those nights back.

He navigated carefully around the debris as he moved to Aaliss's bedroom, and hesitated at the doorframe, recalling how territorial she was over her *space*. She hated when others entered her room without permission, so he paused out of habit and remembered the night she had decided to become a Guardian. Stunned, he'd tried to argue with her, urging her to go into politics or buildings or anything safer, but she was resolute.

Once she made up her mind, no one could persuade her differently.

He'd grudgingly accepted the decision. Every night since, he'd prayed to the Creator to keep her safe.

Piers had made a pact with Aaliss the night before her first patrol in the Zone, and they created a secret hiding place where she left her *final words.* They laughed about it at the time, but he knew she was serious and the small precaution made her feel better. In truth, it made him feel better, too. If anything happened to her, he would find her *final words* and hear the farewell she would have told him in person.

He shoved the metal bedframe a few inches toward the windows, wincing as it scraped against the wooden floor, and found the loose board three slots in from the bedpost. He tapped it with the end of the flashlight and breathed a sigh of relief.

The Monks had missed it.

He used a paring knife to easily pry up the wooden board. When he flashed the light into the hollow space left behind, he found two neatly folded pieces of paper.

The first had Piers written on top in Aaliss's script. He opened it with a shaky hand.

Dear Piers:

I guess you were right. The Zone was too dangerous for me! I don't regret my decision. Stubborn until the end I guess. I owe my courage to you. You're the strongest person I know. No one cares about the scars as much as you do. Don't let them limit you! Be the person I know you are.

You're going to have to take care of our Wilky. He has gotten much more independent over the years, but he can't go it alone. Always make sure he has smooth soap. I know he's in good, strong hands with you.

I'll see you in the next life.

Love Always,

Aaliss

He exhaled. He hadn't realized he was holding his breath while he read the note. He folded it slowly and neatly before looking at the second one.

Wilky had addressed it to him in precise block letters. Surprised that Wilky knew about the hiding spot, Piers cautiously unfolded the note, his hands no less shaky than before.

Piers:

Username: Piers

Password: David

Love,

Wilky

Piers pondered Wilky's note for a long moment. David had been their father's name. The note had to be a clue, a breadcrumb to follow so he could learn the truth.

He pocketed both messages in his robe, and spotted a photograph of Aaliss and Wilky on the floor that made him grin. Aaliss smiled grimly for the camera while Wilky had a blank expression on his face. She kept an inch of space between them.

He laughed — Wilky hated to be touched — but the laughter turned to anger and he slammed his hand against the wall.

I'm the oldest! I should have protected them.

Just then, the door to the dwelling opened. He heard whispers and the sound of glass breaking under foot.

He was trapped.

On a whim, he removed Wilky's note, ripped it into shreds and tossed it across the room. The small pieces fluttered in the air, and blended in with the rest of the chaos. He retrieved his paring knife in one hand and held the sturdy flashlight in the other.

The crunching sounds became louder as the footsteps grew nearer.

He frowned at his inadequate weapons. Jacob would have to guide him.

Summoning up his courage, he stood taller and lurched out of the doorway, switching on the flashlight at the last second in an effort to blind the intruder.

Two figures darted forward, and a large, strong hand grabbed his wrist, twisted it behind his back, and slammed him against the wall, face first with a crunch.

Piers dropped the flashlight.

"Drop the knife, Priest, or I'll break your wrist."

A trickle of warm blood flowed from Piers's nose. He let the knife fall and heard it clatter against the floor.

The Monk spun him around and stood close, his beady black eyes glimmering dangerously. "What are you doing so far from your quarters, Priest? I guess you didn't notice the J on the door."

A second Monk stood behind him. She had red hair and a face full of freckles, which did nothing to lessen her hard edge. She stood a head taller than Piers and looked to be in her late twenties.

"So what are you looking for?" she asked.

"I-I ju-just wanted a photograph of my brother and sister. A keepsake. I've got it in my pocket." Piers smiled, trying his best to look contrite, hoping the Monks would let him go. As a Priest he usually enjoyed some privileges, although he suspected those days were gone forever.

The male Monk shoved him into the bedroom and swept his

flashlight across the room. "I hate traitors. You know what I would do if I got my hand on those traitors, Sarah? I'd burn them good and crispy."

Sarah chuckled. "Not bad, Mark, but a fire would be too good for traitors. They'd die too quickly. I'd bleed them and leave them in the pigpen. Let the pigs have fun with them. It would take all night, and it wouldn't be pretty. They'd happily go to hell and join the Dark One to get away from the pigs."

Mark poked Piers hard in the chest. "I hope you get the idea, Priest. Now what did you find? You wouldn't want us to think you were a traitor."

"Really, I was just looking for a keepsake." Piers glanced from one hard face to the other.

The beam from Sarah's flashlight stuck on the loose floorboard.

Piers had forgotten to replace it when he heard the door open. *What a fool!*

"Take a look at that board. I don't remember it being popped open when we searched the place." She squatted down and examined it. "It's perfect for a hiding place."

Mark swung his flashlight into Piers's stomach, and Piers doubled over. "My, you are a thin one. I bet I can break your ribs without even trying. Now turn out your pockets, and let's see what you found."

Piers gasped as he sucked oxygen back into his lungs. Having no choice, he turned his pockets inside out, and the photograph and the note from Aaliss fluttered to the floor.

"What do we have here?" Sarah bent down and picked up both. She read the note out loud, laughed, and handed it to Mark, who also snorted in amusement.

"What a touching message," sneered Mark as he popped the note in his mouth and started chewing. "Too bad we can't let you keep it. It might have had a code from the Dark One. Tell you what? I'm going to take pity on you, Priest. You can have the photo to remember your traitor brother and sister."

He took the picture from Sarah, crumpled it in his fist and handed it to Piers in a ball. "You should go to bed, Priest. I'm sure you'll have a big day tomorrow." He slapped Piers hard on the back and handed him his flashlight.

Piers moved past him.

Before he left the room, Sarah squealed, "Oink, Oink, Priest." When he jumped, she laughed and said, "I'll see you tomorrow, Priest."

CHAPTER 21
FINTAN

Fintan stared hard at the yellowed paper in his hand. Someone had torn the page from a book and scratched a message onto it with gray ash. He hoped that if he stared at it long enough the words would change, but he re-read them for the tenth time, and they stubbornly remained the same:

> *Prince Fintan:*
> *I heard you speaking with the Captain last night. Meet me by the Naming Tree after the bells ring tonight.*

The bells had just finished tolling, their echo dying in the wind. They rang twice a day, at midday, and at midnight when the last grains of sand tumbled from the giant sandglass. Four times a year the timekeepers reset the sandglass by using the sundial in the Courtyard, a practice that stretched back further than anyone could remember. Fintan never gave it much thought before, but now that he'd dreaded the bells tolling, he wondered who had come up with the system.

His head ached. Just a few hours ago, the Feasting Hall had been full and festive, and he had basked in the glow of a conquering hero for the first time. He felt alive and had practically floated in the air. Finally, he had earned the tribe's respect.

Eamon, of all people, had persuaded Dermot to open casks of wine usually reserved only for holiday feasts. Fiddlers, guitarists, and drummers filled the Hall with bright, happy music. They played all his favorite songs: the Stronghold and the Siege, the Seven Shield Walls, and the Merry Maiden. The festivities almost reminded him of Dermot's victory celebrations. But this had been better—this celebration had been about him. And for once, more women lined up to dance with him than for Dermot and Eamon the Handsome.

As the wine flowed, Dermot had hopped on top of his table, and silenced the Feasting Hall with a wave of his arms. "Lord Fintan, please join me," he shouted loud enough to be heard by everyone in the Hall.

Fintan smiled sheepishly and jumped on the table with him.

Dermot wrapped an arm around his shoulders. "Please regale us with the tale of how you saved our fair sister, the princess. Leave out no details or heroics for modesty's sake."

The crowd chuckled at that, which pissed Fintan off, but he wouldn't let the crowd's reaction ruin the celebration. He made believe it didn't bother him, exaggerated a low bow, and gladly entertained the Hall with his adventure. So what if he didn't lead his horse through the blue flames? And it might have been a stretch to say that he snatched one of those toy bolts right before it would have sunk into his chest, but he did no harm, and everyone cheered and laughed at the right times. Even some of the old-timers in the King's Guard nodded their heads respectfully.

The feasting went on well after the usual time, and they slid tables to one side of the large room to make room for dancing. A spirited game of dice broke out on one end of the hall as some members of the tribe gambled hard-earned coin against each other.

After the music and merriment stopped, Fintan and Cormac had laughed their way back to the Royal Hall. Fintan, still in high spirits, flung open the door to his room. Waiting for him was a note perched on his bed. At first he'd expected the message to be congratulatory, maybe from Dermot, or a thank you from Gemma.

It had taken three readings before his cloudy mind understood the words, and his spirit sank like a heavy stone tossed into a river. Just when the tribe had recognized him as a hero, this note blindsided him and threatened to take it all away. That was when the pounding headache began.

Fintan shook off the memories and sullenly studied the Naming Tree from the far side of the Courtyard, cloaked in deep shadows. The tree glowed silver with an otherworldly shine in the moonlight. The founding members of the tribe had built the Stronghold around that ghost tree. The tribe had no record of it, but nothing else made sense, so the tribe accepted it as truth.

The founders had carved their names into the trunk in large block letters. Every child learned those names along with the other tribal heroes: Langdon the Large, who successfully held the Stronghold against a siege when the Stronghold had just been completed; Helena the Healer, who found a cure for a disease that threatened to kill the herd; Oisin the Omnipresent, who established the Outpost in the North. They told stories about a dozen more, and the tribe would undoubtedly add Dermot to the list after he went to the heavens.

As a child, Fintan playfully added his name with those heroes—*Fintan the Famous*. As an adult, he obsessed over it.

If he looked carefully, he could see his name carved into the bark. The tree carver placed royal names in the center of the main trunk, so those names did not stretch as high as the others.

Even though the night seemed unusually quiet, it was never *completely* silent. The King's Guard walked the stone wall that protected the city, their boots tapping against the palisade. Others had nighttime business. The Nursery always had life, horses neighed in the Stables, and lovers laughed in the distance. Still, an unusually deep and heavy quiet had settled over the enclosed settlement, as much of the Stronghold had gone to sleep, feeling the drowsy effects of the wine and the merriment.

Fintan shifted his eyes around the deserted Courtyard, sighed, and left the shadows to trudge toward the Naming Tree and whoever waited for him.

Dermot is old. Even without the poisoned berries, how much longer can he last?

He had almost reached the Naming Tree when a young woman slid from behind the wide trunk. She looked familiar, and Fintan wracked his brain to remember where he had last seen her. Then he remembered tripping the Little One at breakfast, and he recalled her—the girl with brown eyes who had been staring at him.

She twisted her hair and swayed in place.

She must be anxious.

He grinned. He could use that against her. "Are you the one who sent me the note?"

"Yes, Prince Fintan. I overheard your conversation with Cormac about your feelings for the King and what you're planning to do."

The mousy girl's voice sounded stronger than he'd expected, with an unexpected edge of malice.

He beamed a bright smile. "You know, I've been watching you. You work in the Nursery, right?" He leaned toward her as he spoke.

The girl blushed and swayed in her spot, her dress puffing outward. "You know who I am?"

He inched closer to her. "I do. I've been watching you. I saw you today at breakfast." He paused and shot her his most sincere look, his eyes wide and unblinking. "Being a royal prince is hard sometimes. Everyone is always watching me. It's hard for me to talk to the special girls."

Her eyes narrowed. "You're not angry about the note?"

"Angry? How could I be angry?" He leaned forward until only a few inches separated them. "Without the note, I might never have gotten the courage to talk to you. The way I see it, this is fate."

She returned his smile, but it looked calculating and not fully genuine.

"I've always known you were special." He gently brushed a loose strand of hair from her cheek.

She trembled at the touch.

Encouraged, he continued. "I need a special girl like you—someone smart and ambitious. Meet me tomorrow morning. We'll sneak away so we can get to know each other, far from the prying eyes of the Stronghold. Just you and me."

"But I have to work in the Nursery." She made a sour face and wrinkled her nose when she said *Nursery*. "The Master will be very angry if I don't show up. Unless someone important speaks to him and tells him that I can be excused for the day."

The tone in her voice conveyed her unspoken message—that she hated the Nursery and never wanted to go back.

"Someone special like you shouldn't be working in the Nursery. I'll talk to him myself before we go. I'll make sure it's all right." He gently stroked her hair, brushing against her ear, and saw heat blush her cheeks. "Now, my sweet, did you tell anyone else about my conversation with Cormac?"

"No."

"It's important that you don't tell anyone we're spending time together. We'll have to act like strangers until later, when we can be alone. If the other women know how much I'm interested in you, they'll do everything they can to keep us apart. They can be so jealous. We'll have to keep our relationship a special secret between us for just a little bit. Deal?"

She nodded.

"Tomorrow at first light then. We'll leave from the Stables." Fintan kissed her on the cheek.

She turned her head, but he backed away a moment before she could reach his lips.

He turned to leave, and she tugged on his leather cloak, spinning him around. "My name's Cattie."

"Oh, yeah, Cattie's a lovely name."

He turned, but she twisted him around with another pull.

"I am no fool."

"That's why I like you so much. You're special. I'll see you in the morning." He turned his back and left the Courtyard without looking back. As he returned to the shadows, he smiled at Cormac.

"Is she the one who overheard us?" Cormac asked.

"No, she's just someone who happened to be waiting by the Naming Tree."

"Really?"

Fintan sighed. "No, not really, but don't worry. I have a plan to deal with her. We'll have to wake at first light." He clapped him on the shoulder. "When will Scotty return with the poisoned berries?"

Cormac shrugged. "It's hard to say. They're not easy to find. Probably a couple of days."

"Good."

"I don't like the looks of her."

Fintan laughed and shoved his big friend. "Neither do I. Leave the planning to me."

He sauntered to his room feeling better than he had when he first read the note.

CHAPTER 22
AALISS

Aaliss fumed over all the mistakes she had made since she overheard the High Priest's plans to murder Wilky and her.

I should have killed that blubbery pompous good-for-nothing High Priest and my worm of an uncle before I went to Wilky's lab. I should never have camped in the terrawk nest or set that trap, or....

She angrily paced the small cell—four strides from the bars to the wall and four back again. She had lost count how many times she had completed the circuit, but the repetitive motion made her feel better, as though she was doing something positive.

After they surrendered, Fintan and his party had brought them to the Stronghold on horseback.

A Guardian captured by Soulless. What would my instructors say?

Never in Eden's long history had a Guardian been taken captive. A few had died while fighting Soulless, but none taken. The Guardian's code could not be clearer:

Better to die than be taken. When a Guardian dies in service to Eden, all his or her sins will be forgiven. The fallen Guardian will stand as a hero with Jacob in heaven, and will want for nothing. A captured Guardian will spend eternity in hell, and his or her torment will know no end.

There's no doubt about it now; she was damned. But it probably didn't matter, since she couldn't be damned twice. Her eternal soul was in no worse shape than it had been when she fled Eden and removed the gasmask.

At least Wilky had made it to the Stronghold safely.

Aaliss had experience riding, but her brother had never ridden a horse before, and he shook even when they held the animal steady.

One beefy horseman reached toward him to hoist him onto the saddle, but she shielded him with her body. "I'll help him." Even with her hands bound, she managed to push him into place before she mounted herself.

Luckily, they didn't tie Wilky's hands, so he clutched her waist, pressed his face against her back, and closed his eyes to the world.

She sighed. *It's better that way.*

The one they called Cormac held their horse's reins while the other riders penned them in. The arrogant one they called Prince Fintan rode at the point, leading the party triumphantly back to the Stronghold.

The ride took no longer than a few hours, but the going was rough and awkward. Her back and legs ached, and she knew Wilky felt worse, but he didn't complain. She added the uncomfortable journey and shabby treatment as one more thing she'd make Cormac pay for—that and the cut on Wilky's neck.

She curled her hands into fists just thinking about it. Her list of paybacks had started to become long.

They cleared the forest and the Stronghold sprang up suddenly in the near distance. A tall stone palisade ringed the crest of a good-sized hill. The roofs of stone buildings rose high above the stone wall, and the branches of a ghost tree towered over the buildings. A wide wooden drawbridge provided entry over deep ditches dug at the base of the walls. The slope of the hill and the ditches made the fortifications appear taller than they were.

Aaliss had the odd feeling that the Soulless city was older and more solid than the Compound, even though she knew that could not be true. The Book of Jacob identified the Compound as the oldest remaining human settlement—built when the Red Death first plagued the Soulless, after God allowed the Dark One to curse humanity for its wickedness. Still, something about the stone looked tested and secure, and made her certain that men had died in vain attempts to breach its defenses.

A large flag with a jeweled sword, blood dripping from the tip, greeted them as they trotted over the wooden drawbridge toward the tallest stone hall. Along the way, she caught glimpses of the small city in the twilight: a courtyard, an old ghost tree, numerous stone buildings in which she could only guess at their functions.

People stopped to gawk at them, and a few pointed at her. They all looked so young it made her feel uneasy. She kept expecting to see gray hair, or the bent backs of the aged, but she saw none here. She should have expected this, but she had never contemplated how the Soulless lived without elders. Here she would be among the adults, which seemed strange, since in Eden she was considered young.

Fintan reined up close to Cormac. "Let's take our prizes directly to the Basement. I'll determine their fate at my leisure."

When they dismounted, Fintan led them inside a wide, short building, and Cormac pushed her from behind.

She skittered to a stop in front of a heavy wooden door with iron deadlocks. As Cormac threw the door open, the stench threatened to overwhelm her. It smelled like death, but not death alone—death mixed with other foul, evil smells.

She gagged, and cursed herself for the sign of weakness.

Cormac chuckled and shoved her in the back. "You don't like the Basement? I'm sorry if it isn't up to your standards."

"It smells better than you," she answered defiantly, bringing laughter from others in their party, as well as a cuff to the back of her head from Cormac as they plodded down the stairs.

Fintan reached the Basement floor first and barked at the fat jailor. "Keep a good eye on my prizes, Redmond the Round. We freed

Princess Gemma from them. Watch out—the girl with the boy's hair is a wild one."

The jailor squinted his eyes and seemed to grasp his keys tighter in the presence of such important charges. Sweat started to bead on his face.

Aaliss thought he looked far more used to drunken ranchers than prisoners captured by a prince.

She glimpsed the rest of the Basement before Cormac pushed the siblings into the cell and the metal gate slammed shut, locking them inside. The clanking sound of metal locking against metal felt like a punch to her midsection.

The long hallway had cells on both sides. Murmured conversations drifted on the stale air and, toward the far end, weeping. Two oil lanterns provided the only light, one placed on either side of the hallway.

She fought hard against despair, focusing instead on her anger to give her strength.

Better to be angry than hopeless.

Time had crawled since. No one had visited them or paid them the least bit of attention.

Only the fat jailor sat at the far end of the hallway near the staircase, not far from their cell, his eyelids heavy as his head nodded forward sleepily until he snored himself upright again.

"We need to find a way out of here," Aaliss whispered to Wilky. "If the jailor would come close enough, I could cut his throat. He must have the keys to these doors on that giant ring of his."

She touched the short, razor-sharp blade she had secreted inside the folds of her jumpsuit, standard equipment for Guardians. These Soulless fools had never bothered to search her. She could throw the knife and sink it into his throat, but he'd die where he sat, and that was too far away for her to grab the key ring.

She studied the jailor, an unkempt, overweight, unattractive man with greasy hair, acne, and stubble dotting various parts of his face. She smiled and called out in her best, most seductive voice. "Hey, jailor, I want to show you something."

Redmond opened his eyes and turned his head. "I can see from here, if you want to put on a show."

"Come closer. I want to tell you a secret." She playfully tugged on the zipper of her suit.

Redmond grunted and closed his eyes.

She spun, stomped her foot, and returned to her pacing. Their cell had two empty wooden buckets and two raised wooden platforms with loose straw thrown on top. She refused to think about the buckets and turned toward Wilky.

"Why bother with wood platforms? The floor would do as well." As she finished talking, a small rodent with a long, thin tail scurried through their cell.

"You sit on top of that," she told Wilky as she pointed to the platform bed.

With Wilky safely off the floor, she continued pacing. "I don't understand why they're treating us like this. Gemma should have told them that we saved her by now. They should be thanking us."

She turned to Wilky for confirmation, but he just looked at her with his big eyes, quiet and calm. He said so much without ever speaking.

Some of the steam blew through her. "I know, Wilky. We don't treat them awfully well in the labs either, but that's different."

She tried to think of all the ways the Edenites treated Soulless prisoners better, but she really couldn't come up with much. In many ways they treated Guests far worse.

"Besides, could you imagine a place like this in Eden? The Priests would go crazy. All of this *filth*." She snorted, happy to have at least one thing to feel superior about.

The night crept along. She rattled the bars, but they held.

The jailor opened his eyes long enough to sneer at her before closing them again.

The prisoner across the hall snored incessantly, which had started to drive her crazy. She looked for something to throw at him. She eyed the bucket but it wouldn't fit through the bars.

The Basement door opened and whined on rusty hinges. Two sets of footsteps grew steadily louder.

The jailor woke from his stupor and rose from his chair.

Aaliss wrapped her hands around the metal bars and waited.

Gemma appeared first, followed by a young man her age. Tall, he had shaggy brown hair that reached the tops of his wide shoulders. When he turned to look at her, he had smoldering sapphire eyes that sparkled in the flickering lantern light. He resembled Fintan, but his features were more pleasing, and he had no trace of the arrogant smugness Fintan sported in abundance.

Not many people in Eden had blue eyes.

What is that silly saying? If his eyes are blue, then he'll be true. Does the saying work for Soulless eyes?

She bit her lip, and the pain helped her focus.

I can't become distracted by a pleasing face and blue eyes. What does it matter if his eyes are blue?

Everyone she met was an enemy until proven otherwise.

Redmond the Round stood stiffly and sounded nervous. "Good evening, Prince Eamon. I wasn't expecting any visitors at this time of night."

"Believe me, this is the last place I expected to be tonight, but I've displeased Dermot. For punishment he sent me here to relieve you and watch our prisoners for the rest of the evening."

Redmond squinted at him. "And Princess Gemma? Is she also being punished?" The question in his voice made it clear he doubted Dermot would punish Gemma in this fashion.

Gemma stood in the shadows watching them, smiling shyly at Wilky, swaying back and forth.

Eamon laughed. "No, Gemma couldn't go to sleep unless she had a chance to curse at her captors. I'm sure she'll get bored in a little while and go back to her room."

"Well, I'd sure like to go to bed and leave this lot, but the Master won't like me leaving. This is my last day on Basement duty, and I'd hate to anger him." Redmond shifted his weight and gazed uncertainly. "I don't want to serve additional time in the Basement. He only has the one arm, but he's quick with that whip he keeps coiled at his waist."

He rubbed his cheek, caressing a faint scar.

"You will do as I say," Eamon said. "King Dermot will be a lot angrier than the Master Jailor if his orders are ignored. You know how he gets. Of course, if you want to ask him yourself, you could go to his room." He winked. "I wouldn't suggest it. He wasn't alone the last time I saw him."

Redmond grabbed his key ring. "As you wish, my lord. They'll give you no problems." He nodded toward Aaliss. "She just paces back and forth. I wouldn't get too close though. She's got a crazy look in her eyes."

He handed Eamon the keys and trudged up the stairs.

Once the Basement door closed, Eamon and Gemma approached the cell and stood an arm's length away from the bars.

If he moves a little closer, I can grab him and use my blade to persuade him to free us.

Wilky hopped from the wood platform and stood beside her.

Gemma grinned and said something to Wilky that Aaliss could not understand.

Eamon stood quietly, studying them both. After a long moment, he took a step closer to the bars.

Aaliss glared at him and inched her hand toward her hidden blade. Almost without realizing it, her eyes focused on the key ring in his hand.

Just another foot and she'd have him.

CHAPTER 23
EAMON

Eamon studied the siblings. The boy seemed harmless, his mind elsewhere, but the girl was a different story. She looked lethal and very present, and a jolt of energy zipped through him. Something about her posture made Eamon wonder if she could spring forward at any moment and slide effortlessly through the bars of her jail cell.

She stood, arms crossed, her lips pinched together, her eyes narrow and intense. A black suit fit snugly over her athletic body.

He had never seen a garment made of skins like that before. Pieced together seamlessly, it gave the illusion that it served as the girl's second skin.

A few freckles scattered across her nose and cheeks dotted her cream-colored face, but her eyes took his breath away. They were deep pools—nuanced and dangerous. They sparkled sapphire-blue with specks of gray.

He glanced away, embarrassed by the current that raced through his body and worried he might fall too deeply into those waters. He wasn't usually absorbed by looks, but something about this girl was different. More than her physical beauty pulled at him. He instinctively knew he had never met anyone quite like her.

He turned his attention to the boy, in part to avoid the girl's withering gaze. "What's my name?"

"Eamon."

"How do you know my name?"

He shrugged one of his small shoulders. "I saw it."

How can he see a name?

Perhaps a subtle difference in language between tribes explained the odd word choice.

He regarded the boy more closely. His face looked unlined, showing no sign of distress or deceit. He had the same coloring and straight black hair as his sister, but his gaze lacked any sign of danger. Something else replaced the danger, however. When he looked carefully, the boy's eyes appeared as if they folded in on themselves, creating an infinite loop—the most complicated pattern he had ever seen.

He pulled back and questioned him. "You have me at a disadvantage. You know my name, but I don't know yours."

"I'm Wilky, and my sister is Aaliss."

Gemma twirled her dress and clutched a small scented cloth to her nose to mask the Basement's stench.

No use playing at word games. The time was late and he needed to know. "Have you discovered a cure to the Red Death?" Eamon spit to ward of bad spirits.

"Yes," the boy answered simply.

"You'll need to free us before we tell you what it is." Aaliss grabbed the bars and leaned forward. "We'll need to work together to find the ingredients to make it."

"But you attacked my brother, Fintan. The way he tells it, you shot a bolt at him that he snatched before it sank into his chest. You're his prisoners to do with as he sees fit. He's very angry at you."

Aaliss's face burned scarlet, and her left eye twitched. "I never attacked him! If I did, he would be dead right now. I just offered an invitation to fight, which he turned down, being the miserable coward that he is. I'd gladly give him another chance, and that large, overgrown, imbecile he's friends with, too. If they're afraid, I'd fight them both at the same time."

He heard no bluster in her words, which meant she was either crazy or confident, both equally dangerous. "Watch your tongue! That's my brother you're talking about."

He tried to feign anger, but made a poor show of it; the edges of his lips betrayed him, having turned upward. The thought of the ever-confident Fintan reluctant to face the girl amused him. He wished he had seen it.

"Well, my condolences. Hopefully, cowardice doesn't run in the family."

Eamon glanced at Gemma, who giggled and spoke in her special language. "She speaks the truth, and I said you would like her. I can tell by the way you look at her."

"*Right*," he said, and then turned back toward Aaliss. "Why should I free both of you? I can keep your brother hostage. You and I can look for the cure together, and if we can't find it, your brother's life will be forfeited."

Wilky's eyes widened, and Aaliss stepped toward him protectively. "No deal! Only Wilky knows the components for the cure. He'd be useless without me, and I'll never leave him. You'll have to free us both or you'll never get it." She sounded and looked sincere—no bluff in her eyes.

He whispered to his twin sister, "What do you think? We don't have much time. If we're wrong, Fintan and Dermot will be angry with us. I'd likely spend the rest of my life down here on guard duty."

He scowled at the filth and the stench. He could think of no worse job in the Stronghold.

Gemma spun in a carefree circle. "Why ask me? You must do what is right, Brother. Besides, your mind is made up anyway."

He had persuaded Dermot to serve wine at dinner so the Stronghold would be sleepy tonight and sluggish tomorrow. If Dermot's eyes had already flickered, Eamon had to move now or face losing him. He sighed. If he had any chance to save his brother, he had to take it. He really had no other choice. The conditions were as good as they were going to get. Tomorrow would be too uncertain and perhaps too late.

He turned from his sister and faced Aaliss. "If I free you both, I'll have your word that we'll work together to get the necessary items for the cure? You'll promise not to run off or kill me in my sleep?"

She answered for both of them. "We swear it on Jacob's life."

He had no idea who this Jacob was, but no matter. "If you're lying, it will not go well for you." He inserted a key into the metal lock, twisted, and swung open the gate with a creak.

Aaliss smiled. "That sounds better than Jacob's Choir. Where's our stuff?" She glanced around the Basement with a frown on her face.

"A friend has it. We've got to sneak out without anyone seeing us. It's late and few people should be out. The guard by the drawbridge will conveniently look the other way when we cross. Once we leave the Stronghold, we'll meet up with my friend, who has horses and supplies."

"And our stuff?" asked Aaliss.

"Yes, but first tell me what we need to make the cure." He rested his hand on the hilt of his sword. While the two seemed honest, he would be stupid to trust them, and he was not stupid. "We'll need a destination after we leave the Stronghold."

"The cure is made from a mixture of a flower and a mushroom," Aaliss answered confidently.

"Okay, but what flower and what mushroom? We'll need a direction and a plan."

Wilky pointed at Gemma.

"What does my sister have to do with it?"

Wilky shook his head and touched a flower on her yellow dress. "This flower."

Gemma giggled. "How lucky for us. It blooms in the fall and has the loveliest blue and red petals. It smells like fresh dew in springtime. It's one of my favorites, but you'll have to hurry. You won't find many left."

Eamon's heart started racing.

Can this be true? Did these strangers find the cure to the Red Death? Can I truly save Dermot?

He turned back to his sister. "Where do these flowers grow?"

"You'll need to find the old creek to the east and head north. They bloom along its banks." Gemma whirled in a circle, a broad grin on her face.

"What about the mushroom?" asked Eamon, hoping the answer would be as easy.

Wilky shrugged. "It grows this time of year, but I can't see where to find it."

Eamon waited but when the boy said nothing else, he asked, "Is that it? We need more to go on than that. Half a cure is no better than none."

"I can draw it. I'm a good artist. I just can't see where to find it."

"*He can't see it.* What does that mean?" Eamon glanced at Aaliss. "How does he *see* things?"

Aaliss stepped between the two. "It means that we get the flower first and go after the mushroom second. We have a destination. That's enough for now. After we're free, we can talk about the mushroom and where to find it."

Eamon stared at Wilky for a moment. He had hoped that the mushroom would be as easy as the flower, but at least they had a destination. And maybe he'd know how to find the mushroom after Wilky drew it. Standing in the Basement any longer certainly wouldn't get them closer to the cure.

He had no choice. "So be it. Lets go."

He led them up the staircase, taking the steps two at a time. He inhaled deeply as they shut the door behind them, trying to flush the jail's stench out of his system, but it still lingered like slime left behind by a slug.

He kissed Gemma on top of her head. "Go to bed and tell Dermot it was all my doing. I forced you to come down into the Basement, and you don't know where we went. Remember, it was all my fault."

"Bring back some of the flowers for me. They're my favorite." She turned and raced upstairs.

Eamon whispered as he led them out of the hall and into the night. "Follow me. Keep close and quiet."

He glanced around the Stronghold. The only home he had ever known looked foreign to him now. The light from the moon and the torches cast shadows on the stone buildings, making them look sinister. The strong walls he had always found protective now appeared hard and unyielding. The Courtyard felt like a graveyard, and even the Naming Tree, his favorite place within the Stronghold, appeared like a giant skeleton raised from the dead, or like a giant tombstone, the names written proudly across the tree's trunk nothing more than lives it had claimed.

He jumped when the bells started tolling. With no one in sight, he swallowed hard, grabbed Aaliss's hand, and pulled.

She felt warm to the touch, steady, and fearless. He drew courage from her strength as he sprinted from one building to another. When she started to stray to his left, he yanked her hard to keep her safe.

"What's that for?" asked Aaliss.

He pointed to the ground. "See those four white stones. They mark the corners of a trap. We have a number of them spread throughout the Stronghold. It's really a false floor. If you step on it, it'll give away. There's a steep drop with spikes at the bottom. This way, if the walls ever get breached, we have some nasty surprises for invaders."

He resumed his sprint, stopping only when he reached the bakery. He breathed in deeply, soaking in the last scent of bread that lingered in the air and driving away the remaining stench from the Basement.

A blackbird with a splash of red on its claws perched on the roof opposite them. Squawking loudly, it shattered the quiet. He waved his hands at the bird and it reluctantly flew off. Eamon watched it go, but he had the uneasy feeling that the bird had been spying on them.

He pushed onward, leading from one building to the next, keeping as deep in the shadows as he could, with Aaliss and Wilky breathing heavily at his heels.

Close to the drawbridge, he heard footsteps. Two people, lost in conversation, approached from the Courtyard, and he squeezed himself tight against the edge of the Nursery.

Flickering torchlight brushed against Fintan's and Cormac's faces.

Eamon froze. There was no place for them to hide.

Aaliss tensed her body and narrowed her eyes. He put his arm in front of her to restrain her, but she knocked it away sharply. Still, she held her place, although he could tell it took all her willpower not to confront the two.

Fintan and Cormac walked only a few feet away from them. If either of them glanced in their direction, they'd be caught and all would be lost. Eamon smelled traces of wine and saw the tight expression on Cormac's face, and heard Fintan's easy laughter.

He held his breath. He could touch them, or stick out his leg to trip them if he wanted.

Cormac looked up, but Fintan whispered something and shoved him. The push propelled Cormac past where they stood, and the two friends didn't notice them.

Eamon exhaled, took Aaliss's hand, and led them to the drawbridge. She stood close when they stopped, and he felt a surge of electricity ripple through him. Heat singed his fingers where their hands touched.

When he spoke, his voice sounded breathless and husky. "We walk across the drawbridge. Try to be quiet. When we reach the other side, we will cross the bridge and run to the woods. It's not far. My friend should be there with the horses."

She pulled her hand from his. "I think I can manage from here. We'll be right behind you. No offense, but I'm happy we're leaving, and I don't plan on returning."

He led them across the drawbridge and chanced a look back at the guard, and noticed his friend, Kiernan, looking in the opposite direction. Kiernan would answer truly when asked whether he saw them cross the bridge. Eamon had bailed Kiernan out from some large gambling debts last month. The man would keep his silence.

They cleared the drawbridge and plunged forward into the moonlight. Dirt turned to grass, and before they reached the river and the wooden bridge that spanned it, Eamon turned back to look at the

Stronghold one last time. He saw it with fresh eyes, its walls impressive, strong, daunting, and unyielding.

I wonder if I'll be welcomed back.

He crossed the bridge and spotted the walking path easily enough, having taken it too many times to count, and heard the sound of nervous horses before he saw them. When he turned around a cluster of trees, he found Jillian waiting with three horses in a small clearing.

"Thank the heavens!" she said. "I was worried you were going to get caught."

"No one saw us. All is quiet." Eamon had no idea how Jillian stole the horses and supplies, but he *knew* she would be waiting for him. She always came through for him. "Jillian, meet Aaliss and Wilky. They've agreed to help in return for their freedom."

Jillian's eyes lingered on Aaliss, washing over her in a slow dance. She pursed her lips. "I'm coming with you."

"But you can go back. We agreed. Only Kiernan knows of your involvement and he'll keep quiet. If he said anything, he'd only be implicating himself. It's not safe. You need to go back." He hesitated and then added, "Besides, who will look after Gemma?"

Jillian grabbed the reins of a gray mare. "She can take care of herself for a spell. This was my idea as much as yours. I'm not leaving you alone." She spoke to Eamon, but her eyes never wavered from Aaliss.

"We only have three horses and there are four of us." Eamon argued what he could, but he knew he had already lost.

"Wilky rides with me," said Aaliss. "He doesn't have experience with horses."

Jillian mounted the mare and stared down at Eamon defiantly. "Don't we have someplace to go? I imagine we should get moving."

As Eamon grabbed the reins of a chestnut colt, a blackbird called from a nearby tree. He got the weird feeling this was the same bird he had seen from the Stronghold.

A shiver crept up his spine.

Blackbirds were evil creatures, known to do the work of the Dark One.

CHAPTER 24
AALISS

A aliss decided she had no love for riding horses. Her back and legs started to cramp.

At least Eamon proved to be good company, pointing out trails they did not take and where they went. He even added a story or two about different hunts, and one about a red bear that had surprised him and a trading party one night by a campfire.

She added a few stories of her own, always filtering them so she didn't reveal too much about Eden or her life as a Guardian.

The conversation waned as they traveled for hours, past rock formations, an old burial site, heavily wooded forests, grass fields, and finally to the bank of a small creek. Luckily the night sky was clear and the moonlight bright enough for them to find their way.

Aaliss couldn't shake the feeling that this forest wasn't as dangerous as the Zone. Perhaps the absence of the Guardians made a difference, or maybe it was Eden itself.

When they reached the creek, Eamon pulled his horse to a stop. "In this darkness we could pass an entire field of flowers and never know. We have enough of a head start on anyone from the Stronghold who might come looking for us. They shouldn't realize we're missing until morning, and even then it'll take time before they send out search parties. Let's make camp and grab a few hours of sleep."

Wilky groaned but didn't complain as Aaliss helped him off the black mare. He moved stiffly, as if he had a boulder stuck between his legs.

She frowned. *Where does all this strength and courage come from? Did I underestimate him from the start?*

She anchored his hammock to the sturdy branches of an oak. When he fell asleep, she found Eamon and Jillian by the campfire.

They warmed their hands by the fire and spoke quietly with passionate voices.

The discussion ended as she approached. She sat beside Eamon, and she could swear Jillian shot her an unfriendly, suspicious stare, but she couldn't see clearly in the dark, the light from the fire uncertain, so she shrugged it off. She wanted to make the cure, inoculate Wilky, and devise a plan for what to do next. She didn't need friends but....

Allies would come in handy, and she had no desire to make enemies.

The dry wood crackled and filled the night with a sporadic beat and unpredictable rhythm.

Eamon turned toward her, his voice friendly. "So tell us something about your tribe and where you're from. Gemma says you live in a tube in the earth with weird white light and boxes with glowing words." He shrugged one of his shoulders, which seemed his way of explaining that Gemma had a vivid imagination, and he didn't believe a word of her story.

"It's all true. We live in a series of tubes, dig for gold with big picks, and sing songs all day."

"Really?" Jillian hooted.

"I think she's having a little fun with us." Eamon chuckled, his blue eyes glowing in the firelight.

Aaliss leaned back from the fire. She needed to be careful. It would do her no good if they knew the truth about Eden. "Wilky and I come from a tribe to the north and west. It's far from the Stronghold."

At least it seems far way.

"How did you find Gemma?" Jillian's gaze pierced through the firelight.

"Alone in the woods."

She left out many of the more difficult details, like the part where she captured Gemma and dragged her to Eden to be a test subject. Some particulars were better off not spoken and, technically, she hadn't lied. She just focused on a few select facts.

"Wilky and I brought her to that meadow where we ran into Fintan and his merry men of kidnappers."

Eamon shook his body as if a chill had settled into his bones. "The Witch's Woods is a very dangerous place. Strange creatures lurk in that forest, and many people have gone missing. I can't imagine Gemma alone in those woods. We're lucky you found her."

Aaliss felt her face heat. She *was* one of the reasons those woods were so dangerous. The faces of the Soulless she had either killed or gathered flashed through her mind—ten faces, nine if she didn't count Gemma. Now it all seemed wrong. *Purity, Faith and Strength*—the three pillars of Eden. How many times had she uttered those words? Now, other words came to mind—*Fear, Self-Righteousness, and Weakness.*

She considered confessing her sins and shedding her secrets. Thoughts swirled in her mind like notes in one of Jacob's hymns.

What would Eamon say? Would he blame me for doing what I was told was right? Why does it matter to me what he thinks?

Eamon broke the spell. "Why did you leave your tribe?" He looked pensive and brushed shaggy hair from his eyes. Only the smallest trace of stubble on his chin marred his otherwise smooth skin.

"It was time for us to go." She picked up a stick and started to prod the ground. "Tell me about *your* tribe. What's the deal with your brother? Why is he such an...." She thought better of finishing the sentence. She sensed that Eamon knew the truth about Fintan; however, they *were* brothers. She didn't want to fall through thin ice.

Eamon tossed a branch onto the fire. "Fintan can be a little *harsh*. He has many things on his mind." He grinned and his eyes twinkled in the firelight. "But life has been good under my other brother, King Dermot. We've lived in peace for the last four years and the herds have been strong. Besides, we're completing the Books of Wisdom, which should last us generations."

They know how to read?

"The Books of Wisdom? What's that?" Aaliss tried unsuccessfully to hide the surprise in her voice.

Eamon's face lit up, and the enthusiasm added a youthful charm to his features. He was handsome; Aaliss could not deny it.

"They're Dermot's idea. We're writing the Masters' collective wisdom into three books so future generations won't repeat the same mistakes we've made, and the tribe can advance. It's brilliant."

"Eamon's in charge of the whole thing," Jillian added with more than a little pride in her voice.

Aaliss fell silent. Children in Eden joked about life without adults — hollow words from scared children. The Red Death saturated every aspect of life in Eden. The Book of Jacob warned about it on almost every page, and the Priests told frightening stories of how the Dark One cursed all humanity. Vivid descriptions of disease, famine, pestilence, and pagan worship punctuated the sermons on a weekly basis. One famous passage told of human cannibalism. Now it seemed that the Priests might have been totally wrong — this tribe wrote books to share wisdom with future generations.

According to the Priests, God spared only the Edenites from the Dark One, and only Edenites have souls. They also taught that one day, when the people of Eden were judged worthy, Edenites would become immune to the Red Death and re-make the world in Jacob's name.

Now that Wilky has discovered the cure, has that day come? Are the Edenites now worthy?

It certainly didn't feel that way.

She glanced up and noticed Eamon watching her, so she asked the first question that came to mind. "What about your parents? Did you know them?" The words tumbled from her mouth without her thinking about how silly they might sound to him. Everyone he knew died, or would die, in their early twenties. What type of relationship could he possibly have had with his parents?

Eamon frowned. "I am the youngest, so I have few memories of my mother and father. I know father ruled the tribe briefly before I was born. I grew up in the Nursery like everyone else, but Dermot has always been there for me. He's five winters older than me. He's been my guide."

She did the simple math in her head and realized Eamon's predicament. "So Dermot is close to the end of his time and you want to save him. Is that why you freed us? To get the cure for him?"

Eamon glared into the flames. "Dermot has been a great king. He deserves more time. It would not be right for him to be taken so soon."

Jillian squeezed his arm.

A heavy silence hung over the small campsite, broken only by the babbling sound of the creek and the hooting of an owl in the distance.

"What about my short sword and crossbow?" Aaliss asked. "I don't want to sleep without them. These woods could be dangerous."

"I don't think so," Jillian said, and Aaliss practically felt a blast of winter air hit her in the face. "How do we know you won't attack us in the night?"

Eamon stared into the flames, refusing to look at her, his face tinting pink.

So now I know what they were arguing about before I joined them at the campfire.

Aaliss deftly removed the knife from inside the folds of her suit. With the blade in hand, she darted behind Eamon, grabbed his shaggy hair, and pressed the blade close to his face. She held the sharp side safely in the other direction from him and gripped his hair lightly in her fingers.

Jillian's mouth formed a perfect "oh" as her jaw dropped.

"You mean like this?" She shot Jillian a sharp look. "If I wanted to, I could have killed you both a dozen times. I gave you my word and that should be enough!" She pinched her eyes together, but she felt a sharp point jab her stomach.

"Ouch," she said.

Eamon playfully poked her with a dagger and chuckled. "I'm not that easy to kill."

She released him, surprised at his cunning. So few people surprised her. She had not seen the dagger, and joked, "I guess we'd both be dead and where would that get us?"

Eamon laughed. "We'd go to the next life, and they would be left on their own to mourn us."

"That's not funny," said Jillian.

"Aaliss's word is good enough for me. I'll get your gear. We'll all be safer with you properly armed." He jumped to his feet, leaving Jillian and Aaliss alone.

Jillian glared at her. "You better not hurt him. I'll make you pay for it."

Even in the darkness, Aaliss could see the malice in Jillian's eyes. She let the threat hover in the air like a dark storm cloud. Unsure why Jillian disliked her so much, she didn't want to snipe back and make a full-fledged enemy of her. Maybe Jillian just wanted to protect her boyfriend, and how could Aaliss fault her for that?

Eamon returned with Aaliss's short sword and her crossbow, which he handed to her. He also retained something in his own hand that she had a hard time seeing in the darkness.

"What else did you bring?' she asked.

He settled between the two women. "This is a book. I always read before I sleep. It's become a habit for me. I don't think I can fall asleep otherwise."

"Does everyone in your tribe know how to read?"

"Everyone is taught the basics up to their thirteenth winter after their name carving. Those who are suited go on to more advanced study."

Aaliss arched both eyebrows. The Soulless were supposed to be primitive, just barely able to dress and feed themselves, yet Eamon's tribe created Books of Wisdom and everyone knew how to read. She realized she knew nothing about life outside Eden.

"Where'd you get a book like that?" she asked. It looked old and familiar.

"We found a vault in the ruins to our east. It contained dozens of books that could still be read—weird stories about life during the time before tribes. Some even had pictures, pictures you could otherwise only see at The Exchange. We added them to our library above the Nursery. We must have thirty books by now. This book was in a special metal box."

"What's it about?"

"It's hard to explain. It's about everything. I didn't fully understand it the first time I read it, so I'm reading it again. It talks about life and old men with beards and a time long forgotten. Something about it speaks to me." He smiled sheepishly. "According to this book, there is only one God, not a different one for each season like we believe. The book gives me hope that there's a better way to live. Perhaps we could go back to life as it was before the curse if we remember this ancient God."

"How do you know any of it's real?"

"I don't." He sighed. "It just feels real to me. That's all I have."

"What's it called?"

He lifted the tome. "The cover page is faded. I just call it The Book."

"Read me something from it," Aaliss asked.

He grinned and looked happy to oblige. "Sure. I've been trying to get Jillian to read it, but she hasn't taken me up on it."

"I would if I had time." Jillian's face turned a light shade of pink.

He opened the book to the beginning, his voice confident. An experienced reader, he could easily have been a storyteller back in Eden. "In the beginning God created the heavens and the earth. Now the earth was formless and empty, darkness was over the surface of the deep, and the Spirit of God was hovering over the water—"

"And God said, 'Let there be light,' and there was light." Aaliss had memorized many verses from The Book.

"You know this book?" Eamon's mouth dropped open as he let the book fall softly to his lap.

Aaliss chuckled. "I've read it before." She thought of the Priests back home, even Piers.

How would he react if he knew a Soulless was reading the Book?

Eamon surprised her.

How could he have no soul?

"Shouldn't we get some sleep? Tomorrow will be a long day." Jillian sounded irritated and noisily prepared a sleeping place by the fire close to Eamon.

The woods turned abnormally quiet and a chill swept through the forest.

Aaliss whispered, "Do you hear that?"

"I don't hear anything," answered Jillian, her words biting.

"You're right. It's too quiet." Eamon's eyes darted around the campsite.

"Look over there." Aaliss pointed toward the creek.

Three hazy, silvery figures on silver horses rode in silence. They shimmered as though not quite fixed to this reality, and moved so quietly the horses' hooves could not possibly be touching the forest floor. They floated above the earth.

She swallowed hard. "They're Ghost Riders. I've seen them once before. They're not fully of this world."

"I don't see anything," said Jillian.

"If you look closely, you can see silver shadows. Are they dangerous?" Eamon reached for his sword.

"They ride in silence. They never notice the living. Don't try to touch one. It's said those who touch a Ghost Rider become part of their world and not ours."

The lead rider turned his head and looked directly at the small campfire.

Aaliss's heart thundered. She could only make out a vague outline of a face, but for a moment she thought he stared at her. Then she realized he looked beyond her and toward Wilky. Alarmed, she stood and reached for her sword, but by the time she unsheathed it, the riders had vanished. The normal forest sounds returned, and the air turned warmer.

"Will they come back?" asked Eamon.

"I don't think so." Aaliss stalked from the campfire and set up her hammock close to Wilky, even though she felt a little silly.

It must have been my imagination. Everyone knows Ghost Riders don't see the living.

CHAPTER 25
FINTAN

Fintan trudged to the Stables. The first rays of sunlight had just started to brighten the horizon, casting the sky in a dull grayish hue that matched his mood perfectly. The sky looked ominous as his steps fell heavy, slow with anxiety and lack of sleep. His head pounded from the wine he'd consumed last night, and he silently cursed Eamon, who'd wanted to celebrate his heroic rescue of Gemma with spirits.

I'll get you back for that, Brother.

He had tried to sleep, but the many doubts that churned in his mind kept him awake. He'd acted rashly when he devised his plan under the Naming Tree, probably another result of the cursed wine and another dirty trick he'd make his brother pay for. He wanted to dispatch the blackmailer quickly. Now, with dawn's first light, he realized he should know more about Cattie before he enacted his plan: who were her friends, did she have family at the Stronghold, and most importantly, did she tell anyone about his plans?

He wasn't like Eamon; he didn't waste his time paying attention to the common people, the simpletons who were of little use to him. Under normal circumstances, he wouldn't have noticed Cattie in a hundred winters.

He would be happy to rid himself of her, that was plain, but when they talked last night, the sparkle in her eyes caused him concern. She had intelligent eyes, and he doubted whether she had fully bought into his charms.

She wanted to believe that he liked her, and maybe that would be enough. He knew convincing people of things they wanted to believe was easy. But if she told someone else about his plan to kill Dermot or their meeting together this morning, he might have a tricky time extracting himself from that mess. They didn't call his brother *Dermot the Just* for nothing.

At least he had Cormac. If events turned particularly sour, he could blame everything on him.

He rounded a corner and saw Cattie standing by the Stables, the only wooden building in the Stronghold. She wore a blue cotton dress with yellow flowers scattered across the collar and the hem. It looked new and probably cost her all of her savings, which he took as a good sign—she wanted to impress him. She also wore a leather cloak over the dress to guard against the morning chill that nipped in the air.

He forced a smile as he stepped toward her. "What a promising day for our adventure. Did anyone see you?"

She shook her head.

"So no one knows we're headed off this morning?"

"I've kept it a secret just like you asked."

He studied her for a second and thought he detected a slight tremor in her eyes.

Is she lying?

He couldn't tell, and the brightening sky meant he needed to hurry. Soon the Stable Master would arrive and that would spoil everything. He had not choice now but to see through his plan. "Great. I'll be back in a second with our horse."

He ambled inside the Stables and found Cormac's favorite horse—a gray colt. He saddled the steed, made sure to don the hood on his cloak to hide his ponytail, and swung on top of the large animal. From the drawbridge, the guard would mistake him for Cormac in the dim light of dawn, so if asked, he'd think Cormac took Cattie from the Stronghold.

He rode out of the Stables and lowered his hand to Cattie. "My lady, let us take our adventure."

Cattie smiled and he lifted her light frame in front of him so she could ride sidesaddle. He kicked his heels into the horse's sides and the animal galloped away from the Stables, through the cobblestone streets, and out the drawbridge.

The Stronghold still slumbered due to last night's festivities and the early hour, so he passed no one on his way out, which meant that at least *this* part of his plan had worked.

Cattie turned her head to face him. "Where are we going?"

"To Whitewater River, my lady."

He pushed the horse to a fast gallop, found the trail that led to the water, and raced another few minutes to a little-used bend in the river. Here the water narrowed and turned decidedly rough, as white caps splashed over rocks.

He slowed the horse to a stop and dismounted. "This spot is perfect. No one will disturb us." He offered his hand to Cattie, who eagerly took it, so he helped her from the horse.

He added as much honey to his voice as he could muster. "So, Cattie, tell me more about yourself. Do you have any family?"

She frowned. "I thought you were watching me. Didn't you notice my sister, Maeve?"

He bit his lip. He didn't want her to have family, someone who might miss her. He deserved some good luck for once. "Maeve, of course. I was just making conversation. I'm a little nervous."

"You're nervous?"

He nodded and lowered his eyes toward the ground. He could playact if necessary.

"There's no reason for you to be nervous, my prince." She stepped toward him, but before she could touch him, he heard the sound of a crow behind a weeping willow.

He smiled. *Just in time.*

Cormac emerged from behind the tree and took long looping strides toward them.

The color drained from Cattie's face. "Why is he here?"

"You didn't think I was going to let you get away with blackmailing me, did you? I mean, the thought of you and me together turns my stomach."

Cattie reached inside her cloak, pulled out a sharp dagger and held it to Fintan's chest. She caught him completely off guard as she pushed the tip of the blade through his shirt and nicked his skin.

He lifted his hands in the air and Cormac stopped.

"Stay away from me," the girl yelled. "I'll stab him if you take another step."

Cormac looked between the two, his mouth slightly open. Finally, his gaze settled on Cattie and he shrugged. "Okay, don't do anything stupid. We just wanted to scare you a little."

"*Right*. I'm not a fool."

The gray colt snorted and stomped its hooves at a small snake in the grass.

Cattie glanced at the horse, and the half-second distraction did her in.

Fintan snatched her wrist, bent her arm behind her back, and twisted.

She let go of the dagger, which fell harmlessly to the ground.

"That's two days in a row a girl has wanted to kill me. I must be losing my touch." He pushed Cattie toward Cormac with a hard shove.

She fell to her knees and glared at them with angry eyes.

Fintan sidled next to Cormac. "Tell me the truth, and I'll let you live. Did you tell anyone about our plans, or about our little meeting this morn?"

Cattie shook her head. "No one. I told no one. I can keep a secret. I won't tell anyone about your scheme. I can help if you want."

Fintan wanted to believe her, but he didn't. She spoke too quickly and had a mischievous gleam in her eyes. He nodded at Cormac, who unsheathed his longsword and placed the tip at her throat.

"Are you sure you didn't tell Maeve or anyone else?"

Tears formed around the edges of her eyes. "Leave my sister out of this."

He smirked. "I don't know, Cormac. I've heard tell of a Maeve at the Stronghold who is quite beautiful. *Maeve the Magnificent*, some of the men call her. Maybe I should pay her a visit tonight. I'm sure I can get her to talk and tell me all her secrets."

"You're a monster and a coward." She spat on Fintan's boots.

"That's just not nice." He kicked his foot and sent the spit flying. "Since you won't tell us what we want to know, I guess we'll just have to kill you."

He smirked at Cormac. "What do you think? Shall we kill her or give her another chance to tell us the truth?"

"Kill her." He plunged his sword into her throat.

Cattie clutched her neck, but she could do nothing as blood seeped through her fingers. Her eyes still fired brightly, but the light faded and she fell face-first to the ground.

Fintan felt anger bubble up inside of him. "Why did you do that, you idiot? She hadn't told us the truth yet."

Cormac shrugged. "You said we should kill her. That was the plan. You said that was the plan this morning."

Fintan ran his hands over his face and tried to steady his breathing. "I thought we would threaten her a bit so she'd crack, you moron! Now we don't know if she told anyone."

"Oh. You should have said something to me. You can't blame me for that. I'm not a mind reader."

Fintan groaned. Scotty the Snake would return with the poisonous berries in a couple of days. This secret would have to last until then. Once he became king, no one could touch him. Even if Eamon suspected he had killed Cattie, he'd make sure his brother would do no more than suspect.

"Did you give the note to Shane to hand to the Master at the Nursery?"

Cormac nodded. "He wasn't happy waking up so early, but he did as I told him."

Fintan grinned. Shane would keep a secret *unless* Fintan wanted him to talk. Then he'd say that Cormac had written the note and given it to him to pass on. Fintan wrote it in Cormac's chicken scratch and even misspelled a few common words. The note said that Cattie was headed to the Outpost. The Master of the Nursery should believe it came from her, but if Eamon investigated, it would be easy for him to point at Cormac as the culprit.

"Shall we bury her?" asked Cormac.

Fintan looked at the morning sky and then the fast moving river. "Let's throw her in. The river will take her away. We should head to the Feasting Hall and breakfast before we're missed."

The two wrestled with Cattie's body and tossed her as far toward the middle as they could. She landed with a splash and the current swept her lifeless body down river.

Fintan clapped Cormac on the shoulder. "I brought your horse. You can ride him to the Stronghold. I'll wait here for a few minutes, and then I'll take the other one back."

The plan had gone reasonably well. At least he was rid of Cattie, although he wondered whether Maeve knew the truth.

What shall I do about her?

CHAPTER 26
PIERS

Piers studied the last remaining bite of his breakfast. The forkful of eggs stared back at him until he summoned his willpower and choked it down a moment before the bell rang. It was a sin to waste food, and even though he'd only grabbed a meager portion of scrambled eggs and a few apple slices, he had difficulty finishing the meager meal.

He glanced down the table and found every plate wiped clean as usual. No one wanted to be caught sinning. Sinning was never a good idea, even a small sin—no sins were small in Eden.

Piers ate amongst the novices at long, crowded tables, the seating close. Arms and legs bumped into other arms and legs, but today Piers had ample space, as though a contagious disease had infected him.

Ordinarily a talkative bunch, the novices usually discussed the day ahead or some theological issue, and Zeke could always be counted on to blather away about something. Either he prayed or he talked and talked and talked. The two Great Silences the Priests celebrated each year seemed physically painful for him. The other novices avoided him on those days, knowing their presence made the temptation almost too much for him.

No Great Silence was required today. Zeke ate with his head down, silent as a mouse.

Piers caught his eye for a brief moment.

Zeke smiled weakly in return, and averted his eyes back down to his clean plate, as if he had never seen the plain white plate before and its plainness fascinated him.

Being branded the brother of two traitors made Piers notorious, dangerous even, as if traitorous behavior flowed in his blood and could be transmitted as easily as the Red Death. The other novices seemed to have decided on silence and space as the best ways to deal with him. He briefly wondered if they had a meeting about it or whether they all came to the same conclusion independently.

It didn't bother him much; Aaliss and Wilky had to deal with much worse. Besides, this situation would only be temporary. Once he proved their innocence, he'd find some way to get them back safely and things would return to normal. At least that's what he told himself. He had to vindicate them. As the oldest, it was his responsibility.

He stood with the rest of his table and followed the wave of humanity into the main Compound. He moved stiffly, his ribs aching, his arm still sore, his mind exhausted, and his spirits low. After returning to bed last night, he had lain awake lost in a tumult of thoughts, his mind racing from one idea to the next, never settling down long enough for slumber.

He knew what he *had* to do. He had to break into Wilky's lab and use the password and username that Wilky had left for him. The *how*, however, baffled him. How was he going to steal a key to the Labyrinth? Only researchers, Guardians, and Monks had keys. He prayed on it, but Jacob sent him no answers, leaving him with nothing but his own ideas, as deficient as they were.

Someone shoved him and he sputtered forward, almost losing his balance as his feet tripped over each other. When he steadied himself, he balled his hands into fists and spun to find the culprit, but all he saw were bland expressions and Edenites eager to start their day. He scowled at no one in particular and resumed his trudge to religious studies class, his limp slightly more pronounced than it had been a moment earlier.

He reached the open classroom door on the first floor of the Compound and peered into a long windowless room.

Three Clerics taught the group of novices from a raised platform at the end of the room. All three were Blood Relations, with gray hair, long years of study, and ample helpings of arrogance. They wore the simple white robes of Priests with the black slash, but they added gold piping to their robes so everyone knew their elevated status.

Piers had quickly distinguished himself as a star student among his peers, often held out as the ideal. He had a near perfect photographic memory. Wilky was the only person he knew who had better recall, and he suspected Wilky's gift extended beyond the written word to every aspect of his life. He'd asked Wilky about it, but his brother could not explain it.

He always said the same thing: he *saw* the answer.

Still, Piers's extraordinary gift allowed him to remember every chapter and verse from the Book of Jacob and every other religious text. His photographic memory, combined with a highly intelligent mind, made him a rising star in the academic world — the one place he felt special.

Before he entered the classroom, the hair on the back of his neck stiffened. He surveyed those around him. Nothing looked unusual, the faces familiar, but he couldn't shake his uneasy feeling. He had never realized it before, but eyes were always watching you in Eden — whether they belonged to Priests or Monks or government officials. He knew of only a few places where one could truly be alone.

Just when he thought he might be mistaken, he spotted Sarah, the tall red-haired Monk from the previous night, grinning at him. He realized instinctively that his happiness was inversely correlated to her happiness, and she looked practically giddy.

His stomach soured.

"Good morning, Priest." She grabbed his arm and dug her nails like talons into his flesh. "You're not attending class today. The High Priest would like a word with you."

He shook his arm free and forced confidence into his voice where none existed. "What a pleasure to see you again, Sarah. I wondered when we would next meet."

She chuckled. "Oh, I think we'll see much of each other from now on. I'm thinking about furthering my religious education, and I think you should be my personal Priest." She pushed him toward the circular staircase that led to the Parsonage.

After a difficult climb, Piers waited outside the High Priest's office. The Parsonage buzzed with activity—Priests and government officials moved with urgency and purpose.

Eden Day was fast approaching. All five thousand Edenites would descend on the Compound for the daylong festivities. The outdoor religious service would begin at midnight, attendance mandatory. Great bonfires would light the night sky until morning. The High Priest and the President would stand on a vast platform to officiate the services, with the High Priest playing the starring role.

Eden Day was the only day during the year when the Priests relaxed Eden's many rules. The Sacred Drink flowed like a river as the Edenites celebrated the gift of life and the joys of living, and the feasts were exorbitant. Numerous tournaments, sporting activities, and festivities lasted well into the next night. Virtually no sin was unforgivable on Eden Day, and from the activity in the Parsonage, it looked like the planning for this year's feast was extensive.

Finally, the heavy office door swung open and Sarah emerged, looking sullen. She waved Piers in and shut the door behind him, leaving Piers and the High Priest alone.

A plate with a half-eaten breakfast sat on the side of the High Priest's desk, steam still spiraling up from the dish.

Piers's spirits sank as he moved toward the desk. He'd hoped that the Monks wouldn't report his nocturnal adventure, but now he chided himself for his stupidity. He should have known that they would report him. He had no friends here.

"I understand you had trouble sleeping last night. I'm told you went for a rather long stroll and ended up in your siblings' apartment."

The High Priest spoke in short, curt words, and he twisted the large gold and ruby ring he wore on his pinkie finger. The rubies formed an elaborate capital J, which functioned as Eden's symbol and flew on the flags above the Compound—flags Edenites hoped only they would ever see.

"Yes, your Grace. I wanted a photograph of my brother and sister to remember them. I should never have left without your permission." He lowered his gaze to the highly polished black and white floor.

"No, you should have come to me!" Perhaps the High Priest's voice sounded angrier than he wanted, because he paused, pressed both of his beefy hands flat, rested the fingertips against his lips, and continued more softly. "You need to be careful, Piers. Your brother and sister are traitors. If you continue with this bizarre behavior some will doubt your loyalties. We wouldn't want that, would we?"

"No, your Grace. No one should worry about my loyalties. They are pure. I am, as always, your humble servant, sworn to live in the service of Jacob."

"Wonderful." A smile spread across his round face. "For now I want you to work in the Orchard. Report to Father Luke at once. A little manual labor might help you sleep at night." He dismissed Piers with a wave of his hand.

Piers bowed low and turned to leave the office. He headed down the spiral staircase slowly, lost in thought. He swung past the rear doors of the Compound, squinted against the bright sun, and could see the edge of the well-developed grove of apple trees in the distance.

The High Priest used the Orchard as punishment, and though the Priests generally supervised the manual laborers, at times they did the work themselves. Piers had no illusions over what his day would be like; he would work the fields or sort the recently harvested apples until he couldn't stand any longer.

He strode along the stone path that cut through a lightly wooded forest and ended at the Orchard facilities a half-mile from the Compound. Apple trees stretched in long, neat rows, for nearly a mile. Abundant in Eden, apples made up the largest portion of their diet. The sun felt refreshing against his skin, and his black robes fluttered around his legs as he walked.

He paused with the facilities just in sight. He could make out a half dozen workers unloading a wagon filled with casks, a horse pulling a cart piled high with apples, and two men walking briskly toward the Orchard, long poles slung on their shoulders to knock ripe apples from the higher branches of the trees.

He sensed that someone was watching him again and spun, half expecting to see Sarah leering at him, but he found no one. Feeling foolish, he continued along the path until he heard an odd whistle to his right, followed by a hushed, "Piers, over here."

He looked in the direction from which the voice had come and strained his eyes, but couldn't spot anyone.

"Come on, Piers. It's Michel. I'm behind the oak."

Piers saw a shadow behind the tree and wandered toward it.

"Here." A tall, reed-thin man with walnut-colored hair stepped from behind an oak. Michel was Piers's age, friends with Aaliss and trained as a Guardian. He wore a black ostrich suit, which helped him blend in with the shadows cast by the tree.

Piers trampled a patch of long grass and joined him behind the oak, hidden from the path and the Orchard. "How did you know the High Priest banished me to the Orchard?"

Michel's long, thin face looked tired with dark circles under his eyes. "Nothing is a secret in Eden. And besides, where else would they send you? They send everyone they want to punish to the Orchard."

"Good point."

Michel clenched his jaw. "I don't understand what in Jacob's name is going on? I can't believe what they're saying about Aaliss and Wilky. They're not traitors! There's not a dishonest bone in your brother's body, and I know Aaliss as well as anyone. I just don't believe it."

Piers sighed. He had not realized how lonely he had felt until now. It seemed that no one believed in Aaliss and Wilky but him. "Neither do I. The High Priest has made a horrible mistake. They're innocent. I know it." Just saying the words made him feel better.

"I'm not the only one who believes in them, either. A group of us offered to go into the Zone and bring them back alive, but they refused to let us. I'm grounded. Forbidden. Gabriel and Jonas went in after them." He frowned. "Your sister is one tough customer, but the Viper is the scariest thing in the Zone. If he finds her.... I don't want to even *think* about what would happen."

He glanced at his feet. While he didn't want to think about what would happen to Aaliss, by the expression on his face and the dark circles under his eyes, Piers knew he had spent much time imagining the worst. He knew Aaliss and Michel were friends, but seeing him like this made Piers wonder if they shared a deeper relationship.

I have to trust someone.

"Look, Michel, last night I went to their apartment. Wilky left me a message in a secret hiding spot. I need to get to his computer in his lab. He left some clue for me to follow. Maybe it will prove their innocence before...."

Michel whistled softly. "Whoa... Jacob's braid! That's not an easy thing to do. There's been tons of activity in the Labyrinth lately." A calculating look sharpened his eyes. "There's only one way. We need to break in late at night when everyone else is asleep. It won't be easy getting around the Monks, but I have a key, and once we get into the Labyrinth's maze we should be all right."

Piers whispered, "Just give me the key and I'll sneak in. You shouldn't put yourself in harm's way. I'll tell you what I find." He reached his hand out, palm up for the key.

This is my responsibility. I am the oldest.

Michel stared at the hand for a few seconds before he turned away. "Meet me at midnight by the door to the Labyrinth. Be careful. Stay in the shadows. I'll find you."

Michel left Piers standing by himself, hand still outstretched and empty.

Piers saw movement in a nearby tree and found an odd-looking blackbird watching him. He thought it must be his imagination, as surely the bird had no interest in him, but then it cocked its head as if to get a close look at him.

CHAPTER 27
AALISS

Aaliss woke tired after a restless sleep.

At least Wilky looked fine. He had survived another day outside of Eden.

Eamon waved them over to the campfire and handed them strips of dried beef. "Sorry that breakfast isn't a little better, but this is all we brought for provisiosns."

Aaliss smiled. "I've eaten worse." When patrolling as a Guardian, she usually ate dried apples for breakfast and foraged for her other meals. The beef, while dried and rough, was tasty and satisfied her morning hunger.

They broke camp and led their horses on foot along the banks of the creek as it meandered northward. Wilky explained that the flower was too small to be seen on horseback, so they formed a ragged line on foot, head down, necks straining, eyes studying the ground as closely as they could.

Everyone except Wilky, who seemed lost in his own thoughts and spent more time looking at the sky than at the ground.

They moved slowly, and after traveling hours, had found no sign of the flowers. Most of the morning conversation burned away like dew.

Tension replaced the words as each mile melted away and the sun rose in the sky.

Jillian, who hadn't said much the entire trip, asked, "Did everyone in your tribe take the cure?" The tone in her voice practically froze the words in the air.

The question worried Aaliss. She had concocted a thin story, and if Jillian pushed hard enough, she would rip a hole right through it. In no rush to answer, she studied the forest unfolding before them.

"Well, is your tribe free from the Red Death?"

Aaliss realized she could stall no longer. "Not exactly." She hoped the conversation would move to something else. To help it on its way, she added, "I hope the weather holds up. It looks like it might rain."

"What *exactly* happened? How do you know that the cure works?" Jillian shot invisible daggers at her in rapid fashion with her eyes.

Aaliss had started to rethink her position on creating enemies. Jillian's attitude grated on her nerves, but Aaliss had to admit she asked fair questions. If their roles were reversed, she would have asked more difficult ones, and probably at the tip of a real dagger.

She glanced at Wilky, who nodded. "Wilky gave the cure to a *Sou...* to a person with red eyes, and it worked. It cured him, and he stayed cured."

"So, if he became cured, then how come the whole tribe didn't take it? Why did you run?" Jillian pressed her, those invisible daggers ready to draw blood at the first sign of weakness.

Eamon stopped to look at her, his hopeful gaze falling heavily upon her. She knew he so desperately wanted the cure to be real he would believe anything, but Jillian presented a tougher obstacle. She would not be so easily fooled.

"The tribe thought Wilky used dark magic to make the cure, which is totally ridiculous. They were scared and destroyed the cure, so we ran. They called the man Wilky cured a demon and burned him at a stake. If we didn't get out, they would've killed us for certain."

She met Eamon's gaze sincerely. While a twisted version of their story, just enough truth remained that she told it convincingly. Still, the deceit made her stomach twist.

Maybe later I can tell him the truth — later, after we make the cure, after Wilky and Dermot are safe, after I have a chance to breathe.

Aaliss asked Jillian her own question, her voice matching Jillian's frosty tone. "So how long have you two been coupled?" She glanced at Eamon and her stomach somersaulted.

Why do I care?

Jillian's face reddened as she bent down low to inspect a common weed by her foot.

"We're not coupled," Eamon explained. "We're just close friends."

Did he seem just a touch eager to tell me?

"Oh," Aaliss said. The word lingered in the air, transforming from sound to something physical... like a dense fog. She smiled to herself, not certain why their uncommitted status made her happy, but it did, and something lighter and bubblier replaced the acid in her stomach.

After that, they ambled in silence for a stretch.

The morning had turned into early afternoon when Eamon pointed to the far side of the creek. "Look over there! That's the flower from Gemma's dress."

Two small plants with a plethora of tiny flowers stood just a foot from the edge of the creek, the flowers little puffs of blue and red.

"Wilky, is that what we want?" Aaliss asked, holding her breath.

He grinned. "Yes."

Eamon and Aaliss raced forward, splashing through the creek to the far bank while Wilky and Jillian stayed behind with the horses.

The cold water lapped past Aaliss's boots and splashed on her legs. Only the two small plants swayed in the breeze; no others bloomed in sight.

Eamon reached the bank first and looked back at Aaliss with pure joy on his face. He turned toward the flowers, and as he reached for them, a blackbird swooped down and grabbed both plants in its claws and flew off. Dirt dropped from the plants and toppled onto Eamon's head as the bird soared in the air.

He cursed and ran after the thief with Aaliss at his heels.

The blackbird rose above the trees.

Aaliss raced forward, moving swiftly and gracefully. She passed Eamon and weaved her way under branches, around trees, and over short thorny hedges, all the while keeping one eye on the blackbird.

The bird beat its wings a few more times and perched in the high branches of a maple, the flowers clutched firmly in its red-tipped claws.

Aaliss and Eamon skidded to a stop.

The thief stared back at them, taunting them as if it knew something they did not.

She leveled her small crossbow and took aim.

He whispered, his breath brushing against her ear. "That's one hard shot from here."

"It'll be a lot easier without you talking." Pulling back the elastic cord, she steadied her hands, aimed, and pulled the trigger.

The bolt clipped the blackbird's wing, freeing the two plants, which twisted around each other in a slow graceful dance as they floated to their outstretched hands.

It was the most stunning flower Aaliss had ever seen. The blue and red colors wove around each other creating an intricate swirling pattern.

She lifted it to her nose. "It does smell like dew."

Eamon smiled at her with his shaggy brown hair falling in front of his eyes; a few strands of copper mingled with his unorganized mop.

A tidal wave of happiness and relief overtook her. She was one ingredient away from making the cure and keeping Wilky safe.

She looked upon Eamon and her body warmed as he stood close, his eyes earnest and happy. She imagined what it would feel like to throw her arms around his neck and pull him toward her.

What would his lips taste like?

She felt herself inch toward him and his smoldering blue eyes when she heard a scream.

Jillian screamed.

Aaliss froze and her heart skipped a beat.

Jillian and Wilky were out of sight on the other side of the rushing water.

CHAPTER 28
EAMON

E amon followed Aaliss as she retraced their path to the creek, his heart firmly lodged in his throat.

She grabbed his arm and pulled him to a stop before they reached the water. "We have to be quiet," she whispered. "Stay behind me."

He nodded, feeling numb.

Aaliss moved shadow-cat quiet and confident. The rushing water masked the little sound they made as they bent low and peeked through a web of branches and thorny vines across the water.

Jillian knelt helpless in the tall grass. A large, ragged looking man held her hair in his left hand and waved a curved knife at her in his right.

Eamon's heart vaulted and his legs turned to liquid.

"Where's your friend?" the ragged man shouted.

Sprawled on the ground, twenty feet from Jillian, Wilky spat blood from a cut lip.

A tall, lean, wild-looking woman stood over him. She held a simple spear and wore a torn leather cloak patched with an odd assortment of furs and skins. So much dirt and filth blended on her that Eamon could not tell the difference between skin or dirt or leather or fur.

Two other men rummaged through their saddlebags by the horses.

"They're outlaws," whispered Eamon. "Tribeless. They poach cattle and steal whatever they can to get by. The King's Horsemen run them down whenever they stray too close to our lands, but I've never seen these ones before."

The ragged men by the horses clutched heavy wooden clubs with steel spikes through them, but Eamon's eyes gravitated toward the curved knife that fluttered close to Jillian's neck.

The bear-sized man sneered down at her. A wild beard clung to his chin, a thin scar zagged down his left cheek, and his bulbous nose bent at an unnatural angle. "Tell me where the third rider is or I'll cut you."

The wild woman laughed gaily, clapping her hands. "Cut her! Cut her!"

"It's just us two," Jillian sobbed. "There's no one else."

Eamon's blood raced and his head filled with the sound of his pounding heart. He unsheathed his long sword and bent at the knees, anxious about the knife hovering so close to Jillian's throat. He had to stop that brute from hurting her.

Aaliss whispered, "We can't cross the creek here. It's too wide. By the time we reach them it'll be too late. I'll sneak around to the left and cross the water over there. You go to the right and sneak up on the guys by the horses. We should have just enough time. Call like a crow when you're in place. I'll take one out with the crossbow, and then we'll have to do the rest with the swords."

Eamon nodded and watched Aaliss sprint away, admiring her calm. He wished he had felt calm as he turned and dashed through the forest, weaving his way around trees and rocks and through mud slicked by the creek. The water wound around a rock formation large enough to hide him from the tribeless band, so he scampered across a natural stone footpath.

Relieved to be on the right side of the world, his adrenaline kicked in and details exploded—colors burst around him; the burbling of the creek sounded like a waterfall; and odd smells mixed with cool sweet air to fill his lungs.

He strained his ears, fearful of hearing Jillian cry out, fearful of that knife. Hearing nothing unusual, he pushed on.

He concentrated on his footing and resisted the urge to run recklessly forward, mentally assuring himself they would not kill Jillian. He repeated the same thread in his mind.

They're probably just scaring her. They want information. Why kill her if she's harmless?

Anxious horses snorted nearby and he slowed. He said silent prayers to all the gods of his childhood, until he remembered the God from The Book, and he prayed to him also. He had never faced a warrior in battle before, never spilt blood. He thought of Dermot, found strength from within, and pushed forward, trying his best not to make any noise.

He heard one of the two rogues by the horses before he saw them. He sounded raspy and impatient. "Just cut her and let's see if she'll sing."

Eamon circled the horses, taking only a few steps until the small clearing came into view. He stood no more than fifteen feet from the two thieves who held the horses, their attention firmly fixed on Jillian. The bear-sized man had released her hair, but he feared the angry look on his face and the tightening grip on the knife.

He gave his best crow call without thinking. Time slowed. A bolt flew from the other side of the clearing and plunged into the chest of the bear-sized man, but it scored a moment late; the ragged man had already looped the knife toward Jillian. Luckily, the bolt changed the blade's arc, so instead of Jillian's neck it sliced into her arm and splashed the ground with her blood.

Jillian's blood!

He charged from the edge of the forest and swiped his longsword at the nearest outlaw, who noticed him just in time to block the blow with his heavy club. Eamon pressed the attack by slashing his sword at the rogue's stomach. His extra practice time had proven useful. He moved without thinking and the sword felt comfortable in his hand.

When the outlaw jumped backward to avoid Eamon's sideswipe,

Eamon spun forward and sliced his blade into the man's side, cutting through his furs and into his flesh.

The outlaw shouted and darted forward with his club raised over his head.

Eamon sidestepped the awkward charge and thrust his sword into the charging man's stomach, the blade sinking in deep.

Blood bubbled from the tribeless man's mouth. He dropped his club harmlessly, and groaned as he tried to keep his innards from spilling out of his body with his hands.

Before he hit the ground, the second outlaw charged Eamon, swinging his club at his head, trying to drive the spike into the side of his face. With little time to react, Eamon dropped his sword and grabbed the man's wrist before the spike gouged him. The point inched its way toward his face, and the outlaw laughed.

Eamon struggled with both arms. Sweat drenched his body and his hands shook with effort. Despite using all his strength, the spike crept ever closer. The red tip inched toward his eyes, a hairsbreadth from him. All he saw was that tip. The world melted away and was replaced with that tip.

Is it red because of rust or blood?

"I'm gonna spike your head," growled the tribeless man, his breath stinking of rotten meat. He was a weird-looking person, with a long horse-face, rotten teeth, and an odd bald patch in his hair that looked as if someone had ripped hair from the side of his head.

Eamon pushed hard with his hands, but he might as well shove against one of the stone walls back home. The spike continued to slide toward him, and he felt the tip against his eyelashes.

He didn't want to die. He had to save Jillian and Dermot. He steeled his resolve and the spike paused right before the tip would have punctured his eye.

A black blur swooped by his side, and he knew Aaliss had joined him. He heaved against the club with all his remaining strength—one last shove that bought a couple of inches of separation—all she needed.

She struck quickly, her short sword slicing into the man's neck.

Hot blood splattered across Eamon's face. Shock filled the tribeless man's eyes, and for just a moment he looked young, younger than Eamon, before falling lifeless to the ground.

Eamon fought back the urge to vomit as he sucked in air and tried to stop his hands from shaking. He had survived his first real fight, yet he couldn't decide whether he should feel elated or sickened. He had never seen death up close before. It didn't look anything like the songs the singers sang about victory and battle and glory. It looked sad and final and pointless.

Still alive, the first outlaw Eamon had faced groaned and clawed for Aaliss's boots.

She knocked him unconscious with a stomp of her right foot. "Some people don't know when to die."

Eamon grinned despite his unsettled thoughts.

At least Aaliss had no doubts about death or battle. Sword in hand, blood splattered on her suit, face flushed with color, she looked as if she were born a warrior.

When her expression changed—her face turned tight and the color drained from her skin—he knew something was wrong and spun to look upon Jillian and Wilky.

The wild woman held the boy by the neck, the point of her spear pressed against his side. She screamed a wild cackle, and tear tracks ran down both sides of her face, creating little streams through the dirt on her cheeks. Her hair resembled a tangled bird's nest with pieces of carved bone used to push it from her face. A bolt from Aaliss's crossbow jutted out from her chest, yet she seemed unharmed and shrieked, "Come near me and I stick 'im!"

Aaliss lowered her sword and spoke calmly. "No one is going to come near you. Everything is fine." She started to edge away from Eamon.

"Everything's not fine! You killed Bobby!" The woman nodded toward the bear of a man whom Aaliss had shot with a bolt.

Aaliss continued to circle away from Eamon, making it difficult for the woman to keep an eye on both of them.

Clever.

He followed her lead and moved in the other direction, then added as much hope in his voice as he could muster. "Maybe he's not dead?"

Spit flew from the woman's mouth. "She shot 'im in the heart. Look at 'im." Sadness, more than anger, weighed down her voice.

"She shot you in the chest and you're not dead?" he offered, thinking he had made a strong rebuttal.

A new batch of tears sprouted from her eyes. "That's because of Bobby! His love protected me."

The bolt had pierced a small, decorative wooden pendant that draped over her neck on a worn leather strap. The other colors and dirt made it hard to distinguish, but now that she pushed it from her chest with the point of her spear it was plain to see. "You see how he loved me!" Her sobs came in a typhoon.

Out of the corner of his eye, Eamon noticed Aaliss grab the small knife she kept secreted inside her ostrich suit.

I've got to distract the woman and give her a chance to throw her blade.

"It sounds like Bobby really cared about you. If you kill Wilky, we'll have to kill you, and then what would happen to him?"

"He's already dead! I don't wanna live without him." She gripped the spear tighter, her knuckles turning white as she twisted them in anguish on the wooden shaft. A light breeze rustled her tangled hair.

Aaliss was still too far away to throw her blade, but Jillian rose from the ground with Bobby's curved knife in her hand. A small red stream dripped from her arm and splashed the grass, her expression vacant and otherworldly, as if she had been transformed into a ghost.

"If we have to kill you, we'll just leave him where he is, and he'll be food for the firefoxes and the wolves. I'm sure you love Bobby more than that." Eamon grasped for straws. "He would want to be buried properly and honor whatever gods he served. We can bury him for you if you want. Just put down the spear."

Jillian rolled toward the woman like fog over a meadow, silent and graceful.

A blackbird squawked at the ragged woman, and her tears

stopped. A look of calm spread across her face as an eerie smile twisted her lips upward. "Bobby wouldn't care what happened to him after he was dead, but he would want blood. Blood for blood!" She pulled back the spear, readying it to plunge into Wilky's side.

Wilky closed his eyes, but Jillian slid directly behind the woman and slashed the knife across her throat with one smooth stroke.

The woman dropped the spear and clutched her neck, blood gushing through her fingers as she fell face-first into the dirt.

Jillian collapsed to her knees.

Eamon sprinted to her. "Are you all right?"

She looked at him with unfocused eyes and did not respond.

After a moment he said, "Let me see the arm." He gently removed her leather cloak and ripped open the sleeve of her shirt. The gash appeared deep and nasty and bloody. He did his best to stifle the gasp that threatened to sneak past his lips.

Aaliss and Wilky moved next to him.

"Get my medical kit from my satchel," Aaliss said, and Wilky ran off toward the horses. "It looks bad." She sounded feathery. "She's lost a lot of blood."

"She'll be fine." Eamon fixed his eyes on her arm, and all that blood — Jillian's blood. "I should never have let her come with us. This is my fault."

Aaliss grabbed him roughly by the shirt. "Listen to me. I can sterilize the arm and bandage the wound, but we're going to need something to close that cut. The bandage will only work for a few hours. We need a needle and some thread or something else. Do you have anything?"

Wilky skidded to a stop and handed a small black pouch to Aaliss.

"No, nothing like that," Eamon said.

"To give her a chance we must close that wound soon. In a few hours she'll lose too much blood, and it will be too late." Aaliss applied a salve from the bag to Jillian's arm and wrapped it tightly with a white cloth bandage.

"We're too far from the Stronghold. There's only one place I can think of where we could go."

Jillian snapped awake, her gaze focusing suddenly. "No, Eamon, it's too dangerous! There has to be another way."

"What is it?" Aaliss turned to face him.

"A red witch lives off the ancient road not far from here. She's supposed to be a healer, but I've heard stories. She's dangerous."

Aaliss rose. "So are we. Let's go see this witch."

CHAPTER 29
JONAS

J onas strode into the High Priest's office, his shoulders swaying aggressively, his gait limping and otherwise slightly off from the half bottle of Sacred Drink he'd swigged upon returning to Eden.

The High Priest stood with his back to him and gazed out the windows at the setting sun. A decorative green robe loosely embraced his great bulk like a tent. Cool air swept through the cracked-open windows, adding a chill to the air.

Jonas paused, feeling trepidation about his meeting with the High Priest. All had not gone well in the Zone, and the High Priest didn't take bad news well. He didn't want to find his head on a chopping block.

The High Priest glanced over his shoulder at him and sounded somber. "Where's Gabriel? Were you successful? Is the deed done?"

"No, your Grace. A tribe of Soulless devils captured the girl and boy. Horsemen from the Butcher tribe surrounded them at the last moment. The Viper went after them."

Jonas left out how Aaliss shot him with a poisoned bolt and how the Viper strung him up in his hammock until the poison wore off so the wolves wouldn't get him. No need to bother his Grace with details. After all, he was a big picture type of guy.

The High Priest's face pinched together. "You allowed them to be captured by Soulless."

"There was nothing we could do."

The High Priest sighed. "I am disappointed. Too much is at stake for failure now."

"Gabriel went after them. He'll find a way to end them. He's never failed before."

"I hope so. We've spread the story that Aaliss killed Samuel and his team. If they somehow make it back into the Zone, any Guardians they'll meet will dispatch them. You're in charge of the unit for now. Make sure any who might be sympathetic to Aaliss stay in Eden until Gabriel returns."

Jonas nodded. He didn't want to be responsible for the Guardians. All he wanted was enough Sacred Drink to drown himself. He'd have someone else do the schedule and make it sound like a promotion. Maybe he'd find a bright side to this assignment: he could trade favors for more apple wine. Favors were valuable.

"Soon we will fulfill Jacob's true calling." The High Priest turned from him and faced the window. "I love the way the light sparkles off Eden River, don't you? It looks so divine, as if God created the river and sunlight just so I can see its beauty from this window."

CHAPTER 30
KALHONA

K
alhona traced the outline of the scarlet fish with her fingers and then glanced behind the tree. A worn path led off into the distance. If she had not stopped to inspect the ornament, she would never have noticed the trail.

Someone keeps it up.

Convinced P'mina would have taken the trail if she had seen it, Kalhona took one last look at the old road, found it as foreboding as ever, and followed the new path, stumbling slightly over a tree root as she started out.

The trail meandered through heavily wooded forest, and just as she started to think she had made a mistake, she turned a corner and found a small stream and a stone cabin in the distance.

The roof, originally made of slate, looked in disrepair with thatch replacing missing tiles. An ill-fitting red door hung crookedly on its hinges, and wood boarded all the windows except for one. A simple red fish that matched the ornament was painted on the wall next to the door.

A thin gray finger rose from the chimney and reached into the sky, beckoning her forward. Someone must have lit that fire, which meant someone lived in the cabin. She stared hard at the small building, and for the first time in ten harvests, she thought about seeing her mother again.

During her trek she had thought exclusively about P'mina and bringing her home for the Renewal Feast. Usually, she imagined hauling her home with her hands locked around her throat. Now that she saw the cabin, other thoughts rifled through her mind.

After all these years, will I really see my mother again? Will she even recognize me? Does she ever think about me?

She shook her head to chase those childish thoughts from her mind. Lingering on them would do her no good. No longer a child, she'd made herself into the best Artist in the tribe, and she had a toddler of her own. She had already mourned her mother, and whether she lived here or not, Kalhona had forged an independent life without her. Nothing she'd find in that cabin would change anything. All she needed was her sister.

She warily crossed the stream on an old wooden plank that bent as she stepped on it, and headed for the front door. The sounds of a goat braying tempted her to turn back, but she stiffened her resolve and took another tentative step forward.

The door seemed far away, and at her current snail's pace it would have taken her half the night to reach it, but as she inched forward, an unfamiliar voice called out, "State your business!"

Startled, Kalhona jumped forward and almost pitched onto the ground.

A witch had crept from behind an oak with her bow drawn.

Kalhona trembled, her eyes wide with terror. Words stumbled out of her mouth, as if uncertain that they should make the trip at all. "I'm looking... for my... sister."

The Witch kept the arrow trained on her. "You'll have to speak up! I can't hear like I used to."

Kalhona summoned her courage, straightened her back, and lifted her head. She tried to see the Witch clearly but the shadows cloaked the woman's features. All she saw was the bow and the pointy steel tip on the arrow. "I'm looking for my sister. She came here searching for our mother."

The Witch lowered the weapon and stepped from the shadows. "You're looking for your sister, you say?"

The Witch wore a loose-fitting, black-hooded robe that sagged over her shoulders. The last rays of sunlight lit her face and a spider web of lines stretched over her cheeks and forehead. She shuffled forward with a stooped back, and her hand shook as she used the bow as a walking cane. Bits of red speckled her eyes, but a pasty film covered them and dulled their shine. Her long, lush, and blood-red hair afforded her the last vestige of youth.

"Yes, my sister. She's looking for our... mother."

"What's the problem?" The Witch cackled. "Am I the first witch you've seen?"

Kalhona dipped her head not sure what to say. She had never seen anyone older than twenty-three harvests before, and the Witch did not look as she had expected.

The Witch spoke with a coarse, raspy voice. "We better go inside before the stew boils over." She shuffled past Kalhona and into the small cabin, leaving the door open.

Kalhona followed a step behind.

A short, fat bulldog ran up to the Witch, wagged its tail, and licked her hand. "So you decided to come out from under the table. Some guard dog you are. I should add you to the stew." She reached down and rubbed the fur on its head.

The fragrance of rabbit stew wafted from a kettle hung above the flames in the fireplace. A small, round, wooden table with a thin crack down the center stood near the fire with two stools.

"Sit down while I check on the stew," the Witch said.

Kalhona sat and dropped her satchel by her feet.

A red and black finch, which must have snuck into the cabin through a hole in the roof, began tweeting loudly.

The Witch paid it no attention and joined Kalhona at the table — her face gaunt, her cheeks hollow and lined from age.

"Is my sister here? Did she come to see you? "

"A sister, you say. No, no one's been here for a week."

Kalhona dropped her head into her chest. "I was hoping she would've come this way. I need to find her and bring her back before the Renewal Feast."

"What's so important about a feast?"

"It's the *Renewal Feast.*" Kalhona stared at the Witch, expecting recognition to dawn on her face, but found none. "Once every ten harvests we have a special feast with the Orion Tribe, where we swap girls of age."

Kalhona expected the brief explanation to have cleared everything up, but the Witch just nodded her head and said, "Oh, so your sister was supposed to be swapped and ran instead?"

"Yes, and if I don't get her back in time the family name will always be a disgrace. It'll be terrible all over again." Moist tears brimmed her eyes and stood dangerously close to falling.

"It sounds terrible to me. She has to leave her family and friends to join a new tribe just because of her birthday. I see why she ran away."

"You don't understand. It's a great honor to be swapped, and when our mother became a witch it was awful. Everyone shook their heads at us and thought we were bad luck. I trained to be an Artist, but no one wanted me to paint them. I had to work twice as hard as the other girls. When they played, I'd stay behind and work the needles until my hands ached. Even then only a few people risked getting my tattoos, and I had to do them for free." Pride swelled in her voice. "Now I have the longest lines, but it'll be ruined if she doesn't go to the feast. Things will go back to the way they were. I'll have to start all over again."

This time the tears fell in a quick rainstorm. When the storm passed, Kalhona wiped the remnants away with her sleeve.

The Witch returned to the fireplace and stirred the stew. She clanged the wooden spoon against the sides of the pot harshly. "Why did your sister come looking for your mother here?"

"Last year a trader told me that a red witch lived off the Ancient Road. I told my sister about it the other day. She must have gone looking for her, but you aren't the witch that the trader described. She looked... different."

The Witch grinned. One of her yellow front teeth was missing, which caused an unattractive gap. "By different you mean young, don't you? Not old and rotting like me?"

Kalhona nodded her head solemnly. She did not want to insult the Witch, but the truth was plain for anyone to see. If she lied, the Witch would surely know.

"Let me tell you some things about witches. We don't age like everyone else. Sure, there are minor changes over the years, but they're small and barely noticeable, until one day when everything changes. There is no predicting when that day will arrive. Some Sisters live for two hundred revolutions before they change, and others make it only thirty. Last moon I could have been your sister, appearing only a few years older than you. Now look at me! My back has bent, my eyes have clouded over, my face has these ugly lines in them, and my hands have knotted up like the roots of an old tree." She lifted her hands, which were indeed knotted and twisted and scarred with age spots. "I've lived sixty revolutions and now my body's given up. I could barely draw the bow."

Kalhona whispered, "What happened? Did you anger the Dark One?"

The witch smirked. "You Painted Ones and your fears. Yes, the Dark One chooses us, but we do not have to choose him back. When the eyes turn red, more than just their color changes. It gives us the *Sight*. We can see the forces around us, those you cannot—good spirits and evil ones too. We can communicate with them, not always in the way one person talks with another, but they make their meanings clear to us. They teach us magic and share knowledge that has been lost for ages. It's up to the witch to choose which spirits she follows. It is not always easy, my child. I have tried to listen to the ones blessed with light, but there were times when the darks ones misled me."

Kalhona swung her head around the room nervously. They appeared to be alone, but she didn't know what spirits looked like. "Are spirits with us now?"

"Yes, one is with us. Spirits sometimes possess the lower animals, temporarily inhabiting those creatures to communicate with us." The Witch nodded toward the finch. "That bird is trying to persuade me to poison you. He wants me to slip the sleeping plant in your stew. He says I will be justly rewarded. My youth would come back to me. Your death will help the Dark One capture a boy he wants."

The bird squawked at the Witch, hopping up and down on its claws.

"But I will not do it!"

The bird flew off.

"I knew your mother," the Witch said abruptly. "She was so lost when she turned. I helped her the best I could."

The bulldog barked and snarled at the door.

CHAPTER 31
EAMON

E amon slowed his horse to a walk.

Where's the witch?

Only Crazy Reilly had admitted to seeing her, and they had good cause to call him crazy. Reilly never said why he visited the witch or what he had learned from her, but he became even more odd after he returned. He moved to the Outpost, rarely bathed, and often muttered to himself. When questioned about how to find the witch, he just repeated the old instructions that had been passed down from prior generations.

Find the ghost;
Look for the nose to see your host;
The tip points to the devil's fish;
Follow it up stream to see the witch;
Answer her question correctly and all is clear;
Speak false words and you'll have much to fear.

Light had started to fade at an alarming rate and, even worse, Jillian's breathing had become shallow, her chest moving ever more slightly with each breath. She had fallen asleep, and he could not wake her. The bandage around her arm had turned moist as fresh blood seeped through it.

He feared she had little time left and wrapped his arms around her. *The witch has to be around here someplace!*

Eamon spotted the ghost tree off the road to his left, its towering silver branches impossible to miss even in the dead of night. "This has to be the *ghost* we need. Now we have to find the witch's nose. It has to be near."

He'd never known a world without Jillian in it and could not imagine such a dark place—did not *want to* image such a place. He searched the trees hoping for a sign, his heart threatening to pound straight through his chest, but all he saw were ordinary trees and branches, nothing that resembled a nose.

Aaliss spotted it first. "Look up ahead on the right, just off the road." She pulled her reins sharply, bringing her horse to a stop. "If you look at it sideways, it looks like a face with a sharp nose. I've always been told witches have long pointy noses. That could be it."

He stared hard at the branches until he saw it also. At least he hoped this was it. Darkness had prevailed over light as shadows faded into the blackness around them. He could not be sure of anything at this point, but he'd believe anything to save Jillian.

Aaliss and Wilky dismounted.

"What's the rest of the instructions?" she asked.

"We need to look for the devil's fish and follow it upstream. It's supposed to be in the shadow of the nose." Eamon stayed mounted, feeling the faint tapping of Jillian's heartbeats.

"There are no shadows in the twilight." Aaliss shot him a look.

Wilky closed his eyes, and when he opened them he pointed to the left side of the road. "Up there." He strode purposefully to an oak where they found a small, scarlet fish ornament.

Hope flooded through Eamon for the first time in hours. "There's no doubt about that!"

"Good work, Wilky. How did you see that in the darkness? I had to practically touch the thing to find it, but where's the stream?" Aaliss spun. "Give me a moment." She glided away from the road and onto the path behind the tree.

Eamon could see no stream. He whispered, "We're almost there, Jillian. Don't give up. The Witch will fix you up. Everything will go back to the way it was."

Quiet blanketed the forest, which only amplified the slight sounds of Jillian's breaths.

He held her tighter, convinced her breathing had gotten more shallow and sporadic. He counted the seconds in between breaths, and with each one, he reached a higher number. Panic rose up in him. Even the tired horse sensed his despair as it started to dance nervously in place.

Aaliss returned with a smile. "There's a path beyond the tree. It's just wide enough for a horse. I followed it a short distance and heard a stream farther ahead. This has to be it."

"We need to hurry." Eamon poised his heels at his horse's side when Aaliss blocked his way.

"We need to be careful. You said the Witch is dangerous. We probably shouldn't just march up to her front door and start knocking."

"We don't have time for caution. Jillian is slipping away. I feel it."

She nodded. "Okay, you ride ahead. I'll move through the woods off the path just in case. Wilky will follow on foot with the other two horses. If there's any danger, I'll figure something out."

"Done." He spurred his horse ahead at a fast trot.

In no time, the surefooted animal splashed through the stream and stopped just outside of the red front door.

"Witch, we need your help!" Eamon scanned the cabin, looking for signs of life.

The Witch crept from her hiding spot, her bow drawn, her hand shaking from the effort. "State your business!"

Eamon could not see her in the darkness. "My name is Eamon and my friend Jillian is hurt. I need a healer."

The horse snorted its agreement.

The Witch could not see the two visitors. In the dim moonlight she had to rely upon her *Sight*, which had also become weaker by the day. All she could see were the aura of two people, one weak and one strong.

Before she could answer, she felt the sharp tip of a sword at her back.

A young woman growled at her. "Lower that bow, old woman, before you hurt yourself."

"Even the Sight fails me!" She lowered her weapon. "A month earlier no one could sneak up on me. The Sight would sing out like a beacon. Many had tried and they all failed. I promise you that!"

"Come on, old woman, we need your help. Our friend has been wounded, and we need you to stop the bleeding. She's already lost much blood. We don't have much time." The young woman sheathed her blade and marched past the Witch toward the cabin, unafraid of the bow.

A boy joined them a moment later with two horses in tow.

The Witch shrugged. At least she could still do good; she could still heal. She still had knowledge to share. "Bring her inside and we'll see what can be done. The boy can tie the horses to the post in the back."

She shuffled after the young woman, who glanced back at her with an impatient expression on her face.

"I'm coming! It takes me a little longer than it used to!"

"Hand her to me." The young woman waved her arms at Eamon in encouragement.

Eamon gently slid Jillian from the saddle and lowered her to the young woman, who held her steady. He hopped down from the horse, scooped up Jillian, and carried her inside the cabin.

The Witch hobbled inside after them.

The newcomers simply nodded at Kalhona in greeting.

"Grab that table!" She pointed to a long table at one end of the cabin far from the fireplace.

The young woman and Kalhona dragged it from the wall, and Eamon gently placed Jillian on top. She looked ashen and weak, her eyes closed.

Eamon bit his lip.

The Witch handed a lantern to Kalhona. "Light that with embers from the fireplace. Be careful, we don't need the place to go ablaze." She turned toward Eamon. "You, rip away the shirt. We need to see what is what. Be quick."

He did as he was told, and Kalhona returned with the lantern.

The Witch cut away the bandage, revealing a deep slash in Jillian's arm. Blood still flowed from the wound.

She clicked her tongue. "Not good, not good." She leaned in close, no more than two inches away from Jillian's arm to see it clearly. "We must close the wound, but look at the vein. If we puncture it, all will be lost."

Eamon swayed on his feet. "Can you heal her?"

"I have the needle and thread. It's possible still, but I cannot do it." She lifted her twisted and gnarled hands to prove her point. "There was a time when these fingers would do my bidding, but this is very delicate and needs a deft touch."

Eamon looked at the young woman. "Aaliss, do you have the skill?"

Aaliss shrugged. "I can try, but I've never done anything like this. I'm worried that I'll mess up."

He leaned against the table, his face white, and lifted his hands in frustration.

The Witch saw tremors shake them.

"I can do it," said Kalhona. "It's not nearly as delicate as my art."

The Witch handed needle and thread to Kalhona and grabbed a dried, dark, green leaf from a bin on a nearby table. "I'm going to give her the Sweet Leaf. It will help with the pain." She crushed the dried leaf in her hand and slid it into Jillian's mouth.

"If you poison her—" threatened Eamon.

"Yes, I know. You will kill me most grievously. It is always the same with men—threats and more threats. Make yourself useful and bring me that container." She pointed to a ceramic jug that stood on a shelf by the fireplace. "We need to clean the wound."

When he returned with the jug, the Witch poured onto Jillian's arm a clear liquid that bubbled up angrily.

Jillian stirred and moaned, yet her eyes stayed closed.

Kalhona effortlessly threaded the needle and looked toward the Witch for instructions.

"It's just like you're piecing together thick fabric. Make sure you don't go down too deep. We can't puncture any veins."

Kalhona's nimble fingers went to work.

When she finished, the Witch said, "Nicely done! Almost as good as I used to be. That's the best we can do." She wrapped a white cloth around the arm and the wound. "The Sweet Leaf will dull the pain and let her sleep. She's very weak. Bring her to the straw and lay her down, but gently, careful not to disturb the arm. Re-open the wound and we'll never close it again in time."

Eamon and Aaliss lifted her off the table and gently placed her on the straw bedding on the floor.

"Will she make it?" Eamon kept his eyes focused on Jillian as he spoke.

The Witch saw the pain in his face: the clenched jaw, the tight muscles in his shoulders, the creases in his eyes.

"It is in the hands of another now," she said. "We've done all we can. I can't say if she'll live. She's weak, but there's life in her still."

The Witch turned to face the boy. She had wanted to study him from the moment she felt his presence. A spark of excitement burned in her old blood. She had never seen another person with an aura so white, and she smiled to herself.

Finally, he arrives. I thought I might die before I saw him.

She hobbled over to the kettle and lifted it off the metal bar. "Come on, there's plenty of stew for everyone."

Aaliss watched as Eamon hovered over Jillian like a dark cloud on a stormy day.

She squeezed his shoulder. "This is not your fault. There was nothing else you could do."

He shrugged her off. "I should never have let her join us. She isn't cut out for this type of adventure."

"If I remember correctly, she didn't give you much choice. Jillian made up her own mind." She knew he wanted words of reassurance, but Jillian looked weak and she would not lie to Eamon now. She had lied to him too much already and refused to add to that list. She liked him too much to utter false words.

"I should have stopped her," he muttered quietly. "She looks so... weak."

The bulldog ambled over, flopped its tongue from its mouth, and nuzzled Eamon's leg. He cracked the smallest trace of a smile and rubbed the fur on its head. The bulldog barked as it settled at Eamon's feet and enjoyed the attention from his new best friend.

The old crone shuffled toward them, her voice sounding as if the words were dragged across sandpaper. "Sit and eat some stew. There's enough for everyone. You only make matters worse by hanging over her."

He glanced at her. "*Really?* How could I make things worse?"

"Who's the witch? She will sense your unease and anxiety and that will only weaken her. Go to the table and eat. You need your strength. I suspect your travels are only beginning."

The bulldog barked playfully, licked his own nose, and padded off to the table as if the matter had been decided.

Aaliss tugged on his arm. She hadn't eaten anything hot since she left Eden, and the stew did smell awfully good. Besides, the Witch was right—they needed their strength, and who knew when they would eat something hot again.

Eamon looked at her, pain scribbled across his face.

She wanted to lessen his hurt but she had no idea how. She pulled on his sleeve again, and this time he gave in and allowed her to tug him toward the table, where Wilky and the woman who stitched Jillian were already sitting.

Small wooden bowls were set on the round table for everyone. The Witch carried the kettle in one arm and slopped rabbit stew in each bowl. The kettle shook in her hand from the effort. Small amounts of stew splashed over the sides of the bowls and onto the table.

Eamon faced the stranger who stitched up Jillian. "I'm in your debt. Your fingers are deft. You must be a great Artist."

She smiled. "They call me Kalhona, and I came here looking for my sister. You didn't happen to pass her along the Ancient Road, did you? She's younger than me and has light-colored hair and skin."

He frowned. "We came from the north and passed no one."

She sighed. "She must have gone the other way."

"The other way?" questioned the Witch. "You think she went south along the old road?"

"If she's not here and they didn't pass her, then she must have gone south. It's just like her to make things difficult on me."

The Witch settled in her chair. "The south is dangerous. There's a red witch named Santra who lives that way. If she's grabbed your sister, she will be in real danger. She flies the banner of the red raven and keeps company with firefoxes." The Witch turned toward Aaliss. "And you... what brings you out on the Ancient Road?"

Aaliss touched the leather pouch in her pocket, which held the two small flowers they had retrieved earlier in the day. "We're looking for a particular mushroom. It's known for its healing powers."

"My sister is an expert on plants," Kalhona added. "If anyone knows where to find it, she would. I just need to get her back first."

Eamon nodded, his blue eyes somber and dangerous. "Then it is settled. I will help you find your sister and free her from this witch Santra if need be. It is the least I can do to repay you for your kindness toward Jillian. And then your sister might point us in the right direction to find this mushroom."

Aaliss grabbed his hand and squeezed hard. The contact sent a current racing through her body. "No. *We* will help save your sister and search for the mushroom together."

The dog whimpered at the door and the moonlit sky beyond.

"The moon is still bright," the Witch said. "The dark spirits are strongest when under its power. I suggest the quest start tomorrow in the sun's light."

Everyone nodded and the bulldog nestled himself at Eamon's feet.

Even though the moon was no longer full, Aaliss thought it best to avoid it. She had experienced enough of the moon's meddling in her life.

CHAPTER 32
PIERS

Piers cursed the tardiness of the hour. He should be at the Labyrinth door by now, not in bed feigning sleep. Midnight had surely past, yet he was stuck in the sleeping chamber with the other novices. He silently recited prayer after prayer as he waited impatiently. He wanted to be sure that everyone had fallen asleep before he left. It would do him no good to sneak out only to have someone report him, and the other novices were restless. In particular, Anthony was not his usual snoring self.

He suspected dark motives. He thought Anthony wanted to catch him sneaking off, so he could report him and suck up to the Senior Priests.

Anthony had a track record. Neither the smartest nor the hardest working novice, he *was* the most ambitious. Last year he reported Zeke when he slipped up during one of the Great Silences, and he always seemed to have his tongue firmly planted on a Blood Relation's ass.

Piers tried to find the best in people, but with Anthony he struggled.

After silently repeating a common prayer on the virtue of patience for the third time, Anthony finally began snoring—he struggled with sleep apnea, resulting in nighttime serenades that were infamous among the other novices. The other novices called him the *Cat Killer* behind his back, but never Piers. Having suffered his share of name-calling, he knew how hurtful names could be. Even though he disliked Anthony, he wouldn't call him names.

Piers crept out of the chamber, using Anthony's snoring as cover, feeling as if he waded through mud, the pounding of his heart exploding in his head. He was sure he would be caught, but he had no choice. As the oldest, he had to protect Aaliss and Wilky.

When he reached the door, no one stirred. He thanked Jacob, remembered to breathe, and shuffled down the empty hallway toward the staircase. He half expected to see Sarah at every turn, but his luck held true, and he fumbled down the stairs unseen.

The hinges on the door that led to the main floor of the Compound were infamous for their loud squeal. Although everyone complained, no one ever fixed them. Piers had given it little thought until he realized he'd have to sneak through that door, so he had snuck a small vial of oil from the Orchard and carefully greased both hinges.

He held his breath... and the door swung smoothly and quietly for the first time in years.

He limped along in the shadows until he reached the door to the Labyrinth. Boots clattered against tiled floor in the distance, the sound fading as a Monk marched in the opposite direction.

Piers waited for Michel.

Did he give up on me? Does he think I lost my courage? Does everyone assume I'm craven?

He was concentrating on the door when Michel whispered from behind him. "You're late."

Piers jumped.

Michel wore his black ostrich suit, a black mask, and a short sword at his hip. His lean frame blended almost completely with the darkness.

"I couldn't leave any sooner," Piers said. "I didn't want to be seen by the other novices."

"We have two minutes before the Monk returns. Let's go." Michel twisted the lock, which made a loud metallic clank that sounded like breaking glass.

The Monk's steps ceased.

Piers froze, worried that the Monk had heard them.

Michel creaked the door open and whispered, "Hurry through, Piers. We don't have much time."

Piers crossed into the Labyrinth and Michel shut the door behind them.

"I can't tell if the Monk heard us or not, Piers. We should get moving in case he opens the door to investigate."

Small electronic strips lit the rough concrete tunnels. At this time of night, only a few brightened the way for emergencies, and no light came from any of the rooms off the main passageway.

Eden children told many horror stories about the Labyrinth. As their favorite spooky place it easily lent itself to creative nightmares. Most stories involved a Soulless haunting the hallways and killing innocent children in gruesome fashions. The villain always discovered a secret passageway out of the Labyrinth to roam Eden at night. When young, Aaliss was a master at telling those stories, usually to Wilky's dismay.

Piers smiled grimly. *Now I'm the monster lurking the dark tunnels.*

He raced after Michel and noticed a flickering yellow light from one of the side hallways, accompanied by approaching footsteps.

Michel lifted his hand signaling for him to stop. "Someone must be working late. He's coming! Hide behind these crates."

They hunched behind a series of stacked crates, keeping out of sight. The pleasant scent of dew in springtime mingled with the damp and musty odors in the tunnel.

As the footsteps from the side tunnel grew louder, the entrance to the Labyrinth swung open behind them. "Anyone there?" a Monk called out.

Piers recognized the voice as Mark's, the same monk who had caught him in Aaliss and Wilky's dwelling the other night with Sarah.

Michel swung his head back and forth between both dangers, looking uncertain on what he should do next.

Piers sent a silent prayer to Jacob for help.

Michel rested his hand on the hilt of his sword, his grasp firm.

Piers realized what he must do. This was *his* responsibility. No one had to see Michel in the shadows, so he stumbled from his hiding spot, toward the light and the oncoming footsteps, guessing that the unknown danger had to be better than the Monk.

He came face to face with a startled lab researcher he knew as Peter.

"Piers, what in Eden are you doing down here?"

Before Piers answered the Monk called out, louder this time. "Who's down here?" Beams from his flashlight swung from side to side along the tunnel as he marched toward them.

"Wait here." Peter rushed past Piers. "It's only me down here. I've still got work to do."

"I thought I heard the door open to the Labyrinth."

"You must have heard me drop one of these darn crates. Noises echo down here at night. There's no one else but those who're working with me."

"Maybe I should take a look."

"I don't think the High Priest would be happy with you snooping around down here. I'd hate to tell him how you've wasted my time with a tour because you were curious at what we're doing." Peter tapped his foot. "Is that the Sacred Drink I smell?"

A few moments of silence followed and then Mark grunted. "If you say there's no one else, that's fine with me. I was only thinking of your protection." The Monk turned and retreated down the corridor.

Peter returned slightly flushed and embraced Piers with a firm hug. "I'm so sorry I haven't been over to see you yet. They've got me working so much I'm practically locked down here."

"That's all right, Peter. I understand."

Peter was an old family friend. Short and round, he had white hair, a pointy beard, and gray piercing eyes that brightened his kindly face. Piers had forgotten he worked in the Labyrinth, had forgotten he had friends.

"I don't believe a word of this drivel about Aaliss and Wilky," said

Peter. "There are no finer Edenites than your siblings. I'd stake my life on it."

"Thanks. It means a lot. I'm sure there's some type of mistake. I just need to figure out what it is."

"What in Jacob's name are you doing down here, anyway?" Peter's eyebrows arched upward. "You could get in major trouble if they find you. There's a lot of *secret* activity. Even I don't know everything that's going on. They only tell us what they think we *need* to know."

"I'm headed to Wilky's lab." Piers touched Peter on the shoulder. "He left me a clue. I'm hoping there's some evidence in his lab that will clear them."

Michel stepped from behind the crates, and Peter gasped. He shot his hand to his chest and staggered backward. "What in Jacob's world? Jacob's Braid, I thought a shadow had come to life. You almost scared me to death. I don't think the old ticker can take much more. Is anyone else lurking around?" He scrutinized the hallway, looking for living shadows.

"No, just us," said Piers. "Do you have any idea what Wilky was working on? Maybe his research is behind this mistake?"

"I've been thinking the same thing, but I don't have a clue what your brother was researching. I asked around, but no one else does either." Peter stroked his short beard pensively. "Wilky was special. He had his own way of looking at problems, and he wasn't the easiest person to talk to. I showed him around when he first got here, but most of the other researchers stayed away from him—too young and too unusual for them." A trace of bitterness mingled with his words. "They felt threatened by him."

"Is anyone else around?" Michel asked. "Do we have a straight shot to Wilky's lab?"

"I have two colleagues with me in my lab." Peter glanced down the lit hallway. "There's no one else. We're almost done for the night, but I can keep them in my lab for a while longer." He glanced at the crates. "I'll leave one of these behind. Turn it perpendicular to the wall when you leave. This way I'll know the way is clear. I'll keep them busy until you give the signal."

"Thanks, Peter. I owe you."

Peter grabbed Piers by the shoulders. "You're a good man, Piers. I've always seen much of your father in you. Be careful. Strange things are happening."

Piers nodded.

He left Peter and led Michel to Wilky's lab. Finding the lab and the holding pens empty, he awkwardly settled in Wilky's chair and turned the computer on. The flat screen flickered to life, and after a second it prompted him for a username and password.

He breathed deeply, his fingers hovering over the keyboard before he typed *Piers* and *David*. One red file folder blinked ominously in the center of the screen. "Let's see what Wilky left us."

Michel hovered behind him and looked over his shoulder.

Piers clicked the file folder and a series of slides flashed on the screen—close-ups of a particular flower appeared first, followed by a familiar-looking mushroom with a red and yellow stem, and then pictures of Wilky combining the two ingredients with water.

The screen went black and a new series of images appeared—three Soulless drank the concoction, each of them with red eyes; a heartbeat later their eyes looked normal, all trace of the Red Death gone.

The pictures ended and were replaced with another blinking red file folder.

Michel whispered, "Those pictures must be out of sequence. The ones where the Soulless have normal eyes were placed after the ones where they've already had the red eyes."

"I don't think they're out of sequence at all. Wilky's shown us the cure to the Red Death." Piers smiled and turned to Michel. "It's a miracle! He must have discovered the cure, and cured those Soulless. They're probably the ones Aaliss needed the bread for. She told me someone was starving them. Whoever framed Aaliss and Wilky didn't want those Soulless around any longer."

A confused expression clouded Michel's face. "So Wilky figured out a cure to the Red Death and it's a simple combination of a mushroom, flower, and water." He looked incredulously at Piers.

Piers grinned backed at him, feeling giddy despite the dire situation they found themselves in.

"But, if Wilky figured out the cure, why would someone set him and Aaliss up as traitors?" Michel wondered. "He should be treated as a hero, or maybe a prophet."

A prophet.... My Wilky?

Piers couldn't imagine such a thing—not the boy he grew up with who had difficulties dealing with the smallest things. Still, he remembered the prophets God had selected throughout time—none were perfect. And the High Priest wouldn't want a prophet around whether real or imagined. People would look up to Wilky and he'd have power. They might even want him to replace the High Priest some day. No, that would be the last thing the High Priest would want.

He shrugged. "Those in power might not want the cure to be discovered, or maybe they wouldn't want Wilky to be the one to discover it." He couldn't bring himself to speak his suspicions about the High Priest out loud. Just thinking them constituted high treason and blasphemy. He pointed to the screen. "There's still more."

He clicked on the last file folder. The words *Eden Day* flashed on the screen in capital letters, and then a note appeared. It was probably the longest note Wilky had every written him.

> *Piers:*
>
> *I can't tell if the future is set. To learn the whole truth you need to access the High Priest's personal computer.*
>
> *User Name: Jacob1.*
>
> *Password: Serpent.*
>
> *File: Poisoned Apple.*
>
> *Think twice before you do. Once you learn the truth you can't unlearn it. It's up to you.*
>
> *Love,*
>
> *Wilky*

The computer erased the file and shut itself off.

Piers felt the wind knock out of him and he sagged back in the chair. He'd hoped for proof to save his brother and sister, and he only got another mystery and a new clue.

"I don't know what to make of that," Michel said.

"Neither do I, but I know what I have to do next."

He felt hollow.

Once again he knew the *what* but not the *how*.

CHAPTER 33
AALISS

Aliss glanced at her empty bowl. "Many thanks for the hot meal." She meant it. Food would be hard to come by outside of both Eden and the Stronghold, and the stew had replenished her strength.

"It's the least an old witch can do for such important travelers." The Witch spoke to her, yet she seemed to stare at Wilky. In fact, she spent most of the evening stealing glances at Wilky, but Aaliss detected no malice in it, and Wilky paid her little attention.

Eamon sported a sheepish grin. He looked better with a smile on his face, especially the way his cheeks dimpled and his eyes sparkled. "One of my tribe visited you a short while ago. He goes by the name of Reilly. Any idea what he wanted?"

The Witch chuckled. "I remember him. Did he go north?"

"He moved. So what did—"

"Us witches never divulge the wishes of our clients. We have a code, but you can trust that one. He might be important in events that will follow. Yes, he can be... trusted." A faraway look settled in the Witch's eyes for a moment, and then she pointed toward the far end of the cabin where Jillian slept. "There's plenty of room for you all to sleep on the floor. I have some dry straw in the barn to soften the hard edge of the wood. I suggest you get some rest before your journey tomorrow."

She rose from the table with a groan, took one last look at Wilky, and disappeared behind a door on the other side of the cabin.

"Great," Aaliss mumbled.

She looked for a place to string up the hammocks inside the cabin and found none. She considered sleeping outside, but the night looked foreboding and she wanted the safety and warmth of the cabin. And surely Eamon would sleep inside near Jillian, and that weighed on her decision too.

They all grabbed straw from the barn and spread it on the floor near Jillian. At least Aaliss could find no fleas in it. She settled between Eamon and Wilky, and Wilky fell asleep almost instantly.

Kalhona wove a stone over the knuckles on her right hand and through her fingers. When she saw Aaliss staring at her, she said, "This exercise helps keep my fingers nimble, so I can work the dyes." The tip of a tattoo peeked out from the collar of her shirt.

Aaliss had never seen a tattoo before, and it interested her. Painting one's body would certainly be prohibited in Eden. "Would you mind showing me your ink?"

Kalhona rolled up her sleeve.

Aaliss gasped at a tree so intricate and colorful she instantly wanted one. "Does it wash away?"

Kalhona grinned. "Never. This is my tree of life." She pointed to a flower on the top most branch. "This is for my daughter, Tania. She's only two harvests old."

Aaliss dropped her jaw; Kalhona was probably her age and she already had a daughter! The truth hit her hard: the Soulless had no time to wait to have children. For them life was too short, and without the cure her life would also be too short.

"Are you married?"

Kalhona scrunched up her eyes. "*Married?*"

"I mean coupled together with the father."

"No." Kalhona shook her head. "He served his purpose, but that's all he was good for. He died from the Red Death last harvest."

"Oh," said Aaliss. Such a thing—having a child without being married—would be unthinkable in Eden.

Kalhona stopped twirling her stone and closed her eyes, leaving only Aaliss and Eamon awake.

"Does Jillian look any better to you?" Eamon asked.

Aaliss studied her for a long moment. "She looks the same, which is probably a good thing."

Eamon clenched his hand into a fist. "I feel so helpless. There should be something I can do."

"You've done all you can. The rest is up to her. Besides, she seems to be a strong-willed person. I bet she'll pull through just fine."

He nodded.

Aaliss still wrestled with the idea that Kalhona was a mother, and felt her stomach flip when she asked Eamon, "Do you have any children?"

He shook his head. "No, not me. I'm waiting to exchange bracelets."

"Exchange bracelets?"

He smiled. "I forget that you don't know our ways. In my tribe, when two people commit to each other, they exchange bracelets—usually leather cords with a unique design on them. Once two people exchange bracelets they're coupled. If one strays, he or she will be banished from the tribe as a *Bracelet Breaker*. Only half the tribe exchange bracelets. Others live a more *uncommitted* life."

Aaliss felt her face warm and spoke in a breathless whisper. "What about the other half? What do they do?"

"Dermot would never exchange bracelets. He doesn't like to be... *limited*. He has four children with three different women. He thinks I'm silly, but I want to be with that one special girl forever. It's said that those who exchange bracelets find themselves together in the next life, that the leather cords bind them for all time."

Aaliss stole a glance at Jillian and wondered for the hundredth time what type of relationship the two had. She felt weird and unsettled, anxious and somewhat elated at the same time. She couldn't just ask Eamon about his feelings so she settled on more innocent questions. "Tell me about Jillian. What does she do at the tribe?"

"She's working on the Books of Wisdom as a scribe. Her letters are small and precise and her tongue is sharp." He chuckled. "She keeps the masters on subject. When they stray, she lets them know about it."

"So you work with her... closely."

Eamon shrugged. "Sure, but I do lots of other things for the tribe, and Jillian never travels with us when we trade with other tribes and go to other lands."

Other lands? "Do you know a place called the City of Bones?"

Her dream the other night had been eating at her quiet moments. She didn't like the look of those witches, and couldn't explain Wilky's bizarre behavior. She wanted to shake it off as a bad dream and nothing more, but it seemed so vivid and lifelike—unlike any other dream she'd had in the past.

"Sure, I'm familiar with the City of Bones, although we call it Bone City. It's just outside of The Exchange."

"The Exchange?"

"I guess your tribe is farther away from mine than I assumed. The Exchange is a two-week ride on the Freeroad. The *Keepers* run The Exchange. They take a tax on all that is traded there. We barter goods like meat for other items we need. The last two times we went, Dermot let me negotiate the trades. The better we do, the more wine and other supplies we can get in return. Different tribes from all around meet at The Exchange. The Keepers make sure everyone keeps the peace."

"And the City of Bones is near The Exchange? Does it have massive metal buildings, broken down and abandoned?" Aaliss held her breath. If the City of Bones from her dream and this Bone City Eamon mentioned were the same, then her dream was more than just a dream.... It was a vision, and that would make it way more dangerous.

"Yes, it's a wondrous sight to behold. Built during the time before tribes, strange metallic buildings look like monsters that lay wasted on wide streets. Not all the buildings are abandoned though. Many vices can be satisfied in the City—witches sell magic, shadows sell strange drugs that alter reality, women offer nighttime pleasures, people gamble on rat races in the pits—really anything one can imagine, and probably some you can't. It's a dark place. Last time we went to The Exchange, one in our party visited the City and never returned. Dermot and I looked for him, but it's vast and we could find no sign of him. It was if he just disappeared."

Aaliss whispered, "Is there a fine powder on the streets?"

"Crushed bone, hence the name."

Aaliss woke to find the chubby bulldog licking her face, his tongue wet and sticky, his breath sour and hot. She scowled at the furry beast, but the dog stared back at her with a grin of sorts plastered across his wrinkled face. If she didn't know any better, she would have thought he smiled at her, so she shoved his square mug away and the dog trotted off.

Eamon slept next to her, their bodies separated by a few inches, his hair mussed over his face, the slightest trace of stubble on his chin.

She lifted her hand to push his hair away from his eyes, but she stopped herself and brought it back to her side. She had stayed up late talking with him. Much of the conversation after the City of Bones focused on Jillian. The two were close, and at times she felt jealous; however, at other times he portrayed her much like Aaliss might have described Wilky or Piers, which left her confused.

She wanted to know exactly how close the two were, but she couldn't admit to herself why it was so important. She had just met him, after all. Sure, he was funny and sweet in an unexpected way, and his self-doubts charming. Plus, for someone who grew up outside Eden, he was surprisingly smart and learned. He knew more about ranching and farming and how to organize a tribe than she suspected anyone back home did, and that included all the aging Priests.

In a million years she would never have guessed that someone like Eamon existed amongst the Soulless, and yet here he was, sleeping so close to her that the two almost touched. Of course, he also slept next to Jillian, and before Aaliss fell down that waterfall again, she shook her head and forced thoughts about Jillian from her mind.

They discussed other things during the night besides Jillian. Eamon talked at length about Dermot, describing the responsibility he assumed as king of the tribe: the long council meetings, the endless decisions about herds and trading; and the never-ending personal squabbles he ruled over on a daily basis. Dermot had been no older than she was now when he became king, yet his decisions meant life and death for thousands. She would never want that type of responsibility—better to leave that to others.

Her personal slate had started to get complicated and that worried her. The number of people on her *payback* list had grown, but even more troubling, the number on her *owe* list had increased also. She counted Eamon, Gemma, Jillian, Kalhona, and even the Witch as people she owed.

The strings that bound her outside of Eden had gotten complicated, numerous, and tangled, and she didn't like it. She preferred a simple, untangled life. At first, all she had wanted was Wilky's safety and a way back to Eden to clear their names. Now, she wanted something different, but she didn't know exactly what.

Uncertainty was a killer, and that scared her almost as much as the Red Death.

Eamon turned on his side and snored lightly, but his unlined face looked peaceful, beautiful even.

She felt pulled toward him, but she fought against that attraction, knowing no good would come from it. The tide was strong, however, and having never felt that pull toward anyone else, she worried that she couldn't swim against that tide.

She'd never really had any boyfriends back home. Michel had made his feelings for her known, but she didn't share them, so her feelings for Eamon were all new ground, fresh snow without any tracks or any way for her to know how to travel in it safely.

Rubbing her hands over her face, she thought about Piers. He would like Eamon.

Eamon was not *Piers smart*. He didn't have a photographic memory or a well-trained analytical mind, but he thought clearly and was brave, like Piers could be when he let himself... if only he would let himself.

There I go again. I want to think about Piers, and my thoughts turn to Eamon.

When she turned to check on Wilky, her heart skipped a beat. He was gone, and a breeze blew through the open front door.

That door was closed when we went to sleep!

She rose to her feet, resisted the urge to call out for Wilky, headed for the front door, and nudged it open with her foot.

Wilky and the Witch talked quietly, rocking on two chairs side-by-side on the wooden porch. The bulldog, which sat at Wilky's feet, lifted his head for a second, eyed Aaliss with that silly grin on his face, and lowered his mug back down.

"Wilky, are you all right?" Aaliss asked.

He smiled back at her.

Relief soaked into her and she relaxed, though surprised to find him talking to the Witch.

Wilky doesn't chat, and yet there he is talking with the Witch like they're best friends.

"Come join us," said the Witch. "I only have two chairs, but you can settle on the porch."

A sparkle in her red-speckled eyes worried Aaliss. "Sure." She looked pensively at Wilky as she sat next to the Witch and let her feet dangle over the edge. "What are we talking about?"

She knew little about the Witch and did not fully trust her. A cure to the Red Death was valuable — valuable enough to be dangerous in the wrong hands.

"We're not talking about the weather. Wilky has told me about your special *quest*." The Witch smirked. "You understand that your brother has unusual qualities?"

How much does she know? "Well, I'm partial to him, if that's what you mean.

The Witch rocked a half dozen times while she stared at her.

Aaliss got the impression that she looked through her, as if she could see traits that lay underneath, traits that Aaliss might not even know existed. While Aaliss did not know exactly what the Witch looked for, she stared defiantly back; the old crone would not intimidate her.

Finally, the Witch broke the silence. "I like you. You're strong, and that's good because you're going to need strength. We both know there's more to Wilky than his good looks. I have the Sight that all red witches have. We see more than other people. We see the spirit energy thrown off by all living things, and some who have passed from this world many revolutions ago."

Aaliss wrinkled her face. *Spirit energy? None of the teachings in Eden discuss anything like that.*

The Witch grinned. "People with strong characters are enveloped in a bright light, and weak ones, not so much. The light is different depending upon the person. An adept witch can read the aura and know much about a person they have never met. Even in my weakened state I can tell Wilky isn't like other people. He's not the same as witches either. There's something special, maybe even unique about him. I know you must realize it too. He *sees* things—maybe not the way I do, maybe not through spirits like witches but.... I don't know how he does it, but he knows things. *Important* things."

She paused and rocked her chair silently for a long moment before focusing back on Aaliss. "Don't fool yourself. There are dangerous people out here, and you're woven into the fabric of important events. Events much bigger and more important than yourselves."

"I just want to find the mushroom and free us of the Red Curse. After that, I don't have any ambitions but to live a long and happy life with my brother."

A red hue flashed across the Witch's cheeks, her eyes narrowed, and the many lines on her face turned down. "You're too smart for that type of talk. You're not fooling me, and you're not fooling yourself! You have a responsibility. What you do with it is up to you, but you cannot pretend it doesn't exist. If you fail to take it seriously, it will take you, and you will lose all ability to choose your way."

The door opened, and when Eamon stepped outside, the Witch fell silent.

"Jillian looks better," he said, yawning and stretching. "But she still sleeps."

The Witch softened her wrinkled features. "I have bad news for you."

Eamon's face turned white. "But she looks stronger. The bleeding has stopped and the wound looks clean."

"Jillian will be fine. It's your brother, Dermot. He woke with the red eyes this morning."

Eamon looked as if the Witch had struck him across the face. All the remaining color drained from him and his knees buckled.

Wilky frowned and nodded his head.

Aaliss's stomach twisted. She felt the intensity from Eamon's pain as if she stood on the edge of a bonfire.

"How... do you know?" he asked.

"The spirits told me this morning. He's drawn the Circle of Destiny. If you look into your heart, you'll know it's true."

Kalhona joined them on the porch, working the round stone in her right hand.

Aaliss turned toward Wilky. "How long do we have to get him the cure?"

"Two days."

"But you can live with the red eyes for a week after you have them." Eamon looked desperate. "We should have more time."

Wilky shrugged. "Two days."

Aaliss stood. "We have no choice then. We had better get going. Once we save Kalhona's sister, we'll have to hope she knows where to find the mushroom."

"She's our tribal expert." Kalhona pocketed her stone in the folds of her woolen cloak. "If anyone knows, she'll know."

"What about Jillian?" Eamon asked the Witch.

"Her spirit light grows stronger," said the old crone. "She will live. She only sleeps now because of the Sweet Leaf I gave her. She will awaken by midday, but she needs rest. Traveling for the next few days would risk opening the wound again. I'll keep her safe until you return."

"If—"

The Witch waved him off before he could continue. "I know. If I harm her you will burn me at a stake, or cut off my head, or sic the wolves on me. One time, a man threatened to tie each limb to a different horse and send them galloping in four directions. I think he would have enjoyed it. Men always threaten."

Aaliss liked the Witch. She spoke her mind.

Eamon smirked. "If... we don't return in a few days...." He smiled more softly. "Please lend Jillian a horse and help her find the Ancient Road. I'm sure my brother will pay well for the animal."

The Witch's face tinted pink. "Oh... well, I never said I was a mind reader. I have two horses and only need one. When she is ready, I'll make sure she finds her way back home."

A finch landed on a nearby tree and started chattering incessantly.

Kalhona shrank away from the small bird.

The Witch grabbed Wilky's arm. "Don't forget what I told you. It will be important. You have enemies out here."

CHAPTER 34
VIPER

The Viper followed the trail left behind by the Butcher horsemen who took Aaliss and Wilky to the Stronghold. Pausing on the edge of the forest, he gazed upon the stone fortress. This wasn't his first time observing the city; he'd seen it two years ago and watched as torchlight danced against the stone palisade. He thought it crude and wicked and looked forward to the day he could take it and cleanse it of evil.

He felt uncertain. *Is the rabbit inside the stone fortress?*

He could cilimb over the wall and sneak inside to find signs of her, but that would be tricky and risky. Alternatively, he could look for her in the surrounding forest.

He decided to ask Jacob for help. Surely his forefather was with him, leading him, guiding him on this chase.

He closed his eyes and asked for help. Time drifted past. He saw no vision, had no epiphany, but when he opened his eyes, he found a blackbird with talons dipped in red paint staring back at him.

Jacob must have sent the odd bird.

The creature squawked, flew off toward a sturdy red maple tree, and then disappeared into the horizon.

The Viper knew what Jacob wanted from him. He climbed the tree and perched on top of a thick branch hidden from sight, as if he were nothing more than a large raven.

The early morning wind ruffled the leaves around him. A man on horseback approached... as he knew one would.

The only path the horse could take led beneath him, so he waited.

He smiled when he saw the leather cloak drift behind the rider. He needed information and now he would get it. The horseman rode slowly with his eyes fixed on the ground in front of him.

When the horse crossed underneath the tree, the Viper leaped, grabbed the man by the shoulders, and ripped him from the saddle. They both fell to the ground, but the Viper landed on his feet. Before the startled man even knew what had happened, the Viper stood over him with the point of his sword pressed against his throat.

The young man stammered, "Who are y-you?"

"An angel from God." The Viper grinned. "What are you looking for in these woods?"

The man's face turned pink, his eyes darting around wildly before they settled on the blade, but he said nothing.

"Maybe I haven't made myself clear. You have no choice. If I press downward just a little, you'll die." To make his point, the Viper slid the edge of his sword into the man's neck, extracting a small trickle of blood that ran down the man's throat and onto the forest floor. "Don't struggle or the blade will cut into an artery. Your blood will make a mess of this nice trail, and that would be a shame."

The Viper lifted his sword an inch from the man's flesh. "Tell me who you're looking for. It's a simple question. Even a Soulless fool should be able to answer it."

"A couple of prisoners escaped from the Stronghold. I'm searching for signs of them."

The Viper clicked his tongue. "Prisoners, you say. That's very sloppy of you to lose them. Are they the same ones who were captured two days ago? A boy and girl?"

The man's eyes widened. "What type of devil are you? How could you know?"

The Viper beamed his brightest smile. *"Devil?* I'm no devil. I'm an angel. How does it feel to have no soul?"

"What?"

The nerves in the Viper's body fired as if the Creator lit them ablaze in a holy fire. He plunged his blade deep into the man's throat, and enjoyed watching the light leave the young man's eyes.

He collected the horse and tracked the trail left behind by Aaliss. He counted three horses, which meant she must have found people to help her. The trail was hard to track, but he saw faint hoof prints, disturbed dirt, and a few snapped branches. Within minutes he spotted a spent fire and a used campsite.

He dismounted, took a deep breath, and caught whiff of Aaliss and Wilky in the air. He glanced toward the heavens. "The game continues, little rabbit."

CHAPTER 35
AALISS

Aaliss was grateful that the Witch's directions were dead on: a two-hour ride along the Ancient Road by horse, and then a distinctive series of trees—one maple, two poplars, a pine and two oaks—marked the small path to Santra's cabin.

Wilky had spotted the path first. As usual, he'd appeared lost in his own thoughts, but he'd pointed to the narrow path on the side of the road as if he'd been there before, which was surely impossible. He had never left Eden, but sometimes Aaliss got the distinct feeling that he knew more than he should.

Aaliss led the group to the edge of a clearing, where they studied Santra's cabin. The swirling wind left cold little pinpricks on her face and hands, and steam swirled from her mouth when she sighed at their discovery—five men armed with axes, and one witch.

If she didn't count Wilky, and she certainly did not, they numbered only three, and she feared Kalhona would be of little help. The girl had poison darts she could blow through a tube. Aaliss wondered if the darts would work, but the bolts to her crossbow had poison tips, so she figured they probably would. At least Kalhona seemed confident the darts would take down a man, even though she admitted she had never used them on a person before.

One mountain-sized warrior argued with the witch, and three firefoxes wove around Santra's legs, snarling at the big man.

Santra shouted, "You'll pay me a fair price for that girl, Tynchek, or you'll regret it." She crossed her arms over her chest. She looked young and beautiful, but her beauty did not mask the dangers hidden behind her glare—she was a predator dressed in the most unlikely garb.

Tynchek wore a cloak made from wolf fur that covered his barrel chest and massive biceps. A long beard with three different types of hair woven into it dropped from his chin like daggers. He looked like a killer.

Actually, all the men looked like killers. No simple trading party, this group must be a raiding band for a larger group of warriors. They carried no flag, but a red wolf with blood dripping from its jaws was painted on the saddles of the horses, which Aaliss assumed marked their emblem.

Tynchek waved a meaty hand toward Kalhona's sister, P'mina, clear malice darkening his words. "She comes with us as a gift, witch."

Two other men stood by the horses. Both wore wolf cloaks of their own, had unruly beards, and calculating eyes. They looked uneasy, as if Santra and the firefoxes scared them.

A thin, sneaky-looking man leered at P'mina while the last of the warriors carried a wicker basket of sweet leaf from the witch's cabin toward the waiting horses.

All in all, five armed warriors, each with a battleax.

Aaliss swore under her breath. If they were grouped more closely together, she could take down more of them on her own, and rely less upon the others.

P'mina yanked on a chain fastened to her wrists, which looped around a nearby soldier pine. When the chain held, she spat at the thin man who was leering at her, her face red, her hands balled into fists. She shared a family resemblance with Kalhona, but she had a wild look about her that Kalhona lacked, and she was so young—no older than Wilky.

How quickly they grow up outside of Eden.

P'mina had spirit; Aaliss would certainly grant her that much. She would not be taken without a fight, but based upon the enraged expression of the man she had just spat upon, their group seemed to have come just in time.

Aaliss loaded the crossbow, fearing that the girl was in peril. "I'll take out the big one by the witch. Eamon, you come from the right side by the horses, and Kalhona try to sneak behind the cabin to your sister. They'll probably come running once they see Eamon and me. When they do, use your darts to take out the thin guy who guards your sister, and then free her. Wilky will stay back by our horses in case we need to make a quick escape."

"Be careful of the firefoxes," Eamon whispered. "They'll attack as sure as sunrise."

"*Great,*" muttered Aaliss. "When I fire the bolt, everyone strike. With some luck we'll surprise them and have the advantage."

Kalhona shook with fear.

Aaliss grabbed her arm. "You can do this! Just have the poison dart ready when you come around the cabin. They won't have any idea you're there. You should be safe and you'll have a clean shot. Once he goes down, use the axe by his feet to hack away your sister's chains."

Kalhona nodded and left, moving slowly in a wide loop toward the back of the cabin, her steps unsteady, and her hands trembling as she clutched her dart gun.

Aaliss hated to rely on others, and had no confidence that Kalhona would take out the man by her sister. She would have to keep an eye on her and help as soon as she could.

Eamon broke her train of thought when he squeezed her hand. "Thanks," he said, his eyes wide and brilliant.

Aaliss felt her cheeks burn, so she secretly pinched her hand hard to keep her emotions in check. "You would do it for me."

Eamon tenderly brushed his fingers against her cheek.

She saw every detail of his face: the small patch of stubble on his chin, the dimples his cheeks made at the corner of his lips, even the smooth forehead that was now furrowed with concern. He looked as if he wanted to say something, as if words tried to fight their way from his mouth, but he turned and sprinted off without uttering another word.

She watched him race away, angry for not telling him more. *What* she would have said, she had no idea, but certainly something.

What if I never talk to him again?

She drove away the negative thought with effort. Negative thoughts were dangerous in a fight; they had a way of coming true.

She turned toward Wilky. "If things don't work out, you ride back to the Witch's house."

He nodded bravely, but he looked as scared as Aaliss felt. Five armed men, an angry witch, and three firefoxes were a lot to take down. She wished she had a better plan, but wishing for a better plan wouldn't give her one, so she turned back toward the cabin. Her heart hammered as the firefoxes snarled by the witch's feet.

Aaliss squinted her eyes, steadied the crossbow, and breathed through her nose. Events moved in slow motion as she felt adrenaline flood her body. Her finger rested lightly on the trigger. She aimed for Tynchek's wide chest right below the three long strands of his beard. She took one last breath, and started to pull the trigger....

One of the firefoxes jumped toward the big man. He swatted the animal away with his arm, and the witch moved in the way.

It was too late for Aaliss to adjust her aim, and she fired the crossbow. The bolt missed Tynchek and struck Santra in the shoulder instead.

The witch staggered backward, but Tynchek still lived.

Eamon dashed from the forest and attacked one of the men by the horses. The sound of metal against metal rang out as the man deflected Eamon's sword with the blade of his axe.

Aaliss dropped the crossbow and sprinted toward the cabin with her short sword at the ready.

A short, wide-chested warrior spotted her and charged.

She closed the distance in a heartbeat. He swiped his axe at her stomach, and she sidestepped the cut and swung her sword at his barrel-chest.

Quicker than he looked, the man parried the blow with his axe, but he stumbled off-balance.

She spun and slashed him in the neck. The ground splattered red, and he fell at her feet.

Another warrior leaped at her and swung his axe at her side.

She whipped her sword against the blade just in time to block the blow, and spun, raking her blade against the axeman's unprotected back. He groaned and turned, but she had anticipated that and had already spun to her left and slashed the man's thigh.

He went down in a heap, clutching his leg.

Breathing heavily, she glanced up just in time to see the spinning edge of a sharp blade fly toward her. With a flick of her wrist, she knocked the blade away with her sword a moment before it would have plunged into her chest.

There's a sixth warrior!

Sweat stung her eyes as she searched in vain for the knife thrower. He must be hiding at the edge of the clearing, but she couldn't find him.

Eamon grunted and Aaliss turned toward him. His blade had lodged inside a beefy warrior's chest. He heaved with both hands, but he could not free it.

Tynchek raced toward Eamon. The monster dwarfed Eamon, a determined grin on his ugly face as he swung his axe at Eamon's head.

Eamon released his sword and skipped backward, but the blade sliced into his shoulder. Eamon rushed the giant before the beast could ready his axe for another cut, and they went down in a tumble of body parts.

Aaliss tasted bile. She started toward Eamon, but one of the firefoxes launched itself at her throat. She protectively threw up her arm, and the creature bit into her flesh with its powerful vise-like jaws. Pain exploded through her forearm as she flung the beast hard against a tree. A second firefox poised to jump, but she slashed open its side with her sword, and the third ran off with its tail between its legs.

By the time she turned back toward Eamon, he and Tynchek had gotten to their feet and had started grappling.

Tynchek drove an elbow into the side of Eamon's head, which staggered him backward. Tynchek used the advantage to rush Eamon, and took him down hard on the ground. The big man twisted on top of Eamon.

Tynchek grabbed his battleax from the ground while still on top of Eamon. "You will bleed well."

Eamon locked both of his hands on the handle, but the behemoth was stronger and had leverage. The axe inched downward; Eamon had only a few moments left.

"Hold on, Eamon, I'm coming!" Aaliss leaped over a large rock and skirted a small maple tree, holding her breath as she ran, but she didn't see the slick moss. She slipped and toppled head-first onto the dirt and grass.

Tynchek heaved downward, sweat dripping from his beard. The axe's blade gleamed lethally, inches from Eamon's face.

Eamon's arms shook. He had seconds left to live.

Aaliss jumped to her feet, knowing she would never reach him in time, but she had to try.

Tynchek grimaced... and the axe slowed. He twisted and exposed a poison dart jutting from his neck, but he still pushed, still used his weight and remaining strength. The blade cut Eamon's cheek when Tynchek lost all his energy and slumped forward.

Eamon managed to push the blade to the side and heave the man off him with a shove.

Aaliss inhaled, surveyed the clearing, and counted dead warriors: she saw the two she had cut down, two bodies by Eamon, and one prone figure by P'mina. *Five dead.*

Kalhona clanged an axe against P'mina's chains.

Clank!

Kalhona swung the axe down a second time, another loud *clank*.

Where's the sixth warrior?

Wilky had brought the horses toward the cabin.

P'mina shouted a sharp warning and pointed at the edge of the clearing.

Aaliss found the knife thrower. When she saw him, her heart felt as if someone had stabbed it.

The knife thrower hurled a dagger at Wilky. It spun in the air, as if in slow motion.

He's going to die.

A cold frost swept the clearing.

"Look out!" Aaliss screamed.

Three ghost riders streamed past Wilky and toward the knife thrower. The blade, which surely would have claimed Wilky, disappeared in their slippery light. In a *whoosh* the riders ran over the knife thrower, and he too vanished.

CHAPTER 36
EAMON

E amon stared with his mouth open at the spot where the knife thrower had just been, and his tongue threatened to roll out and smack the ground.

What in the heavens happened? The killer just disappeared.

He felt a frost in the air and saw the same shadows he'd spotted at the campfire the other night. He remembered what Aaliss had said then—she called the shadows *Ghost Riders*—but, in truth, he wasn't totally convinced they were real. She'd also said they didn't pay attention to the living, but this could be no coincidence.

He locked eyes with Aaliss, and she shrugged. If she knew what had happened and why, she did a good job of faking it.

Kalhona groaned, and he spun to find a knife protruding from her hand, blood flowing from it like a small stream. The knife thrower must have hurled one at her before he disappeared.

P'mina reached for her sister, straining against the chains, but she couldn't touch her.

Eamon appreciated the girl's spirit, but if she continued to pull against the chains, she'd only hurt herself. He marched toward her and grabbed the axe. "Let me help." He swung the blade down hard and freed her with one swing.

When the shackles fell away, P'mina darted to her sister's side. The knife was still lodged into Kalhona's palm, her fingers curved and unmoving, blood darkening her hand, wrist, and washing down her arm.

"Oh, Kally, that's your artist hand." Tears rained down P'mina's face. "You should have let the knife hit me. It's all my fault."

"You're my sister. I couldn't let you die out here in the woods! What would I tell everyone?"

Aaliss and Wilky joined them. Both looked unharmed.

"We need to remove that knife from your hand," said Aaliss.

Kalhona nodded, her face lit with pain.

The wound would not kill her, but Eamon doubted she'd ever regain full use of her hand again. "I'll hold her and you pull out the dagger." He wrapped his arms around Kalhona's shoulders and held her tight. "On the count of three. One, two—"

Aaliss pulled the knife out and Kalhona screeched.

When Eamon released her, P'mina tried to hug her sister, but Kalhona shrugged her off. "You promised me that you'd behave before the Renewal Feast. Now look what you've done."

"I just wanted to find our mother, and I got lost. I never meant—"

"You never mean for bad things to happen, P'mina, but they have a way of following you around."

P'mina cringed and looked as if her sister had slapped her.

Aaliss helped Kalhona to her feet. "Let's clean that wound." She led them to the stream, where she washed the wound with fresh water.

When she'd finished, Wilky handed P'mina a cloth he had cut from one of the axemen's shirts.

P'mina wrapped the fabric around her sister's hand.

Kalhona winced and clutched her hand at her side.

"You should see a healer," Eamon suggested. "Perhaps the Witch? She's knowledgeable. If anyone can help you get the use of your hand back, it'll be her." He didn't think the Witch could help, but he realized how important Kahona's art was to her, and thought just the slight bit of hope would make her feel better.

P'mina's voice jumped with eagerness. "You met another red witch?"

"Yes, P'mina! She told us where to find you. And no, she wasn't our mother! We will never see her again. The Dark One probably dragged her to hell by now!"

P'mina looked as if she would cry, but the young girl had nerve and no tears formed in her eyes.

Eamon broke the ensuing awkward silence by introducing himself, Aaliss, and Wilky.

After a moment, P'mina regained her wits and gushed her thanks for their help in freeing her.

Aaliss cleaned his shoulder, wrapped the wound with a cloth, and dotted his face with the water from the stream.

The cut in his shoulder stung, but he had full use of his arm. "How bad is it?"

Aaliss grinned. "Probably won't scar."

"Too bad. I've heard women like men with scars."

"Not all women." She smiled and winked at him.

A jolt zipped through his body. It seemed to start somewhere around his head and burn straight through his body to his toes. He had never felt anything like it before.

She was strong and fearless and smart. She was also sweet, although he was sure she would never admit it, and would probably deck him if he mentioned it. Her eyes burned with an intense light, and he felt giddy when near her, as if he had stumbled upon a secret book that no one else had ever read before—one that would change everything.

How'd Gemma know I'd fall for her so quickly?

Wilky retrieved dried beef and pears from the axemen's saddlebags, and they ate lunch by the stream. By the time they finished, it was midday, and the sky darkened quickly as a cloud blocked the sun.

The darkness brought thoughts about Dermot, and Eamon's stomach turned. He sought out P'mina with his eyes.

She sat next to her sister and furtively glanced at Kalhona's hand every few seconds.

He should have asked about the mushroom by now, but part of him was afraid to ask. The young girl was his only chance at finding the mushroom in time to save Dermot.

He swallowed a lump in his throat. "P'mina, your sister told us that you are knowledgeable about plants."

"Yes, I studied under Loiana, who was the wisest when it comes to all things that grow from the earth."

"We need to find a particular mushroom," said Aaliss "It has a red and yellow stem. We think it grows around here someplace. We don't have much time. Do you know where we can find it?"

P'mina smiled. "Sure, come with me."

Eamon did his best not to get his hopes up too high. There must be a dozen mushrooms with that type of stem. Still, his lips turned upward and butterflies swirled in his stomach.

P'mina led them inside Santra's cabin, and on the way, she made sure to stomp on Santra's arm. "I saw some among the witch's stores." She shuffled through four baskets until she found one full of mushrooms with red and yellow stems. "Are these what you're looking for?"

Wilky nodded. He took the basket from her, sat cross-legged on the floor, dumped the mushrooms into a neat pile, and studied each one carefully.

Eamon's heart soared, but he had the sick feeling that Wilky looked oddly disappointed.

CHAPTER 37
AALISS

Aaliss wondered what in Eden her brother was looking for.

Wilky placed all the mushrooms neatly back into the basket except for *one*. He lifted that last one close to his eyes for a careful inspection. It appeared no different from the rest.

For the last hour, he'd examined each mushroom, twirled it in his fingers, and dropped it back into the bin.

Aaliss could see that with each one he rejected, Eamon grew more agitated. He started to huff and bounce his legs, and looked as if he might explode.

After Wilky spun the mushroom around six times, Aaliss finally asked him, "Do you have what you need?"

Wilky glanced at his audience as if he had woken from a dream. "This one will work."

Eamon exhaled with an audible woosh. "What do you need to do to make the cure?"

Wilky spoke slowly. "Boil the flower and mushroom."

"What exactly are we creating?" P'mina asked.

"The cure," Wilky said.

Aaliss sighed. She wasn't sure it was a great idea to tell P'mina and

Kalhona about the cure, but they *had* fought together, and it was too late now anyway, so she continued for her brother. "I know it sounds crazy, but Wilky has discovered the cure for the Red Death. It combines a flower and this mushroom."

"It doesn't sound crazy to me. Plants can cure all types of ailments." P'mina bounced toward Wilky. "I'll help you build the fire, so we can create the tonic."

Kalhona dozed in the corner under the influence of the Sweet Leaf P'mina had given her.

With nothing to do but get in the way, Aaliss pulled Eamon from the cabin to let the two youngsters do their work.

Once outside, Aaliss squinted against the sun's glare as she surveyed the carnage from their battle. "We might as well clean these axemen of anything valuable or useful while we wait."

They worked mostly in silence, making two piles: one for weapons and a second for any valuables, such as coins or jewelry.

When they had finished, Aaliss studied the two mounds.

The valuables pile looked short—the witch had a heavy coin purse on her, Tynchek wore a silver armband, and one other axeman had a copper ring. The weapons stacked substantially higher.

"Not bad." She pointed to the larger pile. "They brought a lot of steel." She lifted one of the battleaxes. "It's heavy and well made. I wouldn't want to get stuck on the receiving end of that blade, but it's too bulky for me. I prefer a short sword and quick strokes."

Eamon had been unusually quiet, and glanced up at the darkening sky with a frown on his face.

Aaliss couldn't tell if he had heard her, but even if he had, she knew his mind was with his brother. She moved close to him. "Wilky will make the cure and we'll be on our way. There's still time."

"There has to be. He has to live on. The tribe needs him."

He looked down at his feet to obscure his face, but she saw enough and knew that look. Yes, the tribe needed Dermot, but Eamon needed him more. He might be worried those feelings made him appear weak, but she thought the opposite.

A few moments later, Eamon looked up. "If Fintan becomes King, he'll start a war with the Painted Ones. He can't wait to attack *someone.* If Dermot doesn't get that cure in time, all of this will have been for naught. And Jillian would never have gotten hurt."

Aaliss grabbed his arm. "The Witch said Jillian will recover. You saved us from that brother of yours, and we freed P'mina from Santra and those axemen. That's not bad for a couple days' work." She shoved him on the arm and that brought a reluctant grin.

"True. But I have a feeling you would have found some other way out of that Basement."

"And *we'll* get the cure to Dermot in time to save him and stop your brother." The words tumbled from Aaliss's mouth without her thinking much about them.

Since when did I decide to go back with him? Wilky and I are safer on our own and not tangled with the Butcher Tribe.

When she peered into his blue eyes, she felt her heartstrings tug.

She tried to convince herself that she'd go just long enough to see Dermot cured, but it wasn't working terribly well.

Eamon turned to say something, but stopped when P'mina emerged from the cabin.

"We're finished!" she said.

Wilky and Kalhona sat cross-legged in the center of the small house on the wooden floor, dust swirling around them. In front of them were two wooden cups and a tall yellow candle made from beeswax. The smoke smelled like lilacs.

P'mina waved at the floor around them. "Sit."

They settled in a makeshift circle with the cups and the lit candle in the center.

Aaliss sat beside Wilky. His eyes looked sad, his lips turned downward. Glancing at the two cups, she understood what had happened. "So there's just enough to make two doses of the cure?"

He nodded.

"It's your cure," Eamon said. "You should take one, and I'll bring the other to Dermot."

Wilky shook his head. "No."

Aaliss glowered at him. *What does he want?*

Since they discarded their gasmasks, she had fixated on making the cure and protecting him from the Red Death. Now a cup stood inches from him filled with the cure, and he simply says, *no*.

Wilky pointed to the two cups. "There are two tribes."

Aaliss's heart sank as she understood what he wanted. "Is this really necessary?" Heat flushed her face. He could be so frustrating. "Who knows when we'll get these ingredients again? I want you to take it."

Wilky shook his head. "The two must bond together. It's the only way. A new enemy comes."

"A new enemy," said Eamon. "Who? These axemen?"

Wilky looked at him, his eyes glowing. "I see it."

"What do you see, Wilky?" Aaliss asked, her voice breathless.

He closed his eyes, and spoke in a flat tone as if he were merely reporting events he just now saw.

A chill washed through Aaliss. She had never seen him like this.

"They march along a long road that swirls around them like a cloud. The clay falls upon them, turning everything red. A man rides a horse at the front of the war band. He has broad shoulders and a long beard twisted with many different-colored hairs. Two battleaxes are slung over his shoulders. They call him chief but he does not lead them. A witch rides on a red horse next to him. She has the power. She has the vision. She dreams of a world ruled by witches. They carry two banners, the bloody wolf and the red raven."

"How many are they?" asked Eamon.

Wilky paused for a long moment. "They form a river that stretches farther than I can see. The ground shakes from their footsteps. A bloodlust hovers over them. It's the witch's making. They do her will. They're coming for you."

Wilky blinked a few times and snapped back to the present.

Could he have seen a vision?

In Eden only the High Priest could see the future or hear from God.

Anyone else claiming to see a vision was immediately branded a liar and burned for blasphemy. But Wilky never spoke false. She glanced at the other faces around her, certain that everyone believed what he had told them.

"Are you sure they're coming for us? Both tribes?" Eamon leaned closer to him.

Wilky nodded.

"How much time do we have?" P'mina asked.

He shrugged.

"The clay road has to be the Freeroad that leads to The Exchange and the City of Bones." Eamon glanced at Wilky for confirmation, but received none, so he continued. "In that case, they might be two weeks away."

Aaliss knew Wilky would say no more. Perhaps he knew nothing else. Still, she understood what he wanted, and sighed. "The two doses are for the two tribes, one for each leader—Dermot for the Butcher Tribe, and one for the leader of the Painted Ones, to bind them together so they can unite to face these invaders."

Wilky nodded.

Eamon grabbed a cup. "Thank you for the gift of life for my brother. Dermot is deserving."

P'mina seized the other one. "Our Tribal Mother will be honored to receive this tonic."

"We should swear an oath to join the two tribes to defeat these axemen," said Eamon. "I swear on my ancestors, who live in the heavens, to bring the tribes together and defeat this threat as one."

When Eamon finished, P'mina, Kalhona, and Wilky all swore to the same quest. Once they finished, all eyes turned toward Aaliss.

She felt the heat from their collective gaze and turned toward Wilky, who stared at her with that stubborn *look* in his eyes.

Not this time.

She stormed from the cabin without uttering a word.

The cold wind whipped across Aaliss's face. Perhaps it was just her imagination, but she smelled war and death in the air.

Wilky joined her, a sad expression darkening his face.

"Wilky, what have you done?"

"The tribes must unite."

"How do you know?"

"I *see* it. And we are to help."

"This is not our fight. How can we return to Eden if we're helping these tribes?"

"We can't."

Aaliss looked away. All she had wanted was to protect Wilky from the Red Death and find a way back home. Now everything had twisted together. She had met Eamon and his blue eyes, and Wilky had that stubborn look on his face that meant he'd never change his mind. She had no choice now. She would plunge into the middle of the two tribes and this war without any idea where it would lead them.

Can I keep him safe in the middle of a war?

CHAPTER 38
HIGH PRIEST

The High Priest waddled as he walked, the blubber rolling from one side to the other with each step, his knees creaking in protest. He refused to limp or grimace as that would show weakness. He had to be above weakness. As Jacob's chosen one on Eden, he must be infallible. Once people questioned his physical condition, they might question his relationship with Jacob and his infallibility. He could never let that happen, would never let that happen. Charles the First had let them question his infallibility, and they burned him at a stake. No, he would never let them see weakness.

He longed for his electric cart. Eden only had a handful of carts left: one for him, one for the President, and two others in case of emergencies. They had to carefully maintain the battery-operated vehicles. They retained the technology to fix them, but they lacked the necessary natural resources, which lay outside Eden. All that would change. Soon, he'd recreate life on the planet the way it had once been, only better. With the Red Death as his tool, all power would concentrate in him and his clergy.

He had looked forward to the walk to the Orchard, hoping that the exercise would do him good. He knew there would be much walking in his future—one of the small, necessary inconveniences he had to face. Still, halfway through his stroll, he wished he had brought the cart.

He hadn't always been fat. There had been a time, before his father died, before he became High Priest, when he was lean and strong and fit. Everything changed when he became High Priest. He had to become more than himself. He had to become Jacob's representative in Eden. He had to become infallible and swim in the murky waters of politics and crises and stress. The pounds added up over the years, as did the scheming.

The late afternoon sun beat down on his head but did little to warm the crisp autumn day. His orange full-length robe swished as he walked. A blue circle with a capital J in the center was embroidered on the right chest.

Two Senior Priests followed in his wake, content to carry a skin of cold fermented cider in the event he became thirsty, dried apple slices in case he grew hungry, and to attend to whatever other needs he might have. Neither of them was a Blood Relation and therefore could never progress beyond Senior Priest to a Cleric. Still, they were diligent and loyal, and would soon be rewarded when he successfully enacted the *Eden Day Plan*.

One of the High Priest's children usually attended to his needs, but not today. He had six from his two wives, ranging from five to thirty years old, the oldest being his son and successor. He had to keep them in the dark about his plans for Eden Day and beyond. His oldest was ambitious, and the less he knew about the future, the less of a threat he would be. When the High Priest slept, he often dreamed of his oldest sneaking up behind him with a knife in his hand. No, the less his offspring knew, the better.

For a short time he might have conferred with his first wife, but that trust had faded away when he married his second one. Now he grew weary of both women he called wives. In Eden, only the High Priest could have multiple wives. God had told Jacob that, as guardian of the human race, he must procreate, so Jacob had taken three wives and had twelve children. Since then, not only did the members of the

Community expect polygamy from their high priests, they required it from them. Since Jacob took three wives, it was an unwritten law that subsequent high priests should limit themselves to two. After all, no one could compare with Jacob... until now.

The High Priest smiled.

After Eden Day I will be all powerful, rivaling Jacob himself. Not only will I take many wives, but polygamy will be expected from all Blood Relations.

He pictured scores of young men with braids ruling over the Soulless, all owing their very existence to him. He liked to daydream as he walked. It took his mind off the ache in his knees. He grinned and slowed his gait as the gravel path ended at the large, wooden doors of the Orchard's facility.

One of the Senior Priests jumped in front of him and swung the door open.

"I shouldn't have to slow down for you to open the door! My time is too precious to be wasted."

"Yes, your Grace." The man's voice trembled.

The High Priest ignored him, strolled through the portal and entered the warehouse. It smelled of oak, apples, and sawdust. Harvest season for the Orchard had started a few weeks earlier, so the facility burst with apples and activity. Workers sorted different types of apples into large wooden crates that threatened to overflow, the apples rolling onto the floor as if they had minds of their own. Casks of apple juice were neatly stacked in massive pyramids, and he heard the steady clanging of the apple press in the distance. He had never seen the facility bursting with more fruit — undoubtedly a sign from Jacob that he would have all he needed for his plan.

He scanned the building and found Father Luke.

The aged priest directed two workers who pushed large wheelbarrows filled with apples. "Those go in the crates on the west wall. If there's no room, just leave them in a pile on the floor. I'm having more crates made." Father Luke's voice sounded nuanced with age, as if his deep tan and the lines on his face had embedded themselves in the timber of his voice.

The facility functioned as the depository of the apple harvest, the distillery for the fermented apple cider, and the storage area for the Sacred Drink.

The High Priest turned toward his two assistants, who looked eager to please him. "One of you should fetch my cart, and the other should stay here. I want to commune with Father Luke privately."

He tottered his way to Father Luke, already looking forward to tonight's massage, when his young masseuse would work out the aches in his legs.

Father Luke glanced in his direction, and flashed a stoic expression on his leathery face. The man was short, allowing the High Priest the luxury of looking down at him.

When they were boys, the High Priest and Father Luke were best friends. In truth, he was the only friend the High Priest had ever known. As they grew past their teenaged years, they started to quarrel. When the High Priest's father died unexpectedly, thrusting him into the role of high priest, the relationship grew troublesome. He could not have a member of the clergy question him, even if they were childhood friends. But Father Luke had a way with the old apple trees. Even when he was young, they bore fruit for him in greater abundance than they would for anyone else, so the High Priest banished him to the Orchard, safely away from the Compound.

"Good afternoon, Father Luke. I hope Jacob has enlightened your day." The High Priest flashed a fake smile as he spread his arms wide in an awkward blessing. The robe flowed off his limbs and his large frame.

"As I hope he has for you." There was no affection in Father Luke's voice as he completed the customary greeting and response expected of senior clergy. "It is always an honor when you bless us with your presence, your Grace. Have you decided to tour the Orchard and stroll through the trees? It might take some time. I hope you brought your walking shoes."

His voice dripped with sarcasm. It had been years since the High Priest had last made an inspection, and they both knew that one would serve as his last.

The High Priest ignored Father Luke's sarcastic tone, and clasped his right hand firmly on the man's shoulder. "No need for that. I trust the Sacred Trees are in good hands. I just wanted to see the casks for Eden Day, and give them a blessing."

"Why certainly, if you feel the calling, but I don't recall you ever blessing the casks before we've delivered them in prior years." Father Luke's eyebrows arched high above his deep-set eyes.

"Jacob has appeared to me in a vision and told me that this year is special. He wants me to bless the casks today." The High Priest shrugged. "I'm only an instrument of his will."

Father Luke rolled his eyes and turned his back on him. He moved quickly, giving the impression that he had little time for this foolishness.

That was fine with the High Priest. He wanted to spend as little time in the Orchard as possible—the dust bothered his breathing. He followed behind Father Luke, trying hard to keep up with his short rapid steps. They weaved their way around crates of apples, humming conveyor belts, and large oak tanks that they used to ferment the apple cider to the storage area in the back of the facility.

Twelve massive barrels were lined up neatly in a row. The High Priest hummed as he inspected each one and settled on the one furthermost down the line. Eleven of the barrels had a green apple stamped on their side. The last one had a red apple. He smiled. Everything was in order.

He had to make sure for himself. "You seal the barrels tomorrow, correct?"

"Yes, as it is written. They are always closed two months before Eden Day. I will place my seal on each barrel to certify its purity. I've been doing this for thirty years. I think by now I've got it down right."

"Good. Everything looks like it is in the proper order." The High Priest raised his arms above the barrels and mumbled a short blessing. When he finished, he turned and left without another word to Father Luke.

Piers had watched the two from the shadows. After the High Priest and

Father Luke left the storage area, he limped to the barrels. He noticed nothing unusual at first... until he saw the small red apple stamp on the last cask, the one where the High Priest had paused.

Odd.

All the other barrels had a green apple stamped on them.

CHAPTER 39
VIPER

The Viper stalked toward the prone body of a large, haggard-looking young man by a creek. He waved his arms to scare away the crows that had already started pecking at the dead man's bloated face, and swatted away the flies.

"Good." He ripped the bolt out of the corpse's chest. "My rabbit has teeth."

He squatted low and noticed a separate pool of blood near the deceased man. He followed the crimson trail to a dead woman. "Interesting. One of her new friends is hurt."

He tracked the blood to the edge of the clearing and found hoof prints. "The trail heats up."

He frowned at the darkening sky, mounted his own horse, and followed after them.

CHAPTER 40
AALISS

Weary from all the riding she had done recently, Aaliss smiled as they approached the Witch's home. "At least we made it before nightfall."

She glanced at Eamon, who stared ahead and said nothing.

He had barely spoken to her since they left Santra's cabin. In truth, he really hadn't *looked* at her either.

She balled her hands into fists. *I know he's angry because I refused to take the stupid oath, but if he keeps this up, I'm going to punch him in the face.*

Halfway along the trek back to the Witch's cabin, P'mina found the spot where she first entered the Ancient Road, and told Kalhona another dozen times how sorry she was about her hand before she trudged toward her village.

Kalhona gave no ground. She only told her sister to try and not mess things up any more than she already had.

The Witch stood on the porch and watched them rein up the horses. She leaned heavily against her bow as the bulldog paced anxiously next to her. "I told you they'd come back tonight. I don't know why you always doubt me."

The dog barked once in response, stopped pacing, and wagged his tail.

When Aaliss climbed the creaky steps, the bulldog brushed against her legs. She smiled despite her weariness and rubbed his large wrinkled head in greeting.

At least he's *happy to see me.*

"How's Jillian?" Eamon asked.

"She's recovering. She woke around midday, but she's still in a lot of pain. I gave her more Sweet Leaf to blunt it. She sleeps now and is cool to the touch. She can't travel for a few days, but she'll heal." The Witch nodded toward Kalhona's bandage. "Better come inside, so I can take a look at that hand."

The group followed her into the cabin. Chickens boiled in a kettle over the fire, and the smell of freshly baked bread filled the air with a sweet scent.

Jillian was sleeping on the straw bedding, and to Aaliss's untrained eye, she did look better.

Eamon lifted the purse heavy with coins they had taken from Santra. "Payment for all you've done for Jillian, and to help heal Kalhona's hand."

The Witch laughed, which deepened the lines in her face and made her appear not just old but ancient. "I'm not helping you for coins. That's a poor bargain. I'd receive more by betraying you, but the one true God has made his wishes clear to me. My reward will come in the next life, and that reward will be great."

She motioned for Kalhona to lift her hand so she could examine it.

"Dinner is ready. Clean yourselves by the creek. You smell like horse," the Witch said tersely. "Except you, Kalhona." The Witch held Kalhona's hand in hers, brought it close to her face, and clucked her tongue. "Now let's peel back that bandage and see what's been done."

Aaliss watched as the Witch led Kalhona outside and made a salve from an assortment of plants and mud from the creek. She told Kalhona she might regain full use of her hand and fingers, that she knew a spell she might try, but it would require a few days to prepare.

Still, Aaliss heard no certainty in her voice and doubted a spell could fix Kalhona's hand.

They ate mostly in silence, answering only the direct questions asked by the Witch.

After Eamon told her about the northern invaders, he mentioned the oaths the others took, and then looked sullenly at Aaliss. "I release Wilky from his sworn words. You've done your part. You didn't take the oath. We had a deal, and you lived up to it. You shouldn't come back to the Stronghold with me. Fintan will be unhappy to see you. He will likely want your head as punishment for your escape."

Aaliss snorted as she strangled the fork in her hand. "Thanks for being so chivalrous, but I make up my own mind. If I want to see this through, then I'll do just that. I'm not worried about your brother."

The Witch smirked. "I guess that's been decided."

"Yes, I guess it has," said Aaliss. "We'll have no more talk about us staying behind." She noticed that Eamon looked pleased.

He must care about me at least a little.

Afterward, the conversation flowed more easily, and they talked at length about the axe-wielding warriors and the strange bloody wolf markings on their saddles. Eamon confessed that he had never seen the symbol at The Exchange or in the City of Bones.

Jillian woke when they finished the meal, and Eamon rushed to her side. He chatted with her, held her hand, and smiled gently.

Aaliss felt a clamp squeeze her heart. *What did I expect? I have no claim on him.*

He loved Jillian—that was plain to see—and she had been foolish for imagining anything different. Nothing more than a great big fool.

She turned away from the two and found Wilky engaged in a whispered conversation with the Witch by the fireplace. She twisted again to find Kalhona asleep on the straw bedding. Standing by herself, she felt utterly and completely alone. The feeling was not unusual, but this time it felt worse, heavier and more complete than before. Needing to escape, she trudged outside, settled on one of the rockers, and moved in a steady rhythm.

How did I get myself caught in this web?

In Eden, she'd lived a clean, simple life. She'd had Wilky and, to a lesser extent, Piers to worry about, and that was enough. She had no desire to owe anyone, to need anyone, or to have people in her debt. Now, everything had changed. Wilky refused the cure, a war was brewing, and Ghost Riders seemed to notice him.

How can I keep Wilky and Eamon safe when I don't even know the dangers?

She barely realized that keeping Eamon safe had somehow slipped into her thoughts, but it seemed as natural as her desire to shield Wilky from harm.

To forget about all the dangers she imagined and those she could not, she composed mental lists of all the people she needed to pay back: the High Priest, Uncle Aibel, the Viper, Fintan, and Cormac all stood prominently on her payback list. It felt good to stew on those she'd seek revenge on, imagining a just punishment for each. Yet the feeling was fleeting.

She sighed and glanced at the moon. "What other tricks do you have for me?"

The door opened and the Witch strolled out and settled into the rocker next to her. "There's nothing to fear about the moon, child."

"You sound like my older brother. He told me the same thing a few days ago. I don't think he was right. We've been thrown into this storm ever since the last full moon. It has been one trial after another."

"What color is the moonlight?"

"It's silvery. Not quite white, but somewhere between white and gray."

"That's right. It's neither white nor black. It's neither good nor bad. The full moon amplifies what already exists. That's why witches use the full moon to converse with those spirits who are the hardest to reach. Where there is good, the moon makes it better, and where there is wickedness, it makes it worse."

The Witch threw Aaliss a pensive stare. "When you fled from Eden, the wickedness was already there. You escaped and that was the good."

"What do you know of Eden?" A jolt ripped through Aaliss's body. As angry as she was with the High Priest and her uncle, she still called Eden home. Piers lived there, and no good would come if the Soulless knew of Eden's existence. "What has Wilky told you?"

"He just confirmed what I long suspected. I've dealt with a veiled stranger in the past, who I knew lived too many revolutions for this world. The veiled one tried to hide his face from my eyes, but the wool could not conceal his aura from my Sight." The Witch shuddered as if the memory of this veiled person had shaken her. "Don't worry. I will keep the secret."

A veiled one?

The Priests prohibited all contact with the Soulless. A few days ago, she would've dismissed the notion of a veiled one from Eden as a fable, but now all she could do was nod and accept it as possible. "I'm surprised Wilky talks with you so much. He usually finds it hard to communicate with words."

The Witch rocked steadily, the chair creaking rhythmically. "We see the world differently from normal people. The Sight lets me perceive things ordinary people can only glimpse in the shadows or during twilight. He too sees things differently from others. Not the same way as I do, but different from those around him. The difference binds us and helps me understand him in a way few could."

Aaliss exhaled in a long sigh. Sometimes she felt as if she spent her whole life trying to understand Wilky, and the Witch had made more progress in two nights than she had in thirteen years.

The Witch spoke in a soothing tone. "He loves you dearly, and understands all you've sacrificed for him."

Aaliss curled her hands into fists. She needed someone to confide with and her instinct told her to trust the Witch. "Wilky says a war's coming. I don't want him thrown in the middle of it, but how can I protect him against this war when I don't even know the dangers?"

The Witch chuckled, but not in an unkind manner. "The way I see it, he's been protecting you."

What is she talking about?

Clearly she had been protecting him all along. That was her role, her responsibility ever since the fire. Still, she knew truth rattled in the old woman's words, but she dismissed it without thinking more about it. It would mean the world had truly turned upside down, and that could not be.

"I like things clean and now everything is messy," she said. "I can't rely on other people. They disappoint you in the end, and now I'm in the middle of this mess and Wilky's so stubborn. He won't leave it alone! This is madness!"

"Oh, dear, you have to choose. There's nothing else you can do, child. Fate has already written that tune. Your life is out here now, among these people. Your future is woven with theirs. Either you help Eamon and the others, or you ally with the invaders coming from the north. Those are the only two alternatives. No one is an island by herself. Believe me!" The Witch rocked faster. "Besides, the war is the least of your concerns. You have time before that begins."

"What do you mean?"

The Witch stopped rocking and stared at her. "You will be tested when you return to the Stronghold. Eamon will not be welcomed by everyone."

"Great," Aaliss muttered.

The Witch grinned. "You are given no more than you can overcome. Besides, when you're in love, everything gets messy."

"What do you mean, old woman? I'm not in love. I've just met him." She shot the Witch her best nasty look, her eyes narrow slits, her face suddenly hot.

"Time doesn't move in a straight line. You know enough to understand what's in his heart." The Witch rose with a groan. "You can deny it all you want to me, but don't fool yourself. Even without the Sight I can tell the signs. I was in love once myself, long before I became a witch. He was a baker."

For a second the Witch's eyes shone with youth, and Aaliss imagined what she'd looked like when she was young and beautiful, and thought she would have been breathtaking.

"What happened to him?" asked Aaliss.

"Taken too early like everyone else but us witches. It's a horrible thing to watch someone die and know there's nothing you can do to save them."

The Witch continued, a sheen drifting in front of her eyes. "He died so long ago I can't remember his face, but the smell of freshly baked bread always brings back memories. Mostly good."

"What difference would it make anyway?" Aaliss folded her shoulders and lowered her chin against her chest. "He's already chosen. I can tell the way he looks at Jillian that he loves her."

The Witch chuckled. "There are all types of love, dear."

She grabbed the Witch's hand before she could leave. "Ghost Riders saved Wilky at Santra's cabin. What do you know of them?"

The Witch leaned against the rocking chair. "You can see them, child?"

She nodded. "The chill always comes first, but then I can see them. I can't explain it, but it seems like they've taken an interest in Wilky. Are they good or bad?"

"Neither." The Witch shook her head. "Happenings here, in this realm, affect life in their world. Whether you wish to believe it or not, Wilky is at the center of events. I had hoped they wouldn't notice him, not yet anyway. Whatever you do, you cannot let them take him. Time moves differently in their realm. Wilky might not come back until it's too late, if he returns to us at all."

The Witch turned and left the porch, her back bent, her steps slower than they had been just a few moments ago.

The bulldog joined Aaliss and plopped his large belly on her boots, looking up eager for affection. She obliged by running her fingers against his head, and within seconds he fell asleep and began snoring.

A rustling in a small bush a few paces away woke the dog with a start. He barked and bolted toward the noise to investigate, moving faster than Aaliss would have thought possible for his short fat body.

Aaliss darted after him and drew her sword. "What's wrong, dog?"

The dog stopped a few feet from the bush and started snarling and growling.

Aaliss peered into the thicket and saw two amber eyes staring back at her, but discovered, the animal turned and scooted away. Aaliss thought she saw the wide fluffy tail of a firefox.

Could it be the same animal from earlier in the day?

As the creature bounded off, the bulldog ceased barking and licked his own nose with his tongue.

Great, now I owe the dog.

The firefox howled.

She shuddered and couldn't shake the feeling that she should have killed that firefox.

CHAPTER 41
P'MINA

Upon her return to the village, P'mina went directly to the Tribal Mother's living space, which her people simply called *Home*. It was the largest living space in the tribe — over thirty people fit comfortably inside. The large fabric roof was the color of summer grass. All members of the tribe were permitted entrance into Home no matter when they called, although few arrived this late.

P'mina shifted her weight back and forth as she waited outside the Tribal Mother's hut, her palms sweating and her stomach fluttering.

Two guards, one man and one woman, armed with steel-tipped spears, stood on both sides of the entrance. Both wore gray roughspun woolen cloaks over their emerald tunics and brown pants — the uniform of Protectors.

"Is the Tribal Mother alone?" P'mina asked.

The female Protector frowned. "Is she ever alone? The Vestals hover near her always. Three are with her now, buzzing around like flies. I'm sure the remaining three will show up sooner or later."

P'mina's stomach lurched. She adored the Tribal Mother — the smell of wildflowers followed her like a train on a long dress — but the Vestals caused acid to bubble in her stomach. They helped the Tribal Mother govern, and P'mina felt no fondness for them—they talked with their noses in the air and had unshakeable opinions on every subject.

She wished she could see the Tribal Mother alone.

A Vestal poked her head through the golden flap of fabric that operated as a door and waved for P'mina to enter with a short, quick arm motion. She looked annoyed at being bothered so late.

As P'mina entered the chamber, the thick scent of cinnamon and lilacs made her head swim. A round firepit made from river stones sat in the middle of the hut. A pot filled with incense swung over a small fire, and smoke swirled above the flames, forming a fragrant cloud that hovered toward the ceiling.

The Tribal Mother and three Vestals sat in twine hammock chairs suspended from great oak beams near the firepit. The Tribal Mother swung in the middle; her long, braided blonde hair fell to the left side of her face. Once, when asked to describe her by a visiting entertainer, P'mina just uttered the word, "More." Beautiful, she had wide shoulders and womanly curves, and a tattoo of a vine crown with red roses circled her forehead. Only the Tribal Mother could have that tattoo.

"Come closer, P'mina." The Tribal Mother smiled. "We were worried about you and your sister. Has Kalhona returned with you?"

P'mina looked toward her feet. *Kalhona's injury is my fault. If I hadn't run off, she'd be painting the center of the Banner for the Renewal Feast. She'll never forgive me.* "No, Mother. Kalhona hurt her hand and has gone to see a healer."

The Tribal Mother frowned. "This is very bad news indeed. I was saving the center of the Banner for her. Now I will have to give the honor to a less deserving Artist. Is this the news you have brought me?"

"No, Mother. The news is worse still." P'mina paused. Running away before the Renewal Feast was a serious crime. Once she warned them of the upcoming attack, they'd know her offense. Still, she had no choice. She had to think of others before herself. "Invaders from the north intend to attack us. They're marching toward us."

One of the Vestals, known as V'ronica, leaned forward. She was the Tribal Mother's younger sister and P'mina liked her least of all. She had never paid Kalhona for the tattoos she did for her, and scarcely said a kind word to anyone. She smirked at P'mina as if she accused her of lying without speaking the accusation. "How do you know this?"

P'mina's face reddened and she confessed in one quick burst, "I ran away. I didn't want to be swapped with the girls from the Orion Tribe. I know I was wrong, but it's unfair." Tears formed on the edges of her eyes, but she would not let them drop. Instead, she balled her hands into fists and clenched her jaw as she described the red witch that poisoned her, and her subsequent rescue. Finally, she said, "The one called Wilky warned us of the attack."

"How could he know? We've had no word from our scouts," said V'ronica. "Did this stranger see these invaders? How many are there?"

P'mina shook her head. "He didn't actually see them. They came to him in a vision. He would not say how many, but he did say they stretched as far as the eye can see. I know he spoke truth."

"You want us to believe such a crazy tale?" V'ronica quipped. "All this nonsense is to cover up your own treachery. Running away when you have a duty! It is an honor to swap with the Orion girls!" V'ronica's shrill voice became higher pitched until it could only be described as a shriek. "I knew you were no good! Did I not warn you, sister?" The Vestal turned toward the Tribal Mother. "She attempted to shame the entire tribe, and now she covers it up with lies." V'ronica pointed at P'mina. "She is a *liar!*"

The incense clouded P'mina's thoughts, and her head spun in circles. "It's all true. They're coming. We must band together with the Butcher Tribe to defeat them. Please believe me!" P'mina's eyes skittered amongst the Tribal Mother and the three Vestals. Her skin turned clammy and bile rose in her throat.

The incense made her thoughts foggy, hazy, jumbled.

"Join with the Butcher Tribe!" screeched V'ronica. "They're barbarians who want to steal our lands. How can we join with them?"

A second vestal started to circle P'mina. "We should punish her! Tie her to the Holding Tree. Let her stay the night alone. In the morning she will tell us true."

"No, you must believe me! It is all true." P'mina's face flushed with anger. She wished the others were here.

The Tribal Mother ignored the Vestals, leaned forward and beckoned for P'mina to approach with a wave of her hand. "Come here, child."

P'mina took halting steps until she stood in front of the Tribal Mother, who cupped her face in her soft hands. "Is this story true? Nothing good will come from falsehoods."

"I speak true."

The Tribal Mother sighed. "I believe her. Every word she's spoken is pure."

"We can't trust the Butchers," V'ronica snorted. "They're a warring people who're looking for an excuse to attack us. We'd be better off on our own. I think—"

The Tribal Mother stopped her with a glance. "I remember Dermot. He made the peace with us and that peace has lasted. I could make a treaty with him."

For the first time, P'mina wondered how many harvests the Tribal Mother had lived. The Red Death would overcome her soon, and that reminded her of the cure.

"There's more!" she added hastily. "I almost forgot. The brother and sister have discovered a cure to the Red Death. I helped the boy make it—the one who had the vision of the invaders. There's just enough for you and Dermot to take. I've brought it with me." She removed a leather traveling skin from her satchel, her hand trembling.

"What type of evil witchcraft is this?" asked the last Vestal, who stood shoulder-to-shoulder with the other two Vestals. "There's no cure for the Red Death! It's always been and always will be. We can't trust this daughter of the witch."

"I bet Kalhona is with a witch right now. What healer *did* she see?" charged V'ronica.

The Vestals started circling P'mina again, coming closer with each revolution.

"Only a witch would make a potion like this. We should burn it," cried V'ronica.

"We should cast her out!"

"She's no good just like her mother!"

The accusations buffeted against P'mina like an incoming tide against a rock. Her head ached, and her body felt numb.

"My mother has nothing to do with this!" She stomped her foot.

The Tribal Mother took the skin from P'mina's shaking hand. "Quiet!"

The Vestals obeyed, but they continued circling and looked like hungry wolves about to attack.

"You forget the stories of old, when hair turned gray. The time before tribes." The Tribal Mother looked suspiciously at the skin. "Was dark magic used when you made the potion?"

"No, it's simple enough. I would drink it if we had enough. Please, trust me! It will bind the two tribes together, so we can fight off the invaders." The incense made P'mina's legs weak, and she swayed backward.

The Vestals stared hard at her, six eyes unblinking, filled with hate and suspicion and malice.

The Tribal Mother tipped back the skin and swallowed the drink whole.

The world slowed. The leather pouch tumbled to the ground. The Tribal Mother's face turned red, her eyes closed, and she collapsed backward, unconscious.

"It can't be," screamed P'mina.

The Vestals shrieked.

P'mina stomped her foot angrily. "It can't be!"

"She's a traitor!" Spit flew from V'ronica's mouth. "Guards!"

P'mina saw red and ran at V'ronica. She wanted to strangle the nasty Vestal, but V'ronica darted behind one of the hammock chairs and P'mina ran past her. By the time she turned, the guards had bolted into the hut.

V'ronica pointed at her. "Grab her! She's poisoned our Mother."

"I did no such thing!" P'mina darted at V'ronica, hands outstretched.

The female guard moved quickly and swung her spear into P'mina's legs.

P'mina crashed to the ground, but she never took her eyes away from V'ronica. She tried to lunge at her, but the male guard grabbed her arm. P'mina bit his hand and drew blood. He screeched and she spun out of his grasp.

She had a clear shot at V'ronica, and a smile crept across her face. Revenge would be hers. She reached for V'ronica's neck, but before she could grab her, the female guard bashed the butt of her spear into P'mina's forehead.

P'mina's legs turned to water.

She thought she heard V'ronica call her a witch before blackness took her.

CHAPTER 42
MAEVE

Maeve's legs hurt from all the searching she did around the Stronghold for her sister. She had not seen Cattie for two days now. No one had seen her at the Feasting Hall, the Naming Tree, the Courtyard, or anywhere else she might have gone. The Master of the Nursery said she had gone to the Outpost, yet none of her stuff was missing. Why would she go to the Outpost of all places, and why leave all her possessions behind? It made no sense.

After two days of searching, Maeve had the dark feeling that something bad had happened to her sister.

She enlisted help from her friend Eric, but he also failed to uncover any trace of Cattie. None of the horses at the Stables were unaccounted for. She could have gotten a ride with one of the traders headed in a wagon to the Outpost, but that sounded farfetched. It was as if she had vanished.

Maeve and Eric sat on Maeve's bed in the room she shared with her sister in the female residence hall.

Eric leaned his broad shoulders against the wooden headboard, concern scribbled on his handsome face. He served as a member of the King's Guard, had thick arms and a broad chest. He wore a leather shirt and pants and a full-length leather cloak that swept over the longsword sheathed at his hip.

Maeve felt safe when she was with him. Soon they would be coupled—once she saved enough for a dress, made a bracelet, and summoned the courage to tell Cattie that her younger sister would be coupled before her.

"Maybe she did head north to the Outpost," he said. "She's certainly not in the Stronghold. We'd have found her."

"Cattie in the Outpost?" Maeve shook her head. "I can't imagine it, and how would she get there? She has no money saved for passage."

"She could have *borrowed* the money from you. She's done it before."

Cattie had never shown any interest in the Outpost, but Maeve couldn't absolutely dismiss the idea as impossible. Besides, the alternative frightened her—Cattie had messed with Fintan, and it had turned out poorly.

She grabbed onto the last shred of hope. "Okay, turn around. I don't want you to see my hiding spot."

"*Seriously?* We'll be coupled soon."

"A woman is entitled to her secrets."

Eric grinned and turned.

Maeve found the small mouse hole in the plaster in the corner of the room that operated s her hiding place, squeezed her hand in and took out her leather pouch. When she lifted it, she knew something was wrong. It weighed far too little.

She brought the pouch to the bed and opened the drawstring. Instead of the few coins she had saved, she found a folded piece of paper. Hand trembling, she removed it and read it out loud, her voice shaky.

> *Dear Sister,*
>
> *I'm meeting prince Fintan by the Stables, and borrowed your money so I could buy a new dress. If you're reading this note, then something must have gone wrong.*
>
> *I overheard Fintan and Cormac planning to poison the King. They sent someone named Scotty to fetch the red berries. That's all I know.*

I'm sorry I wasn't a better sister. I liked to make you cry, but I was jealous because you're special and I'm not.

Love,

Cattie

When she finished reading the note, Eric crossed his arms against his chest. "What haven't you been telling me?"

Maeve explained all she knew about Cattie's plans, which wasn't much more than her sister had written in the note. Her voice broke when she finished. "Fintan must have k-killed her after they met by the Stables. We have to find Dermot and demand justice."

She shifted her weight to stand, and Eric grabbed her arm. "Hold on a moment. We have no proof against the prince except this note. That won't be good enough. The Circle of Destiny has been drawn. Eamon's not here to oppose Fintan, and even if he does, Fintan is likely to be our next king. We can't just bring this note to Dermot and accuse the prince without more."

Maeve shook off Eric's hand. She would not let Fintan get away with this, and Dermot was the only one who could bring him to justice. Still, she couldn't deny the truth of his words either.

Then an idea formed in the back of her mind. "What about this Scotty? Do you know him?"

Eric nodded. "Scotty the Snake. He's a real nasty one. Cormac sent him north. He's supposed to return today."

"That's our proof. Fintan must have sent him to fetch the red berries. If we catch him when he comes back—"

"We can grab him! He'll have the berries in his saddlebag. That plus Cattie's disappearance might be enough."

Maeve folded the note and put it back into her pouch. "It *will* be enough. It has to be."

CHAPTER 43
EAMON

The hard ride from the Witch's cabin to the Stronghold left Eamon's back and legs stiff, but the adrenaline pulsing through his body chased away those aches. Each passing mile brought him closer to giving Dermot the cure, closer to saving his brother's life. He entered the Stronghold at a gallop and barely slowed his spent horse as he whipped through the winding streets. When he reached the Residence Hall, he jumped from the horse and sped up the staircase, taking two steps at a time.

He banged against Dermot's door with three heavy blows.

"Enter," Dermot called from within.

He stormed into the room.

Dermot, who stood by the windows gazing at the Stronghold, turned and grinned at him. "I was worried I would never see you again. I'm happy you've returned before I move on. I see you've made new friends." He nodded toward Aaliss and Wilky, who'd just entered the room. "I imagine they're Fintan's prisoners you freed from the Basement? I should be angry with you, but I see things differently now." He pointed to his red-specked eyes.

Eamon's heart plummeted. He knew what he would find when he

saw Dermot, but knowing something and facing it were two different things. He threw his arms around his brother, slapping him hard on the back. "All is not lost. This is Aaliss and Wilky. I've fought alongside them. We've saved each other's lives."

Dermot faced the siblings. "Then I'm in your debt. I pardon you from any crimes my brother, Fintan, may have levied against you, but you would be wise not to remain when he becomes king. He's unlikely to be as forgiving as I am."

"You don't have to die! Wilky has discovered the cure to the Red Death and we've made a potion for you." Eamon spit on the ground and removed the small leather skin from the folds of his cloak, holding it steady in his hand.

Dermot looked at the leather pouch as if it were filled with rotten meat. "What type of foolishness is this?"

"No foolishness, Brother. We've made the cure. All you have to do is drink it." The strength in his words faded as he recognized the hard expression in his brother's eyes.

Dermot placed his hand on Eamon's shoulder and softened his tone. "I know you wish it to be so, but this is not the way of things. My life has come to an end. It's Fintan's time to rule, and your place is to serve him. Let's not talk about cures or dark magic. We're about to go to war with the Painted Ones. Fintan is convinced it's the right thing to do. We could use your wise counsel."

Eamon's eyes grew wide. "No, we can't! We're facing northern invaders. We need to band together with the Painted Ones before it's too late."

"Northern invaders?" Dermot squinted. "Tell me about these *invaders.*"

"Wilky saw a vision. They're coming from the Freeroad. They number many, but if we combine to stop them, we might have a chance. Wilky created two cures, one for you and the other one for the Tribal Mother. They will bind us together to fight our common enemy. This is our way forward." Eamon pushed the cure closer to his brother.

Dermot glanced out the windows, and after a short pause he said,

"So you haven't seen this *war band* with your own eyes? You take the word of this boy who saw a *vision*."

"We fought six of them along the ancient road. They carry the flag of a bloody wolf. They were real enough, Brother. I killed one myself."

When Dermot turned, he looked sad, long lines dripping from the corners of his mouth. "I believe you, but there's nothing I can do now. We must hope this vision doesn't come to pass. Fintan will not change his mind. We are strong. Our swords and shields will hold against these *invaders*."

Wilky spoke softly, but everyone heard him. "No. It will be too late."

Dermot regarded him sourly. "How could you know? I don't believe in *visions*." The veins in Dermot's neck pulsed. "I thank you for helping Eamon, but you should be leaving now."

Aaliss stepped between Dermot and Wilky. "My brother never lies. He has a way of knowing things. The cure is true. You don't have to die. You can lead your people through this. They need you."

Dermot snorted. "No one but witches survive the Red Death. And to what end? I would grow old while I watch those I love perish around me. No! My place is in the stars with the rest of our ancestors, where I can look down on the tribe. I'll guide them from above. I want no more talk of this foolishness." He turned back to the windows.

Eamon grabbed his arm, but Dermot yanked free with a violent twist. Eamon searched for the right words, but he could think of none that might change his stubborn brother's mind. Despair had crept into his body, and his spirit was almost broken when a series of loud raps pounded against the door.

The door opened before they could answer. Maeve and Eric stood in the doorway. Dark circles ringed Maeve's eyes. "I'm sorry, my King, for interrupting, but I have urgent business."

Dermot answered tersely. "What's so urgent that you barge into my private residence?"

"We've found treachery and murder. Prince Fintan and Cormac murdered my sister. They planned on poisoning you. When she discovered their plan, they murdered her to keep her quiet."

Dermot's eyes narrowed as he rose up taller, straightened his back and lifted his head high. "These are very serious allegations. Do you have proof?"

Eric stepped forward. "Yes, my King. We have this note from Maeve's sister."

Dermot took the paper from him and read it. "This isn't enough. I need more than some poorly scribbled note."

"Cattie has been missing for over two days, and we grabbed Scotty the Snake as he rode into the Stronghold," said Maeve. "He had the red berries in his saddlebag."

Dermot spoke but there was no strength or conviction in his voice. "He could have acted on his own."

"The Snake confessed and told us that Fintan and Cormac ordered him to bring back the berries for you." Maeve fought back tears, but her eyes burned hot. "I urge justice before the Circle of Destiny closes!"

Dermot ran his hands through his hair and retrieved the Sword of Power from his bed. He moved slowly and looked old. "*Dermot the Just* they call me." He sighed. "Sometimes I believe it was a curse to become king. I hope it never becomes your burden, Brother. Gather the Masters. I will deliver justice one last time. We'll hear all the evidence and decide the truth of the matter in one hour by the Naming Tree."

Eamon felt the wind knocked out of him. Had Fintan conspired to murder Dermot? It was possible. Fintan wanted to rule, but did he want it so much that he'd kill Dermot?

Eamon wished it was not so, but Maeve and Eric looked certain. And he did see Fintan and Cormac conspiring together when he helped Aaliss and Wilky escape.

Why else would they be out so late?

CHAPTER 44
AALISS

A aliss stood close behind Eamon under the protection of the Naming Tree's wide branches.

Wilky stood beside her.

She studied the Courtyard, where the Circle of Masters was formed. Twelve made the Circle, eleven men and one woman. Armed members of the King's Guard ringed the Masters.

Eamon whispered, "Dermot's picked the members of the Guard himself. They're the older ones, who are less likely to favor Fintan or Cormac."

He must suspect that Fintan is guilty.

Fintan and Cormac sat cross-legged in the center of the Circle as the accused. Fintan twisted a long strand of grass in his hand and looked nonplussed.

Maeve and Eric joined them only a few feet to their left.

Aaliss pointed to a flickering torch and a long wooden spear that were planted in the grass next to Dermot. "What are those?"

"The Tools of Justice," said Eamon. "If Dermot suspects someone of lying, he can light the end of the spear and burn the truth from the witness. He rarely uses them, but just having them ready is usually enough to get the truth."

Eamon excused himself and moved to stand beside Dermot along the Circle's edge.

Aaliss thought of Eden's High Court, with the High Priest as judge and six Priests as jury.

Advisors help both sides, but is there any justice in it? If Wilky and I stood before the High Court, what chance would we have?

She'd rather take her chances here with Dermot. Although crude, she thought this Circle simpler and closer to justice and truth than the High Court in Eden.

Dermot started the proceedings. "May the herd forever be strong!"

The Masters repeated the prayer.

Dermot continued. "The accusers will recite the crimes."

"Yes, my King." Maeve faced Fintan and stared fearlessly at him. "I accuse Prince Fintan and Cormac of murdering my sister, Cattie. They also ordered a Horseman named Scotty the Snake to retrieve the red berries, so they could poison our rightful king."

Aaliss detected no deceit in her voice, and from the expressions on the Masters' faces, they believed her.

Fintan chuckled. "These accusations are ridiculous. It's some ill-conceived plot by my brother, Eamon, to take over the Tribe. If he believes he's worthy, he should throw his sword into the Circle of Destiny. We can battle in combat the way it is written. I'm innocent of these baseless charges. We should be planning our attack against the Painted Ones, not wasting our time with fairytales!"

A few Masters turned their gaze toward Eamon, who remained silent in the face of the accusation.

If he accused me like that, I'd kill him before he could say another word!

Aaliss wanted to defend Eamon, but caution held her tongue. Still, she realized that it was an effective argument, adding an element of doubt, creating a motive for false charges where none would have existed.

Dermot addressed Maeve. "What proof do you have of your accusations?"

"We have this note written by my sister, which explains everything. Cattie has gone missing, and I'm sure she's dead. We grabbed Scotty when he entered the Stronghold earlier today and he had these." Tears brimmed in her eyes as she pulled out a handful of red berries from a leather saddlebag.

One of the masters gasped.

Maeve pointed at Fintan. "He's a murderer!"

"Why would I murder this girl?" interrupted Fintan. "I don't even know this *Cattie*."

"Because she overheard you and Cormac plotting to kill the King the night of the full moon! She tried to use that information to force you to couple with her, but she knew too much to live. You wanted her dead, as if she didn't matter! As if you could just throw her away!"

"If only she were here to accuse me herself! I deny all of it." Fintan laughed. "This is a scheme to put *Eamon the Handsome* in charge of our tribe. Without a witness, I cannot be judged guilty. This is all a waste of time."

Fintan sounded arrogant, and Cormac kept silent with a confident smile plastered on his face.

Aaliss knew fear from her time in the Zone. She had smelled it, tasted it, even welcomed its ice-cold embrace. No fear oozed from these two, and that meant trouble.

Eric spoke for the first time. "Scotty the Snake is in the Basement. He's a witness to your crimes."

"Bring him here then, and let's see what he has to say." Fintan shared a confident look with Cormac, which bordered on smug.

Dermot ordered two of the King's Guard to fetch Scotty from the Basement.

When the two Guards returned alone, the taller of the two was red-faced. "My King, Scotty is dead. He hanged himself in the Basement."

"They killed him!" accused Eric.

Fintan ripped a clump of glass from the ground. "And what other crimes are you going to accuse me of without evidence? I was nowhere near the Basement. There are many witnesses to my whereabouts. I don't know why Scotty killed himself. Maybe he killed your sister too. It could have been a lover's quarrel, but there's no evidence that links me to this girl. Perhaps she tired of her work in the Nursery and ended her own life? We have more important things to do than waste our time on false accusations."

Eamon thought back to the morning after the Counsel meeting and the full moon. He remembered the brown eyes that followed Fintan into the Feasting Hall. Those eyes belonged to Cattie, and she *did* work in the Nursery.

"How do you know she worked in the Nursery, Brother?" Eamon's words lingered in the air.

Fintan looked nervous for the first time, his eyes jittery as they danced around the Circle. "What are you talking about? Who said anything about the Nursery?"

"You just said she might have tired of her life in the Nursery. If you do not know this girl, then how did you know she worked in the Nursery?"

"You see how this is Eamon's plan." Fintan waved his arm toward him. "I don't know anything about this girl. I had just guessed."

A murmur rose among the Masters.

Dermot grabbed the Spear of Justice and everyone grew quiet. He held the tip to the fire until it blazed bright orange. "And you, Cormac... what do you have to say for yourself?"

Cormac looked as if he had woken from a trance, his eyes locking on the tip of the spear, his face covered with sweat. "I'm innocent just like Fintan says."

Dermot stepped toward him, bringing the glowing point of the spear close to his face. "Did Fintan know this girl before she died? Tell me the truth of the matter."

Cormac focused on the point of the spear as if frozen in place.

Eamon nodded. *He'll break if Dermot uses the spear.*

Cormac's voice shook, and sweat rolled down his face in rivers. "I've never met... her before."

Dermot brought the tip of the spear inches from Cormac's face, close to his eyes. "I'll give you one last chance to speak the truth. I will be very harsh if you lie to me."

Cormac glanced at Fintan, who shook his head slightly. He returned his gaze to the glowing point of the spear and locked onto it. "We're... innocent of these... crimes."

Dermot lifted the spear over his head and thrust it down sharply. The point dug into the ground an inch before Cormac. "Without Scotty there are no witnesses against my brother. I have no choice but to judge him innocent. Let this settle the matter. May the herd forever be strong! Now go."

The Circle broke. The Masters left first, their steps heavy and grave.

Fintan and Cormac followed, but not before Fintan shot a murderous look at Eamon.

Eric consoled Maeve, who wept in his arms.

"You know he's guilty of these crimes!" Eamon growled at Dermot.

"Guilt could not have been written more plainly across their faces," Aaliss added.

"What would you have me do?" Dermot leaned against the spear. "I cannot judge him guilty without a witness. I cannot throw our laws away now! Let the matter end for the good of the tribe."

Eamon leaned close to him. "What of the cure, Brother? Will you take it?"

"I will not." Dermot looked away. "You take it."

"You leave me with no choice. Tomorrow, I throw my sword into the Circle of Destiny to fight Fintan."

Dermot flinched as if he had been struck. "You promised me you would not face him! You swore it!"

"He just accused me of being a liar. I can't let that stand. Everyone will think I am a coward. Better to die in combat than live as a coward." Eamon's face flushed with heat. "You leave me no choice."

Dermot hunched his broad shoulders and stared hard at his younger brother. "Give me the skin."

Eamon handed him the leather pouch.

Dermot stared at the potion long and hard before lifting it to his lips and tipping it back.

CHAPTER 45
AALISS

Aaliss watched Eamon hover nearby. He refused to take his eyes off of Dermot for more than a few moments, except to occasionally glance at Gemma and sigh.

"He looks pale. Is that what's supposed to happen?" Eamon asked Wilky for the third time.

After Dermot drank the cure he became dizzy and complained of a splitting headache. They helped him to his room, where he fell asleep.

Wilky shrugged.

"The Circle of Destiny closes tomorrow by midday. Will his eyes clear by then?"

Wilky shrugged again.

Eamon groaned and waved his arms in the air, looking a little like a large bird that was having a problem taking flight. "Against long odds, we finally succeeded, made him the cure, forced him to drink it, and now this. I don't think I can take much more."

Aaliss took his hands to distract him before his head exploded, and led him toward the windows. "So tell me about this Circle of Destiny. How does it work?"

"Once a king suffers the red eyes, he draws the Circle in the

Courtyard from calf's blood. He sends news of the Circle throughout the kingdom. Three days later, the Circle closes. Any eligible heir can throw his or her sword into the Circle. Whoever does, fights to the death. The winner rules."

She frowned. "So the fastest sword rules the tribe?"

"It's the way we have always done it. Past rulers in the heavens influence events and help the most suitable person become the next king. Often only one sword stands in the Circle, so no combat is needed." He brushed hair off his face. "How does your tribe select a ruler?"

In Eden the President is elected every four years by general election. No term limits existed so Aaliss's uncle had served for the last twenty years. Even so, the real power lay with the High Priest, who was appointed for life and must be a Blood Relation. When she boiled it down, it didn't seem any better than the Circle of Destiny.

Thinking it best to leave out the details, she simply replied, "We have a similar process."

A sly smile swept across her face. "Is it only those with royal blood who can toss their sword into the Circle. Can anyone do it?"

Eamon grinned. "No, Aaliss, you cannot throw your sword into the Circle and fight Fintan."

"I was just checking." She slapped her palm against the stone wall. "I'd love the chance to pay him back."

"Don't underestimate Fin. He's been practicing his whole life for this contest. His sword is quick and his shield strong." He averted his eyes and gazed out the window, a defeated look darkening his face.

She guessed at his thoughts and frowned.

Self-doubt in a fight will kill him. He has to believe in himself.

She claimed both of his hands. "You fight well. I've seen it. You are quick and strong."

"Not as quick as you. I would have died if you hadn't saved me with the tribeless outlaws. And then Kalhona's poison dart saved me again."

She dropped his hands. With the fight scheduled for tomorrow, she had no time to coddle him. "No, you're not as quick as me, but if we can find someplace to train, I can teach you how to move faster. With a few changes to your footwork, you'd give me a run for it." Her smile broadened. "Are we going to wait here and hope Dermot wakes, or increase your chances with Fintan just in case? By the time I'm done with you, Fintan won't stand a chance."

He gazed at Dermot with an uncertain look in his eyes, and then turned to his sister.

"Go with her," said Gemma. "Dermot would want that. Wilky and I will stay with him. We'll let you know when he wakes."

CHAPTER 46
P'MINA

P'mina stood on the Ancient Road, the sky dark, the moon dim.

How did I get here?

The last thing she remembered was the Tribal Mother's reaction to the cure.

Did they banish me?

At least she had her spear. She glanced down both sides of the road, uncertain which direction to travel. Her breath froze in her throat.

A red wolf stalked toward her. Red wolves were smaller than their brothers but more vicious, and way smarter. Add a red wolf into a regular pack and it transformed them into an efficient killing machine.

The wolf howled and P'mina turned and ran. She raced recklessly forward, but a pack of wolves charged her from that direction. Luckily, she spotted the turn-off from the road that led to Santra's cabin and barreled along the path.

If I can make it to the cabin, I can lock them out!

She ran as fast as she had ever run before, the wolves gaining on her with each step. She could almost feel their teeth bite into her flesh.

She turned around a bend and found the cabin. A small fire burned in front of it, and a cloaked figure stood by the door.

It can't be Santra. She's dead.

Her heart froze. She didn't want to face the witch again, but with the wolves closing in on her she had no choice. She raced until she was four paces away, lifted her spear, and aimed it for the woman's chest.

Three paces and the woman lowered her hood.

Two paces and P'mina realized it wasn't Santra at all, but her sister.

One pace and Kalhona lifted her right hand to block her spear.

P'mina tried to stop but couldn't halt her momentum, and the steel tip ripped through Kalhona's hand and plunged into her chest.

P'mina cried "No!" and the world spun.

She came out of her haze and found herself chained to the Holding Tree like a dog. A tall wooden fence circled the ghost tree to keep out large predators. A howl drifted across the darkness and she shuddered. The fence bent inward as something large threw its weight against the wood. It held, but P'mina scooted backward toward the trunk of the tree. She had no place to run.

Another howl and this time a red wolf jumped over the fence and landed gracefully on the other side, not more than a dozen paces from her.

Her heart raced. She shouted for help, but no one came to the Holding Tree at night. That was part of the punishment.

The wolf raced toward her, its red-tipped fur burning in the moonlight.

P'mina balled her hands into fists.

The beast opened its jaws, and its sharp teeth and red-tinted eyes gleamed.

P'mina lowered her shoulder and charged at it. If she were going to die, she'd go down fighting.

The beast leaped, and mid-pounce transformed into a witch, laughing as she passed right through P'mina's body.

P'mina bolted upright and gasped for breath. Her head ached. She lifted her hands and found them weighed down by heavy chains. She was chained to the Holding Tree, after all, but the wolf and the witch must have been bad dreams.

She yanked on the chains, to no avail, and sighed. It would be a long night.

Her imagination created all types of monsters lurking just beyond the fence. One time, the fence shook as something crashed into it. P'mina would have cried out, but her head hurt too much to shout.

Still, the larger creatures were not as bad as the flying bloodsuckers that swarmed around her whenever she stayed still. Rats also scurried back and forth all night, growing bolder whenever she nodded off. All in all, she preferred the butt of Santra's spear and the inside of her cabin—at least she'd gotten some sleep.

At daybreak, V'ronica strode stiffly toward the fence, tired bags under her eyes. "What did you do to our Mother? She cannot be woken."

P'mina pulled hard on the chain. "I gave her a cure for the Red Death. It's just a mushroom and a flower combined." She knew the ingredients. They were harmless. She had eaten the mushroom herself and used the oil from the small flowers to keep the flying bloodsuckers away.

Perhaps when they are combined they become poisonous, but Wilky was so certain. He would not lie to me.

"Let me see her," she pleaded. "Have you tried the rousing plant?"

"You don't think we've tried that already!" V'ronica sneered at her. "You're not going anywhere. The Vestals see the hand of the Dark One in this. If she fails to wake soon, we'll burn you as a sacrifice to Mother Earth. Maybe then the Dark One will loose his grip on our Mother. A life for a life." A sly smile slowly replaced V'ronica's sneer. "Unless you can wake her now, *witchborn*. Maybe then we'll just banish you."

All the years of shabby treament because of her mother bubbled up inside of her and exploded. "You can pound dirt! My mother was good. She never cursed anyone! If I could find a witch, I'd have her curse you!"

"Is it the Butcher Tribe then? Have you sold us out to them? You persuade us to form an alliance while they attack us, all because of some *northern invaders* we've never heard tell of." V'ronica folded her arms over her chest and glared at P'mina for a long while.

For a heartbeat, P'mina forgot about Kalhona, the Tribal Mother, the northern invaders, even the chains that held her. She lunged forward to scratch out V'ronica's beady black eyes, but the chains jerked her back.

V'ronica laughed. "You have a few more hours, but the next time you see me, I'll be leading a witch-burning party. You had better pray that the Mother wakes unharmed. Even that may not save you. Your time is numbered, *witchborn*." V'ronica huffed haughtily and left her alone.

Time languished slowly. P'mina closed her eyes and sleep came, but it was a troubled sleep and there was no rest in it. She dreamed of fire and laughing amber eyes and spears and V'ronica.

She had no idea how much time had past when Merina rattled the gate.

"They're building a Witch Pyre." Merina frowned. "They say you're a witch and in league with the Dark One. Some say your witch mother cursed our Tribal Mother. Others say you're a traitor and secretly in love with one of the Butchers. No one knows where you go to collect your plants. Maybe you met a Butcher during your wanderings. Either way, they mean to burn you."

"This is crazy! I'm not a witch or a traitor. You know me! I just gave the Mother a cure to the Red Death. It was to protect her, to bind the two tribes together." P'mina slumped back against the Holding Tree. "Does the Mother stir?"

"No. I knew you were up to no good when you went into the forest alone. You told me you needed dyes for Kalhona." Merina glared at her. "Why did you lie?"

P'mina groaned. "I didn't want to be swapped with the Orion girls. It's not fair, and you were so happy with the idea. I just wanted to run away and—"

"And you couldn't trust me. I thought we were friends. I would've helped, if you had trusted me." Merina frowned and puffed her lower lip out sadly.

"I'm sorry, truly." P'mina realized Merina was a true friend. "I should've trusted you, but I have nothing to do with witches or the Dark One or anything bad. I was just trying to help."

"So, are we still best friends. You won't lie to me again?"

"No more lies. We're best of friends." P'mina rattled her chains. "But not for long."

Merina lifted a shiny metal key.

"Where'd you get that?"

"One of the guards favors my sister. He left it behind in our hut."

"Left it behind or you stole it?"

"It might have fallen from his pocket." Merina smiled and tossed the key over the fence.

P'mina caught it but hesitated before she put it into the lock. "If I use this key, you could get in real trouble."

Merina shrugged. "I'll say you cast a spell on me. They might get mad, but they won't burn me."

P'mina twirled the key in her fingers, uncertain what she should do. A few days ago she would have used it without thinking, but much had happened since. She'd seen bravery and real sacrifice.

Then she heard it—a low rumble that grew increasingly louder.

"Burn the Witch! Burn the Witch!" they chanted.

"Hurry!" shouted Merina.

If she hurried she might have time to escape, but they sounded so angry she thought they'd burn Merina instead.

She dropped the key and kicked it away. "Make sure they don't bring Tania. She can't see me burn."

Merina nodded and raced away.

V'ronica held a lit torch and led a long column of Painted Ones.

"Burn the Witch! Burn the Witch!" V'ronica's onyx eyes shined brightly, her face animated by the flickering torchlight. A wicked smile creased her lips.

"Burn the Witch!"

CHAPTER 47
P'MINA

The Vestals all wore green wraps the color of summer grass, as if it were a sign of unity. Led by Veronica, they triumphantly marched P'mina to the Witch's Pyre, a ten-foot tall, cone-shaped stack of split wood. They had built a wooden cross in the center. Dry kindling surrounded the bottom of the Pyre to form the base of the cone.

P'mina moved stiffly and absently. The fight had left her.

She didn't even protest when V'ronica tied her to the wooden cross with a thick cord—first her arms and then her legs. She stood three feet above the ground, her arms stretched wide to the sides, her feet resting on a small wooden step. Although still dressed, she felt naked before the tribe.

"Burn Her! Burn Her!"

The mob chanted as men hammered out a steady beat on massive leather-skinned ceremonial drums. The chant and the drumbeat filled the ceremonial space, building upon itself, shaking the ground, rising in volume and fervor like a tide before a storm.

P'mina didn't struggle. She had spent her whole life fighting those who saw her as a *witchborn* and nothing more. She was surprised they had waited this long.

They will not see me cry. I'm stronger than tears. They did not burn my mother, so now they will burn me.

She scanned the angry crowd and studied the people.

She found Storum, who had such bad teeth she'd brought him a special mint plant to blunt the pain; and Lulia, who needed the purple berries to help her fickle stomach; and Kokopia, who needed the Mother's Assistance plant to have children. Kokopia stood next to her sister, who so desperately did not want to have any children that P'mina had given her the Sour Plant to prevent conception.

She barely recognized the faces—foreign, twisted by anger and hate and fear. The number of people she had helped stretched on, but they all chanted just the same.

Jacarto, a Protector who had always been sweet on her, waved the Painted Ones flag by the drummers and shouted, "Burn her!"

"Burn her!" they all shouted.

How can they hate me so much?

V'ronica stood tall, her head held high and her shoulders back while the other Vestals milled around her. When she stepped forward, the drumming and chanting stopped.

Her wrap fluttered around her as she spit out her venom. "We know P'mina was *witchborn,* and now we know she's in league with the Dark One. The evidence is unquestionable. We must burn her to cleanse our tribe!" She paused for a moment to let her words sink in. "She has poisoned our Mother, and concocted stories of northern invaders just to let the Butchers attack us from the south...."

The words blended together in one long stream of hatred and lies, but P'mina stopped paying attention. Fall was her favorite time of year, and the leaves on the trees had just started to turn. The maples in the distance blazed a fiery red.

Is that a bad sign?

A cool breeze ruffled her hair. She let go of her rage and felt oddly calm.

V'ronica stepped toward her, lit torch held high.

Its heat pressed against P'mina's face like a passionate embrace.

V'ronica yelled at her. "Do you have anything to say, *witch?*"

P'mina barely heard the question. She wondered who would paint this scene on the Banner — the day they burned an innocent girl.

Will they ask Kalhona to paint it, or will they burn her also?

A hushed quiet settled over the crowd as they waited to hear her last words. They wanted her to say something incriminating.

In truth, she knew it would matter not what she said. Whatever her words, they would gather around afterward, and find a way to twist it into proof she was a witch, proof they had done the right thing. For a fleeting moment, she thought to curse them and admit to the folly. That would give them something to talk about, but that was what V'ronica wanted, and she would not give that beast what she wanted.

V'ronica's eyes shined with hatred in the flickering torchlight, her hand moments away from tossing the torch onto the pyre.

She's waiting for the perfect moment to light the pyre. I wonder if she believes I am truly a witch, or if this is just a way to get the tribe to rally around her, so she can replace her sister as the next Tribal Mother. She's probably already counting the votes.

Through the eerie quiet came a horn blast carried low in the wind. Those in the back turned.

The horn grew louder as horses galloped toward them. The crowd parted and six horsemen raced toward the Witch's Pyre — four armed Protectors and two members of the Orion tribe. One Orion held their banner high above his head, depicting an archer drawing his bow. A strong-looking Orion, thick of arms and chest and chiseled jaw, rode beside the bannerman, his expression hard as he spurred his horse.

The group reined their horses within a few feet of V'ronica at the base of the Witch's Pyre.

The other Vestals parted and stepped away from their leader.

Snakes! They cower at the first sign of trouble.

V'ronica stood her ground, her thin face pinched together. "What's your business here, Orions?"

The well-muscled Orion pulled hard on the reins of his horse, which danced in a tight circle. "I bring news. A war band approaches from the north."

Someone in the crowd shouted, "P'mina speaks the truth!"

Another person called out, "She tried to warn us!"

After that, the voices blurred together as a loud, unsettled murmur built among the tribe.

"It makes no difference!" V'ronica held her torch dangerously close to the Pyre, which quieted the crowd. "She gave our Tribal Mother a witch's brew, and now we cannot wake her. We must burn her to save our Mother! She will be a sacrifice for the Earth Mother. Only they can defeat the Dark One and save our Mother from damnation. A life for a life!"

A rustling sound started from the rear of the crowd, and it parted like a rolling wave as Merina raced forward. "Wait! Our Mother wakes! She's coming. Wait!"

P'mina saw the outline of the Tribal Mother in Merina's wake, striding with long, angry strides, her braid bouncing behind her, her face skewed into an angry scowl.

"Put that torch out!" she commanded.

V'ronica looked at the torch, and back at P'mina, as if she considered tossing it on the pyre.

The Tribal Mother bellowed, "Put it out, or we'll burn you!"

V'roncia snuffed out the flames on the ground and began pleading. "But we thought she was a witch. We thought if we burned her, then the Dark One would release you."

The other Vestals melted away from V'ronica to make a clear path for the Tribal Mother.

V'ronica stood alone.

The Tribal Mother barely slowed as she approached and slapped V'ronica hard across the face, sending her skidding to the ground. "What type of craziness is this? Have you lost your mind? No one is going to be burned while I am your Mother!"

The crowd gasped.

As far as P'mina knew, no one had ever seen her strike another person.

The Tribal Mother faced the crowd, her voice loud. "P'mina has spoken true. We must prepare for war!" She hesitated for a moment. "We will teach these northern invaders what it means to face our fury!"

The crowd cheered and started chanting, "Mother! Mother!"

The drums started again, this time in a steady war beat.

The Tribal Mother turned toward P'mina and whispered, "I'm sorry, child. They didn't understand." She cut P'mina loose and held her in a tight embrace.

P'mina closed her eyes and smelled wildflowers.

For the first time since her mother left, she felt whole.

CHAPTER 48
AALISS

Aaliss studied Eamon and tried to suppress a chuckle, with little luck. They had left the Stronghold to practice at a deserted clearing along the banks of Whitewater River.

"Why are you laughing?" Eamon asked, red-faced.

"What are you wearing?"

He had donned a fine metal mail tunic. The small rings covered his arms, torso, and flowed down to his knees. He held a round shield in one hand and his longsword in the other. The shield was made from dark wood covered with boiled leather and had a metal spike jutting from the center. A jeweled sword was painted on it with blood dripping from its tip.

Eamon glanced at his shirt. "The rings protect us. We use these shirts for battle."

Aaliss stifled another chuckle. "Okay, let's see what you've got. Don't go easy on me." She playfully waved her sword.

Eamon lumbered toward her, swinging his longsword wildly: sideswipes followed chops, which followed more sideswipes, and a couple half-hearted thrusts.

Aaliss parried each without difficulty.

After a few minutes Eamon stopped, breathing heavily, sweat raining down his face.

"That was good, really," encouraged Aaliss.

It wasn't a complete lie. He had talent, and with some training would make a reasonably good swordsman. He needed to harness his skills, but that ringed shirt had to go.

"Are you required to wear that ridiculous metal shirt?"

"No requirement. It's traditional. I'm sure Fintan will wear one."

That's the best news I've heard so far.

"You've got to dump it. It makes sense in a battle where blows could come from anywhere, but in single combat it will only slow you down. You'll have the advantage just by shedding it."

Eamon reluctantly removed the ring shirt, and it made a loud thump as it hit the ground.

"Okay, we're making progress. Now toss me your sword."

Aaliss snatched the longsword by the hilt and swiped a few strokes with it. "It's not bad, but mine is much better. It's lighter, more aerodynamic, and the steel is stronger and sharper. It'll cut those metal rings into shreds. It's shorter, but you'll be quicker and more effective with it."

She tossed her short sword to Eamon.

He sliced it through the air with a flurry. "It's so light. I can't imagine it's stronger than mine."

Aaliss grinned. "Give it try."

Eamon sliced the air with the sword using quick, sharp strokes.

Aaliss worked hard to parry them with the heavier weapon; the sound of metal clanging against metal rang out in the small forest clearing.

After a few minutes, Eamon stopped with a wide grin on his face. "It sings through the air, but I can't borrow it. You should take it back."

"Why? You'll get used to it quick enough."

Eamon looked toward his feet and spoke into his chest. "You should leave before the Circle closes. If Dermot isn't cured by then, it'll be up to a battle between Fintan and me. If I lose, Fintan becomes king at that moment. He could order you arrested or worse. You took no oath. You don't need to stay."

The big oaf doesn't get it! I can't let anything happen to him.

"You don't decide what I do. Only I decide my own actions. You can't make me leave, and I'm not going anywhere."

"You and Wilky fulfilled our bargain. We made the cure. You're free to go. Nothing is binding you here." He kicked the dirt.

Aaliss struggled for words, unsure what she wanted to say or what exactly she felt. "Don't be an idiot. I... need to see this through. Besides, I want to watch while you best your pompous brother."

He glanced up at her, his eyes moist and wide, and let the silence build for a moment. Finally, he bared the truth behind his worry. "It's too dangerous for you to stay. Fintan's the best swordsman in the tribe. Everyone knows it." He shrugged one shoulder. "I've spent much of my time with books. He's always beaten me in the past. If I lose...."

"After I'm done with you, you'll have an easy time with him. He's a bully. When you cut him, he'll panic. Keep that sword and let's get back to work. We've got a lot to do. You can give it back to me after you best Fintan and you're king."

He cast a somber look, his eyes twinkling sadly.

She knew he wanted her to leave.

"You could go to the Witch's cabin. I'll meet you there after."

"You talk too much! That's your problem. Always talking! Come on, we don't have all night." She waved the longsword at him, her mind made up.

She didn't know when it happened, but she'd chosen Eamon. Even if he loved Jillian, it didn't matter. For the first time in her life she needed someone else. She wasn't going anywhere until he was safe. She couldn't go even if she wanted to.

From now on, my life will be complicated.

Eamon flipped the short sword in the air and caught the hilt when it fell back into his hand. "Okay, if you're certain. What's next?"

Aaliss shoved him with two hands and spun him in a circle. It gave her just enough time to wipe away a tear that had formed unbidden without him noticing.

"No more talk about losing! We've got to work on your footwork and leverage." She glanced at the darkening sky, hoping that the moon would help her and shine brightly.

CHAPTER 49
PIERS

The hot tea sloshed inside the white porcelain cup, threatening to escape over the lip and spill onto the wooden tray. Piers tried hard to make sure that none of the tea toppled over the sides. The High Priest would be angry if the outside of the cup became wet.

The Priests ate their dinner in a private dining room in the Parsonage, a simple room with long wooden tables, tall ceilings, and long benches upholstered with red velvet cushions.

Most nights, like this one, the High Priest preferred to eat alone in his office.

Piers carried the dessert tray and the tea. A thick slab of apple pie and a bowl of apple ice cream competed for space on the tray with the tea.

The Pantry, where the Priests prepared their food, connected to the High Priest's office by a heavy swinging door. A small copper bell hung above the door, which the High Priest rang with one tug of white twine. The unwritten rule: five seconds — if he waited more than five seconds, he became surly, and that always spelled bad news for the tardy novice. A different novice manned the small kitchen each night, all night, just in case the High Priest wanted something to eat, which he commonly did when he had trouble sleeping.

Tonight, Piers had drawn Pantry duty.

He backed through the swinging door and into the High Priest's office carrying the tray and limping slightly.

The High Priest sat behind Jacob's Desk with his back to him, gazing out the windows. His computer was on, but the screen showed only wavy lines.

Piers breathed easily as he successfully placed the tray on the desk without spilling a drop of tea.

Still facing the window, the High Priest said, "We're a lot alike, you and me." He turned. "We're both true believers. Jacob's blood flows through my veins and not yours, but you have a real devotion. Very admirable."

I'm nothing like you.

"Yes, your Grace. I wish to follow your example, although I could never reach your level of knowledge or your communion with Jacob." He spoke hollow words that almost choked him as he uttered them. He had to say them; the High Priest expected to hear them.

The High Priest smiled thinly. "True, Piers. I'm happy you understand. Not everyone does. Eden Day this year will be very special. Jacob has sent me visions, but they are not complete." A touch of melancholy drifted in the High Priest's voice as if doubt troubled him. "Sometimes Jacob's will is hard to discern. It takes patience."

"Visions, your Grace?" Piers's heart skipped. Eden Day had to be at the center of the High Priest's plans, but how was it connected to his siblings and the cure?

The High Priest faced him for a long moment, his gaze inward. Finally, he said, "The visions are not complete yet. I'm not sure what they all mean, but I will before Eden Day, and I promise it will be special."

Piers felt a cold shudder whip through him, and then he noticed the drapes by the window had blown in the wind. "Do you want me to shut those windows for you?"

"No, Piers, I always keep them open. I don't even know if they close. The fresh air helps me connect with Jacob. That will be all."

He left the tray and retreated through the swinging door and back into the Pantry. His heart raced and his hands shook. He leaned out a window and saw the open windows to the High Priest's office. Fifteen feet separated them, not a far distance. The wall, made of coarse stone, had plenty of handholds and footholds.

It's only fifteen feet. If I climb that distance, I can access the High Priest's computer.

A crow landed on the window ledge and squawked at him. In the old stories, crows were always bad omens.

He did not believe the old stories. He believed in The Book.

Still, the bird's squawking unsettled him, and he shooed it away with a wave of his arm.

Will I be brave enough?

He looked down and saw the long plunge to the ground, and his stomach lurched. The fall would shatter him.

I'm the oldest.

I'm responsible.

CHAPTER 50
VIPER

T he Viper, riding high on the horse he'd stolen from the Butcher horseman he'd killed, followed the trail in the slippery moonlight. Dawn had almost arrived, and he hadn't slept since he left Eden, but he felt no fatigue. Exhilaration coursed through him as he sensed the electricity in the air, knowing he neared his destination.

These woods were not entirely unknown to him. He'd traveled here when alone, always alone. Even Jonas had no idea hed spent such time amongst the Soulless. Only the High Priest knew of his adventures.

He wore a woolen veil, careful to keep his face and gasmask concealed. Sometimes he tortured Soulless for information about the world outside of Eden. Other times he traded with witches, bargaining with them for news about the Soulless that would come in handy after they had a cure, when his life would truly begin. He always knew Jacob would deliver them a cure—always knew the battles would commence—and soon he could purify the world and have everything he wanted.

First, he needed to kill the girl and her brother, and then he would be unstoppable.

Over a year had passed since he had visited this particular witch, but the rabbit's trail led through the small creek and to the old cabin. The wind swirled in short gusts, blowing frigid air against his ostrich suit and flapping his veil against his face. The branches in the trees swayed, and some gave up loose leaves that swirled to the ground.

The cabin looked much like it did a year ago when he last came here. He chuckled. The witch who lived here had always accommodated him in the past. She would help him now.

If he found the rabbit his search would end. If she had moved on, the Witch would know where she went and would guide him. Either way, he closed in on Aaliss and her brother.

He dismounted and warily approached the front door with the crude red fish painted on it, wondering where the Witch hid with her bow.

The door swung open before he reached the porch. The Witch and her bulldog walked through it; one shuffled and the other waddled.

The bulldog barked and growled at the Viper. The Witch silenced him by rubbing his head with her gnarled fingers.

"What has happened to you, Witch?" He continued walking toward her as he spoke. "You look weak and old and bent at the waist, as if you were an old horse that needed to be put down. Is this how the Dark One treats his followers? Only last year you looked young and beautiful."

"It is a blessing you could never understand, *Veiled One.*"

He looked beyond her and into the cabin, but saw only shadows. "I'm looking for two travelers, a girl and a young boy. Where are they?"

"I've seen no one. No one visits an old witch."

He started to grin, but before his lips turned into a full smile he seized the Witch by the throat with one hand. "I know they were here. Tell me where they are."

The Witch grabbed his hand and tried to pull it from her neck, but he locked on her like a vise. The bulldog sank its teeth into his leg, but he kicked the dog and sent him flying across the porch.

The Viper snarled and released the Witch's throat.

She sputtered and sucked in air. "You... have... no power of life and death over me."

The bulldog ran at him.

This time he grabbed the dog and lifted him with both his arms. "I'll snap his mangy neck if you don't tell me where they are."

The Witch frowned, tears glistening in her eyes, yet she stayed quiet.

"Did they return to the Stronghold?"

The Witch's gaze fluttered from the dog to the moon.

The Viper laughed. *The small tell gives you away.*

"You've told me all I need to know." He twisted the dog's head, snapped his neck in a vicious yank, and dropped the lifeless animal to the ground.

"You're a fool, Veiled One. That was no ordinary dog you killed." The Witch paused for a heartbeat and cocked her head to the side, as if she were listening to a voice on the wind. "You have one last chance. Leave the girl and boy alone. Repent and follow the one true God, and you will be saved. You can still be saved."

"Saved." He laughed. "I don't need saving from your god. Jacob provides for me. Once I kill the rabbit, I'll have everything I've ever wanted."

The Witch shook her head. "You follow a false god. Jacob is not the prophet you believe him to be. He sits in darkness. Your plans will fail."

The Viper ground his teeth in rage. He lashed out both of his hands and clutched the Witch's throat. "What do you know of my plans? What did the girl tell you?"

He dug his fingers into her flesh, but she did not struggle. Instead, a tranquil expression graced her face.

"Why are you smiling? I'm going to choke the life from you!" He relaxed the pressure on her throat so she could speak.

"I smell freshly baked bread."

"You have lost your wits and now your life is forfeit." He grunted and squeezed her throat again. She closed her eyes, and an overwhelming rage filled him. He crushed her throat, and she stopped breathing.

When he let her go, she fell, and a bright white aura left her body. Like a shooting star, it rose to the heavens and swirled out of sight—one last illusion by the Witch.

Still, he shivered as a cold wind blew through him, and turned from the cabin without searching it.

He had no time to waste. He had a rabbit to snare.

CHAPTER 51
EAMON

E amon had trained with Aaliss throughout the night and until morning. He marveled at her skill and gracefulness. He'd never seen anyone move so quickly—always in control, always a step in front of him, always calm and clear-eyed and lethal. He had learned more in the one session from her than a year on his own, but when the light started to brighten, they returned to the Stronghold.

Midday approached and he was in Dermot's room. His brother still hadn't stirred, his eyes remaining stubbornly closed, and quiet anxiety covered Eamon like a shroud....

...until Fintan and Cormac burst into the room.

"Where's Dermot?" Fintan's eyebrows bunched together when he saw him in the bed. "Is he dead already?"

"He lives still. I gave him something to drink for his... health, and he does not stir."

"Good job, Brother! You've poisoned Dermot!" Fintan laughed. "You should have been the one on trial!"

"He's not poisoned. He's just sleeping. I'm sure he'll wake shortly."

"It matters not to me, Brother. Midday is almost upon us. The bell will toll and the Circle will close with my sword in it. If you want to face me, you're welcome to throw yours in with mine. I don't recommend it. The contest is to the death, and I will not accept your yield, even if you beg."

"Don't you think we should wait for Dermot to wake? He's sure to rise soon."

"Rules are rules, Brother." Fintan's face turned hard. "I'm sure *Dermot the Just* would not want us to break the rules. After all, he felt obligated to try his own brother for murder and treason! No, no, no! Rules are meant to be kept, little brother, and keep them we shall!"

"We need to ally with the Painted Ones to defeat the invaders from the north. We can't fight the Painted Ones now," urged Eamon.

Fintan chuckled. "Oh yeah, the mysterious invaders from the north no one has seen."

Cormac followed with a forced laugh and sputtered in a high-pitched falsetto, "The b-bearded ones with he-heavy battleaxes."

"We've seen them. Eamon killed one when we faced them." Aaliss took an angry step toward Fintan.

Fintan hesitated.

A year ago, Fintan and Cormac claimed to have killed three tribeless in the forest. Both suffered minor injuries, but no witnesses could confirm the deed.

Perhaps he fabricated that story. Maybe he hasn't seen death up close.

"These *axe people, if* they are real, will only make my job easier. They'll destroy the Painted Barbarians for us." A smug look graced Fintan's face. "By the time we face the northerners, they'll be weak. We will defeat them, and I will have what I want."

"You play a dangerous game, Fin!"

"Don't worry, Brother. I'll save a place in the front of the battle for you. We can burn those silly books you've been working on, and you can do some real manly work." Fintan laughed arrogantly. "Perhaps *Eamon the Handsome* will prove his worth at war. Try to duck when they swing their axes at you. I'd hate to see your pretty face get lopped from your neck."

"You're making a mistake," added Aaliss.

Fintan scowled at her. "Are you still here? I will be known as *Fintan the Famous*. No one will remember *Dermot the Just*. He will pale in comparison. Songs will be written about me! My place in the stars will be bright. Glory will shine upon me!"

"This is all about *your* glory?" accused Aaliss. "You'll risk your entire tribe just to measure up to Dermot?"

"I've heard enough from you! Don't think I've forgotten *your* crimes. Dermot may have pardoned you, but his rule ends when the Circle closes." Fintan paused, and let the threat linger heavily in the air, before he turned to his brother. "I expect you to be at the Circle when the time comes. I want you to be first to bend his knee to me as the new king!"

Fintan whirled and left the room with Cormac a step behind.

"That one's a real charmer," muttered Aaliss.

"There's still time for you and Wilky to leave." Doubt wove into Eamon's voice. "Fintan's threat is real. Who knows what he'll do when he becomes king."

"*If* he becomes king, but that won't happen. You'll beat him. And besides, I've already talked to Wilky, and we're staying."

Wilky nodded.

"Look!" Gemma practically jumped to her feet. "He's waking."

Dermot groaned, twisted and blinked his eyes open.

They're brown!

His brother's chestnut eyes were the most wonderful things Eamon had ever seen.

"I had the weirdest dream," said Dermot. "I met Father... at least I think it was Father. He looked just as I remembered him, only broader in his shoulders. Next to him stood a tall man with a beard and a great, round belly."

"Was it Grandfather, Finnegan the Fat?"

Dermot smiled. "Your guess is as good as mine, but I think so. They were angry with me. I could tell by the look on Father's face. He always had the same pinched look when he was angry with us. I rode a silver mare toward them. At first I rode hard, and then I slowed the horse to a canter and finally stopped in front of them. Father grabbed the reins with that look on his face. I tried to ask him where I was, but the words never left my mouth. Before I said anything, he turned the horse and grandfather slapped it hard on the romp. The horse bolted away from them, and I woke."

Dermot scanned their anxious faces. "Why so worried? What time is it?"

"It's almost noon," answered Gemma. "Your eyes are brown again!"

"I know. I feel different. The Red Death has left me. We better hurry or the Circle will close." Dermot hopped out of bed as the bells started to chime.

The twelfth bell had just rung when Eamon reached the Circle.

Dermot had beat him there and held the Sword of Power in his right hand. "The Circle remains open!"

A gasp spread throughout the crowd.

"His eyes are brown!"

"He's been cured!"

"What type of magic is this?"

A hum rippled through the tribe. Some sounded relieved and others scared, as if the tribe were torn between the two emotions. A hushed, uneasy silence replaced the voices as the tribe collectively tried to determine what Dermot's recovery meant.

Fintan shattered the silence. "What type of witchcraft is this? No one is saved from the red eyes."

"No witchcraft, Brother." Dermot smiled. "It's simply not my time yet. I met our father in the stars, and he sent me back."

"No, Brother, your time is over!" Fintan shouted so everyone could hear. "The twelfth bell has rung! In accordance with our laws, you've resigned and a new king is birthed from combat. It matters not if your eyes have returned to brown. I've thrown my sword in the Circle. It is too late for you. Your rule has ended."

"Surely you see the providence in this miracle. I've been sent back from certain death."

More than half the crowd grew angry, shouting encouragement for Dermot, but Fintan would not relent. "We are a tribe of laws, are we not? I demand the Circle close. I am the rightful king!"

Other voices, led by Cormac, sided with Fintan. Swords scraped against scabbards as the declarations grew louder and angrier. Two Guardsmen jostled each other, shouting insults.

Dermot scanned the angry mob and looked soulfully at Eamon.

He doesn't want to rip us apart. Eamon felt a pit in his stomach.

The tribe was uncertain. Fintan and Cormac could rally enough people to make a fight of it. Many in the King's Guard looked as if they would fight for Fintan.

Eamon hung his head. He should have anticipated this reaction and spoken to the Masters. With them on Dermot's side, the tribe would rally behind him, but now it was too late. He was a fool.

"You're right, Fintan," Dermot said. "No man is above the law. My time has passed. The Circle will close, and you will be king."

Dermot lifted the Sword of Power. Once he thrust it into the ground, the Circle would indeed close and Fintan would rule.

Eamon's senses sharpened.

Gemma screamed, "No!"

He noticed the edges of the leaves on the Naming Tree had started to turn color. In a week's time, each would have the color it had chosen for itself, and all would drop to the ground.

Dermot's hands rose to strike the sword downward. His muscles tensed before the thrust.

"Wait!" shouted Eamon. "I throw my sword into the Circle!" He tossed his sword high into the center of the Circle. It revolved slowly before it fell, blade first, plunging into the grass at Dermot's feet.

Dermot stared at him, the Sword of Power still raised in his hands, sadness written into the corners of his eyes.

Eamon could not remember their father's look, but he knew Dermot's. The accusation remained unspoken: *You broke your promise.*

Dermot thrust the Sword of Power into the ground. "The contest will begin at midnight within the Ring of Fire, as it is written!"

A cheer roared from the crowd.

Eamon wondered if they approved, or if they just wanted to see a fight.

Either way, I fight to the death.

CHAPTER 52
AALISS

Aaliss stared at the torches around the Ring of Fire. They blazed bright and hot and bathed the Courtyard in flickering firelight.

As the final bell tolled, Fintan strolled toward the Ring. Aaliss cursed to herself.

The chain mail flowed naturally over his wide shoulders with no sign of the added weight. Even worse, he moved with grace and confidence. He swung his longsword in looping circles as if the weapon were an extension of his arm, while carrying his shield lightly in his other hand.

She looked for weaknesses and, if she were honest with herself, she would be wary about fighting him. She'd defeat him, but he demanded a certain level of respect and caution she'd failed to notice before.

After yesterday's moonlight training session, she had convinced herself that Eamon would best his older brother. Now her confidence slipped, and she felt numb. A tourniquet squeezed her heart tight. Eamon might be fighting, but it felt like *her* life was at stake, and she *was* helpless.

The Witch's warning rang in her ears. This was the test. Everything had led to this moment. Fear rippled through her, not because Fintan might seek vengeance on her or Wilky if he beat Eamon. She could take care of them, but she could no longer imagine living without Eamon.

And that terrified her.

Eamon ambled over to her, the first time he'd appeared since sunset. He'd wanted to be alone to gather his thoughts.

She whispered, "Just concentrate on what we worked on last night, and you'll be fine. He's a bully. Once you cut him, he'll crumble."

The importance of first blood could not be overstated. It meant everything. It would sow doubt in Fintan's mind and add confidence to Eamon's.

We need first blood.

Dermot moved toward them, his gait stiff with worry. When Eamon threw his sword into the Circle, Dermot had seethed and stomped from the Courtyard without uttering a word. He might have said nothing, but every step screamed his displeasure as if he shouted from the top of the stone palisade.

His eyes now looked soft in the firelight as he faced Eamon. "Are you sure you want to go through with this? I can still talk to Fin. If you withdraw, he might accept it."

"I don't have a choice. Fintan will destroy the tribe if he becomes King, and I will not be thought of as a coward."

Dermot sighed. "No, you are brave, and now both my brothers will fight to the death. What can I do to help?"

"Make sure no harm comes to Aaliss and Wilky."

Dermot nodded. "Done. They will be safe while I'm alive."

"And don't forget about Jillian. Aaliss knows where to find her, so you can bring her back."

"I will. She's like a sister to me. Now, are you sure you don't want to wear the metal shirt? And are you positive you want to use this... *short sword* instead of your normal blade?"

Eamon nodded. "I'm much quicker without the shirt, and Aaliss's sword sings through the air."

"It's time. I have to start the contest." Dermot leaned close to

Eamon's ear and whispered just loud enough so Aaliss could hear him. "How many times have you seen Fintan spar with someone?'

"Too many times to count."

"How does he start every session?" Dermot didn't wait for the reply. He merely slapped Eamon hard on the back, turned, and left.

"What does he mean?" asked Aaliss.

"To start every sparring session, Fintan bangs his sword hard against his opponent's shield with an overhead chop." Eamon grinned. "It's a habit. I'm sure he'll do the same against me now."

"A habit," she said mostly to herself. Habits were dangerous things. Her sword master beat all her habits out of her with a cane.

She smiled. "That's great. When he pulls back to make the strike, raise your shield to meet the blow, spin, and slash at his right leg. You'll have to guess at the timing, but that should give us first blood." Hope started to crowd out the fear she felt a moment ago, but something looked off in Eamon's eyes. "What's wrong?"

Eamon shrugged and looked away. "It's all becoming so real. I've known Fintan my whole life, and now...."

Aaliss grabbed him roughly by the shoulders. "Look at him!" She spun him so he faced Fintan. "I mean... *really* look at him. I'm not sure who he was as a boy, but that man standing there will kill you the first chance he gets. He won't be thinking about your fifth birthday! He killed Maeve's sister and plotted to poison Dermot. Either you're all in, or withdraw right now!"

Eamon's face hardened. "I'm in."

"Good, now don't forget about Fintan's temper. Use that against him. If he gets angry, he'll get sloppy. Take advantage of it."

Eamon nodded, and she pounded hard on his shield for good luck.

Dermot whistled and waved for his brothers to join him.

Eamon smiled at her. "Dermot will be good to his word. He'll make sure you're safe."

"Don't worry about me." She brushed a few strands of unruly hair from his eyes.

She wanted to say something profound or encouraging, but a large lump formed in her throat that no words could circumvent. So instead, she kissed him lightly on the cheek, her lips just brushing his skin, and she turned away before he could see her moist eyes.

He went to join Dermot, and she scanned the crowded Courtyard. Small children sat on adult shoulders, and a few torches burned on the outskirts of the field. One tall man with wide shoulders and big arms, who looked like a smith, waved the Butcher's flag.

She imagined the crowd wanted Eamon to win, but she really couldn't tell whom they favored. Clearly, those around Cormac were ardent supporters of Fintan, but everything else was an uncertainty. She didn't even know whom Gemma rooted for—both were her brothers.

What am I doing here?

The thought kept popping into her mind with alarming frequency. Each time she pounded it downward with a mental chop.

Her eyes followed Eamon. She would rather face terrawks or a Devil's Storm or tribeless rogues or Axemen or even the Viper, than have to watch him fight Fintan. This was worse than the fire that took her parents. Now her own life felt like it was on the line, and she was helpless.

She looked to the moon and said a prayer to the Creator, one she hadn't spoken in quite some time. She hoped He was listening—at least this once.

CHAPTER 53
EAMON

Eamon joined Fintan and Dermot in the center of the Ring. He remembered watching Dermot in the Ring of Fire when it was his turn to become king. No one opposed him. Before that, his uncle and two cousins battled to the death. He didn't remember that much about the actual fight but he did recall cheering when the fight ended and his uncle won. Now he couldn't say why he'd cheered then. Maybe he was happy it was over, or maybe he just followed the crowd. He was too young to recall his father's contest.

Dermot told him stories that made his father seem like the best warrior that had ever fought, although Eamon was pretty sure Dermot made those stories up. He noticed how they changed over time, but Eamon never pointed out the inconsistencies. Now, he wondered what tales would be told about his battle. Certainly no one would remember him as fondly as they did his father — if anyone remembered him at all.

Fintan shattered his thoughts with his mocking tone. "Where's your ringed battle shirt? I'll let you borrow one of mine if you've let yours go to rust from lack of use, or maybe you lost it among all the books that keep you company." Fintan laughed, but his eyes looked cold and calculating in the firelight as he twirled his sword gracefully in his hand. "You might as well fight me naked."

Aaliss is right. He'll kill me first chance he gets.

"Eamon is free to wear the chain mail or not. It's his choice." Dermot stood between the two brothers, separating them. He lowered his voice so only they could hear. "Is there some other way for us to settle this dispute? We don't have to rely on combat. We could forge a new path, one where no one dies."

Fintan arched his back and erupted in a full belly laugh, his body shaking with mock amusement. "Maybe we can have a reading contest or something with numbers? You'd like that, wouldn't you, Dermot? No, we must rely upon the old ways and settle matters amongst the flames at midnight. The law stands. Only one of us will leave the Ring alive, and I have plans later this evening." Fintan paused for a heartbeat and continued with a snarl. "If he gets on bended knee right now and proclaims fealty to me as king, I will let him live."

Eamon remembered the doubt that flickered in Fintan's eyes when he talked about the axeman he had killed.

"Let it be said that you gave Fintan a chance to withdraw," he said with a wide grin. "It's one thing to twirl a sword in practice, Brother, but another when your life depends upon it."

Eamon had added as much feigned confidence as he could muster into his voice, and he saw Fintan's demeanor change from unbridled self-assurance to something less. Exactly what, he could not tell in the uncertain light.

He has doubt. I've got to use that.

"What about that toy sword?" Fintan pointed at Aaliss's sword in Eamon's hand. "He should fight with a real weapon. That's our custom. I don't want that toy to mar my victory."

"What's the problem, Fin? Are you afraid of this short sword?" Eamon slashed it in the air. "I thought I'd give you an advantage with your longsword. You're going to need it." He glowered at Fintan, inched closer to him, and rose up to his full height, which lifted him just slightly higher than his brother.

"I've had enough!" Dermot's face flushed angrily as he lifted the Sword of Power, blade pointed to the heavens. "I had hoped there would be some brotherly love here at the last, but I guess that's asking too much." He faced Fintan. "The law requires each combatant to use a sword and shield. Eamon is free to choose whatever sword he wants. When I plunge the Sword of Power into the ground you shall begin the combat. The winner can claim the Sword of Power and will be our next king."

Dermot stalked away from his two brothers and spoke to the crowd. He turned in a slow circle so everyone could see him. The torchlight enveloped him and made his face shine with an otherworldly glow. "The Circle of Destiny is closed and the Ring of Fire is open! Our next king will be determined through battle and blood, as it is written. I call upon our ancestors to guide the contest and choose the best king for the tribe, as they have throughout time. May the herd forever be strong!"

The tribe repeated the prayer in a thunderous explosion: "May the herd forever be strong!"

Dermot plunged the Sword of Power deep into the earth.

Eamon bent at the knees, shield high in his left hand, sword in his right. His heart pounded as he tightened his grip on the leather hilt and tried to recall Fintan's sparring sessions.

What exactly does he do? A mental picture formed. *He hesitates, smiles, and darts forward to batter his opponent's shield with his sword in a chop.*

Fintan snarled, "I never liked you, *pretty boy*. I'm not going to make it quick."

Eamon focused on the details, his senses working overtime.

Fintan's knuckles turned white on the hilt of his sword. Then he smiled.

That's the smile.

Eamon lifted his shield high to meet the chop as Fintan started the blow, and spun in a tight circle when Fintan's sword clanged off his shield, raking a short sidestroke across Fintan's exposed right calf. The blade ripped through Fintan's leather pants, leaving a ragged gash behind. Fintan turned and backslashed at Eamon's head, but Eamon darted backward, just out of reach.

Fintan groaned and glared at his leg and the blood that seeped onto his boot. "What type of trick was that? You've cut me!"

Eamon knew the wound was superficial, but for the first time he actually believed he could win, and that belief fueled him. He felt lighter, stronger, quicker than before. "That's the point. You'd know that if you had ever been in a *real* fight."

Fintan sneered and leapt at him, sending a flurry of strokes at him. They came fast, seemingly from all angles: backstrokes, overhead chops, sideswipes, and thrusts. Some were aimed at his legs and others at his head.

Eamon labored to deflect them, but Fintan's attack was sloppy, driven by anger rather than technique, and Aaliss's sword seemed to jump through the air.

Frustrated, Fintan started breathing heavily and slowed.

"Is that really the best you can do?" Eamon said. "I bet Cormac is a lot better. At least, that's what everyone says."

Fintan's eyes narrowed and he lunged forward, delivering another barrage of heavy strokes with renewed energy and muster. They rained down on Eamon's shield.

Each one shook his arm and wrenched his shoulder—one after another.

Thud! Thud!

Fintan's rage grew stronger, the blows heavier and less balanced.

Thud!

Bits of Eamon's shield chipped away from the onslaught, but he held it firm.

Thud!

"You swing the sword like a cattle butcher!" teased Eamon. "Perhaps you missed your true calling!"

Fintan reared back to put all of his strength and weight behind a vicious chop in an attempt to cleave Eamon's shield in two, but Eamon anticipated the blow and stepped back as Fintan brought the sword down.

Fintan saw Eamon move too late. He couldn't control his momentum and staggered past Eamon awkwardly.

Eamon seized upon the opportunity and kissed Fintan's back with his blade. The super sharp steel tore through the metal rings and into Fintan's flesh.

Fintan spun and slashed at Eamon, but once again, Eamon jumped backward, outside of his reach.

Fintan winced in pain, fear and doubt clouding his eyes.

Eamon's heart tightened. He felt none of the exhilaration he had experienced when he had killed the axeman or the tribeless outlaw. Everything seemed clear and straightforward then: he had to kill. Now, his world turned cloudy, as he could not bring himself to hate his brother. Rather, he felt sorry for him.

"This isn't happening. I'm supposed to kill you!" Fintan shouted, and charged forward in a full rage, crashing his shield hard against Eamon's.

The clash staggered Eamon backward, and Fintan pressed the attack with his shield again. This time Eamon pushed his shield against Fintan's, thrusting the two into a deadly game of push. Sweat rolled off both of them.

Fintan suddenly stopped shoving against Eamon's shield, hoping to throw Eamon off balance, and swung his sword at Eamon's side.

Eamon moved quicker. He deflected the attack with plenty of time to spare.

Fintan growled, sounding inhuman, desperate. He stomped hard on Eamon's foot, pegging him in place, and when he shoved with his shield, Eamon wobbled off balance. Fintan slashed at Eamon's sword arm, scratching through Eamon's stiff leather shirt.

The blow stung, but Eamon spun to his left and drove the spike in his shield into his brother's exposed right bicep. The sharp point pierced the metal rings and bit into flesh and muscle.

Eamon twisted the shield, and Fintan dropped his sword in pain, his eyes furious. Eamon kicked Fintan off his shield with his boot. "You can yield, Brother."

Fintan dropped his shield in shock. Much of his blood stained the ground, his face drained of color. He held his damaged arm with his good one and rocked unsteadily on his feet. "I'm hurt bad. I don't understand. I'm supposed to win. I've been practicing my whole life. I'm better than you. It's my time!" He staggered backward toward the center of the Ring.

"Yield, Brother. Don't make me kill you. We can work something out."

Fintan toppled to the ground, looking young and innocent.

Eamon remembered how they used to play when they were children, before swords and books got in the way, when their uncle was king and life was simple.

Eamon had concentrated so intently on the fight, that he only now heard other sounds and saw other sights. The crowd cheered but he couldn't make out words, just noise and energy. He peered through the flames and turned toward Dermot and Gemma, not sure what to do.

Dermot's face looked stoic, but tears stained Gemma's cheeks, a silent "oh" formed by her open mouth. Kelly stood beside her, pigtails flapping in the breeze with her hands covering her eyes.

Eamon lowered his sword, and then he heard Aaliss's voice knife through the crowd. "Look out, Eamon!"

He spun.

Fintan lunged at him with the Sword of Power in both hands. The longsword cut through the air; flames gleamed off the highly polished steel and fired off the jeweled handle.

Eamon slid to his right and lifted his own sword to block the blade just before the steel carved into his head. He felt the weight of the collision and worried that Aaliss's sword would shatter, but it held, a few inches from his throat.

Fintan brought the heavy blade back again, but he had no strength and it clattered to the ground behind him. "I yield, I yield," he blubbered, and fell to his knees. "Don't kill me. *Please!*"

The Sword of Power belonged only to the victor. No one was allowed to touch it during the combat. It was the one rule of the contest within the Ring of Fire.

Angry, Eamon pointed his blade's edge at Fintan's chest. "Tell the truth about your plan to kill Dermot!"

Fintan's hands flew to his face, covering his tear-streaked eyes, his face ashen, his body shaking. Blood stained his shirt and he mumbled into his hands. "It was all Cormac's doing. He wrote the note for the Nursery. He took the girl by Whitewater River. I didn't know about it until it was too late. Don't kill me. He is the one to blame."

"Louder, so everyone can hear!" Eamon pressed the point of his blade against Fintan's chest. "Did you plan to kill Dermot?"

Fintan threw his head back and shouted, "It was all Cormac's idea. I can prove it. He killed that nothing girl and wanted Dermot gone so we could be heroes!"

Eamon kicked the Sword of Power away from Fintan, who collapsed, weeping.

The energy ebbed from him. Weariness heavier than anything he had experienced before bore down on him. A breeze rustled the leaves on the Naming Tree, and he lifted his head to see the names burned from its bark. Traitors could not stay on the tree. Now Fintan's name would be charred off.

A commotion rose from one end of the Circle, where Eric restrained Maeve.

She screamed, "She was not a nothing girl! She was special! She was somebody! She was my sister, you murderer!" Eric held her firm, and her shouting transformed into a hurricane of tears.

Eamon heard a new scream rise from behind him.

What now?

He turned.

Cormac had burst into the Ring with his sword drawn. He looked like a demon running through the flames.

He's moving so quickly.

He knew he should lift his sword, but he was too exhausted to move.

Aaliss bolted forward, her knees pumping to her chest. She moved fast, but knew she could not reach Cormac before he would strike Eamon. Tears blurred her eyes as she pressed forward.

A blood chilling scream ripped from Cormac's throat.

Eamon stood statue-like, as if stone had replaced his flesh and bone.

One stride left.

Cormac lifted his sword.

Aaliss felt her heart explode, air coming in bursts. "No!"

At the last second, Cormac swerved past Eamon and jammed his blade into Fintan's chest. The quick thrust took only a few seconds, and then he yanked his weapon free and spun toward Eamon.

The diversion gave Aaliss just enough time. She reached Cormac before he could strike down Eamon, and made a sliding, foot-first tackle that sent the large man sprawling headfirst.

His face uprooted turf as he crashed violently into the ground, and his sword tumbled from his hand.

Aaliss jumped to her feet first and launched a roundhouse kick that connected flush with his face. The blow sent him backwards to the ground, unconscious.

She stood over his prone body and felt all her anxiety bubble from her. "That's payback!"

Dermot and Gemma joined Eamon, and all three siblings stared at Fintan's lifeless body.

Cormac had stabbed him through the heart.

Aaliss would like to have said she felt remorse, but Fintan got what he deserved. The world would be a better place without him.

After a long silent moment, Dermot held the Sword of Power outstretched, hilt first, to Eamon, and bent on one knee. "The Sword is yours, King Eamon. The heavens have spoken. May the herd forever be strong!"

The crowd cheered and began chanting Eamon's name. Each Master around the Circle lifted a torch and knelt in a show of loyalty to the new king. The rest of the crowd dropped to bended knee while still chanting his name.

"King Eamon! King Eamon!"

Eamon raised the Sword of Power high over his head, triumphantly, and the chants grew louder.

Aaliss's heart swelled. *Eamon deserves this moment. He will be a good king.*

Cormac stirred and struggled to his knees.

Eamon's eyes narrowed as he marched to him. "As king, I pronounce you guilty of murder. You must pay the ultimate price."

Cormac looked at him with watery eyes. "We just wanted to be heroes."

"And now you will go to the next life as traitors." He chopped down with the Sword of Power, and the big blade carved through skin and bone and freed Cormac's head from his neck.

The crowd cheered and chanted Eamon's name with renewed vigor.

He walked back toward the circle and quieted the tribe by thrusting the sword in the air. "This Sword of Power is not for me. It is for you, Brother, King Dermot. Dermot the Just! The Blade of the Butchers! The best king the tribe has ever known. May the herd forever be strong!"

When he handed the sword to Dermot, the tribe started chanting, "King Dermot!"

Aaliss saw strength in Eamon's face as the torchlight reflected off his blue eyes.

She could not imagine a more handsome sight.

CHAPTER 54
PIERS

Piers smoothed the lines in his robe as he glanced at the digital clock that hung high above the Pantry door. The blue neon numbers read 1:15 in the morning, well past midnight and the usual time the High Priest requested food from the small kitchen. He smoothed his robe again. 1:00 was the time he had set for action, yet he still sat motionless, afraid to move, afraid to act, afraid of what he must do.

Only five digital clocks existed in Eden. Piers had not given them much thought before, but now this solitary clock in the Pantry stood out as an unnecessary extravagance, contradictory to Jacob's teachings. Piers had started searching out the contradictions and found them everywhere: the abundant food the Priests ate for dinner, the Monks who favored the Sacred Drink, the electric carts the President and High Priest used. The list stretched on and could be found in the smallest aspects of life in Eden. If one looked close enough they were obvious, and he had started looking.

He wished he hadn't.

The Pantry was as quiet as the Cathedral during meditation, and that silence brought his mind to far-reaching places. Before the fire, he had been a good athlete.

Before the fire.

Piers often cleaved his life in two—before and after the fire. The fire changed everything.

A few years ago, Aaliss had quarreled with him. She shouted for him to snap out of his funk, her face red with anger. She said no one cared about the scars and that it was time for him to start living again.

If he closed his eyes, the words echoed in his mind. She had been right, but he'd turned his back on her, leaving her angry and alone. The scars did not hold him back. Well, not the external ones, but the internal ones shackled him—the ones that had shaken his belief in himself and God.

He believed only two explanations for the fire existed. Either he had angered God, or God did not exist. The latter so terrified him that he assumed the fault must be his. He must have so angered God that He caused the accident, and God took his parents, to punish him.

As a boy, he had no love for religion, shunning numerous rules and beliefs. God took notice and had punished him for his failings, and those he loved most paid the ultimate price. That was why he had turned to the priesthood. He needed redemption. He needed to follow Jacob's rules, so God would not punish him again—because next time, Aaliss and Wilky might suffer His wrath.

How could he face the world if something bad happened to them or Rebecca because of his failures? Without a choice, he'd turned to the priesthood and followed every rule.

Now, Aaliss and Wilky needed him—required him to be the Piers he once was, and not the shaken, scared, shell of a man he had become.

Without realizing it, he had swung the casing window outward and peered into the dark night. Clouds, heavy and dark, filled the sky, blocking out stars and moon alike. He leaned over the window and glanced down. It was a long way to the ground. No trees or hedges would cushion a fall.

He turned and surveyed the Pantry. Everything was in its proper place, as he'd left no food out. Only a paring knife lay on its side on a long oak table. He had almost forgotten about the knife. He'd thought it prudent to bring something he could use as a weapon if need be. He reached the table and took the knife by the small wooden handle. The blade was only three inches long, but it was razor sharp and fit neatly in the pockets of his robe.

With the knife secured and silence on the other side of the swinging door to the High Priest's office, he returned to the window and recited Jacob's prayer.

> *Jacob, the guardian of power and might;*
> *May he guide us to do what's right;*
> *He saved us from the Red Death;*
> *So we can breathe God's breath.*

He chuckled when he finished. Every child was taught those words among their first, Piers being no exception. Most people believed he was devout, his faith as strong as Eden River, but he knew the truth. He believed in The Book and God, but had a tenuous relationship with Jacob. He wanted to believe, and sometimes that was enough; sometimes he even thought he *did* believe.

Tonight was not one of those times. Tonight he'd have to move on without Jacob.

He swung open the window and stepped onto the sill. The cool night air gusted. The window to the High Priest's office was only fifteen feet to his right, and the old pitted stone was rough, with many places for him to wedge his feet and to grasp with his fingers. He inhaled deeply to let the cool, fresh air fill his lungs, and searched for his first foothold in the darkness.

Only three feet away from the window, Piers pushed the tip of his boot against it. He followed with a handhold, and then another foothold and handhold, until he reached the High Priest's window.

No light came from the office, just another room bathed in darkness, but he knew truth hid in this office, if only he could reach it. The wind gusted, ballooning his robe outward, threatening to blow him off the wall. He clutched at the stone with all his strength, and felt oddly whole, as he had before the fire.

He pulled against the window but it didn't budge. Panic snaked through him. The High Priest always kept the windows open. He could not remember a time when he saw them locked. He searched the window frame with his left hand and felt the casing where the window connected to the frame. A small gap separated the window from the stone — the wind had wedged the window closed. He pulled hard with his left hand, but it stayed stubbornly shut.

Hands sweating, his body started to cramp in his awkward position. Doubt swept through his mind, but he refused to give in to it. He thought of Wilky and Aaliss.

I am the oldest. It is my responsibility to protect them.

As he shifted toward the window to try to pry it open again, the sharp edge of the knife stuck him in the side.

He slid the small knife from his pocket, jabbed the blade into the crack, and pried hard on the handle. At first the window did not give, but he pulled harder and the window flew open.

The sudden lack of resistance pushed Piers from the wall. He hung precariously by two feet and one arm. The cool wind froze the sweat on his face. He dug the fingers of his right hand in deep against the stone. He looked down and saw nothing but darkness. With courage he thought he had lost, he looked up and stared at the window — the top only a few inches from his hand.

He summoned every bit of strength he had and grabbed the top of the window with his left hand, and swung his feet into the High Priest's office, breathing heavily and feeling safe... for the moment.

CHAPTER 55
PIERS

Piers's eyes adjusted to the darkness, which was not as complete as it seemed from the outside, and shapes formed around him. Blue neon numbers glowed from the clock on Jacob's Desk, and a small, round pinprick of light shone from the computer screen resting next to it. More than enough light for Piers, who recalled every last detail about the room from his visit earlier that day.

Still, he had never stood behind Jacob's Desk before. The room looked longer from this vantage point, and felt heavy with responsibility. The paintings on the walls were more imposing, the eyes in the portraits fixed on the desk and the man who sat behind it as if eternally judging events, silently assessing the High Priest but offering no advice.

For a moment he almost felt sorry for the High Priest, but that moment passed quickly.

Butterflies swirled in his stomach. He closed his eyes and fought back the acid in his throat. If caught, he would be branded a traitor. He had entered the sacred High Priest's office without invitation, and had placed his soul in jeopardy of eternal damnation.

He glanced back at the window. Retreating would be cowardly, and although he might be many things, a coward was not one of them.

He steadied his nerves and crept toward the desk, its surface smooth and clean. He studied the computer screen, recognized the green *on* button, and pressed it firmly. A picture of a spinning globe replaced the dark screen, the colors bright, clear, and sharp.

Piers looked for the keyboard but....

Does the High Priest remove the keyboard?

He doubted it. The High Priest would believe his office secure. He would never worry about someone breaking in.

A green light peeking through the cracks in a thin drawer underneath the computer caught his attention. It hadn't been there before Piers started the computer. He tugged on the drawer but a simple brass combination lock held it firm. The lock appeared original to the desk. He tugged harder and felt the wood give. He could force it open if he needed, but then the High Priest would know someone had broken into the desk, and Piers would be at the top of the suspect list.

The combination required six numbers from zero to nine.

The combination must be a date.

His head began to spin with dozens of possibilities as he studied the rest of the desk and looked for some clue, anything that might point him to the correct date. The desk's surface was smooth except for a small engraving on the drawer itself. It read simply: *Jacob's Desk.*

What date would Jacob use? Two dates jumped to mind. *What if I use the wrong one? Will it trigger an alarm?*

He said a prayer, not to Jacob, but an older God, one that felt true and honest. He twisted the brass numbers until it reflected Jacob's birthday, which was not Jacob's Day. Jacob's Day was the day when an angel told him he was God's divine messenger and the guardian of the human race. The date he was born was older and less known.

When the last number rotated into place, Piers held his breath and slid the small brass clasp to the left. The lock released and the drawer sprung open.

He exhaled, removed the keyboard, and placed it on top of the desk. After he pressed the escape key the globe stopped spinning, and dozens of electronic folders popped up around the edge of the globe.

He scanned them looking for one named "Poisoned Apple." He studied every file, but none bore that name. He clenched his hands into fists and tapped the desk with his knuckles.

Wilky wouldn't send me here with the wrong file name.

He scanned the files again looking for a name close to "Poisoned Apple," something Wilky might have mistaken for that name. Nothing worked. Finally, he studied the familiar globe in the center of the screen. He had seen this picture dozens of times, as they used it in every astronomy textbook. At first glance the globe looked ordinary, but he got the unsettling feeling something looked out of place. He contrasted this globe on the screen with the one from his memory banks. His photographic memory paid off and, finally, he saw it—the clouds in the center formed a small apple shape, which looked as if blood dripped down the sides. None of the textbooks had that cloud formation. It must have been added to this image on purpose.

He worked the mouse until the pointer covered the unusual cloud formation and clicked. The globe and the folders vanished, and a blank screen stared at him with two blinking prompts: "User Name" and "Password." He typed in "Jacob1" for the User Name and "Serpent" for the Password, but he hesitated before pressing the enter button.

Wilky's message had come with a warning: *once you learn the truth, you can't unlearn it.*

Steeling his nerves, he clicked the mouse and a box appeared in the center of the computer screen. The name "Poisoned Apple" flashed as the header, and the word "PLAY" in all capitals blinked ominously in the center. Piers plugged a small flash drive into the slot on the screen and pressed the copy key. He planned to save the file, retreat to the Pantry via the window, and later find a time to safely study the file with Peter and Michel.

The plan was a good one, but, as the progress bar marched slowly across the screen, he became increasingly curious as to the file's contents.

What could be so important?

A bell pinged and the screen read "Copying Complete." He

removed the flash drive, tucked it into his pocket, and looked for the exit key. He found it, but his eyes kept returning to the screen and the blinking word "PLAY."

It taunted him. He didn't need Peter and Michel. This was his responsibility. He was the oldest.

He clicked on the word and an image filled the screen. It started with a picture of a rotten apple with blood seeping from the core—a strange image that looked oddly familiar. He thought hard on it and remembered where he had seen it before—inside the facility at the Orchard. He waited for the rest, feeling woefully unprepared.

CHAPTER 56
PIERS

Piers stared at the screen as the video began.

A woman with long blonde hair and fair skin sat behind a light-colored, sleek, wooden desk. Beautiful, she had bright red lips, a small nose, and high cheekbones. She leaned on the desk confidently while interviewing a young man dressed in a white lab coat, with military medals pinned on his chest, wearing a green and black camouflage beret on his head.

He recognized the young man immediately. He was Jacob.

Although younger than in any picture Piers had seen of him, he had the same angular features, the small birthmark on his left cheek, and those bright, brilliant, emerald eyes. This video must have taken place over eight hundred years ago, before Eden was created, and before the Red Death plagued the world.

The woman asked, "So, Colonel Jacob Smith, you head the army's scientific research division?"

Jacob sat comfortably on a couch across from the desk, his legs crossed crisply, an easy smile resting on his face. "I do, Cindy."

"You look so young to have such an important position." She

smiled, her eyes wide and her lips moist. "Tell me about your cancer treatment breakthrough. It sounds so fascinating."

Jacob leaned forward. "I've discovered a trace element that's embedded in almost all cancer-forming cells. It converts normal cells to dangerous, cancerous ones. Now that I've found this element, we've developed a counteragent that stops the process. A simple vaccine will prevent virtually every type of cancer from emerging."

"So, you stop cancer cells from multiplying before they actually form?" Cindy's smile widened, her teeth an impossibly bright white.

"Exactly! With this treatment we can wipe out ninety percent of the harmful cancers. No one will have to be subject to them again." Jacob leaned back into the couch, looking pleased and confident.

"Will other researchers use this technology to battle other diseases?"

Jacob furrowed his eyebrows. "It's possible. I expect this may lead to many cures."

"Amazing. You've changed life for potentially hundreds of millions of people." Cindy's smile melted from her face. "What about this rumor that the military was going to keep this discovery secret? If it weren't for the leak, would we know about this breakthrough?"

Jacob maintained his pleased expression while he spoke. "Utter nonsense. As scientists we only disclose breakthroughs once we are certain they're repeatable. It was always our plan to release the vaccine. A treatment like this one is too important to humankind to keep secret."

Piers leaned close to the screen and scrutinized his face: his smile remained, but tiny crease marks around the eyes had appeared. He was lying.

Cindy's grin returned like the sun breaking the horizon. "Well, I'm happy that's out of the way. Now tell me about the actress, Jessica Roberts. I hear you two are quite the item. Can we expect to see you on the silver screen soon?" Cindy chuckled and the image changed.

This time a new interviewer appeared, a man in his late fifties wearing a gray suit, red tie, and white shirt. He sat behind a round glass table with an older version of Jacob across from him.

Jacob wore a white lab coat, a different assortment of medals pinned to his chest, and the same green and black beret on his head. He still looked younger than Piers had seen him before, but cracks appeared in the façade—faint creases dug into his forehead and around his eyes; his skin did not have the same youthful glow it had before; and his shoulders were rounded slightly.

The interviewer's voice sounded smooth but serious. "So, General, tell me about the organ replacement experiments. I understand they've had mixed results."

Jacob appeared less comfortable than he had in the earlier interview, his body stiff and his smile forced. "We've been able to grow most human organs in the lab, creating replicas of the ones originally grown in the body, and have successfully transplanted them into patients. We've only had problems on a few occasions, and with time, we will overcome those."

"I understand you're a religious man. What about the accusations leveled against you by some religious authorities that you're playing God and, let me paraphrase them here for a moment, 'Are stepping on His divine toes?'"

Jacob chuckled, but there was no genuineness in his mirth. "These people offer a false choice between God and science. No difference exists between the two. All science stems from God. My job is simply to determine the divine will already embedded in the DNA. Just like the preacher whose job is to interpret the messages in the Bible."

"What other experiments are you doing at this *Eden*? Eden is what you call your lab, right?" The interviewer raised his eyebrows, making his disapproval clear.

Jacob shrugged disarmingly. "Yes, we call the facility Eden because we are trying to uncover God's will when he created the world. It is really just a play on words."

"And the other experiments? Some say your experiments are dangerous and secretive, that we should open Eden to the public. Congressman Tish has been very outspoken."

"Congressman Tish and the American people have nothing to fear from our research in Eden. We seek only the divine truth and to further God's will."

Piers saw the same strain in Jacob's eyes. He was lying again.

The image changed, and an anchorwoman spoke solemnly. "Today marks the twentieth anniversary of the Smith Cure for cancer, which made possible treatments for a number of different diseases. Overpopulation problems stretch mankind's ability to feed and cope with rising populations. Wars have broken out on every continent to some degree, including the increasing violence south of our border. We tried to contact General Smith for an interview, but the reclusive soldier and scientist remains unavailable. The army tells us his work in Eden is too important to be interrupted. Speculation grows about what he's working on. Some believe Eden has been turned into a biological weapons research lab."

The anchorwoman paused and smiled at the screen. "Other sources say they're working on a drug that will let man live forever. Hopefully, the reclusive General will provide some information about his research shortly."

The screen turned black and flickered back to life. An image of Jacob, looking much like the photographs Piers was familiar with, appeared on the screen. He sat alone behind this same desk in this office. Gone were the lab coat, the military medals, and the beret.

Strange how the Book of Jacob fails to mention his military past.

He wore a scarlet robe, had short black hair, and his features looked gaunt, his cheeks hollow, the mole on his face darkened. "I tried explaining to them what would happen if we released the cancer vaccine, but they would not listen. I knew others would pervert it to cure other diseases. The treatment was meant for only those who deserved it, those who were pure. Now, the world might cave in under the weight of the worthless."

Jacob drummed his fingers against the desk and shrugged. "Oh well. That's in the past, and we move on. The world must be cleansed. Even the dimwitted should see that now. God spoke to me through the DNA, through the molecules. He told me it must be done, so I will do it for humanity and God, as guardian of the human race. The virus is ready. I've sent angels to far-reaching corners of the globe. Even though they're unaware of their role in God's plan, they are His instruments. They will sit at his right hand in the afterlife. They're infected with the new plague. It should take three months before the entire planet is under the influence of the disease, and the great cleansing can begin."

He paused for a moment and tapped his fingers on the desk in silence.

The pause unnerved Piers.

Jacob's eyes jittered, and he looked unstable, as if he were close to shattering. "Is it any different from Noah's Ark? We have everything we need to survive in Eden, to continue after humanity is cleansed and purified. The river is mined. We will be tested over the next year, but we'll prove pure. I'd rather have completed the cure first, but recent events required me to speed up the plans. Meddling government officials!"

Jacob's eyes twitched again. "I'm only one small breakthrough away and God will deliver us. Once the cure is finished, the virus will provide immortality to those who are pure, those I deem worthy." He smiled slyly for the camera.

After a short pause another video flickered to life. This time Jacob appeared ragged, his robe dirty and torn, his thin gray hair oily, his face taut, old, haggard, and his skin yellowish.

He whispered, "They keep me locked up here in the Labyrinth, but some are still loyal. They say I've gone crazy, but they don't understand. The cure is just outside my grasp. It's maddening! I want to kill them all. If I kill them, God will reward me. He will grant me immortality to start over with the pure. I know this to be true."

Jacob's fingernails were yellowed and long. He scratched at his left arm, and Piers saw old rips in his flesh that had scabbed over. "I hear them. I hear the cries, billions of cries of those who perished. I know the Dark One tempts me. He sent those boats of children down Eden River. I had to kill them for God! God knows I was right! He commanded me to kill them!"

He laughed maniacally, his eyes skittering. "They've told everyone I've gone to the mountain to save Eden, to prevent a horde of Soulless from invading. They plan to kill me."

He frantically pushed his hands over his ears. "Can you hear them crying? They cry so loud."

The video went silent, and Piers stared into Jacob's green eyes. They still fired brightly, but now the green twitched with madness.

The screen returned to the globe, and the electronic files that were on it earlier reappeared.

Piers went numb. Everything he had been taught was a lie—Jacob was a madman, the Red Death his evil invention.

How can it be all so wrong?

He stared at the computer screen, still lost in the vastness of the lies, the wrongness of Eden and Jacob, when he noticed a small red apple icon. The apple looked like the red one burned into the cask the High Priest had looked at in the Orchard.

Piers clicked on it without thinking.

A simple list popped on the screen titled "UW."

What does that mean?

Underneath the title were one hundred and thirty-three names: the first name was that of his uncle, the second himself. As he scanned further down the list he saw other names he knew, names of people who were friendly to his parents and whose views differed from the High Priest.

He saved the file on the flash drive and tucked it into his robe. The blue neon clock read 2:26 A.M.

He pressed the exit key and heard voices coming from outside. Frozen, he saw the latch twist and the door open. Orange lantern light filtered into the room.

The High Priest and Jonas stood in the doorway.

He ducked under the desk, hoping they had not seen him.

CHAPTER 57
WILKY

W ilky peered into the torch's soft flames, trying not to lose himself in the intricate colors that twisted and changed. Alone and exhausted, he could not rest. His loneliness felt deeper and more intense than usual, as if he had fallen into a deep well with slick walls he could not climb.

Aaliss did not understand him; he knew it was his fault, but fault wasn't the issue.

He yearned for the simple, white walls of his lab and apartment in Eden. If only he could shut out the world for a short time, so he might rest. Maybe with rest he could see things clearly. But even if he shut his eyes now, his mind would continue spinning like a top, bouncing off thoughts and ideas as if they were solid obstacles. Besides, there were things he needed to know, so he stared into the flickering torch and let the flames guide him.

Aaliss had asked him, "Who's going to win the upcoming war? What's our role in it?"

He couldn't answer.

She didn't realize the complexity of that question. Besides, she had asked about the war, but she really wanted to know about Eamon, and Wilky had no answer for that.

He tried to see who would win the war, but the images appeared muddled. Now he stared into the fire, to see beyond the flames, watching intensely as the flickering streaks of yellow and orange danced their mysterious waltz. Since he had left Eden, the visions had come to him more frequently and more clearly than before. At times he lost track of where he was, what realm he was in—reality or a vision. Those times scared him, but the Witch had counseled him to accept the visions, which seemed wise.

The flames took him away. He no longer sat in the room in the Stronghold. He stood along a clay road, where a fire much like this one danced in front of him. Images formed and unformed in rapid succession, and finally he saw a pair of eyes that glowed in the darkness—blue with red flecks—witch's eyes.

They looked powerful and angry and they frightened him. These eyes belonged to the witch from the City of Bones. She led the northern invaders, and she too searched for a deeper meaning behind events. A blackbird perched on her shoulder and a firefox wound its way around her feet.

He ignored the animals and focused hard on the eyes. When they blinked, he pulled back.

They were looking at *him*.

He shook his head to clear it, then wandered to the window and gazed at the Stronghold. The stones gave the impression of strength and permanence. There were, however, things stronger than stone and more permanent. He touched the rough edge of the windowsill and the details started to overwhelm him. Each stone in the wall varied in size and shape. The one he touched was mostly dark gray but contained streaks of white and silver. The next stone was the largest in the line, at least a full finger longer than any of the other stones, but not the widest.

He glanced back out the window, noticed a shadow in the street, and his heart skipped a beat.

CHAPTER 58
PIERS

Piers heard the High Priest's heavy footsteps at the far end of the office. "We still have time to add names to our list of the Unworthy," he said. "We can purge more of the impure from our ranks."

Piers inched to the side of the desk to glimpse what they were doing.

"There are better ways to get rid of the others we don't want," said Jonas.

The High Priest placed the lantern on a short table by the door.

Piers suddenly understood the High Priest's plan. It all made sense.

UW from the computer list stands for Unworthy. On Eden Day he will give those on the list ordinary apple wine without the cure – wine from the cask with the red apple. When they expose everyone to the Soulless, those who drink the wine with the real cure will live, and the Unworthy will die. The High Priest will claim Jacob judged the dead as impure. Who will refute him? All power will consolidate under him.

"I'm happy the experiments are over for now." The High Priest rotated his head on his neck. "It's so inconvenient to do them this late."

Jonas grinned. "The new virus worked perfectly. Our researchers have outdone themselves. The uncured Soulless died instantly while those with the cure were unaffected. The person's age doesn't matter. They all die instantly from our new virus. With it as a weapon, we will conquer the local tribes in a few days. They will be powerless to stop us."

The High Priest smiled and clapped his hands together like a child who had just received a toy. "Yes, now if we make enough, we should be ready by Eden Day. This calls for a celebration." He waddled toward the desk, stopping inches from Piers. He smelled like an unpleasant mixture of apples and body odor as he opened a drawer from a short cabinet.

"I'll pour," said Jonas. "It's bad luck not to fill the glass to the top for a toast so important."

Piers heard the tinkle of glass and the sound of wine splashing into goblets.

"Just the one drink tonight, Jonas." The High Priest sounded annoyed. "I have much planning to do in the morning."

"Of course. You're the boss."

Glass tinkled against glass and the room grew quiet. Piers took light shallow breaths, fearful they might hear him breathe.

After a long moment Jonas broke the silence. "Why is your keyboard on top of your desk?"

Piers felt as if someone had ripped his heart from his chest and slammed a sledgehammer into his stomach. *What an idiot!* He had forgotten to grab the keyboard when he ducked behind the desk.

"I don't know. I never leave it out." The High Priest shook the door to the Pantry. "The door is still locked."

Volcanic rage bubbled up inside Piers that he could no longer contain. Rage at the lies behind Jacob and the religion, at the billions of lives lost because of a madman, at his parents' death, at his scars, and for Aaliss and Wilky. His siblings were probably already dead, and he had been fooling himself. He was the oldest and he failed to protect them. He had failed at the one job in which he couldn't fail!

He rose from his hiding spot with his head high, his back straight, and his right hand clutching the small paring knife. *They won't find me cowering behind the desk!*

The High Priest's mouth dropped in surprise, and Jonas smiled.

"How did you get in here?" asked the High Priest incredulously.

Piers shrugged.

The High Priest scanned the office, obviously confused until a gust of wind blew open the window curtains. "How about that, Jonas? Our little Piers grew wings and flew through the window. Who would have guessed the *Scarred One* could have summoned the nerve?"

Jonas lumbered toward the desk, every step lethal.

"So you plan to give us Wilky's cure on Eden Day and pass it off as your own?"

The High Priest clapped his fat hands together. "You are a smart one, Piers. Why don't you put down that knife? We can talk about this in a more holy way."

"You want to murder those on the list. The *Unworthy Ones*, right?" Piers pointed the knife at the High Priest's chest, the blade trembling.

"Jacob has judged them unworthy and has commanded me to do it. That's how he works. He speaks to me, and I'm commanded to follow." The High Priest grinned, his voice sounding sickly sweet, like honey dripped over something rotten. "You must understand."

Jonas edged closer to Piers until only the desk separated them.

"Why can't the cure be enough? You could save them. You could cure the Soulless." Piers inched his way back from the desk. "You're sick and unworthy!'

The High Priest's face reddened. "The cure was never enough! The Soulless are wicked, nothing more than sheep for me to use. They are not human! They have no souls. Jacob commands me to use the cure, so I can rule over the wicked forever." A twisted smile spread across his face. "I have the Second Book of Jacob, one you've never seen, one only for high priests. It's clear. I must follow his will."

Piers staggered backward and remembered what one of the newscasters said: "*Some say he's working on a drug that will let man live forever.*"

"Forever? You've changed the cure to provide immortality?"

The High Priest folded his arms across his wide frame. "You really are special, almost as clever as your father. Now I will have to kill you, just like your parents."

Piers stumbled back against the window frame, the world closing in on him. "You started the fire? All this time I blamed myself."

"Me, Piers?" The High Priest pointed to himself. "No, not me. Now... Jonas might have a different answer."

Jonas shoved the desk to one side and lunged at Piers, grabbing his wrist. He twisted hard and Piers dropped the knife.

"I enjoyed it," Jonas sneered.

Piers's vision clouded over angrily. He swung a wild, looping punch at Jonas's head, but the big man blocked the blow with his elbow and drove his right fist into Piers's stomach, doubling him over.

Piers fought to get air back into his lungs, and stuttered, "You're as mad... as... Jacob was."

The High Priest rolled next to him. "What craziness are you talking about? Jacob saved Eden by sacrificing himself in the Forbidden Mountains. Everyone knows this."

Piers saw the spark of insanity in the High Priest's eyes. "You don't know about the file." He laughed. "In the end, Jacob was as mad as you. He died in the Labyrinth under the ground, far from Forbidden Mountain. He died alone, scared and crazy, just like you will."

"Blasphemy!" The High Priest slapped Piers in the face with the back of his hand.

Piers reeled from the force of the blow. The High Priest's jeweled pinky ring had cut his cheek. "You're sick, and Eden is rotten. You could save mankind, but instead, all you want is power. I'd prefer to live among the Soulless."

"I'm sorry but you don't have that choice."

Piers felt dizzy and heard a voice in his head: *"I love you, Piers. I've always been proud of you."*

It sounded like Wilky's voice, but stronger, more confident and warmer than the Wilky he had known.

"You've done enough. You've made a difference."

Fear and pain and anger vanished from Piers like water through a drain. A feeling of peace and strength washed over him.

"And you'll share your parents' fate." The High Priest turned toward Jonas. "It's a shame that Piers committed suicide. He was always such a fragile individual." The High Priest nodded toward the open window. "I guess he couldn't handle having traitorous siblings."

Jonas grabbed Piers and heaved him toward the window, holding him perilously close to the edge.

Piers smiled. He felt whole and strong and at peace with God and his faith. Refusing to struggle, he lifted his arms out toward his sides.

"Don't you want to plead for your life? If you beg, maybe I'll let you live?"

Piers called on a mental picture of Wilky and Aaliss on a crisp autumn day before the fire. They raced in the great meadow during an Eden Day long forgotten. Aaliss ran in the lead with Piers running at Wilky's heels, urging him to go faster and catch up.

Jonas frowned.

"What's wrong?" questioned the High Priest.

"He won't scream or beg. I like it when they beg. Oh well."

He shoved Piers out of the window and into the darkness.

CHAPTER 59
AALISS

A aliss watched as the bonfire roared. Orange spikes soared toward the heavens and danced to what seemed like a jubilant tune.

The night was cold but the heat from the flames and the closeness of other people warmed the Courtyard. After Eamon passed the kingship back to Dermot, a massive celebration had erupted. Young men rolled out casks of wine, a pig roasted above a firepit, and musicians played light and airy music. The Stronghold exploded in song, many of which described Dermot's greatest victories. The Singers also composed a new song about *Eamon the Short*, which was the name they dubbed him since his reign was the shortest in tribe history.

Lost in the midst of the celebration was the grief that Dermot, Gemma, and Eamon tried to conceal. Yes, they drank and toasted and even sang. Eamon had a sweet clear voice, while Dermot's rumbled lower and raspier in quality. Still, when Aaliss caught them alone, they looked sad, their eyes ringed with red. Whatever Fintan had been, he had also been their brother.

Wilky had returned to the residence hall early in the night. It was best that way. He couldn't deal with all the people and stimulation of the feast.

Aaliss closed her eyes and let the energy from the celebration rejuvenate her and seep into her soul. She thanked God for delivering Eamon. Her world, so close to imploding, had held together and now even seemed bright. She could make a life among the Butchers. She'd have to find the ingredients for the cure, but she had time. She even pushed aside her worries about Eamon's relationship with Jillian. She felt free and had found happiness in a most unlikely place—amongst the Soulless.

The slightest trace of dawn brightened the horizon and brought an edge of gray to the silky darkness in the distance. The party still had life, but most of the tribe had disbanded. Couples broke off to be alone—shadows in the distance colliding into each other passionately, clinging to the short time they had together. Others, who tired of drink and celebrating, staggered back to the residence halls.

Eamon walked up to her and stood close. "My teacher and savior, fearless, strong and... beautiful." He brushed her cheek with the back of his hand.

Heat seared her skin. She smiled at his deep eyes and the shaggy hair that fell across his face. She had only met him a few days ago but she felt as if she had known him her whole life. He was unlike anyone else she had ever known, and he stood only inches from her, his eyes locked on hers, wide and curious.

He smiled. "Without you I would—"

Aaliss pressed her finger to his lips. "Without me you would still have found a way."

"I don't—"

Aaliss kissed him gently on the lips. He tasted like honey and wine. She pulled back just enough that her nose rubbed against his. "You would have found a way," she whispered.

He smiled and she pushed against him, locking her lips onto his. This time she felt passion build from her toes and explode throughout her body. It was a feeling she had heard others describe but thought imaginary. Now she knew better as she reached for him and pulled him close. Lip to lip, body to body, they were one, joined in a way that melted her heart. They shared the same space and were completely entwined together.

Aaliss pushed him back to catch her breath. She gasped for air and grinned at him. "So that's what it's like to kiss a king?"

"You mean former king," he said with a smirk. "I'm *Eamon the Short*."

"Same thing to me."

He circled his fingers around hers and chuckled. "Maybe to you, but I think the tribe's happy how things worked out."

"I don't know. I'm sure some of them wanted *Eamon the Handsome* to rule."

"Hey, I don't go by that name!" He protested but his eyes told a different story. "Shall we go back to the halls? The sun will be up soon."

Aaliss glanced at the coming dawn—a new day was indeed starting, full of possibilities she had never dreamed of before. She smiled shyly at Eamon. "Sure. I should check on Wilky. Our room is on the same floor as yours, right?"

"No one ever accused me of being stupid."

She chuckled.

They started back to the halls, winding their way through the tight cobblestone streets. When they neared the Royal Hall, Aaliss noticed a prone figure lying on the ground against one of the buildings. "Who's that?"

Eamon shrugged. "Someone who can't hold his wine. Let's see."

A young man lay face down.

"Hey, wake up!" Eamon used his foot to flip him over. Blood splatters covered the man's shirt, his eyes lifeless. "What in the world?"

Aaliss's instincts sang a cautionary tune. She felt a jolt of adrenaline as she surveyed the empty street around her. Then she saw a shadow move from the side of a building and heard the *whiz* of a spinning throwing star head toward them.

"Eamon!" She tried to jump in the way of the spiked disc, but she moved too late.

The star lodged in his chest. He glanced at it and then back at her.

"Run!" He staggered backward, clutched the star, fell to his knees, and looked back at her. He tried to say something, but he had no wind and toppled to the ground.

Aaliss's eyes stung, a scream frozen in her throat. For a heartbeat she felt her legs turn weak. Her hand almost moved to brush his hair, but she pulled it back and glared at the shadow. Tears burned her eyes and her breath turned ragged. Anger shoved aside her grief. She would make him pay for this. A million deaths would be too good for him.

The Viper stalked toward her, armed with both his short swords. "Time to end the chase, rabbit. You can't run any longer."

Aaliss's vision tunneled around the Viper and the night tinted red. She drew her sword and sprinted forward. She wanted to kill him, to avenge Eamon more than anything—more than finding a cure for Wilky, more than returning to Eden, more than her hatred for the High Priest and her uncle who started her on this journey. Her footsteps fell hard against the stone street.

She slowed a step before she reached him, swinging her blade in an angry sideswipe for his head. He deflected it with the sword in his left hand and cut at her with the one in his right. She moved just in time and the night air rang with the sounds of their steel dance—Aaliss powered by her anger, and the Viper no doubt by his self-righteousness.

She moved quicker and felt stronger than ever before, but the Viper always moved a second ahead of her. She tried everything she had been taught, but none of it was enough.

He snickered. "You learned well, but who do you think taught your sword master?" He feigned to his left. When Aaliss shifted, he sliced her left shoulder with the sword in his right hand.

She hadn't lost a sword fight in years, yet he was toying with her. He had no weaknesses and no tells. Whenever she thought she could anticipate his next move, he did the unexpected and she labored to cover. He had already scored half a dozen nicks on her body, and she hadn't drawn his blood.

She began to tire, so he switched from mostly defense to offense and pressed her toward the Royal Hall. "You have talent. Too bad I didn't spend more time with you. I could have made you into something truly valuable."

"I'd rather wrestle with the Devil in hell!"

He swiped at her stomach.

She danced back but not quickly enough. The tip of his blade turned red and left an angry line behind.

He chuckled. "Once I kill you, I'll murder your brother. Him, I'll finish off quickly."

She breathed hard, trying to get enough oxygen in her lungs. The cuts had weakened her. She knew her end neared, and then she saw the first light of dawn reflect off a white stone on the other side of the street.

What did Eamon say about those white stones again? They're traps!

She danced backward to avoid a vicious cut at her neck.

The trap was her only chance to defeat the Viper. She had to get him to chase after her. Only if he thought he had defeated her would he fail to notice the false ground.

Clanging her sword against the one held in his left hand, she let it linger for a second longer than she should have.

He sensed the opportunity and bit his blade into her arm. She dropped her weapon, and he grinned.

This was her only chance. She bolted for the trap, the Viper hot on her heels. When she reached the stone marker she leaped and cleared the false floor. She turned and saw the Viper skid to a stop, his toes beyond the imaginary line between stones as he studied the ground before him.

"You must think me a fool," he said. "This ground is untrod upon. Jacob would never let me fall for such a trap." He swerved around the stone markers and hemmed her in against a building.

Despair filled her now. She looked at Eamon, who hadn't budged since the star hit him, and then she backed away from the approaching devil. She had nowhere to go and her shoulders bumped against stone. Her plan had failed. He had her trapped, and now he would kill her, and then he would kill Wilky. She had failed everyone she cared about.

He paused, bent his head back, and looked toward the heavens.

"Jacob is with me! He embraces me." When he focused on her again his eyes had an ethereal glow about them, and his smile had an eerie quality. He tensed his legs for the last deadly plunge.

If she was going to die, she wanted to look one last time on Eamon. She glanced toward him, and she saw Wilky standing in the street instead.

He leveled her crossbow and squeezed the trigger.

A heartbeat later, the bolt ripped into the Viper's chest, and he froze. His eyes shot wide. "It can't be. Jacob—"

"Isn't with you. Maybe you'll find him in hell?" Aaliss kicked him in the chest and toppled him into the trap.

The false ground gave way, and he landed on a spike. Blood bubbled from his mouth.

Aaliss pulled her eyes away from the Viper and ran toward Eamon, who did not stir.

CHAPTER 60
MICHEL

Michel watched from the shadows, invisible in his black ostrich suit. He wanted to help, to scale the wall from the Pantry to the High Priest's office, but Piers would not allow it, and without Piers's help he could not gain entry to the Parsonage. He was powerless, and Piers was being stupid.

Michel knew Piers was brave. Even among the Guardians, Piers would stand out, yet since the fire he had an unquenchable desire to prove himself, so Michel waited in the darkness, only the steam from his mouth visible in the cold air. He had the sickening feeling that Aaliss would be angry with him.

He'd held his breath when Piers climbed outside the Pantry window and slid across the wall to the High Priest's office, and his heart had skipped a beat when he almost fell.

Now he waited and watched.

What could be taking so long?

He only needed to copy the file onto the flash drive. Peter said it would take only a few minutes.

Time crawled past. When flickering lights from a lantern danced in the window, Michel knew trouble had found Piers. He considered scrambling up the side of the building, but he understood only the basics about climbing, and the darkness was near complete. He'd never find the necessary nooks in the stone he needed to reach the top floor.

A figure moved to the window. He squinted into the moonlight and saw Piers standing with his back to the window frame, his hands stretched out to his sides. And then he fell, his robe fluttering in the breeze.

Thud!

Michel cringed at the sickening sound. He glanced back at the window and saw Jonas's unmistakable bulk peer out of it. Michel cursed and darted toward Piers, who had landed on his back with his arms out to his sides.

"Are you okay?" he whispered, but he knew Piers had only moments left to live, the light in his eyes growing faint.

"I've got the drive in my hand."

Michel uncurled Piers's fingers and took the small external drive. "I've got it."

Piers sputtered, "I'm the oldest.... I'm responsible...." And the light left him for the last time.

Michel growled. Piers didn't deserve this fate. When patrolling with Aaliss he had promised to look after Piers and Wilky if anything happened to her. He kept his promises, but now he'd failed. A bloodthirsty rage built inside him.

He thought about climbing the stairs to the Parsonage, kicking open the door, and seeking revenge against Jonas and the High Priest, but he hesitated. He'd have to be smarter. He had to get proof that Aaliss and Wilky were innocent of these charges. Armed with evidence, he could clear their names.

He could go after them and bring them back.

He could bring them home.

Michel raced to Peter's dwelling. The aging researcher waited for him but he wasn't alone. Father Luke stood beside him. When Michel explained what had happened to Piers, Peter sank into a chair and Father Luke said a small prayer. Then they went to the Lab together, Michel making sure the way was clear.

They huddled around a computer screen in Peter's office, watching the files from the flash drive, the silence between them thick as the video ended.

"So it's all true," said Peter. "We suspected the origin of the Red Death was man-made, and the Order of the Poisoned Apple was formed at the beginning to pass down that knowledge, but it was so long ago and none of us had any proof."

"Until now," said Father Luke.

"*It's all a lie?*" Michel felt numb. "Jacob was deranged. He wasn't a prophet!"

Father Luke placed his hand on Michel's shoulder. "Not all of it is a lie, my son. God is with us. The God of the Bible. We never would have survived so long without Him."

"Everything makes sense," said Peter. "We've been making the cure for the last week. All those flowers and mushrooms harvested. There's no other explanation."

"Why not just tell everyone about the cure? The High Priest could still act as if it's his miracle. Wilky and Aaliss are gone. They couldn't expose the lie." Michel glanced at the two older men, his mind fighting hard to catch up.

Father Luke shook his head. "He must have tampered with the casks *after* we put the Sacred Drink in them for Eden Day. I knew it was strange that he came by to *bless* them. I took another look at those casks after he left. All of them have a green apple stamped on the outside except one, which has a red apple. That weasel is only going to give the cure to those he wants, and the others will get stuck with the regular Sacred Drink from the cask with the red apple. Once we're exposed to the Red Death—"

"He's going to murder a score of people he'd rather not have around," said Peter. "There's only one way to know for certain. Let's pry open two of the casks. If the cure is in one marked with the green apple and not in the one with the red apple, we'll have all the evidence we need."

"We've got to move on this before he knows the file was copied," said Father Luke. "If what we suspect is true, I'll rally the Priests."

"More than enough guardians support Aaliss," said Michel. "They'll listen to me. The Monks won't stand in our way."

"And the researchers will see the logic of action," agreed Peter.

Michel flung the door open.

Father Luke and a half-dozen guardians, all dressed in their suits with weapons drawn, followed close behind him. Two guardians dragged Jonas with them, a fresh cut across his cheek and the beginnings of a new black eye marring his face.

"What's the meaning of this?" The High Priest stood behind his desk, his face turning to ash as he saw Jonas.

Michel leaped toward him, his sword pointed at his blubbery chest. "You're being charged with murdering Piers and with treason. Make any move, even just blink your eyes, and I'll gut you like a fish." He pressed the tip of his blade against his chest.

"You insolent fool! My power comes from Jacob. You have no authority over me."

Father Luke stepped forward. "Do you really think you can select who gets the cure and who doesn't? Do you think you're God?"

The High Priest glanced between Michel and Father Luke. "I'm greater than God. It's up to me to decide life and death. Piers was a fool, and his meddling sister and brother are more fools who got in the way. You're all fools."

Michel smashed him in the face with the hilt of his sword.

The High Priest reeled from the blow, his head snapping back, blood gushing from his broken nose.

"Do you want to say anything else about Piers?" snarled Michel.

The High Priest wiped his face with his hands and stared at his own blood. He cackled, "This is *his* blood. It's in my veins. I'm doing *his* will. I will rule over all humanity."

"We've heard enough from you." Father Luke produced a six-inch knife from his robe and cut the High Priest's braid off. "There are going to be some changes around here."

"We can make a deal. You can rule with me. We—"

Father Luke nodded at the guardians, who grabbed the High Priest by the arms and dragged him away.

"Take him to the Lab. We've got a special holding pen ready for him."

"No! No! Not that!"

CHAPTER 61
AALISS

Aaliss let the sun streaming through the window warm her face. Since Eamon collapsed, she had felt cold and hollow. The sudden warmth felt good, if temporary.

Eamon lay on Dermot's bed, his chest rising and falling with shallow breaths, his forehead hot and slick with sweat. A short, round man whom Dermot called Hainlan the Healer sat by his side. The healer had soft hands, intelligent eyes, and fleshy cheeks. He'd cleaned the wound and dressed it with a gray cloth.

Aaliss knew he could do little else.

Maybe a medical Priest back home might have been able to help Eamon, but the Master Healer could not. The wound by itself was not fatal, but the Viper had dipped his throwing star in poison. Eamon would have to battle that poison on his own.

An entire day and a half had passed since the attack. Aaliss told Dermot everything: Eden, the truth behind the Witch's Woods, Wilky's special nature. She didn't have to tell him what she felt for Eamon; everyone had seen that plainly written on her face.

Dermot had two trusted friends bury the Viper in the woods. For now, Eden and the cure would remain their secret.

Aaliss had asked Wilky what would happen to Eamon, but he just shook his head.

Not being very religious, she didn't think her prayers to God would work, so she sent a barrage of mental messages to Piers. He was the holiest person she knew, so she silently begged him to intercede with God on her behalf. She promised to do whatever God wanted of her. She'd leave if that was His will. She'd let Jillian have him. She'd repent for her sins. She even offered herself in sacrifice for him. It was her fault he wrestled with death. That star should have struck her instead. She'd change places with him if that was what it took. She'd do anything. If only she knew what to do.

She sat in a wooden chair, her entire body stiff.

Eamon twisted in the bed. He looked as if he was in pain and in the grips of a fierce nightmare.

Her heart cracked in a million pieces.

He tossed his head back toward her and his eyes blinked open.

Aaliss jumped from her seat. "Did you see that? His eyes opened for a second."

Dermot leaned down toward him. "Wake up, Brother. We need you here. Tell Grandfather it's not time for him to have you yet."

Aaliss held her breath, and willed his eyes open, and then they did open, at first unfocused and far away, but they cleared.

Tears rolled down her face. Her prayers had been answered. She thanked Piers.

Eamon sat up in his bed. "Why are you all in my room? What happened?"

"Oh, not much, Brother," said Dermot. "Did you see Father and Finnegan the Fat?"

Eamon nodded. "I did. They said I'm their favorite."

"Come on!" Dermot laughed.

Eamon shrugged and locked eyes with Aaliss.

"I'm sorry, Eamon. He was after me. It's my fault you got hurt." Her voice dripped with emotion.

"I met your brother. Or at least someone called Piers who said he was your brother. He said you can be difficult but you're worth the effort."

"*Difficult* when I get my hands on him!" She grinned and felt light again, as if she had been reprieved. Piers had helped her. She knew she could count on him.

She glanced at Wilky, who was smiling as he looked out the window. He so seldom smiled or showed any emotion at all.

Aaliss took note of it. "What are you looking at?"

"It's light out."

She walked toward him. "Sure it is. It's the middle of the day."

He shook his head. "Light's coming from Eden."

Aaliss looked out the window and could have sworn she saw it also.

---THE END---

Watch for the second installment of the "Red Death" series, *THE GHOST KING*, to launch in the spring/summer of 2017.

RED DEATH: Cast of Characters

EDEN

Eden is a society dominated by religion, physically isolated on a peninsula surrounded by Eden River and a narrow strip of land called the Bridge, which connects the peninsula to the Forbidden Mountain. The High Priest and an elected President rule Eden. Their motto is "Purity, Faith, and Strength," and their symbol is an elaborate capital J for "Jacob," the founder of their religion. Apples are their main crop. Eden is the only known society not affected by the Red Death. They maintain their purity by prohibiting contact with the outside world, or the "Soulless," as they refer to others outside of Eden. Eden's high holiday is known as Eden Day, the one day a year that frivolity and mischief are allowed — at least a little.

Aaliss is the middle of three siblings and a highly-trained Guardian. She patrols the area around Eden known as the Zone, to keep Eden secret from the Soulless. She is seventeen, graduated at the top of her class, and has been a full-fledged Guardian for only one year.

Aibel is the uncle to Piers, Aaliss, and Wilky, and the second most powerful person in Eden as their elected President. He's not one to let family get in the way of ambition.

Estienne is a Guardian who favors the standard issue crossbow to the short sword.

Father Luke is the Priest who runs the Orchard. He was Malachi's only childhood friend, though they had a falling out when Malachi became High Priest.

Gabriel, also known as the **Viper** and the **Priest of the Guardians**, is a direct descendent of Jacob. He holds great power as the leader of the Guardians. He earned his nickname because of his lethalness and his proclivity to spend time alone in the Zone, where he feels closest to Jacob.

John is an apprentice Guardian.

Jonas is a Guardian and the Viper's old instructor. Though past his prime, he remains dangerous. No one would want to get between him and apple wine known as the Sacred Drink.

Malachi, more commonly known as the **High Priest**, is a direct descendant of Jacob and the head of their religion. The most powerful person in Eden, he's also unquestionably the largest. His size provoked a panic at his investiture, when the ceremonial robes had to be enlarged to accommodate his girth.

Mark is a Monk who enjoys patrolling Eden looking for unholy activities. He has a short temper.

Michel is a tall, reed-thin Guardian who is friends with Aaliss, Piers, and Wilky.

Piers is a novice priest with a photographic memory, and the oldest of three siblings at nineteen years. Badly burned in a fire three years ago, which killed his parents, he suffers scars and weakness on the left side of his body.

Samuel is a senior Guardian with a quirky sense of humor.

Sarah is a tall, red-haired Monk with sadistic qualities, who is bitter because she wasn't selected to be a member of Jacob's Choir.

Wilkiford, more commonly known as **Wilky**, is the youngest researcher in Eden's history. He has a way of seeing things. He's also Aaliss's and Piers's youngest sibling at thirteen years old.

Zeke is a novice priest who chats incessantly. Having failed to remain quiet during two of the three Great Silences over the past years, his future as a Priest is suspect.

BUTCHER TRIBE

A king rules the Butcher Tribe. He is chosen from the royal family line through an ancient battle ritual called the Circle of Destiny. The tribe is known for high quality meat they sell at The Exchange. They have three main towns, the Stronghold, the Settlement, and the Outpost, with the Stronghold as their capital, located in the center of their territory. They have vast land holdings for their herds of cattle and sheep, and believe that prior kings help govern them from the stars. They recite, "May the herd forever be strong" at all official events. Their symbol is a jeweled sword known as the Sword of Power, which can only be used by the King. Their main holiday is Naming Day, when the names of all newborn members of the tribe get carved into the vast ghost tree that centers the Stronghold.

Cattie works in the Nursery. She is not well liked and has a habit of making poor choices.

Cormac is a brawny man, the Captain of the King's Guard and Fintan's best friend. He didn't rise to Captain because of his brains, but he's quick with a blade.

Dermot is a popular king, old at twenty-four and near the end of his reign. He is also known by several nicknames, such as *Dermot the Just* and the *Blade of the Butchers*. Early in his reign he led the Butchers through two successful military campaigns, one against the Horsepeople to the south and another against the Painted Ones to the north. His reign has lasted six winters, which is the longest in memory, and he has kept the peace for the last four years.

Eamon, also known as **Eamon the Handsome**, is a royal prince who is in charge of the Books of Wisdom, where Dermot hopes to record the tribe's collective knowledge. He is younger than his two other royal brothers — Dermot by six winters and Fintan by one.

Fintan is a royal prince who is four winters younger than Dermot and the head of the King's Horsemen. He spends most of his time studying war craft and dreaming of ways to unleash his unlimited ambition.

Gemma is Eamon's twin and considered odd. She speaks a weird version of their language that only Eamon and Jillian, her best friend, fully understand, and usually gets distracted by details for hours.

Jillian, best friends with Gemma and Eamon, is often tasked with keeping an eye on Gemma. She also works as a scribe to help record the Books of Wisdom.

Maeve is Cattie's younger sister, who also works in the Nursery, but is well liked and considered beautiful. Few people see the family resemblance between the sisters.

Scotty the Snake, a member of the King's Guard, is known to have psychotic tendencies.

THE PAINTED ONES

The Painted Ones are a matriarchal society that elects a female "Tribal Mother" to govern with the help of a series of females known as Vestals. Only female members can vote for the Tribal Mother. The tribe is known for the female members' distinctive tattoos. On her tenth birthday, each girl gets her own tree of life tattoo signifying that she is now an adult member of the tribe. Most members of the tribe live in small huts with varying colored fabric roofs, the colors and designs of which indicate different family histories. Their grandest celebration is the annual Awakening Feast that they share with the Orions. Every ten years they have a Renewal Feast where they swap girls who are thirteen harvests old with similar girls of the Orion tribe, to further bind the two tribes together and increase understanding of their ways. In addition to their tattoos, the Painted Ones are known for intricately woven fabrics and the poison darts they use to defend themselves.

Kalhona is the best Artist in the tribe and P'mina's older sister.

Merina is P'mina's friend. She is also thirteen and scheduled to be swapped with the Orion girls, but, unlike P'mina, Merina appreciates the honor of representing her tribe.

P'mina is Kalhona's younger sister at thirteen harvests and scheduled to be swapped with the Orion girls of the same age at the Renewal Feast. She is very learned in plants and somewhat of an outcast in the tribe because her mother became a red witch.

Tania is Kalhona's toddler daughter who loves to spin in circles and mispronounces P'mina's name.

Tribal Mother is a robust woman considered extremely beautiful. She is a beloved leader of the tribe.

V'ronica is a beady-eyed ambitious Vestal who serves and advises the Tribal Mother.

RED WITCHES

The Red Death does not kill everyone. Some women wake to find they have transformed overnight into red witches, with thick auburn hair, pale skin, and red-specked eyes. Though they are not all evil, red witches are feared and outcast, if not killed by most tribes. Their magic powers entice the brave or desperate to seek their help in times of need.

Eris is the head of a group of witches who fly the Red Raven banner. She worships the Goddess of the Night and has designs to lead other witches to take control over all the tribes. She currently "advises" the chief of the Bloody Wolf tribe, although many would say she controls him.

Santra follows Eris and is a particularly nasty witch. She keeps the company of firefoxes.

The Witch goes by no formal name. She is near the end of her life and has her own banner of the Red Fish. She tries to follow the light but has been deceived from time to time by dark spirits.

BLOODY WOLF TRIBE (Also Known as the Northern Invaders)

This aggressive northern tribe is ruled by a chief, and divided between warriors and farmers. Because of a drought, their farmland has became barren, so the majority of the tribe has traveled south in search of new lands to conquer. The warriors wear beards they never shave.

They tie the beard with twine, and usually add hair from a victim they have killed. A red wolf head with blood dripping from its mouth is their symbol, and they honor two gods: Baltrix and Feyreh. Baltrix is a male warrior with a red wolf head and a human body. Feyreh is a female agricultural deity who is human above the waist, with a tree trunk below.

Tynchek is a midlevel warrior sent to trade coin for Sweat Leaf with the witch Santra.

ORIONS

The Orions are governed by a leader and his *Circle of Counselors*. The leader always takes the name Orion. Subsequent leaders are chosen by the existing Orion and the Circle of Counselors. The society believes in an omniscient Hunter God who is usually depicted as a man drawing a bow. They are well known as excellent archers and hunters. Young men take a brand on their chest of the Hunter God when Orion considers them of age. Upon the death of a member of the society, his or her name is etched into a stone and tossed on top of the Bridge to the Next World by their family. The tribe is closely allied with the Painted Ones.

Acknowledgements

A book like *Red Death* can only become a reality with many helping hands. Over five years in the making, I can't possibly list everyone who has encouraged me on this project or helped in its creation. Of course my family remains my rock and I'm thankful for their patience and love. I also offer a special thanks to my beta readers who gave me such compelling suggestions and whose passion for these characters have overwhelmed me. I would be remiss if I didn't point out my friend, Melissa Kanovsky and her epic contribution to this book. Her fingerprints touch upon the entire tale. Her encouragement and suggestions were so good, they were worth much more than the sushi lunches we spent discussing the story.

On the more technical side, Lane Diamond, my fabulous editor, did a wonderful job fixing my prose and making the story pop. He's awesome, as is Evolved Publishing. Without them, I'm not sure where I would be as an author.

Mallory Rock, as always, proves why she's the best cover artist in the business. This time she received some help from the talented artist, Sarima, who helped develop the apple for the cover. Mallory and Kira McFadden teamed up to create the amazing map. They basically took an awful sketch and created artwork. I think that's magic!

About the Author

Jeff Altabef lives in New York with his wife, two daughters, and Charlie the dog. He spends time volunteering at the Writing Center in the local community college as a certified writing instructor. After years of being accused of "telling stories," he thought he would make it official. He writes in both the thriller and young adult genres. As an avid Knicks fan, he is prone to long periods of melancholy during hoops season.

Jeff has a column on The Examiner focused on writing, designed to encourage writing for those that like telling stories.

You can find Jeff online at:

www.JeffreyAltabef.com

Via Email at JeffreyAltabef@gmail.com

You can also find Jeff on Goodreads, Facebook, and Twitter!

What's Next from Jeff Altabef?

THE GHOST KING
Red Death – Book 2

Watch for the second book in this dystoian science fiction adventure to release in the spring/summer of 2017.

~~~

Aaliss and Wilky find themselves in the center of a storm. Hunted by powerful forces, will they survive long enough to unite the three tribes against the Bloody Wolf Tribe and the Witches of the Red Raven? Can Wilky find a way to prevent his shocking vision from becoming a reality?

The Ghost Riders hold the key and one will emerge – the Ghost King. But will he be their savior or doom?

~~~

SEE NEXT PAGE FOR A SPECIAL SNEAK PREVIEW:
Chapter 1 of *The Ghost King* (Red Death – Book 2)

SPECIAL SNEAK PREVIEW: *THE GHOST KING*

Chapter 1 – Wilky

The rain fell in sheets. A flash of lightning lit the sky and thunder shook the ground.

Wilky had never seen rain fall so hard or violently before.

A voice shouted, "Reform the shield wall! The devils will be back on us in no time!"

Another flash of light and another boom.

Wilky stood on a hill, charred wood and thrashed buildings spread before him – a ruined village. Flags waved: the bloody wolf and red raven before him; and behind him the jeweled sword, the hunter drawing his bow, and the tree of life.

The air smelled rank, acidic from blood and sour from the foul stench of fear and waste and death. The dead littered the ground around him. He tried not to breathe.

A horn blast carried into the field and was followed by a wild war cry.

Time moved erratically, punctuated by jutting spear points and the whistle of arrows. Steel axes collided with wooden shields as men cried out, cursed, prayed, screamed.

He looked frantically for Aaliss and spotted her in the distance.

She swirled, flashing steel in a tornado of death as bodies fell all about her.

Another flash of lightning illuminated a giant with a multi-colored beard that dropped from his chin like daggers. He stalked toward Aaliss, the ends of his beard glittering whenever lightning lit the sky.

Not him.

Wilky wanted to scream, but he had no voice here. The mud churned with blood under his feet. Death more than hovered over the field. He could see black-winged shades, their leathery skin stretched tight and their eyes nothing but black pools without end, swoop across the small hill. They dragged souls from those who had fallen.

***

Wilky pulled his eyes away, sat up in his bed, and breathed. The air came fast and hot. He should have been braver, and lasted longer to see more of the vision, but he couldn't watch anymore.

If only the images were part of a dream, he could try to forget them, but he knew better. He didn't sleep much these days and this nightmare was no dream; it was a vision that revealed flashes of the future.

Is that future set?

He hoped not. He hoped he could alter it, and thought he could, but he wasn't sure how yet.

He glanced at the bed next to him and saw his sister sleeping, curled around a wool blanket. He wanted to spare Aaliss this future, but that would only happen if he tried harder and found another way. Until then, all he could do was shudder.

A future with light was the most important thing. Some sacrifices would be necessary for that future... and that light.

He strolled to the window. The first rays of dawn had not yet brightened the horizon.

Soon he would have to see the whole story. Soon he'd have to find the courage to know who would win the war, and how he would lead them to the light.

Soon, but not today.

He sighed and glanced back at his sister.

I must find a way. Some sacrifices are too much. I can't let death take her. Piers was enough.

More from Evolved Publishing:

CHILDREN'S PICTURE BOOKS

THE BIRD BRAIN BOOKS by Emlyn Chand:
> *Courtney Saves Christmas*
> *Davey the Detective*
> *Honey the Hero*
> *Izzy the Inventor*
> *Larry the Lonely*
> *Polly Wants to be a Pirate*
> *Poppy the Proud*
> *Ricky the Runt*
> *Ruby to the Rescue*
> *Sammy Steals the Show*
> *Tommy Goes Trick-or-Treating*
> *Vicky Finds a Valentine*

Silent Words by Chantal Fournier
Maddie's Monsters by Jonathan Gould
Thomas and the Tiger-Turtle by Jonathan Gould
EMLYN AND THE GREMLIN by Steff F. Kneff:
> *Emlyn and the Gremlin*
> *Emlyn and the Gremlin and the Barbeque Disaster*
> *Emlyn and the Gremlin and the Mean Old Cat*
> *Emlyn and the Gremlin and the Seaside Mishap*
> *Emlyn and the Gremlin and the Teenage Babysitter*

I'd Rather Be Riding My Bike by Eric Pinder
SULLY P. SNOOFERPOOT'S AMAZING INVENTIONS by Aaron Shaw Ph.D.:
> *Sully P. Snooferpoot's Amazing New Christmas Pot*
> *Sully P. Snooferpoot's Amazing New Dayswitcher*
> *Sully P. Snooferpoot's Amazing New Forcefield*
> *Sully P. Snooferpoot's Amazing New Key*
> *Sully P. Snooferpoot's Amazing New Shadow*

Ninja and Bunny's Great Adventure by Kara S. Tyler
VALENTINA'S SPOOKY ADVENTURES by Majanka Verstraete:
> *Valentina and the Haunted Mansion*
> *Valentina and the Masked Mummy*
> *Valentina and the Whackadoodle Witch*

HISTORICAL FICTION

SHINING LIGHT'S SAGA by Ruby Standing Deer:
> *Circles (Book 1)*
>
> *Spirals (Book 2)*
>
> *Stones (Book 3)*

LITERARY FICTION

The Daughter of the Sea and the Sky by David Litwack
THE DESERT by Angela Scott:
> *Desert Rice (Book 1)*
>
> *Desert Flower (Book 2)*

LOWER GRADE (Chapter Books)

THE PET SHOP SOCIETY by Emlyn Chand:
> *Maddie and the Purrfect Crime*
>
> *Mike and the Dog-Gone Labradoodle*
>
> *Tyler and the Blabber-Mouth Birds*

TALES FROM UPON A. TIME by Falcon Storm:
> *Natalie the Not-So-Nasty*
>
> *The Persnickety Princess*

WEIRDVILLE by Majanka Verstraete:
> *Drowning in Fear*
>
> *Fright Train*
>
> *Grave Error*
>
> *House of Horrors*
>
> *The Clumsy Magician*
>
> *The Doll Maker*

THE BALDERDASH SAGA by J.W.Zulauf:
> *The Underground Princess (Book 1)*
>
> *The Prince's Plight (Book 2)*
>
> *The Shaman's Salvation (Book 3)*

THE BALDERDASH SAGA SHORT STORIES by J.W.Zulauf:
> *Hurlock the Warrior King*
>
> *Roland the Pirate Knight*
>
> *Scarlet the Kindhearted Princess*

MEMOIR

And Then It Rained by Megan Morrison
Girl Enlightened by Megan Morrison

MIDDLE GRADE

FRENDYL KRUNE by Kira A. McFadden:
 Frendyl Krune and the Blood of the Sun (Book 1)
 Frendyl Krune and the Snake Across the Sea (Book 2)
 Frendyl Krune and the Stone Princess (Book 3)
 Frendyl Krune and the Nightmare in the North (Book 4)
NOAH ZARC by D. Robert Pease:
 Mammoth Trouble (Book 1)
 Cataclysm (Book 2)
 Declaration (Book 3)
 Omnibus (Special 3-in-1 Edition)

SCI-FI / FANTASY

RED DEATH by Jeff Altabef:
 Red Death (Book 1)
 The Ghost King (Book 2)
THE PANHELION CHRONICLES by Marlin Desault:
 Shroud of Eden (Book 1)
 The Vanquished of Eden (Book 2)
THE SEEKERS by David Litwack:
 The Children of Darkness (Book 1)
 The Stuff of Stars (Book 2)
 The Light of Reason (Book 3)
THE AMULI CHRONICLES: SOULBOUND by Kira A. McFadden:
 The Soulbound Curse (Book 1)
 The Soulless King (Book 2)
 The Throne of Souls (Book 3)
Shadow Swarm by D. Robert Pease
Two Moons of Sera by P.K. Tyler

SHORT STORY ANTHOLOGIES

FROM THE EDITORS AT EVOLVED PUBLISHING:
Evolution: Vol. 1 (A Short Story Collection)
Evolution: Vol. 2 (A Short Story Collection)

YOUNG ADULT

CHOSEN by Jeff Altabef and Erynn Altabef:
Wind Catcher (Book 1)
Brink of Dawn (Book 2)
Scorched Souls (Book 3)
THE KIN CHRONICLES by Michael Dadich:
The Silver Sphere (Book 1)
The Sinister Kin (Book 2)
UPLOADED by James W. Hughes:
Uploaded (Book 1)
Undone (Book 2)
Uprising (Book 3)
DIRT AND STARS by Kevin Killiany:
Down to Dirt (Book 1)
Living on Dirt (Book 2)
STORMBOURNE CHRONICLES by Karissa Laurel:
Heir of Thunder (Book 1)
THE DARLA DECKER DIARIES by Jessica McHugh:
Darla Decker Hates to Wait (Book 1)
Darla Decker Takes the Cake (Book 2)
Darla Decker Shakes the State (Book 3)
Darla Decker Plays it Straight (Book 4)
Darla Decker Breaks the Case (Book 5)
JOEY COLA by D. Robert Pease:
Dream Warriors (Book 1)
Cleopatra Rising (Book 2)
Third Reality (Book 3)
Anyone? by Angela Scott
THE ZOMBIE WEST TRILOGY by Angela Scott:
Wanted: Dead or Undead (Book 1)
Survivor Roundup (Book 2)
Dead Plains (Book 3)
The Zombie West Trilogy – Special Omnibus Edition 1-3

CPSIA information can be obtained at www.ICGtesting.com
Printed in the USA
BVOW06s2249141016

465133BV00002B/3/P